Anna C. Steele

Gardenhurst

A Novel

Anna C. Steele

Gardenhurst
A Novel

ISBN/EAN: 9783337041335

Printed in Europe, USA, Canada, Australia, Japan

Cover: Foto ©Andreas Hilbeck / pixelio.de

More available books at **www.hansebooks.com**

GARDEN ▮ ST

A Novel.

BY

ANNA C. STEELE,

AUTHOR OF "CONDONED."

NEW EDITION.

LONDON:

CHAPMAN AND HALL, 193 PICCADILLY.

1877.

TO MY SISTER KATIE

(Mrs. O'SHEA).

" A staff to stay, a star to guide;
A spell to soothe, a power to raise;
A faith by fortune firmly tried;
A judgment resolute to preside
O'er days at strife with days."

GARDENHURST.

CHAPTER I.

TAKING POSSESSION.

"The wafted scent of some old garden's flower
Blooming in silence round neglected bower."
H. WHITMORE.

"And round about he taught sweet flowers to grow:
The rose engroined in pure scarlet dye,
The lily fresh and violet below,
The marigold and cheerful rosemary,
The Spartan myrtle whence sweet gum doe flow,
The purple hyacinth and fresh costmary,
And saffron sought for in cicalion soil,
And laurel, the ornament of Phœbus' toil."
SPENSER.

ARDENHURST, formerly called "The Hurst," once belonged to an old X——shire family of the name of Chesham, whose ancestors had lived in X—— as far back as X——shire could be remembered.

Up to the time of Charles I the Cheshams had been powerful neighbours for "weal or woe," but since that period they had been gradually descending in the scale of county grandeur, and now, A.D. 18—, they occupied a small red house called The Holme, situated a few miles from their ancient possession of Gardenhurst.

The latter estate had been gambled away in one night by a young heir of the Cheshams, who, living in the dissolute

1

reign of Charles II, followed the common practices of the youth of that day, most of whom contrived to transmit their estates to their successors in a hopeless state of mortgage, when, indeed, there was any left to transmit.

There is a portrait of this boy, Gilbert Chesham, hanging up in the drawing-room of the Holme. He was only ten years old when Lely depicted his round, guileless face, and his little hand thrust firmly into that of his mother, a stately, mild-eyed lady, clothed in the usual draperies of white satin and point lace. Who, in looking at the fearless blue eyes, and the smooth forehead shaded by a profusion of shining curls that tumble over the lace collar and red doublet, could imagine that twelve years afterwards this angel-faced boy would shoot himself through the head in a gaming-house, filled by a wild passion of fury and dismay because he had thrown his last stake and most ancient possession, Garden-hurst—and had lost it?

His mother was sitting in her window recess one dusky summer evening when she heard the clattering hoofs of a horse gallop up to her door. Her dim eyes peered anxiously through the gloom, for her quick maternal instinct divined that some news of her son might be conveyed by this messenger from London; and when her feeble hands tremblingly broke the cover of the packet that had been sent to her, the first thing her finger touched was a clammy silken curl, which some friend of Gilbert's had hastily severed from the fallen head when it was carried away, hanging heavily over the arm that supported it, with a thick red drop oozing slowly from the forehead.

It was said that in the first ravings of her misery the unhappy woman flung up her arms like one "pierced by a great wound," and prayed that a curse might fall on the new possessor of Gardenhurst, and on all who might hereafter inherit a domain so won by "fraud and blood."

There was a suspicion of foul play attached to the transaction which seemed to justify these passionate words of Gilbert's mother, and a vague remembrance of her curse has come down to the present day, when the country people say, "Gardenhurst always has brought ill luck to its owners, and always will."

Certainly the prophecy has been in a great measure

fulfilled by the ruin of each of its successive proprietors; a fate, however, which perhaps may be ascribed more to the unprofitable nature of the soil than to any ghostly influence exercised by the shadow of the poor grief-stricken mother.

Gardenhurst passed through various hands, and at last, in the year 184—, was purchased by an eminent florist of the name of Ford, who spent all his fortune in cultivating and embellishing to an extraordinary degree that which had become little better than waste land.

Thistles were plucked up to make way for roses of rare beauty; paths were traced through wildernesses of wild shrubs and brambles; smooth velvety lawns succeeded the rugged patches of dandelions that had sprung up round the walls of the old house: and the whole of the once desolate region was converted into a garden such as one dreams of after reading the "Arabian Nights."

It cost Mr. Ford many thousands of pounds, this passion for varied hue and perfume.

He brought flowers from every part of the world to this his great altar to Flora; he imported rhododendrons from India, azaleas from America, tulips from Belgium, peonies from Persia, and slips and cuttings of every description from all the best nursery grounds in England.

He passed a few happy years flitting among his flower-beds, as radiant as the butterflies that lived on their fragrance, drinking in breaths of perfume-laden air, and feasting his eyes on the various tints developed anew every month by the different species of flowers.

At last ruin came; and late one night Mr. Ford departed from his home as quietly and stealthily as a burglar might have wished to enter it.

He unclasped the garden gate, and looked up at the windows of his sleeping household, on which the moon-beams shed their pale light, breathed for the last time the scent of the wax-like magnolias, reared with tender care against his library window, and brushed hastily by his China roses, whose heads hung heavy with night dew; and then— the garden gate fell forward on its latch, the sound of his footsteps soon died away down the silent road, and the curses of angry creditors, and the beauty of his floral

I—2

collection, were the only records left of Mr. Ford's residence at Gardenhurst.

And now for three years' silence and desolation again reigned over the place.

The gravel walks became as patched and irregular as ever, and the lawns swarmed with buttercups and daisies. The swans found ample provision in the green weeds which soon overspread the wide sheet of water that had once been graced by a fairy yacht and small rowing boats.

The last of these lay in rotten fragments in the rushes by the side of the lake, its once bright colours faded to a dirty red.

The broad boundary paths were soon narrowed by the closing over of the untrimmed luxuriant foliage that grew by their sides, and after awhile the space between presented little more than a dim vista through which a few red roses peered here and there, as though striving to assert their former glory and supremacy in the place.

Within three years of Gardenhurst being dismantled, a rumour went through the county that the place had been taken by a gentleman from London, a Colonel Lisle, who would shortly bring down his wife and family to inhabit a small house close to Gardenhurst, which would serve as a temporary residence until the larger mansion could be rendered habitable and comfortable.

It was one bright morning in the month of August when this rumour was confirmed by two flys from the station drawing up before the "White Lodge," as it was called, and great was the excitement of the Misses Millwards, two old ladies who lived in an opposite house, when they heard the sound of the wheels rattling past their door.

Miss Eliza, the eldest, who was sitting by her window, peering anxiously down the road in search of any stray carts, little girls, or old women, who might excite her interest, was the first to perceive the carriages. "Virginia!" she said, in a tone of intense excitement, "They are come!"

Miss Virginia dropped her knitting pins and hobbled to the window, assisted by her gold-headed cane.

"So they are!" she said, in a tone of corresponding interest; "and look—look, they've got a parrot in a cage, and they are going to get out."

The two withered faces remained pressed against the window-pane, watching anxiously for the first appearance of the occupants of the carriages. The fly-door opened, and out stepped, with great deliberation, a middle-aged gentleman with a snowy head of hair, and an important-looking expanse of shirt front. This was Colonel Lisle. He was offering his arm with dignity to a grey-eyed, black-haired lady, who was the next to descend; but she, being apparently of an impetuous disposition, jumped hastily out, saying, "Get away, *do*, James, I am nearly suffocated!" Then out swarmed the other members of the family, two curly-headed schoolboys, who were no sooner free from the trammels of the wraps under which they had been buried for some hours, than they set up a wild whoop of delight and dashed round the house, being, like all new settlers, anxious for exploration.

Then came up the next carriage, from the window of which peeped out two restless bright eyes, surmounted by a pair of sharp-cut ears—these appertained to Toby, the Scotch terrier—who was in an agony of agitation until he should feel his paws again resting on mother earth. Holding him in her arms was a little girl of about eight years old—a round-faced, blue-eyed creature, whose thick, silky curls tumbled down in soft profusion round the dark fur boa that was twisted round her neck; her dimpled fingers were half buried in Toby's shaggy coat, in a vain effort to restrain his transports. This was Christine Lisle, the youngest and fairest of the party. Close to her sat another child about four years older than Christine : this was Esther, or, as she was commonly called, "Esty;" then came Flora, the eldest sister. These and the old nurse, Dolly, formed the complement of the Lisle party.

The Misses Millward had an excellent view of the new comers as the flys rolled away from the door of the White Lodge. Christine stood in the foreground pensively sucking her thumb, with a battered-faced doll hanging over one arm. Colonel and Mrs. Lisle disappeared within the door, while Esty ran away after the boys, followed by Toby, the latter making occasional digressions in search of imaginary cats or rabbits.

Miss Eliza sighed as the door closed on their new neighbours, and she and her sister applied themselves to their
little dinner with an additional zest, as they talked over the
probable future doings of the new comers. Meanwhile, the
latter were discussing a sort of picnic repast they had
brought with them, as their servants and luggage were not
expected till a later train. After they had finished their
meal Colonel Lisle looked at his watch.

"We might as well go up to Gardenhurst," he said, and
the children and Mrs. Lisle gladly assented. Esty and the
boys forthwith commenced a race down the long straggling
path which led to what was to be their new home. The
elders followed more slowly, Mrs. Lisle leading Christine,
while the colonel and Flora gazed with dismay at the
unkempt and overgrown condition of the flowers and
brambles that strayed over the pathway. A quarter of an
hour's walking brought them up to the front door—and red,
gaunt, old-fashioned, many-gabled Gardenhurst was before
them.

Mrs. Lisle stood still, feeling all her thoughts soothed to
calm by the beauty of the scene before her.

It was, as I have said, on the afternoon of an autumn
day when the sound of voices and patter of children's feet
came to break the silence and solitude of the old home of
the Cheshams. The magnolias gleamed white amidst their
dark green foliage on the house, while from under the roof
hung down the graceful tendrils of the vine-like Wistaria.
The delicate lilac petals had already begun to droop, and
the window-ledges were covered with their light withered
blossoms. Running up one corner of the house were the
light green leaves and quaintly-twisted flowers of the aristo-
lochiosipho, while the other angle of the wall was completely
hidden by thick branches of ivy, in the dense leaves of
which an occasional rustle gave token of feathered life. A
broad path of what had been golden gravel ran round the
house, but this had been much narrowed by the invading
edges of the lawn.

The dying sunbeams streamed over the tangled flower-
beds where roses, "not royal in their scents alone, but in
their hue," grew side by side with the wild thyme and
dandelions, and over the fragments of the sun-dial, whose

broken face was powerless any longer to record the flying hours, and whose base was buried in long streaming grasses.

The lawn sloped down to a sheet of water where the swans sailed majestically up and down, their snowy wings catching pink and golden reflections as they floated down the western side of the water, where the rosiness of the sunset hues was repeated.

"It will want a great deal of repair," said Colonel Lisle, meditatively. "But we have no money to make improvements with."

"It wants nothing!" said his wife—"nothing outside, at least."

"If I had ten thousand instead of ten hundred a year, I should never wish to have any alteration made in so perfect a scene:

> '. . . . . . The bills
> Of summer birds sing welcome as ye pass ;
> Flowers fresh in hue, and many in their class,
> Implore the pausing step, and with their dyes
> Dance in the soft breeze in a fairy mass,'"

she repeated, softly.

"Oh! there's some of your d——d poetry again," said the colonel, in an aggravated tone. "Ring at the bell, Flora, and let's see if there's anybody alive in this God-forgotten place."

Flora obeyed, pulling at the rusty wire with some difficulty, and the clang of the bell soon resounded within.

After a long pause, during which the swallows had found space to fly out of the eaves in alarm, circle round, and then retreat again, an old woman came to the door, and peered out at the strangers.

"What are yah dooing there?" she said, in the choicest X——shire dialect.

"Open the door! open the door!" cried the colonel, angrily.

"I shayn't," was the prompt reply. "I don't know knawthin about yah," and with that she disappeared in the shadows of the interior.

"What an old catamaran! We had better go up to the lodge again," said the colonel, discontentedly.

But youth, rich in expedients, and unbaffled by defeat,

came to the rescue, and Gerald, their eldest boy, who had
just run up flushed and panting to the scene of action,
suggested that if they went round to the back-door they
could effect a lodgement that way, as he had seen a little
girl feeding some chickens there.

To the back door they accordingly went; and while the
hens fluttered away with loud clucks of alarm, Colonel Lisle
explained to the obtuse old woman that he was the gentleman who had taken the house; and after he had aided her
comprehension by the gratuity of a shilling, she became
profuse in her curtsies and apologies.

Meanwhile the younger ones had effected their entrance,
and were scampering in different directions all over the
house.

Mrs. Lisle followed them more soberly; and, threading
her way through a dark and low-built passage, found herself
in the entrance to the front hall.   An opposite door led to the
drawing-room, on the threshold of which she paused, a little
chilled and depressed by its utterly desolate appearance.
Shreds of paper and plaster hung down from the walls, and
the rats had made big holes in the weakest part of the
wainscot and flooring.   Filling up one side of the wall was
a large and dingy oil painting, representing the murder of
the Dominican Friars, a copy of the picture at Bologna.
Perhaps in the light of morning Mrs. Lisle would have
smiled at the grotesque attitude of the flying monks, but
seen dimly through the fast gathering dusk of evening, their
white flowing garments presented a somewhat weird appearance.

The wind was beginning to rise with the decline of day,
and a Virginia creeper that trailed down the wall outside
the window beat restlessly against the broken panes of glass.
Mrs. Lisle shivered, and felt relieved when she heard the
patter of the children's feet, and the sound of their merry
voices close behind her.

"Oh, mamma!" they exclaimed, almost simultaneously,
"isn't it jolly?"

At that moment the colonel appeared at the door.
Majestically poising his gold-headed cane in his hand, he
looked round the room with a blank expression of dismay.

"Good Gawd!" he said, and there he paused, seemingly

too much overcome by indignation and astonishment to say a word more. Flora was more practical.

"Come away, mamma! come away, children! you'll all catch your deaths of cold. Let's get back to tea. We can finish our investigation to-morrow morning."

"We aint children no more than you!" retorted Gerald, with dignity. Flora was sixteen, Gerald thirteen and a half. The young discoverer had his ear pressed down against a plank of the floor, striving to ascertain the movements of a rat, which had scudded away to its nest under the flooring from the moment of Toby's excited entrance into the room.

Mrs. Lisle cut short the impending discussion by moving to go, and, taking the colonel's arm, she left the room, followed eventually by her whole tribe, only Toby venturing to resist the general mandate, and he remained as it were in a mesmerised attitude for some seconds, his eyes fixed on, and his nose fixed in, the hole in the flooring, and then, seized by a sudden panic as it flashed on him that he was left alone, he rushed through the rooms, and, following the trail, dashed frantically down the long path in pursuit of his friends. Having once regained them, he expressed his delight by making wild gyrations round their feet, and then subsided into that pre-occupied expression common to the canine face.

When the party arrived at the White Lodge, they found a bright fire blazing, a kettle singing on it, and tea set ready for them, while a huge currant cake which occupied the centre of the table caused the faces of the boys to expand into a grin.

The servants, consisting of two women and a man, who had arrived an hour since, had made these preparations; but the cake was a delicate attention on the part of the Misses Millward :—they hoped that if they could supply Mrs. Lisle with anything she wanted that she would not hesitate to apply to them. They would do themselves the honour of calling on Mrs. Lisle on the following day.

"What kind old ladies!" said Mrs. Lisle, gratefully.

"Reg'lar stunners, I call them," agreed Egbert, the youngest boy, stuffing a piece of the welcome gift into his mouth, while Christine gazed at him sadly out of her round, blue eyes, wishing she were big and determined enough to make such a ready and successful raid on the coveted food before her.

"Where's Miss Esty? what have you done with Miss Esty?" said Dolly, the nurse, who, in the cleansing process through which she had put the children, had missed one little face, which it was her duty to make shine—one little head she was bound to scarify with the hardest of brushes and most determined of hands.

"Here I am," said a small voice, rather guiltily; and Miss Esty appeared, her naturally blooming complexion obscured by smudges of dust and dirt, her fingers even more completely begrimed, while her blue pelisse, kept sacred for travelling and other great occasions, had two dismal-looking rents torn down the very middle of the skirt.

"O Lord! O Lord!" cried Dolly, wringing her hands. "What a naughty child you are! I'll tell your mar, directly, I will!"

Mrs. Lisle, however, had left the room, and was absent for some minutes; and by the time she had re-appeared, Esty had persuaded the irate Dolly, partly by real and partly by counterfeit penitence, to forego her intention of complaining to mamma.

Mamma had a practical mode, sometimes, of expressing her displeasure, which although doubtless salutary in its effect, was decidedly painful. This consisted of a sharp box on the ear, delivered with a precision and force which used to make the reeling culprit feel as though all the tinder-boxes in creation were striking sparks before his or her eyes. No wonder, then, that Esty crept away from the sitting-room as quietly as she could, and bore with more than ordinary patience the dabs of yellow soap being ruthlessly thrust into her eyes, nose, and ears, and the unmerciful castigation of the hair-brush, administered by Dolly with unusual energy as a sort of private let-out or temper, and compensation for the sacrifice she had made in not telling of Esty's misdemeanour. When the young lady came down to tea, she accounted for her late appearance by saying that she had been delayed at Gardenhurst by the sight of a large old box of worm-eaten books, which she had seen in one of the attics, and that she had stayed to look at the pictures in one of them. She did not add that, in endeavouring to reach her short arm down to the bottom of the box, she had lost her balance and fallen in head-long, coming out with her head and face in the manner described, and with one of the aforesaid books in her hand.

However, there must have been something suspicious in her uneasy mode of sitting on her chair; for when the meal was half finished, Gerald, the detective, espied the corner of something hard and square peeping out from under the hem of her pinafore.

"Oh, Esty, you greedy pig!" he cried; "you've got a book there; let me see it."

"*You're not to*, Gerald!" screamed Esty, in impotent wrath: "it's *my* book. Mamma, tell him to leave it alone!"

"What is it?" demanded the colonel, aroused from his contemplation of his hot buttered toast.

The book was handed to him, and, flushed and silent, the combatants awaited his decision. The colonel read the title-page, and his blue eyes grew large.

"Good Gawd, Elinor!" he said to his wife; "do you know what book it is your daughter has got hold of?"

He emphasised the *your* as though disclaiming any partnership with his wife in such a graceless offspring.

"I'm sure I don't know," said his wife, impatiently.

"It is the 'History of Tom Jones!'" thundered the colonel; and then he said, in milder accents, "Where do you expect that child will go to?"

CHAPTER II.

LADY RENSHAWE.

"Once was her face bright as the morning sun:
A man could then have loved her for Love's sake,
Nor asked for dowry to enhance the worth
His heart esteemed her at ; but now, whene'er
Her withered hand is kissed, 'tis for the sake
Of that it holds."

A. C. STEELE.

THE lights were out, the children had gone to bed, Colonel Lisle's last grumble was heard faintly through the passages, as he retreated to the little bed-room, made as comfortable as possible by the unwearied Dolly; and Mrs. Lisle still sat with her feet on the fender, in the sitting-room below, her head resting on her hand, and her fine grey eyes staring blankly at the fast dying embers. Outside, the silence was broken by the constant barking of a dog, and this sound, as well as that of the clematis branches beating against the window, came strangely to the ears of the new comer.

Now that the sounds of active life which surrounded the lady all hours of the day were hushed, and there was no further cause for energy, Mrs. Lisle's heart felt heavy and dead within her.

"Always the same," she thought to herself—"always the same ; toil and trouble, irritation that seems irrepressible, which must yet be repressed; labour without profit or pleasure ; labour enough to keep the wolf from the door, but with no power to bring comfort or affluence; a grumbling husband, troublesome children, who will be ungrateful when they grow up. Ah, well !" she sighed, "as I've made my bed, so must I lie on it. I don't wish to complain." Here Mrs. Lisle got up and kicked away the footstool viciously that had supported her feet. " But I wonder why I was ever born ?" with which un- answered question on her lips, she too left the room and went to bed.

She was wearied by the long journey and fatigues of the day, by the incessant calls made on her attention, and the never-ceasing grumbling of her husband, which after a time became as irritating as the tiny feathered shafts of the Liliputians were to their giant enemy; besides, she was too tired out by the struggles of life to feel any of that exuberant delight which filled the hearts of the children as they entered the precincts of a new home.

To them Gardenhurst was an unpenetrated paradise—a paradise because unpenetrated; and their young, fresh, vivid imaginations pictured fabulous delights to be gleaned from the wilderness of woods, shrubberies, and fruit trees. Every over-grown walk contained for them a delicious mystery. Every bird that flew from the bushes, every species of autumn fruit that glowed amidst the red-brown leaves, would prove to them a source of interest and enjoy- ment.

The boys had gone to sleep, with visions of Toby passing swiftly before their eye-sight, in full pursuit of grey cock-tailed rabbits ; while a beautiful smile played round Christine's mouth as she sleepily remembered a long row of strawberry beds, in which she had seen some of the dark-red berries of the Hautbois strawberry peeping out when she went down the path to Gardenhurst.

As for Esther, a different smile lurked round the corner of her mouth, as she tucked up her little feet under her like a dormouse preparing for his winter slumber.

I am compelled to say that her reflections were not of so innocent a complexion as those of her sister, for under- neath that guilty head and downy pillow lay the dusty little volume which had caused Colonel Lisle to utter that forcible

adjuration mentioned in the last chapter. "Tom Jones"
had been laid on a high shelf in the sitting-room after the
stormy discussion had ended to which his ill-timed appearance had given rise; but Esty had never taken her eyes
off the coveted prize, and when the children were saying
"Good-night" in one end of the room, Esty quietly and
deftly jumped on a chair, secured the book, and said
"Good-night" as demurely as though it were still on the
shelf to which Colonel Lisle's parental care had consigned
it.   And now she had got it safe under her cheek, and her
fingers could feel the edges of the volume which contained
so much temptation for her.   The temptation consisted of
a series of engravings, after designs by Gravelot, representing the loveliest and most slender of Sophias, with an im-
possibly small but very graceful head on her falling
shoulders, looking tenderly reproachful at the equally
small and delicate features of her unfaithful lover.   Esty
had caught a glimpse of these perfections in the dim light
of the attic at Gardenhurst, and, as she ran panting up the
long path in pursuit of her relatives, she had perfectly
revelled in the anticipation of the treat the morning's light
would bring her.

"Come, dear, say your prayers!" Dolly had said ere she
tucked up the feminine black sheep that night.

Esty obeyed, and, clasping her hands, went through the
usual formula, concluding with a mechanical blessing for
"Pa and ma, brothers and sisters;" then, turning on her
side, she murmured :—

"I *hate* Gerald; he's a beast!" and so she went off to
sleep.

It is time for me to answer a question that may ere now
have suggested itself to the reader, and which was, at the
time I write of, whispered in every country house in X——-
shire—namely, "Who are these Lisles?—where do they
come from?"   Only one person in the county could have
answered the question, and she lived so secluded a life, was
so impervious to the usual amenities of society, that it
would have required a bolder spirit than any of the X——-
shire people possessed to have induced them to invade her
privacy to seek to gratify their curiosity.   This was the
Countess Renshawe — an old lady who lived in a fine

mansion, called Lynncourt, situated about six miles from Gardenhurst. This Lady Renshawe was, in fact, Colonel Lisle's own aunt, and she was the loadstone that had drawn this large family within her circle.

"Why couldn't they leave me in peace?" the old lady complained to herself when she received that letter from Colonel Lisle, informing her that he was coming to settle near her, as he found London air injurious for his young family, and London rates and taxes equally injurious to his pocket. "James, having spent all his youth and money away from me, comes, now that he is getting poor, old, and cantankerous, to afflict me with his company and that of his children—nasty little savages!—who will go wohooping all over the house."

And the old lady sighed, and took a pinch of snuff impatiently.

Nevertheless, she sent a tolerably civil answer to her nephew's letter, only warning him that she believed Gardenhurst to be very damp and unhealthy, and that there was no skilful physician residing nearer to it than W—— (the county town), which was about thirty miles off, and she only "*hoped* that his poor children wouldn't suffer from the change."

Having despatched this epistle, Lady Renshawe felt that she had done what she could, which was indeed but little, to arrest the blow about to fall on her; and all that now remained was to sit still and hope that some unforeseen accident might occur to prevent this invasion of her domestic peace.

Days went on, and, hearing nothing more from her nephew, Lady Renshawe began to hope that he had altered his mind; and this thought gave such added brightness to her eyes and lightness to her step, that her old servants declared, proudly, "that missus grew younger every day."

CHAPTER III.

ESTY AT LYNNCOURT.

"Where aged elms, in many a goodly row,
Give yearly shelter to the constant crow,
A mansion stands :—long since the pile was rais'd,
Whose Gothic grandeur the rude hind amaz'd ;
For the rich ornament on ev'ry part
Confess'd the founder's wealth, and workman's art."
THE DOWAGER.

EFORE Colonel Lisle turned himself round for his
final nap on the evening of his arrival at Garden-
hurst, he made a significant observation :—
"We must call on the countess to-morrow."
And at breakfast-time the next day, when surrounded by
the jabber of voices and bevy of young faces, after a careful
adjustment of his cravat, Colonel Lisle looked up, and said
" Elinor " to his wife.

" Flora, we must call on the countess to-day."

This announcement was received with a general groan.

" Oh, papa," said Flora, sadly, "we shall be so uncomfortable to-day if we don't get things a little ship-shape ;"
and she looked disconsolately at the rows of unpacked
boxes, and the disordered aspect of tables, chairs, and
mantelpiece, each of which was covered with odds and ends
that as yet had found no local habitation.

" *I* won't go !" said Gerald, defiantly, and he was echoed
by the others, imitative as young creatures mostly are,
whether human or chimpanzee.

"I won't go," repeated Christine, vaguely, stuffing her little mouth the while with a great spoonful of sop.

"Silence, children!" said the colonel. "If I may be permitted to have an opinion in my own house," he continued, majestically, "I should say that it would be exceedingly unwise to let the countess hear of our advent by means of a third person; and some of you had better go over to Lynncourt this afternoon, and announce our arrival."

"Go yourself, pa," audaciously suggested Gerald.

"I shall do no such thing. I have a good deal to do, and shall have my hands full all day;" and, to evade any further discussion of the subject, Colonel Lisle left the breakfast-table and betook himself to his cigar and the perusal of his newspaper.

"The fact is, gov., you funk the old lady!" Gerald cried after him as he left the room; and the colonel, hastening his steps, pretended not to hear the irreverent suggestion, which, perhaps, carried some truth along with it.

"I suppose somebody must go," said Mrs. Lisle. "Flora, we can't do without you here, and as for the boys, they are sure to get into mischief—not but what Esty is as bad, if not worse."

The perplexed mother looked sadly at the row of rebellious faces, and wondered which child was least calculated to tread upon (metaphorically speaking) the aristocratic toes of the countess.

"Esty must go," she said at last, "and, Dolly, you can escort her, and take a note from me to Lady Renshawe."

Esty looked up quickly, as though inclined to rebel at this decision, but a significant glance from Dolly silenced the rising expostulation. Esty thought of her little brown volume, and hung her head; ere another half-hour was over, she and her nurse were walking quickly past dewy hedgerows and down sweet-scented lanes, accompanied by a country boy, who for the sum of sixpence was to conduct them by the short cut to Lynncourt. The gleams of the morning sun lit up the silvery films of the cobwebs that trembled on the bramble, and the drops of night-dew that clung to the fern leaves. Every broken bit of earth, every glistening group of wild grasses, conveyed a sense of

2

freedom and freshness to the little Londoner, who for
two years past had breathed nothing but town fogs and
smoke.

Esty was ecstatic. "Oh, Dolly," she cried, "isn't it
lovely?"

"Well, I'm sure I don't know, Miss," said Dolly,
snappishly. "What *I* like are nice shops, with bonnets and
caps in them, and a nice clean pavement to walk on. I'm
afraid we shall find it very lonesome down here."

"Across the fields" it was only three miles and a half to
Lynncourt, and after an hour's walking—a somewhat long
hour, owing to the difficulty Dolly experienced in keeping
her charge out of such mischief as wetting her shoes, or
adding fresh insults to the injuries already sustained by the
blue pelisse. Their guide informed them that if they would
stand on a knoll of meadow-land close to them, they could
see "the house yonder." They did so, and there, about a
quarter of a mile away, stood Lynncourt, the residence of
the Countess Renshawe, a countess in her own right, the
largest landowner in X——shire, and the aunt of Colonel
Lisle.

There stood grand old Lynncourt, a vast red brick
mansion, flanked by four towers that looked perfect emblems
of feudal strength. The morning sun shone brightly down
their massive sides, and rendered clearly the delicate
greyish-blue tint which time had cast over the once bright
red bricks.

Wave after wave of thick foliage rose behind and around
the house, the graceful masses of autumn trees being well
disposed to throw out the bold character of the noble pile of
buildings they enshrined ; innumerable flocks of rooks gave
out cheerful caw-caws as they passed to and fro in their undisturbed leafy territory, and herds of deer crouched in the
under shadows of the avenues, or passed with slow, halting
steps in line down the more open glades.

"Oh, Dolly, what a great place it looks!" said Esty, in a
subdued voice.

"I wonder what aunt will be like—if she'll be nice or
nasty?"

"Oh, she'll be nice enough," said Dolly, re-assuringly.
"Come along, do!"

They arrived now at a massive gateway, where two stone griffins rested immovable on the columns by the side.

Dry leaves lay lightly between their paws and the pleasant flicker of sunlight coming through the thick foliage overhead played over their grey stone backs, so that their ferocity seemed tempered by the beauty of the day. Nevertheless Dolly, looking up, ejaculated:

" Laws ! what horrid-looking things !"

An old woman opened the gate for them, and the nurse and child found themselves traversing a long avenue of elms and chestnut trees ; thick brushwood and a rich undergrowth of fern formed a shelter for herds of red deer, whose antlers peeped up in all directions as soon as their quick ears caught the sound of approaching footsteps.

This avenue continued for about half a mile ; and then Dolly and her charge, passing through a large iron gate to the open part of the park, found themselves about three hundred yards from the house.

A broad gravel path ran round this, and by the sides stood large vases filled with scarlet geraniums, while over their rims drooped long tendrils of blue and white convolvuli.

Standing close to a rose tree on the lawn they saw the figure of a lady, slightly bent in the back, and wearing a large poke bonnet, which concealed every feature of her face, excepting, indeed, the tip of her nose, which projected like the proboscis of a Roman emperor on a medallion.

Esty turned white.

" Oh, Dolly, I do believe that's aunt herself !"

" Lor, well ! I shouldn't wonder if it is."

Dolly edged off from that side of the lawn where Lady Renshawe stood, and conducted Esty to the low, nail-studded door that formed the principal entrance to the house.

While they are waiting there, and Esty's awe-stricken eyes are regarding the huge escutcheon above the porch, I will devote a few words to the owner of this noble domain.

Fifty years prior to the date at which my story begins, two young ladies—co-heiresses and daughters of the then

2—2

Earl of Renshawe—lived together in sisterly amity and con-
cord at Lynncourt.

These were the ladies Kerriston—Annabella and Clara—
and they were the sole issue of the aforesaid earl.

They were of the respective ages of nineteen and seventeen years (Annabella being the elder), when accident made
them acquainted with a young and handsome man, Captain
Lisle, whose regiment was stationed at W——, the county
town.

Chance commenced the acquaintance, but design continued it, for Captain Lisle soon became alive to the
advantages to be reaped from his intimacy with two handsome women, well-born and rich, and before he had visited
three months at Lynncourt, he discovered that he might
have either of the sisters for the asking.   They were very
young.   Their father had delayed their appearance in the
great world because he feared that their beauty and wealth
might make them too great attractions for the needy and
unprincipled.   And lo! while he was watching the enemy
from afar, a foe had crept in through his gate under his very
eyes, and the earl saw him not.

For a long time Frederic Lisle wavered to and fro in his
allegiance to the two sisters, uncertain whether to be more
attracted by the somewhat imperious beauty and masculine
intellect of Annabella, or by the softer lineaments and ductile mind of her sister.   He sang duets with and attended
Annabella at the tea table, but he walked in the shrubbery
with Clara, and talked sentiment with her under the flower-
ing lilacs and drooping acacias; and at last one summer
morning arrived when Lord Renshawe, hobbling round his
woodland domain, stood still, transfixed by amazement and
indignation : for there in the shady path before him, unconscious of his approach, stood two young people, whose
attitude was eminently picturesque had my Lord Renshawe
been disposed to view them in an artistic light.

The light dress of his daughter fluttered round her lithe
figure, supported by Captain Lisle's arm; her fair head
rested on his shoulder while he laughingly tried to disen-
gage from the tangles of those sunny curls a number of
lilac petals that had fallen in a shower from the branch overhead.

"Why, what the dev——?" But the young couple, startled and terrified as they were, met the surprise bravely, and entreated and prayed so long and earnestly for forgiveness, that the father, always too indulgent to this his favorite child, at last was induced to give some sort of consent to their happiness, only stipulating that no immediate steps to ensure it were to be taken, as "Clara was very young, and might change her mind."

And so Captain Lisle found himself engaged before he had intended it, and accident had solved the difficulty which the choice of beauties had presented to him; but his feelings that night were not enviable, when he felt conscious, by the keen scorn expressed in Annabella's fine dark eyes, that she had heard of and fully appreciated the meanness of his conduct.

She never forgave him, and I do not think she ever, in her heart, quite forgave her sister; although when Lord Renshawe's sudden death, which occurred a few months after, left his sisters alone in the world, Annabella did all that she possibly could to ensure Clara's future comfort and happiness.

She prepared the trousseau, took means to ensure the settlement of Clara's money, so that her husband could in no way touch it, presented the young couple with a superb service of plate to start with, and, finally, saw Clara given away at the altar to her lover, just one year after Lord Renshawe's death and her own discovery of Frederic Lisle's treachery.

The fief was a female one, so it was as Lady Renshawe that Annabella uttered these parting words to her sister:

"Good-bye, dear! I've done my duty to you—have I not?"

"Yes, ye—s," sobbed Clara, and she would have thrown herself on her sister's neck, but the latter put her back.

"I have only to say now that if you and your husband wish to requite any service I may have rendered you, you will do it best by letting me see and hear as little of you as possible. Good-bye!" and with a cold shake of the hand with her brother-in-law, who stood looking inexpressibly perplexed, Lady Renshawe parted for ever from the only near relative fate had left her.

"Thank Heaven, they're gone!" she said, bitterly, as she re-entered her sitting-room, and sat down to a lonely dinner.

But the loneliness, oppressive as it was, was less irksome to the young beauty of two and twenty than the gnawing feeling of jealousy that had never ceased to live in her heart since her sister's betrothal to the man she had hoped to accept her as her own husband.

Guardians, trustees, and would-be chaperons had buzzed round the young countess ever since her orphanage; but like the vindictive ghost in the story of Wild Dayrell, she "scared them all." By her acuteness in business matters and thorough independence of character she soon proved that she could exist without their advice or assistance; and reluctantly, one by one, the would-be sharers in Lynncourt's greatness and Lynncourt's wealth were compelled to abandon both to the absolute control of the astute young lady.

"Of course she'll marry," said the X—— gossips; and "of course she'll marry," they went on repeating, long after the rounded cheeks of the countess had shrunk and faded, and the black hair had become streaked with grey.

Lady Renshawe never married; and she never saw Captain or Lady Clara Lisle again.

Years after, when both her sister and false lover had gone to their last rest, the countess consented to receive their sole surviving child, her nephew James, then a fine young man of two and twenty, a lieutenant in the —— Dragoons. He was handsome in person, and at that time was winning in manner; and, after he had got hopelessly in debt two or three times and had called on the countess's clear head and well-filled purse to aid him in his difficulties, she really became attached to him, finding herself interested in solving the problem of how to keep a good-natured, extravagant, ne'er-do-weel out of the way of mischief. Remember, she was not a mother herself, and therefore not likely to be troubled with any additional black sheep; otherwise, she perhaps would have looked less leniently on a colour that might have tainted the whole flock.

For two years her handsome young nephew was a source of never-failing interest and amusement to her. But at the

end of that time, Lieutenant Lisle's pecuniary embarras-
ments made it necessary for him to take up his residence on
the Continent, and during a stay of two months at Florence
he fell in love with a Miss Elinor Morley, the portionless
daughter of a half-pay officer resident there, married her,
and then wrote and asked his aunt for her consent to that
which was irrevocable.

Lady Renshawe's answer was characteristic.

"My dear James," she wrote, "you have made a fool of
yourself to please yourself: do not expect me to feel any
reflected pleasure from your act of folly; do not trouble
yourself to call on me if you come to England, as I am
growing old, and the sight of fresh faces is irksome to me.
I would recommend you to practice economy a little, now
that you have entered on the expenses and responsibilities
of married life. And I am your affectionate,

"A. Kerriston Renshawe."

James Lisle was twenty-four years of age when he took
unto himself a wife; and it is but due both to himself and
Miss Elinor Morley to say, that they bitterly repented the
rash step they had taken before they had been married
many years.

Not that they did not love each other: they were quite
as much attached to one another as married people
generally are, but they both got rather wearied of their lives
—she, with the incapability of her husband to appreciate
the greatness of the love she had at first lavished on him,
and he, with the shackles of poverty that weighed upon him
more heavily every year as his family increased and his
means grew less.

Time passed away; the rich brown of James Lisle's hair
had changed into snowy white, and he and his wife were
growing old together under trouble and privation, when the
advertisement that Gardenhurst, X——shire, was to let
caught his eye one morning as he sat over a smoky little
fire in his breakfast-room in A—— Street, London.

James, now Colonel Lisle, had considerably aged since
that sunny morning when he walked quickly up the Lung'
Arno with the intention of asking Elinor Morley to

accompany him to the English chapel to make herself one
with him and his fortunes.

His brown curls had become white; the dimples round
his mouth had hardened into deep lines, and the indentations
on his broad forehead spoke of trouble and vexation;
above all, a certain querulousness in his voice, and an
impatience in that of his wife, showed that the days since
their marriage had not flowed very smoothly with them:
still they had their gleams of happiness—who has not?—
poverty, although it nipped, could not repress Mrs. Lisle's
love of art; and she found time, even amidst the drudgery
of housekeeping, stocking-mending, and nursing, to taste
many a pleasure unknown to women of meaner capabilities.
During the weary years of her sojourn in London she found
consolation for the toil and clamour of her household life, by
spending quiet hours in the picture galleries on those days
devoted to artists; and it was no slight pleasure to her to
think, as she laid her weary head on her pillow each night,
of the painting she had left smiling on her easel, and which
would meet her freshened gaze the next morning with what
would seem renewed radiance, while its very defects would
give her as much pleasure to attempt to correct as a lover
feels when he fancies he removes the mental blemishes of
his mistress.

Meanwhile, Colonel Lisle also had his moments of solace
in the shape of daily papers, town gossip, and an occasional
dinner given him by some chance friend at "The Tatters."

But still, as his children grew bigger, and their small
house in A——Street did not enlarge itself in proportion,
and as the expenses of the boys' tuition made it more and
more difficult to pay all the rates and taxes incidental to
residence in a town house, Colonel Lisle came to the
conclusion that some steps must be taken to soften the heart
and open the purse-strings of his noble relative, the Countess Renshawe.

"If the old girl and Elinor could only meet," the colonel
said, in the colloquial style of domestic conversation, "they'd
get on like a house on fire!" And so, a few days after he had
seen the advertisement, Colonel Lisle sat down to his desk,
and penned a letter to his noble kinswoman, in which he
informed her that the white cheeks and thin legs of his

children warned him that a small cramped house in town was not the best residence in the world for a large family, and that he had been compelled to look out for some country-house, where at a less expense he could ensure better accommodation for his "dear ones." A friend had pointed out to him an advertisement, announcing that "Gardenhurst" was to be let; and partly because he had many pleasant reminiscences associated with the dear old place (in his boyhood James Lisle had been in the habit of plundering the Gardenhurst fruit trees and fishing in the long pond there), and partly because he would like to spend his latter years near one whose kindness had so often smoothed away the troubles of youth, he had made up his mind to remove at once to Gardenhurst, and to reside in the lodge until he could make the large house a little habitable!"

"Well, that's a hint for me," said Lady Renshawe, as she paced up and down her gravel walk, with quick, little, irritable steps. "Wants me to go and make the place comfortable for that woman and her brats;—a likely idea!" And my lady sniffed and walked with a more determined step than ever.

Meanwhile we have left little Esty and her nurse standing in the portico of the Lynncourt doorway. In answer to Dolly's somewhat feeble ring, a tall and pompous-looking butler came to the door: he had what seemed to be a white frill of hair standing up truculently round his shining bald head, and he spoke in a strong aggressive voice, which made Esty feel meeker than ever.

"If you please, this is Lady Renshawe's little niece, Miss Lisle, and she's come to call on her aunt, if you please," said Dolly.

"Ho! really!" said the dignified butler (his name was Mr. Lintoff), in a tone of contemptuous surprise. "Didn't know she had one!"

"Well, you know it now," said Dolly, sharply, her spirit rising under the oppression of patronage. "So please don't keep Miss Lisle waiting."

Mr. Lintoff smiled. This great man was magnanimous, and rather admired the retaliation his magnificence had provoked.

"Come hin, hif you please," he said, more graciously;
and then, while Esty gazed subdued and awe-stricken at the
folds of faded tapestry that hung on the staircase wall, and
the dim shields and helmets that were fixed in grim array round
the hall, Mr. Lintoff warned her in solemn accents : "Little
Miss, 'twould be best not to make too much noise walking
over the floors ; Missis don't like no noise but her own !"
He walked before them until they came to a glass-door
overlooking the garden.

"There she is !" and Mr. Lintoff, opening the door for
them, walked grandly back to the region whence he had
come, declining to accompany them down the long walk to
announce them ; for, as he said, the "sun always made is
ead hache."

Lady Renshawe was standing before her favourite red-rose
trees, snipping off with a pair of huge scissors any withered
bud that could be detected peering out among the glowing
blossoms, when she was stopped in her decapitation of the
roses by hearing a little voice at her elbow saying. "Good-
morning, grand-aunt;" and then, like the Lady of Shalott,
she knew that "the curse had come upon her," and, turning
round sharply, the large scissors open in her hand presenting a somewhat menacing appearance, she said :

"Oh, you're come, are you?   And who are you?"

"Esther Lisle, gran'-aunt; and I've come to bring you
a letter, and to hope you're well ; and oh, grand-aunt !" and
here Esty's tone of respect changed to one of intense
anxiety.

"Well, what's the matter, child ?"

"Oh, don't you see Toby's running after a cat, and if he
catches her he'll kill her."   And here Esty's terror for the
safety of the cat quite overmastered the small amount of
manners she had been assuming for the occasion, and she
rushed away down the smooth-shaven lawn, at the bottom of
which could be seen a view in perspective of Toby's back,
as that enthusiastic animal sat barking furiously, his tail
beating the ground and his bright eyes and ears pointing
upwards to the branch of a tree, where stood a large tabby cat,
clawing her perch with tail unnaturally swollen and eyes
flashing fire.

"Toby, Toby, T-o-o-oby," screamed Esty, but with no

effect. Toby remained as immovable as the celebrated American colonel might have done when he stared down the 'coon; and Esty had to pluck him up and carry him under her arm to the door-step of the house, where Lady Renshawe awaited her, speechless with indignation.

" How dare you bring that brute here ? " she demanded. " Nasty little thing, it ought to be shot."

Esty flushed.

" It's quite natural Toby should run after the cat, but you ought to know better than to wish to have him killed."

" Hoity toity," said the old lady — " Teaching your granny. No, never mind, nurse, you needn't apologise for her. Go round and get something to eat, and leave the child with me."

Dolly curtsied and retreated, casting a warning look at Esty.

" Now, child, come and talk to me a little." And she led Esty up to where garden seats were placed by the wall, and half poked, half thrust her down on one of them. Esty sat with her little legs hanging down, and a generally constrained expression on her face. The old lady placed her spectacles more firmly on her nose, and grimly surveyed the little victim.

" You're very plain, my dear," she remarked at last.

" Yes, grand-aunt," said Esty, meekly.

"And very stupid, too, I daresay," retorted her old relative.

" Yes, aunt."

" Well, you don't like me, do you ? "

" No, not much," said Esty, candidly.

Lady Renshawe grinned, and there was a pause.

" Who do you think I'm like?" the latter asked presently.

" Well," said Esty, with a momentary flash of enthusiasm, " I was thinking that you are like the old witch in Jorinda and Jorindel—Gammer Grethel's story, you know."

" Upon my word you're a nice child. Come in and have some luncheon ; I'd better stop your mouth before you say anything else rude," said Lady Renshawe, rising to go.

" Yes, aunt," responded Esty, meekly as before, and with some difficulty she wriggled her legs to the ground, and followed her aunt through the glass-door into the house.

A pleasant room was that dainty little sitting-room into which Lady Renshawe ushered her young visitor; muslin curtains waved at the open windows and clematis clambered over the window-ledge; a table covered with books stood between the windows, and in the midst of these there was a blue china vase filled with red roses and lilies of the valley.

The dove-coloured walls were hung with rich prints and one or two valuable original pictures. Lady Renshawe's quick eyes saw the start and look of admiration in the child's earnest gaze as she looked at one of these.

This was a Magdalen by Guido—a three-quarter face, with eyes looking up and a burnished glory of auburn hair falling softly over the sweet mellow-tinted cheeks, and over the round fingers of the clasped hands.

" What do you think of that?" asked Lady Renshawe.

" Oh, aunt, I think it is beautiful—I wish ——"

" What do you wish ? "

"That mamma could copy it, she would like it so much."

" Ho!" said Lady Renshawe, snappishly, " I daresay ; go and take off your things, child! "

And she pointed to an adjoining ante-chamber, wherein the little pelisse and straw hat might be deposited ; and when the child returned with a pair of blue eyes shining brightly through her unkempt brown tresses, the old lady drew her to the window, and after looking narrowly at the small face for some moments, inclined her wrinkled chin and imperious nose, and for the first time kissed the new comer.

"I don't think I shall mind you much after all, my dear," the old lady said, graciously; and she turned away with a softer gleam in her grey eyes, and a tremulous movement agitating the wrinkles round her mouth. Some look, some chance expression in the child's face, had sent a thrill through Lady Renshawe's heart, reminding her of a summer-day of years past, when she sat with her little sister reading Faëry Tales under the old cedar outside, and when Clara, with eyes as blue as Esty's, had looked up inquiringly to learn the fate of those lost children who had trusted to bread-crumbs to guide their

way and who found that their landmarks had been devoured by the birds of the forest.

Lady Renshawe had not wept when she heard of her
sister's death. The wife of Captain Lisle was a woman
who had betrayed her confidence, and who had been her
successful rival. Time and absence had confirmed rather
than shaken off the bitter impressions left on Annabella's
mind on that day when her sister and lover went forth to
cast their lot together, and for many years after the
remembrance of Clara had only brought a pang of anger
into her sister's heart. And now that it was all over, "the
vain unsatisfied longing," the love and the bitterness of
disappointed passion—all merged in the dead calm of fifty
years of monotonous life—Lady Renshawe looked into a
child's eyes, and felt, for the first time, tenderness and
remorse.

"I was hard," she muttered—"too hard. She had no
mother, and I, who should have acted as one to her, was a
jealous, implacable rival."

And little Esty marvelled, for some moments after, at the
tenderness of her grand-aunt's voice and manner, and
wondered why she had been so afraid of her during that uncomfortable sojourn on the garden seat.

When the shadows were falling round Lynncourt, and the
least streak of crimson had disappeared behind the group of
firs, little Esty and Dolly passed out through the gate,
where the griffins looked darker and more threatening than
in the morning sun.

Esty's hands were filled with rare flowers, and her nurse's
arms were weighed down by a large basket of fruit which
Lady Renshawe had assisted to pack in the cool green
leaves, saying :—

"There Esther, take them to your mother, and say I
should be glad if they would all come and spend the day
here next week; but mind, *you* are to come again to-morrow.
Good-night, dear!"

CHAPTER IV.

OUR HEROINE.

"He has the eyes of youth; he speaks holyday;
He writes verses; he smells April and May!"

MERRY WIVES OF WINDSOR.

WELVE months passed away, and again the rushes that grew so thickly on the margin of Gardenhurst lake began to throw brown shadows into the depths below. This past year had been one of great anxiety and fatigue to the new tenants of Gardenhurst.

If there is but a step from the sublime to the ridiculous, there were in this case very few miles between magnificence and poverty. Lady Renshawe was rich, possessor of lands, carriages, and servants; and Colonel Lisle, the future heir of Lynncourt, was poor, had no carriages, had a tumbledown house, and only three servants.

Lady Renshawe received piles of letters, which as a rule she declined to open, because, she said, they were sure to be begging-letters or circulars.

Colonel Lisle also received many epistles, but his objection (which was very great) to opening them arose from a painful consciousness that they would contain demands for that immediate attention he was so unable to accord them. As they had so little money, and as Mrs. Lisle was a woman of strong practical, as well as of imaginative, genius, she found a good deal of personal labour for herself and her children to accomplish during the time they were moving into their new home.

From six in the morning to six in the evening would Mrs. Lisle toil incessantly, assisting in papering rooms, making carpets, covering chairs ; all labour seemed to come within the compass of her deft fingers and inventive talent. Colonel Lisle would frequently pause in his morning parade before the windows, and take his cigar from his lips, saying : " Good heavens, Elinor, what a rag-bag you look ! " as he witnessed the wife of his bosom, with her dress tucked up decisively round her waist, and her face and finely-moulded arms covered with dabs of paste.

The boys, as usual, did their utmost to retard their mother's progress, by kindly fighting over the heavily weighted slips of paper that had to be handed up to Mrs. Lisle, as she stood in an exalted position on a ricketty ladder, waiting to smooth away the wrinkles as she laid the pieces on the wall. Having one day, in their officious eagerness, nearly upset the ladder, Mrs. Lisle, pastepot, and all, they were dismissed the room, and were succeeded by Dolly, who was a much more effectual assistant.

Meanwhile, Lady Renshawe's ponderous old-fashioned coach had paid many a visit to the Gardenhurst Lodge; it was not always tenanted by the countess, as she was averse to going out beyond the length of her stately garden walks ; but it generally brought some timely gift of fruit or game, together with some civil message to Mrs. Lisle, and an entreaty that little Esty might be spared to come back in the carriage, and spend the evening at Lynncourt.

Lady Renshawe did not easily get over the distaste she had formed for her ungrateful nephew and his unwelcome wife ; but she had taken a strong fancy to the young face that had côme the first to break a solitude of nearly twenty years' duration, and she strove to please the parents for the sake of the child.

So Colonel Lisle was welcome to eat as many dinners and read as many papers as he liked at Lynncourt ; but the former was a privilege he rarely availed himself of, as Lady Renshawe's repasts, although served on magnificent plate, and attended with due solemnity by the great Mr. Lintoff,

were generally of the simplest description, and it suited
Colonel Lisle better to eat a chop served up hissing and hot
by Dolly's clean nimble fingers, than to wait while the same
fare grew cold under the deliberate attendance of the Lynncourt butler.

Besides which, his vanity and sense of dignity were
always being "rubbed the wrong way" by the caustic
remarks of his venerable relation.

"Aha, James!" she would say, with a malicious chuckle,
"you've taken to spectacles uncommonly early, and I do
declare you're more grey than I am," or, "My dear James,
how you walk! Like a porpoise (she meant tortoise), I
declare; look at *me!*" And she would speed down the
path with an activity that gave little promise of her leaving
her high-heeled shoes vacant for her nephew to wear for
many a day to come.

"The catamaran!" the latter would say, indignantly, as
he watched the movements of her poke-bonnet as it bobbed
up and down among the flower beds. "She's immortal, by
Jove!"

To Elinor, Lady Renshawe was more conciliating.
There was much in the character of the high-minded, active
mother that assimilated with the elder lady's acute intellect
and untiring energy; and when one day the countess's
black silk bonnet and Roman nose unexpectedly appeared
in the Gardenhurst drawing-room, and she found Elinor
immersed in the mending of what seemed inexhaustible
holes in the boys' stockings, she said kindly, "My dear,
how can you go on mending those uninteresting pieces of
merino, with that half-finished face looking at you from the
easel?" and when Mrs. Lisle had answered, wearily, that
her work must be finished, as the boys, in the language of
Dolly, "hadn't a bit of sock to their feet," the old lady had
sat promptly down, hoisted the gold-rimmed spectacles, and
worked energetically for about an hour—a piece of practical
kindness which did more to bring the two together than any
elaborate plan Colonel Lisle could have ever hit on to
reconcile his aunt and to pacify his wife.

After this little incident, Lady Renshawe bestirred herself
to confer more substantial favours on her relations than
could be conveyed in presents of hares and partridges, for

which, as Mrs. Lisle used sadly to remark, "she always had to give a shilling to the bearer."

She sent the two boys to Winchester—a step which was much needed for their benefit, although, as the countess remarked, pathetically, "it was money thrown into the sea, as far as Gerald was concerned;" for "it was easy to see that he'd never come to any good." However, both he and Egbert were made the happy possessors of shining black hats, and other little proprieties of costume necessary for public school-"men;" and one sunny morning they departed for the railway station, their little faces looking somewhat woeful as they rolled off in the solemn Lynncourt chariot. They drove their knuckles into their eyes, in a most suspicious fashion, when they caught the last glimpse of Toby's head, as he struggled desperately to get free from Esty's arms, to join his old companions. Esty standing on the door-step that day with her finger in her mouth, and the hot tears welling down her somewhat dirty cheeks, made a resolution born of penitence and remorse.

"If they ever come back," she sobbed, "I'll let Egbert have the biggest share of apple dumpling on Sunday, and I'll never tell Gerald again that he is a sneak for bowling at my legs at cricket." Then turning round to join little Christine, who was busily picking up yellow apples under the apple tree, Esty gave vent to her excitement in such piteous moans and tears, that Christine, quite moved and scared by such unwonted emotion on her sister's part, came up crying too, for company, gently urging the offer of a half-eaten apple on her, as the only adequate means of consolation she possessed.

Peace now reigned in the Gardenhurst household. Mrs. Lisle, less fettered by maternal cares, and having succeeded in transforming the long uninhabited house into as comfortable a domestic residence as their small means permitted, was at length able to rest herself in the enjoyment of more congenial occupations. And now, as soon as breakfast was despatched, and household orders disposed of, she would draw her easel up to the window, and sit for hours entranced in her occupation, and listening vaguely to Colonel Lisle's trenchant but totally inapplicable criticisms, or to Esty's gentle voice, as she sat rolling out big words from Franklin's

3

translations of the Greek plays, words which came oddly
from her little mouth, but which it pleased Mrs. Lisle to
hear, and which did not displease Esty, for, as soon as her
ears became familiarised to the hard words, she was able to
glean some comprehension of the tragic stories and their
dark beauties ; and her eyes used to light up with that look
of glistening enthusiasm one rarely sees but in the eyes of
children, when she read out the mad eloquence of
Cassandra's futile prophecies, or the sad pleadings of
Agamemnon's sacrificed daughter.

Esty was now thirteen years of age, and for her had
commenced what was to be the happiest portion of her life.
Heretofore the companionship of her brothers had kept the
masculine element in her nature almost entirely in the
ascendant; emulation of their boyish feats of strength had
made her as expert a climber of trees, and as fearless a rider
of the shaggy Shetland pony, as Gerald or Egbert themselves ; and she would receive blows on the face from their
hard hit cricket balls with a stoicism that endeared her
much to those unscrupulous urchins, who, by a few words of
commendation as to her "pluck," and her qualifications as
being a "regular trump," could reconcile her to any amount
of physical ill-usage.   "Christine was no good," they would
say, contemptuously, regarding the delicate beauty of their
fairer and more timid sister with great disdain. ·

"If you so much as run after her, she cries and tells
mamma."

And, indeed, this was a species of persecution peculiarly
objectionable to the plump and nervous little girl, who
would run from them, with her feet pattering as quickly as
those of a scared chicken, till she sank on the ground in a
paroxysm of unreasoning terror, beseeching them, piteously,
"Not to !"

But now the boys were gone, and Christine could pursue
her favourite occupation of sucking her fingers and dressing
her doll in peace and quietness.   She would sit still thus for
hours, singing in a low voice tuneless little songs, in evidence
of her content; and Dolly would say of her with admiration,
"her pinafore was the cleanest and her face the sweetest in
the house."

My heroine—for it may be already evident to my readers,

that unkempt, untidy, bright-eyed Esty, is to be my heroine
—had not been, up to this date, an especial favourite of
any one, excepting Lady Renshawe, on whom the burthen
of Esty's faults rarely fell.   The latter was the plague of
Dolly, and the especial annoyance of her father, who
complained that her presence was as baneful to his library
as that of the goblin in fable land, who visited houses for
the express purpose of causing endless trouble and confusion.
If his ink disappeared, be sure it was Esty who had carried
it off, and who would be discovered in a corner, concocting
romances in a weak, straggling hand.   In these early
effusions German barons would behave with great ferocity
to lovely wives, who would assuage their husband's cruelty,
and console their own wounded spirits, by bringing a son
and heir into the world, many months before the time that
more experienced narrators would have allowed for such an
event.

If the books in the shelves were put up the wrong side
upwards, it was Esty who had so misplaced them ; in fact,
she took the position that is generally assumed by cats
among delinquent housemaids, and bore the blame of nearly
all small domestic misfortunes.

At this age she could scarcely be called a pretty child.
The fairness of her skin was generally obscured by sun
tan ; her hands, so small, brown, and thin, might have belonged to a monkey ; and her eyes, blue and bright as they
were, made her face look more weird, shining as they did
from under untidy masses of brown hair.   By the side of
Christine's angelic loveliness, Esty looked what Dolly often
apostrophised her as, namely, an "imp," and her general
demeanour scarcely added much attractiveness to her
personal appearance.   The only person for whom she felt
much affection was Christine ; she enjoyed the meek
homage the gentler disposition accorded her, and she felt
a loving pity, slightly tinctured with contempt, for a child
who couldn't ride two yards unless Esty held her on, and
who couldn't invent any original pastime without her
sister's aid and suggestions.   On more than one occasion
poor Christine nearly fell a victim to her faith in Esty's
prowess.   Colonel Lisle, walking leisurely round the
ground one morning, heard weak cries of distress coming

3—2

from the direction of the round pond, as it was called, a pond situated in a secluded part of the Gardenhurst shrubbery. On arriving at the spot, he beheld his youngest darling's angel face bespattered with chickweed, and her fair hair trailing in company with water weeds, which, like the Naïads' sedgy crowns, surmounted her "ever harmless locks," while Esty, in a still more woeful plight, was making frantic efforts to pull Christine out of the mud in which her white legs were immersed.

The fact was, Esty had persuaded her sister to come on board her boat, the said boat consisting of an old washing-tub, which Esty had purloined from the washhouse; and in this "seasoned vessel," as Esty called it, the two little girls purposed to make a tour round the world,—*i.e.*, round the pond. Fortunately for their ultimate safety, as they were pushing off from the shore by means of a line pole, Christine's habitual nervousness caused her to make a sudden movement to rise, which movement capsized the vessel and its cargo, sufficiently near shore to have no worse effect than to upset the two adventurers into the mud, from which Colonel Lisle extricated them, to the great detriment of his spotless fingers.

"On my word, Esther," said the irate father, giving her an angry shake at arms' length as though she were an objectionable Skye terrier, "you deserve to be well flogged!"

And, indeed, when Dolly discovered the state the children were in on their return home, she applied a hair-brush so vigorously to Miss Esty's shoulders, that she drove that young lady to take refuge in a high tree, from which altitude the prisoner avenged herself by making all the most insulting grimaces at Dolly that she could invent; and in that occupation, so aggravating to her helpless enemy, and so entertaining to herself, she found consolation for her tingling ears and smarting shoulders.

CHAPTER V.

ESTY'S YOUTH.

"Why, what a madcap hath Heaven lent us here!"
                                        KING JOHN.

> "No fountain from its rocky cave
> E'er stepped with foot so free;
> She seemed as happy as a wave
> That dances on the sea."
>   WORDSWORTH.

WHEN her brothers had been gone some weeks, the taste for these freaks gradually died away in Esty's mind, and there began to be born in her that delicious sense of awakening intelligence which makes life such a day-dream of delight to those who have been gifted with souls quick to appreciate the mental fruit they consume with the fresh avidity of youth. Reading had come to Esty very much by the same desultory chance as that to which Topsy imagined her existence was due—"it growed."

Of regular education she received but little, for Mrs. Lisle had been so disheartened by her futile attempts to render Flora accomplished, that she utterly declined to spend money or time on Esty, saying, "if she has talent it will develop itself; if not, what is the good of my spoiling her life and my own by attempts to give her to eat what she cannot digest?" And so she gave her younger daughters no other advantage than that of living constantly in her society—an advantage which Esty involuntarily improved. Impressionable as all young things are, she contracted a tone of refinement and an aspiration for art, rare in ordinary children of that age, but not wonderful in one who possessed a keen imagination and great susceptibility to beauty, and who breathed in that little unfurnished painting-room the very atmosphere of poetry and culture.

Her life at this period was as wild and untrained as the Virginia creeper that clambered round the Gardenhurst windows. Most of her summer mornings were spent in the rushes and long grass by the side of the lake, and she would lie still for hours, drinking in the beauty of sky and earth, and watching the long dragon-flies, with their blue bodies and tremulous wings, as they whirred and gleamed "a living flash of light" through the reeds; or, with a Waverley Novel in her hand, she would read with kindling eyes of the clash of arms that stirred through King Louis's .line of Scottish guard when the Burgundian envoy flung his glove at his royal master's feet, for there was a little of the boy element still in her disposition, and as yet her sympathies ran more with the soldier heroes of romance than with the hopeless lovers. Still she wept bitterly over the dark fate of Edgar of Ravenswood, and his sad-faced Lucy, and she hated Lady Ashton, as only the young *can* hate.

Her days passed away like a pleasant dream, filled with confused fancies, in which Ivanhoe, Harry of Perth, Rebecca, Henry V., and the numberless heroines of the Arabian Nights, figured most conspicuously. It was pleasant to get away from Dolly and the agonies she inflicted by means of frilled muslin frocks that grated the bare shoulders, and shoes which, with a Chinese notion of beauty, she insisted on having too small for Esty's feet. It was pleasant, I say, to get away from these, to kick off the shoes and sit undisturbed behind the library door, where, with the roses peering in through the opened window, and summer insects making soft buzzing noises through the air, Esty could sit crouched out of sight, with her last purloined book in her hand. Like a dog with a bone, she generally preferred privacy for the consumption of her prey, and there, in the very last place Colonel Lisle would think of searching for his audacious daughter, she would sit, peopling the old-fashioned English garden with veiled Georgians, tinkling lutes, gushing fountains, and many other unattainable luxuries described in the enchanted regions of the Arabian Nights.

I am bound to confess that my little heroine hardly made her life so pleasant to others as it was to herself, for in those unquiet hours when she was not entranced in the perusal of some romance, she still retained enough of original sin in her composition to cause much annoyance to the other members of her family : the instincts of youth are generally so much more human than divine !

Esty was alike passiónate and tender-hearted, brave and mendacious. She was truthful under the influence of a kind word, but lied unscrupulously when ruled by severity; she felt exceedingly tender towards all dumb animals ; never herself taking the life of a fly or a worm excepting by accident, and that rarely, for her little feet would move aside for a creeping insect as instinctively as horses spare the fallen men that cumber their feet in battle. " You did not give the life," she would say to Gerald, who was not so scrupulous, " what right have you to take it ? " and when Gerald would reply, sulkily, that she might as well say they " oughtn't to have meat for dinner," the little maiden would answer, gravely " that she wasn't quite sure they ought, but at any rate, Gerald, you don't want to have sparrows or cockchafers for dinner, so pray let them alone."

The feuds of Gerald and Esty had extended over a long space of time, and dated from one of those evenings in town when the boys used to come trooping home from their day-school in the suburbs. On one of these evenings Gerald had been unusually irritating in his manner to his sister, had called her a "miserable tom-tit " in allusion to her diminutive size, and had announced to her that not only he, but his little finger held her in derision ! To add to her indignation, Egbert, her favourite Egbert, had joined in the denunciation, and furthermore had added, " that she was only a girl," and with that parting sneer, the two boys had walked off to bed, leaving their small enemy in a state of fury which would have done credit to a tragedy queen.

She raved, stamped, and clenched her brown hands, and reiterated bitterly, "only a girl, am I? only a girl!" and then she began to meditate vengeance.

When the next evening arrived the boys came back to tea in a more cheerful frame of mind, but Esty received them in sullen silence, which she intended for dignity, and utterly refused all overtures for peace. So they left her alone and went to seek for their own especial means of enjoyment,—Gerald for his favourite knife, Egbert for his equally adored whip-top. They came back from their rooms with suspicion and anger on their countenances; the top and knife had alike vanished; in their place there was nothing left but a blank space, and the gravest doubt of Esty's honesty; but she, on being interrogated by her elders, swore so solemnly that she knew nothing about it that they were compelled to rest satisfied for the while, and to sit down to tea without solving the mystery of the lost toys.

There was a huge cake for tea, and Flora presiding over it with all the dignity of elder sisterhood, cut each child a piece, and handed it to them on a plate.

In the excitement of the moment, Esty, with an impulse purely childish and animal, half rose from her seat, the better to reach her short arm across the table to meet the coveted food.

That movement was fatal; for, relieved from the weight that had kept them on the shining wicker surface of the chair, off rolled the top on to the floor; in another moment, Gerald had pounced on his knife, and Esty sat a detected criminal, with cheeks the hue of crimson. There was an exclamation from Dolly of "Lawk a mercy!" and a pause.

The boys were ready to explode in torrents of wrath, but all eyes instinctively turned towards Flora, as being the superior in age and most unbiassed as an arbitress.

"Esty!" she said in a voice sad but firm, "Esty, how did you come by those things?"

"She took 'em, of course," indignantly broke in Gerald.

"Hold your tongue, do, Gerald," said the elder sister; then she repeated the question.

Esty sat sullen and silent. She would have lied again if she could, but the facts were too strong against her; so she only hung her head and glared fiercely at Gerald.

" It is very evident," continued Flora, solemnly, " that you took these things either with the view of causing wanton annoyance to your brothers, or for the purpose of keeping them for yourself, and thereby committing a theft. My decision is that you shall not have any cake for tea !"

And she ruthlessly took away the culprit's plate ; and, for the tempting mass of currants and plums, substituted a piece of dry bread.

Justice was satisfied. Everyone felt that the punishment was adequate to the offence. Even the boys were content, and Esty sat and sulked, and repented that she had not found a better hiding-place. The method she had taken of concealing her prizes may seem somewhat singular, but it was a common practice with the Lisles' children, who never seemed to feel quite happy about their little household gods unless they sat upon them, after the manner of Rachel !

When Gerald and Egbert returned home after their first half spent at school, they found only Christine and Toby waiting at the gate to welcome them, and in answer to their indignant queries as to "where Esty was ?" they were told that she was gone " to stay with her grand-aunt at Lynn-court," the fact being that Lady Renshawe had observed with pleasure the gradual weaning of her little favourite from all those pursuits which had made her, as Dolly said, " such a tom-boy," and had petitioned Mrs. Lisle to let her take the child home for a time ; and Mrs. Lisle had assented, feeling that the sound of Esty's and Gerald's wrangling was an infliction she would be glad to be free of during the boys' winter holidays. The next day little Esty, sitting in the deep recess of the window in the Lynncourt library, suddenly heard a tapping and whispering going on close to her head.

Starting from her reverie, she turned ; and, behold, out-side there were the rosy faces of her brothers, grinning from ear to ear, as they made energetic signs to her to open the window. This she did with difficulty, as the frost had set the windows fast in their frames, and while the snow blew in against her face she had to listen to their hurried entreaties that she'd come home and have "a lark."

"The pond is frozen over, and it's such jolly sliding," said Gerald.

"The cat has kittened, and there are two kittens kept. Such pink noses! such snowballs, Esty!" suggested Egbert, insidiously; and then, in chorus, "Oh, Esty, do come home; it must be so jolly dull here!" At that moment the apparition of a large black bonnet rose before Esty's terrified gaze. Before her, but behind them, stood Lady Renshawe, her nose looking more than usually prominent, from the red tinge the cold had given it, her feet encased in huge snow-boots, and her general aspect severe and threatening. Esty gave a faint "Oh!" and the boys, turning round, beheld the enemy, and, darting hastily round the corner, disappeared more quickly than they had come. Lady Renshawe looked after them with a smile, as their lithe figures bounded down the avenue, the flakes of snow clinging to their stiff yellow curls.

"No, no, dear," she said when she came in to where Esty sat, looking rather rueful and home-sick; "I can't part with you yet," and the old lady kindly brought down a new book of engravings to engage the attention of her little favourite, and Esty was partly consoled, although she thought a good deal of home that night, of the boys, of Christine's soft voice, of her mother's nightly kiss, and, above all, of the new, white kittens.

And so the days passed happily to Esty Lisle during the interval between childhood and girlhood. What was it to her if her mother looked sad, and her father became more irritable as every post brought in bills, some of them inevitably incurred, others being the ghosts of poor Colonel Lisle's old follies, haunting him with dreadful persistency, finding their way from the club to his former town address, and from thence to the country. What was it to Esty that sugar was forbidden in her tea, and salt butter substituted for fresh! After breakfast-time in the summer she and Christine lived almost entirely on the fruits they themselves collected out of doors; they ate basket after basket full of green apples, and thanks to the digestion of youth, escaped with no other bad consequences than consisted in a few extra scratches on Esty's face and arms, and an additional tinge of brown on her peach-like cheeks. She knew where the first strawberry hung ripening under its shielding leaf; she was quickest to detect the existence of the red-streaked paisons, and would clamber to pluck them down from a height which appeared to Christine wonderful and terrible.

"Oh, Esty, Esty!" her little sister would shriek, piteously, "do come down; 'ool be killed! I know 'ool be killed!"

And Esty would reply by mounting the topmost branch, and clinging round it in the fashion of a cat, and then saying in a faint and exhausted voice, "Oh, Christie, I'm going to drop! indeed I am!" and then seeing Christine toddle off to procure assistance from the house, Miss Esty would descend with immense alacrity, for these feats were apt to be punished by Dolly or Mrs. Lisle in a way more salutary than pleasant to the offender.

Christine regarded her sister with mingled awe and devotion. Esty was to her an incarnation of heroism; wicked, certainly,—for was not almost every act of her life in defiance of righteous authority, but still fascinating! a girl who could climb trees in utter defiance of chances of dislocation of limb; who could ride the pony when he was in his most obstinate mood; and who could pour into Christine's wondering ears such beautiful stories of desert islands, enchanted princesses, and their concomitant dragons: was not this a girl to be worshipped?

Christine thought so: and if it had not been for the occasional castigation with which her sister's ears and hands were saluted in acknowledgment of her faults, I believe she would have considered Esty in the light of something super-human—a beautiful, bold bad spirit, whose daring effrontery and powers of invention lifted her far above the level of ordinary little girls; and even these punishments were borne with such stoical calmness as might easily have led anyone to imagine that Esty had a skin as invulnerable as that of Achilles.

So the hours of Esty Lisle's youth passed happily enough. She delighted alike in the consumption of yellow apples and old-fashioned romances. With one of these latter she would dream away the summer hours among the dense thickets afforded by the sweet-scented azaleas and purple rhododen-drons in the overgrown shrubberies.

There, perched on a knoll of grass, her hand full of wild strawberries, she sat so still that the hare would steal from bush to bush close to her feet and not heed her, and the thrush would pour forth its song of trills close to her ear, unconscious that the motionless downcast head, on which shot such golden-brown lights, was aught human; and then, when tired for awhile of reading the fable in her hand, the girl would put her book down; and resting her head on her hand, listen with a thrill of strange delight to the sighing of the wind through the boughs, and stare up at that blue sky that seemed so far away, wondering whether anything *there* could be so beautiful as the sunny world below in which she was thus passing so many sweet, idle hours away.

CHAPTER VI.

"WHO IS GEOFFRY ADAIR?"

"Though now this grained face of mine be hid
In sap-consuming winter's drizzled snow;
And all the conduits of my blood froze up;
Yet hath my night of life some memory,
My wasting lamp some fading glimmer left,
My dull deaf ears a little used to hear."

OUR YEARS had passed, and again Esty Lisle sat in the recess of the library window at Lynncourt —it was twilight—a dull December twilight, and the snow hung heavily on the gaunt branches of the skeleton trees without, while the deer walked in forlorn lines across the snow-covered sward, their little footprints being rapidly filled up by the thick flakes that kept constantly falling. This time, no little brothers were present to press their rosy faces against the congealed panes and clamour for their sister's return to the charms of home, of white kittens, and long slides. Miss Lisle was now a young lady, for whom the last amusement, at least, had ceased to possess any attraction; while the two brothers, then so careless and rosy, were fast growing into troubled, sharp-faced young men.

Egbert had retained most of his original freshness of complexion and lightness of heart, for he had entered the navy, and being known for a poor man, met with but small temptation to trouble his spirit and empty his pocket; but

Gerald—Gerald, who had been put into the "Guards" in
order, as his father said, proudly, that "the heir of Lynncourt should move in a good set"—to him came many
an anxious care spared to the less pretentious position of
his younger brother, Gerald, who could not look Poole in
the face, who felt nervous and cross when any friend
saluted him with a tap on the shoulder; Gerald, with his
numerous intrigues and complications of every description,
was less to be envied than his sisters, dreaming away their
young lives amidst the pleasant glades of Gardenhurst and
Lynncourt, were wont to imagine. When they saw him
drive off to the station after one of his somewhat brief visits
home, with a faultlessly cut coat, a perfect tie, an incipient
but much cultivated fair shadow of a mustache, and one of
Harding's yellow· rosebuds in his button-hole, they would
retire rather wondering from whence the income came that
could furnish such magnificence, and whose the photograph
could be which they had seen lying on Gerald's dressing-
table the night before; a photograph which represented a
thick-faced woman with dark eyes and innumerable frizzles
of short, black curls, that shadowed the beetling brows, with
a long, pointed collar, a full bust and diminutive waist.
Pondering deeply over these mysteries, Esty and Christine
Lisle would picture to themselves scenes of vague delight
in that far-off London, of which Gerald spoke so carelessly
as "town," and wondered whether fate or chance would
ever lead their steps that way. "Perhaps Flora might ask
them up one day;" but this was not a probable contingency,
for Flora, who had married the curate of the London parish
wherein the Lisles used to reside, was living in a little house
in the suburbs of the metropolis, and, as it was, could hardly
accommodate herself, her husband, and their own servant,
in the narrow confines of " Nutshell Place."

The December evening I have mentioned was the close
of a day which Esty had come to spend with her aunt, and
at this twilight hour Lady Renshawe was snatching fitful
slumbers in the recesses of her arm-chair by the fire-place,
while her niece stared out of the window, watching the
snow-flakes thicken against the pane, and longing for the
time when all this snow and frost would melt off the grass,
and the breath of spring would call out green shoots and

pink buds from the dry stalks in the rose-beds. Now and
then she glanced tenderly at the sleeping form of her aunt,
whose features were imperious as ever when lit by the flash
of her still bright grey eyes, but who, now that the hard
lines in her face were relaxed by repose, looked the very
incarnation of helpless old age. Lady Renshawe's delicate,
high-bred looking feet were cased in black satin slippers,
and her hand rested lightly on the gold-headed cane by her
side ; the fire-light, that played on her snow-white hair and
wrinkled face, showed also, by the light of its ruddy glare,
the portrait which hung overhead, and which represented
the haughty beauty of Lynncourt, with red lips and raven
hair. It was a charming portrait, life-sized, painted by Opie
when Lady Renshawe was seventeen, and its unchanging
beauty seemed to mock the fading life that slept in the chair
below it. Every now and then the sleeper awoke from her
light slumber, and called to Esty in sharp, querulous
tones :

"Esty, come and find my knitting-pins ;" or, "Esty, that
nasty kitten has wrapped itself up in my ball of wool, and
can't find its way out again!" and Esty would come, and,
after hunting the refractory kitten all round the room,
unwind and rewind, with some difficulty, the skein in which
the little creature had involved itself hopelessly, and which
it had drawn at great length round the legs of the table.
Then :

"Esty! now that you've done that, come and read me
some of Jeremy Taylor!" and, with just the faintest sigh,
and a look directed towards the window-seat, where fluttered
the open leaves of "Master Humphrey's Clock," Esty would
sit down on a stool by her grand-aunt's feet, and, while the
fire crackled cheerily within, and the night gathered in on
the glaring snow without, the sweet low voice of seventeen
gave utterance to the quaint, peaceful words of comfort
conveyed in the yellow, ill-printed page before her.

Lady Renshawe sat and listened—listened sometimes to
the sob of the rising wind without—and then her thoughts
wandered far away back into past seasons, when she was
young and her niece was not in existence ; but a glance
at her own withered hand, or at Esty's youthful head, was
sufficient to bring her back to the realities of old age and its

infirmities, and, with a sigh, she told Esty to "put down the book;" then, lifting up her head:

"When I die," she said, musingly, "I shall leave behind me an enencumbered rent-roll, an estate free from charge, and a stainless reputation. And what will it avail me? Your father will muddle the estate, so that my ghost wouldn't know it, if it could come and inspect it twenty years later—(Hold your tongue, child; of course your father expects to inherit the estate, and if he does, of course he *will* involve it hopelessly)—it's ill teaching an old dog new tricks, and James Lisle will always bank his money in a sieve; meanwhile, the appreciation of my reputation for probity and morality will exist only in the nine days that follow my death, while this dead preacher has left a memorial that has lasted from generation to generation— good words that will live when my marble monument (if it exists at all) will not be looked at by any who bear my name, or in whose veins my blood runs. Oh, me! what is the use of it all?" and Lady Renshawe gazed wearily in the fire while she gently stroked the golden brown head by her side.

Esty was troubled by the sadness of her aunt's tone, and, not being able to think of any better mode of changing the conversation, suggested:

"Shall I ring for tea, aunt?"

"Yes!" said the old lady, becoming practical immediately; "and order the muffins to be toasted brown, they were white and leathery last night;" and, taking up her knitting-pins, she intimated by a sign that the reading was to be recommenced.

It had been a very weary day for both guest and hostess. Lady Renshawe, whose mind was still so full of quick intelligence, mourned bitterly the decay of her fine frame. That her once firm step should have become so uncertain, her sense of hearing so dull, was a cause of hourly irritation to the active mind which had outlived strength of body.

She, like Esty, longed that the winter days should pass away, and be succeeded by spring. "I shall feel strong again, then," she thought. "Life isn't life, that exists in bitter frosts and northern winds; if I could only taste a breath of summer-air it would renew me," and certainly, as the snow melted away from the earth, and the buttercups began to force their way through the thick sward of the lawn, Lady Renshawe did seem to taste fresh youth and strength with the spring of the year.

" James, my dear, you must take care of yourself," the old lady observed mockingly, when her nephew came to see her one sunny April morning. "They say that the spring months are very fatal to people who are getting old; now it don't matter for *me*, you know, mine is such a *very* fine constitution, I shouldn't be at all surprised if I lived to be a hundred."

Colonel Lisle could not repress a slight shudder at such speeches as these. To do him justice, he had not any desire that his relative's departure from this world should be accelerated on his account; but still there is a limit to everything, and he could not but think it hard that she should contemplate prolonging her term of existence beyond the usual period only, as it seemed, for the express purpose of annoying him; but as the spring and summer came and went, Lady Renshawe's prediction really seemed as though it were likely to be verified, for her eyes grew brighter again, and she required Esty's support less often than usual during her promenade up and down the terrace. Her eye, too, was keener than ever to detect any disorder in the arrangment of her household, or that portion of the estate that was more immediately around her.

" How true it is that 'one walks in a vain shadow,'" she remarked benignly to Colonel Lisle. "Here am I 'heaping up riches,' and not knowing in the least who 'will gather them.'"

Poor James could only smile blandly and murmur " very true," and it was not until he got home that he revealed his real sentiments to the ears of his wife and daughter. "She's an old cat," he said, indignantly, " and I believe has as many lives as one; she can't cut me out of the title, but she knows that I'm as poor as a rat, and that if she chooses to leave away her personal property, I shall derive very little benefit from her death."

" Never mind," said his wife, soothingly; "she never seems to see or care for any one excepting Esty, so it isn't

4

likely she should leave it away from you ; she only says these things to tease you !"

"I don't know," answered the colonel, gloomily, "she has been talking a good deal about Geoffry Adair lately."

"And who is Geoffry Adair ?"

"You never remember anything I tell you," said the colonel in a testy voice ; "Geoffry Adair is the son of her old friend, General Adair; the father died some two years ago, leaving his only son to the mercy and care of his second wife and her two children by a former husband ; Geoffry, by his father's desire, was put into the Guards."

"Why, that must be the same Captain Adair who is in Gerald's regiment," suggested Mrs. Lisle.

"Of course it is," answered her husband ; "I wonder you never found that out before," and he resumed his cigar with a look of sovereign contempt for his wife's ignorance, not deigning to listen to her asseverations that this was the first intimation she had ever received that any person bearing the name of Adair was in existence. Esty, had she been consulted, could have given her mother some information on the subject, for she had noticed and commented on the miniature of a pretty little boy that hung over Lady Renshawe's breakfast-room mantelpiece, and had been told that it was "the son of a very dear old friend of mine ; this was his only child by his first marriage, and as I knew and liked both the parents very much, I begged to have a likeness of their son ; they sent it to me when he was two years old."

"Then you have never seen the original?" Esty had asked.

"Never; when his first wife (my friend) died, General Adair went and made a fool of himself by marrying a widow, a Mrs. Cadogan, who had two children by a first marriage ; after that they all went abroad, the last tidings I received from General Adair was, that he was living at Florence, and that Geoffry, his son, was pursuing his studies with a private tutor, with a view to entering the army."

"And you heard nothing more of them ?"

"Nothing, excepting that poor Jasper (the general) died about two years ago, leaving the bulk of his property to his wife, which was generous of him, considering that she worried him to death. People said his lungs were affected and that he died of consumption,—*I* know better."

"What did he die of, then?" demanded Esty, wonder-ingly.

"Of his wife's temper!" and for some time after this conversation the countess was so snappish and contradictory of speech that Esty took care not to introduce the name of Adair into the conversation again.

Nevertheless, like the parrot, she "thought the more!"

Here was a fine field for conjecture and romantic speculations opened out, and of course the suggestive mind of seventeen "improved the occasion" as much as possible.

An only and petted child, deprived of his mother at an early age, handed over to the care of a stepmother who possessed a "temper" and two children of her own, left a friendless orphan by the death of his father, deprived of the larger share of his lawful inheritance by the machinations of his stepmother—this was the superstructure of Esty's romance, and many were the inventions and exaggerations her ingenious fancy formed out of these circumstances.

"I daresay she beats him cruelly," she said to herself one day, when she was looking tenderly at the aforesaid miniature ; then, struck by a sudden thought, she looked at the back of the portrait, and perceived that the object of her commiseration must be at least four-and-twenty years of age ; she blushed at her own folly, and for a time put the ideal she had formed of the victimised orphan out of her head.

CHAPTER VII.

EXPECTED VISITORS.

"His father allows him two hundred a year,
And he bets you 'a thousand to one.'"

"ELINOR," said Colonel Lisle to his wife, one June morning, as he inspected the contents of the letter-bag, "here is a letter from Gerald. I wonder what *that's* about; he never writes to me unless he wants something."

"What is it?" demanded Mrs. Lisle, anxiously. But her husband perused the letter twice before he gave her the satisfaction of knowing the cause of the heavy frown that had gathered on his forehead. When he laid down the letter it was with an angry thump of his hand against the table that made the knives and forks rattle and jump.

"D——d cool, I must say!"

"What is d——d cool?" asked his wife, calmly.

Whenever Colonel Lisle used intemperate language, Mrs. Lisle punished him by repeating the offensive words, partly because she knew he didn't like it, partly to give her time to frame a defence against the coming storm.

"D——d cool of Gerald, to expect me to go to the expense of entertaining his friends here, after all the money and trouble he has cost me already! Read the letter out, Christine."

And Christine read as follows:—

"Guards' Club, Pall Mall,
"June —, 18—.

" My Dear Gov.,

" (What expensive paper the puppy writes on !" growled the colonel).

" I am thinking of running down on Saturday to look you up; if you have no objection I should like to bring a friend of mine with me ; he is a very nice fellow, and, moreover, I owe him a few hundreds, so I should like to pay him any civility I can, short of actual cash. I hope you will not mind his putting up at Gardenhurst for a few days. I will bring you down a French cook, and please ask my mother to be sure and get a man in to wait.

" Ever your affectionate son,

" G. L."

" P.S.—We shall bring down a couple of hacks."

" Here is another postscript," said Christine, as she turned over the page, while her mother sat pale and motionless, horrified at the prospect conveyed in Gerald's letter,—a prospect by no means agreeable to the already over-worked anxious housekeeper :—

" I forgot to say that my friend's name is Adair. You have often heard me speak of him ; he is in my regiment."

Colonel Lisle and his wife exchanged glances, while Esty blushed so vividly that Christine, who was a close observer, detected her, and wondered what on earth Esty had been about.

" I shall not permit it," said the colonel, excitedly ; " I am not going to be the means of introducing that young man to ——"

" Hush !" interrupted his wife, with a meaning look at the girls; " we will discuss that when we are alone, James;" and accordingly, when the breakfast-things were cleared away, Mrs. Lisle accompanied her husband to his library, and, I suppose, used some very good argument to induce him to accept of the proposed visit of Gerald and his friend; for when the post-boy left Gardenhurst with the letters that day, he carried with him one addressed to " Gerald Lisle,

Esq.," in which Colonel Lisle expressed the satisfaction it would give him to welcome Captain Adair to his "unpretending household."

When their parents left the breakfast-room, the two girls looked at each other without speaking for a few moments, and then Esty said, significantly:

"Let us go and sit in the strawberry-beds ;" which meant that these young ladies were about to follow the custom of savage tribes, and hold a "palaver."

"Christine," said Esty, solemnly, as they crouched down among the fresh green leaves, and began to pluck the berries from the stalks, "it's the *same !*"

"You mean it's the little boy in the picture you told me of," answered Christine, composedly, as she pounced on an unusually fine, ripe strawberry, and devoured it.

"Well, yes ; no ! but of course he can't be a little boy now, you know," said Esty, rather embarrassed ; "he is in the same regiment with Gerald."

"Do you think he will really come here ? " asked Christine, awe-stricken at the idea of the "little boy " of Esty's romances being converted into a full-grown man like her brother.

"And do you think he will be as disagreeable as Gerald ? because you know, Esty," added Christine, meditatively, "*I* think Gerald is a snob."

"Why ? " demanded Esty, rather astonished at her sister's unusual decision of manner.

"Because mamma told me that snobs were pretentious people, who assume more than they are entitled to ; and while Gerald gives himself all the airs of a rich, fine, gentleman, when he knows how poor he is, I must think that he is snobbish ; besides," added Christine, warming with her subject, "what right has he to expect us to alter our style of living because he is going to bring one of his friends here, and why should he insult mamma with suggestions of French cooks and men waiters ? What is good enough for mamma is good enough for him and his friends."

"But Christy," pleaded Esty, rather disturbed at this digression, which was tending to inculcate a rebellious state of feeling against the proposed visitors. "Captain Adair may be accustomed to live in an altogether different way

from what we do, and that may be the reason why
Gerald ——"

"Then," interrupted Christine, "he needn't come here,
and if he don't like us when he does come, he can soon go
back again," and Christine resumed her search among the
strawberry leaves with such dignity of manner, that Esty
thought it wisest not to discuss the question any further for
the present.

Christine Lisle was now a little more than thirteen years
old, but her grave, gentle manner made her appear older
than she really was; in personal appearance, too, she was
more formed and far more beautiful than most girls of her
age. Braid after braid of bright fair hair was twisted round
the back of her well-shaped head, while her white forehead,
pink cheeks, and deep-blue eyes, presented a most brilliant
combination of nature's colouring. She was slower in her
movements than her more volatile sister, and generally
walked with a soft indolence of manner that would have
been inexpressibly charming to some people, while it would
have driven others distracted with irritation. She was unusually shrewd for a girl so young, and who had seen so
little of the world; but then she had lived in a large family
on small means; and adversity, especially if it be accompanied by brothers and sisters, is an immense sharpener of
woman's "apprehensions," as Mrs. Malaprop calls them.

Esty had spent so many days of the year at Lynncourt,
that she could not realise so well as did her sister all the
rigour of poverty that reigned in the Gardenhurst household.
It was Christine who had seen all the anxious looks of her
mother when the weekly bills came in. It was Christine
who had watched Mrs. Lisle's tears fall on Gerald's un-
receipted "accounts" until her fair young face grew hot
with indignation, and accordingly she was better able to
appreciate and condemn the selfishness that caused her
mother to reduce daily the quality of the meals to such an
excess of plainness, and spend hours trying to diminish
inevitable expenses.

"Christine!" said Esty, in the pause that followed
Christine's outbreak of indignation; "what are we to
wear?"

This was a question to arouse any girl's interest, however

young she might be, and to put all less important considera-
tions to flight.

Christine looked blank. "There isn't much choice," she
said, "we have only these lilac cotton gowns and the white
muslins."

"Never mind," suggested Esty, consolingly. "In most
novels heroines are dressed in white muslins, and look an
embodiment of youthful freshness and beauty to the distraction and admiration of the town-bred lover."

"That's all very well," said Christine, prosaically. "But
if all town-bred men are like Gerald, Captain Adair will be
disagreeably particular as to the fit of your gloves and boots,
and will feel himself personally aggrieved by the wrinkles in
the back of your dress. Oh! I do wish he wasn't coming,
we were so comfortable without him." And in her perplexity she sat deliberately down in the middle of the strawberry bed, much to the detriment of the lilac cotton dress,
and stroked her white nose thoughtfully.

Presently she lifted her head, struck by a sudden thought.

"Do you think Aunt Renshawe would?" she began in
an insidious tone.

"No, I'm sure she wouldn't," interrupted Esty, decidedly;
and so the conversation flagged again for a while. Christine
had no further suggestion to offer; and Esty's thoughts
wandered off into a day-dream—a dream in which she and
Christine figured as the possessors of untold wealth and
fashionably-cut silk dresses. A dream in which Captain
Adair appeared dimly in the background as one of many
worshippers of their surpassing elegance and beauty.

Like the visionary in the Arabian Nights, Esty was rudely
awakened from her flattering meditations.

"Miss Esther, come and feed the chickens!"

And our old friend Dolly appeared in sight, her voice
more tremulous and cracked than formerly, and her manner
quite as aggressive as in the old days when she was in the
habit of applying the hair-brushes to Esty's shoulders.

"Oh Dolly, don't bother," said the latter, pettishly,
"we'll come directly."

Certainly it was irritating to be disturbed at the moment
imagination was supplying Esty with luxuries far beyond
her reach in reality.

Christine got up slowly.

"We're not doing any good here, Esty," she remarked, "so I will go and help mamma to count the linen from the wash, and you might as well feed the chickens as sit there in the sun burning your face."

Esty followed her sister's advice, but when the last grain of corn had been thrown to the chickens, and the hens had ceased to "cluck, cluck," and make frantic rushes in whatever direction they saw her little brown hand moving, she gathered up the basket on her arm, and, instead of going back to the house, returned to the strawberry beds ; and, seating herself under the shade of a large twisted apple tree, resumed the thread of the romance she was weaving, undisturbed this time by aught excepting the' humming of the bees that hovered round the luscious petals of the azaleas, or the soft echo of a distant cuckoo's note.

It may seem strange that with so wealthy a relative living near them, the Lisles should be still suffering from the effects of Colonel Lisle's early extravagance, but when it is remembered that Gerald Lisle inherited all his father's talent for spending money, and indulged this propensity at his parents' expense, it can easily be imagined, to use Lady Renshawe's own words, "that while there's such a leak as Gerald in the ship, she can never be sound."

So, when the countess had paid for her grand-nephew's education, and bought Gerald his commission in the army, and paid for Egbert's naval outfit, she thought that she had done her duty to them. After that, they might "sink or swim," as they liked.

"I've given them enough rope to save themselves," remarked the old lady, grimly. "If they choose to hang themselves, that's their look out ! "

Having thus taken the greater burthen of home expenses off Colonel Lisle's shoulders, the countess imagined (naturally enough) that his income ought to be sufficient to keep himself and his 'family in a moderate degree of comfort, and that "Elinor must have plenty to spare now," more especially as the countess's kindness had not stopped at purchasing the commission, but gone to the extent of making each boy an allowance of £150 per annum. She forgot that the hand of debt once laid on a man is some·

what like the devilish gripe in ghostly tradition that leaves indelible traces on the wrist that has been clasped by its fatal pressure. And the curse James Lisle had laid upon himself in his youth was destined to come home to him in age—reproduced in the person of his son.

It was very rarely, however, that the girls found their poverty any inconvenience to them; their taste in food now was as simple as when they climbed the trees for apples, and thrust their little hands through nut boughs in their search for filberts in the days of their childhood. Their amusements were even a less source of expense now that they had outgrown the taste for wooden dolls and toy lambs that had distinguished them at an earlier period; for whereas Christine had been rather indulged and pampered in her infancy in the way of playthings (on one occasion she had actually been presented with a wax doll, and preserved for many years afterwards a beautiful foot and leg, the sole relic and remnant of the once perfect whole), her amusements were now restricted to the following:

To meet Esty in the summer evening, when the latter returned from Lynncourt.

To pot flowers with her mother in the old dilapidated conservatory.

To feed the pets: consisting of a canary, a pony, and a little pig.

To sing like a nightingale.

To assist Dolly in the household work, even to the making of beds.

To lie still in the sun and read a novel, with a basketful of apples by her side.

These were her amusements now, some of them might be more properly classified as "duties;" but Christine was of such a contented temperament that she generally contrived to make one answer for the other.

Esty was equally satisfied with the occupation which fell to her lot. She was passionately fond of music, of flowers, and of books, and her mother's straitened means had never interfered with the indulgence of these tastes.

Flowers there were in abundance at Gardenhurst; where poor Mr. Ford had planted one rose, there now bloomed a dozen. The shrubbery paths were choked with the exuberance of untrained clematis and honeysuckle, while rare specimens of foreign plants grew side by side with the English dog-rose and flaunting dandelion. In the early summer mornings, while the air was still fresh and sweet, Esty would pick her way down those walks where the gravel was least obscured by moss and weeds, and pluck handfuls of syringa, azalea, and rhododendron blossoms for her flower basket, while in her hand she carefully guarded the more fragile bells of the lilies of the valley, or the fragrant brown bud of the calicanthus.

She would arrange these flowers in every broken vase, or piece of glass she could find, that was capable of holding enough water to nourish the stalks; under the influence of her nimble fingers and her exquisite taste, every dark corner in the old house became bright and graceful, the tazze that stood in the hall overran with tendrils of ivy and branches of Wistaria, while a mass of scarlet geraniums in the centre cup gave a brilliant effect to the whole picture.

Many of the beautiful marble tazze that stand fixed in the polished floors of Florentine palaces look less picturesque than did the plastered imitations of Gardenhurst, when the grey edges of the latter were graced by overhanging leaves of the Virginia creeper; and the bust of Venus, that stood in the niche of the hall window, looked none the less lovely for having a faint glow reflected on her pure cheek from the glass of red roses which stood near her.

As for the books, there were not many more in the library than when Colonel Lisle first took possession of Gardenhurst, but that made little difference to Esty. She loved her old friends among the Novels, and felt as much pleasure in reading "Ivanhoe" and "Old Mortality," for the six and twentieth time, as though they were newly-made acquaintances of the highest sensational type. Certainly they possessed many advantages over more modern works of fiction, the principal one consisting in the fact that she *could* read them again and again, without tiring of them; another was that her thorough knowledge of these works enabled her to proceed at once to the most amusing parts of the book, when she was in haste to be entertained.

As for music, it is true, the pianoforte at Gardenhurst

was rather cracked and uncertain in its utterance. Esty might frequently strike at the treble notes and receive no sort of response from them ; but there was an instrument at Lynncourt of a superior order—a piano soft, full, and sweet in tone. Lady Renshawe did not play herself, but she was very fond of hearing music, or rather of being lulled to sleep by its sound ; and, accordingly, Esty had ample opportunities for indulging her love of soft, low chords and dreaming melodies. She had received very little regular tuition, but her ear was faultless, and the little lithesome fingers that crept in and out among the great ivory keys, rarely affronted the hearer with any false note or awkward discord. Her music-books, like the novels, were of a by-gone school. Rossini was the latest operatic composer of whom Esty had an intimate knowledge. Her favourite pieces were to be found in the works of Beethoven and Handel, Griffin and Viotti.

In the dusk of summer evenings, when Lady Renshawe laid down her knitting-pins, and told Esty to " play some tune till the candles came," the latter would wait until her grand-aunt's hands relaxed their hold of the worsted skein, and her chin dropped on her breast, and then discontinued playing the old country dance, in which Lady Renshawe delighted, and wandered off into odd flute-like melodies, that seemed to harmonise well with the dull twilight, and the silence that reigned in the place—silence that was only broken by the occasional tinkling of a distant sheep-bell, or the twitter of a bird in the branches. Had it not been for the practical nature of their poverty, there might have been some danger of this young girl's becoming a mere visionary. Her intellect was of the wild, untrained nature of her own garden bowers ; she had been uncoerced as to any choice of studies, and had it been in her nature to rest satisfied with such a fate, she might have been almost as ignorant and uncivilised as Casper Hauser. But Mrs. Lisle had not misunderstood her girls' dispositions when she left them to work out the fight of their education in their own way. In the first place, they lived almost entirely in the companionship of herself and Lady Renshawe, their means not permitting them to be surrounded with that tribe of the upper servant class, who generally attended on the children of wealthy parents. Thus they contracted such a tone of refinement and good breeding, that they would have been " fit to hold a court," as old Dolly expressed it, when other girls of the same age would perhaps have been too arrogant or too awkward to do justice to their position.

Then their lives were so solitary, so unaccompanied by any of the ordinary pleasures of youth, that they pursued music, drawing, and reading as recreations; what others might have considered in the light of tiresome studies, were to them boundless sources of enjoyment. Esty's quick, keen intellect devoured eagerly all the food that came in its way, whether the object to be digested lay in music or painting, books, trees, flowers, or stones; and those hours of her girlhood passed at Gardenhurst, when her mind was intent, like the elf in the fable, on turning " Straw into Gold," that is to say, on working through ignorance to knowledge, were some of the happiest and best hours of her life.

So it happened that up to the date of Captain Adair's proposed visit to Gardenhurst, Esty and Christine had rarely been troubled by any reflection as to whether their dresses did or did not come up to the usual require-ments of society. Providing that the tight-fitting cotton frocks did not fit too tightly, and that there was no dis-agreeable " ruck " to irritate their round, white throats, the girls were quite satisfied with their appearance; and until the day when they came upon the photograph on their brother's table, they were scarcely conscious that such gorgeously attired women existed as the one represented there.

To be sure, Phœbe Jenning, the clergyman's daughter, their one solitary " young lady " acquaintance, occasionally made her appearance at Gardenhurst, with variously-coloured velvet ribbons flying from her head, and with brilliant feathers standing up defiantly from her hat; but the effect of this finery was to fill the two girls with mild wonder; and, instead of Miss Jenning impressing them with a sense of her superiority as she fully intended to do by virtue of her gorgeous apparel, their instinctive good taste revolted from the gaudiness of her style; without exactly knowing why, they felt that Phœbe's choice of colours was to be avoided rather than imitated. Of course there were moments of feminine irritation when Esty was not too magnanimous to forbear the wish that she could give Phœbe a good " set down " in the only manner in which the latter could be made to feel such a proceeding, namely, by Esty or Christine possessing a really well-made beautiful dress ; but in the present state of Mrs. Lisle's finances such a contingency was not likely to arise.

CHAPTER VIII.

THE POSTPONEMENT.

" Come care and pleasure, hope and pain,
And bring the fated fairey prince."

HEN Esty returned to Lynncourt the day after the discussion of " ways and means " in the strawberry beds, she was so absent in manner that her aunt had several times to remind her sharply that the teapot was not meant to be suspended long in the air in its transit from cup to cup, and that she would be better employed in doing some plain work than in pulling the rose leaves to pieces that fell from the silver vase on the table.

Esty did not mention to Lady Renshawe the cause of her abstraction. She felt instinctively that her aunt would not be likely to sympathise with any little maidenly flutters on the subject of the proposed visitor to Gardenhurst. " Perhaps it would end in nothing, and he wouldn't come at all," said Esty, mentally apostrophising the curly-haired boy with the ivory face, but in her heart she half hoped that Colonel Lisle's invitation might be accepted, and she looked out with more eagerness than she was perhaps herself conscious for the postman in the morning on which an answer might be expected.

But when Captain Adair's letter arrived, it was found that for the present Esty and Christine Lisle had nothing to fear from the criticism or observation of their brother's friend,

for in large sprawling hieroglyphics the latter expressed his
regret that at "present it was impossible for him to leave
town." If "Colonel Lisle would kindly consent to consider
the visit merely postponed, he would be very glad to avail
himself of Colonel Lisle's kind invitation at some later
period."

By the same post came a letter from Gerald, in which he
said that he could not understand Adair's refusal, as the
latter had so frequently expressed himself very anxious to
make Lady Renshawe's acquaintance, but he durst say his
friend would "run down" when the season was a little more
advanced; anyhow, "he had seemed pleased at the invitation, and Gerald was much obliged to the governor for
sending it."

I think that Mrs. Lisle was secretly a little disappointed
at this answer to her husband's letter, although outwardly
she expressed great satisfaction at being relieved from the
burthen of entertaining a stranger. Even the least vain of
women could hardly be expected to be the possessor of a
precious gem and not desire that some eyes beside her own
should be dazzled by its brilliance; and what mother could
own daughters so rarely gifted and so charming in person as
were Esty and Christine Lisle, and not feel a little motherly
anxiety that such attractions should be seen and appreciated
by some one nearer their own rank in life than Bill Markham,
the farmer's son, who had a red face and a jovial manner,
who rode a hundred guinea hunter to hounds, and who was
wont to stare rather rudely at those delicate beauties when
he encountered them wandering by the hedges of his native
lanes,—looking even to his unrefined eyes like exotics out
of place.

However, the young man was not coming, and there was
an end of it for the present. The transient gleam of speculation faded out of Mrs. Lisle's tired eyes, and in her return
to her ordinary occupations she soon forgot everything connected with the name of Adair. Esty's memory was more
retentive, the name of her hero of the portrait had become
something more than a mere sound to her; but as the days
went on the image of the unfriended, "persecuted orphan"
became more and more dim in her imagination; her books,
flowers, and music were once more paramount in her

thoughts, and while the birds sang and the sun was warm, while the summer days came and went with that dreamy peace which had such a charm to one of her temperament: while Lady Renshawe was not captious, and Christine was gentle and sympathising, Esty Lisle felt that the hours had hardly room for her happiness—happiness none the less complete because it was shadowed by those vague aspirations for something hitherto unattained, that generally pervaded the imaginations of those who are poetical rather than practical. But, although Esty might look with yearnings at the mountain-tops that overhung her "happy valley," and wonder what kind of world it was the sun was shining on beyond, she fully felt the sweetness of the present hour, and looked forward to no future in which anything more charming could be found than her present way of life.

And so, by the time the Virginia creeper that grew outside the Gardenhurst drawing-room had been burnt red by the autumn sun, and the apples were beginning to fall thickly under the trees, Esty and Christine had quite forgotten that their homely dresses had ever been any cause of dissatisfaction to them, and had forgotten also the reason of their having been so. Meanwhile, it shall be seen in another chapter what was the real cause of Captain Adair's declining the invitation of his friend, Gerald Lisle.

CHAPTER IX.

DANGLING.

"Her beauty calm and fresh and bright
As Eastern summers are."

DAVENANT.

"O my heart, my heart,—
It sends up all its anguish in this cry :
Love me a little !"

OWEN MEREDITH.

T was towards the end of June; the sun which was shining with such brilliancy at Gardenhurst, that blossom after blossom, first ripened and then shrivelled, fell beneath its power, was streaming with equal heat through the white blinds of a drawing-room in H—— Street, Berkeley Square.

By the open window, her chair drawn into the shadow afforded by the muslin blind, sat Sophia Herbert, the wife of the conservative member for X——shire.

This lady, if her appearance did not belie her, was young and charming. She had velvet brown eyes—eyes into which there came red gleams of light whenever they were agitated either by anger or pleasure.

She had brown, wavy hair of a colour that might have been called chestnut, were it not too dark and rich in its hue to quite justify the epithet. In the sun, this hair had a golden gleam over its smooth waves, but at night it looked almost black. Now it was gathered in braids round the back of Mrs. Herbert's head and was fastened in its place by a gold pin,—this pin being one of many ornaments that flashed and jingled over her *petite* person. *Petite*, did I say? well! the rounded fingers were small enough, and so was the waist, and the feet would have done credit to a Japanese beauty; but the bust was large and full, and the throat almost too thick to be in good proportion with the small head, the complexion too was dusky, and though it was sufficiently clear to enable her to add a touch of rouge to her cheek with great effect at night, by day it received no further embellishment than what was afforded by a pink sort of face-powder, which Mrs. Herbert used in preference to the ordinary powder, *blanc de perte;* otherwise her skin was like satin in its texture, and no man who had ever once had the privilege of touching that supple hand with his lips would be likely to forget the softness of it.

She had black velvet round her throat, heavy chain bracelets on her wrists, earrings that glittered at every movement of her head, a silk dress that fitted her with such exactness and which was of such thin material, that it showed every movement of her figure. In looking at this dress, you could not but feel, that their are decencies which are less proper than so-called indecencies. No fashionable maiden or matron at an evening party with her neck and back bare and exposed, could look half as suggestively improper as Mrs. Herbert did in these morning dresses which she always had made in Paris.

Not that Mrs. Herbert affected impropriety as her style; on the contrary, she was exemplary in her vocation as a wife and a mother. If on looking round the pretty little drawing-room in H—— Street, you saw no broken toy, no tattered book, to remind you of a child's presence, you could if you liked walk into excellently arranged nurseries, where these luxuries of childhood were strewn in profusion over sofa and chair, and the head-nurse could have told you that "mistress" always visited these regions, four if not six times a day. Then on those evenings when Herbert was able to get away from the House, to dine quietly at home, would not Mrs. Herbert resign any other engagement, however pleasant it might be, for the purpose of making herself as agreeable to her husband as possible,—and were not he

5—2

and she always on the best possible terms? And yet, in spite of her reputation for virtue, a reputation so unquestioned, that even the braggarts of the clubs had not ventured to boast away her good name ; in spite of her three children, her regular attendance at church, and her scrupulosity of speech, there was occasionally a something in her manner (a something hard to be defined even by the person influenced by it, that irritated betrothed women if they saw their lovers exposed to it, and caused the man under its spell to feel as if he were becoming intoxicated by a subtle, indefinable pleasure, which was in some way conveyed to him by the look in Mrs. Herbert's eyes—the low melodious intonation of her voice—and the pressure of her soft fingers. The Herberts had been married ten years, but Sophy was even now in her husband's eyes the most beautiful and loveable woman in the world ; while her sweetness of temper, and the efforts she made to please him, would have rendered her charming, even had she not been so personally attractive.

On this particular afternoon Mrs. Herbert had an anxious expression on her face. It did not amount to a frown, but her eyes were troubled, and whenever the doorbell rang she started and moved slightly on her chair.

Slight as they were, such symptoms of emotion were not common to Sophy. She was of a placid temperament, and the gleam in her eyes I have spoken of was rarely seen even by those who knew her best. But that she was restless and ill at ease to-day was evident, even to the King Charles that nestled in the folds of her soft silk dress, for as soon as he had comfortably gathered up his paws under the shelter of his long drooping ears, he had to uncoil himself again and look with a discontented aspect at his mistress, who (unreasonably as he thought) kept continually disarranging him, that she might get up and press her velvet cheek against the window-pane. Presently a ring resounded through the house, a ring that came from the front-door bell, which must have been pulled by a hand sure of its welcome. Mrs. Herbert probably recognised it, for she sank hastily into a chair, and with an air of listlessness began turning over the leaves of a novel. The sun, that was beginning to turn westward, reached her now, and

the gold-brown threads of hair stirred lightly on her forehead as the door opened, and the servant announced,
"Captain Adair and Mr. Lisle."

For an instant any one looking at Sophy might have
detected an expression of disappointment in her face, but
it must have been very momentary, for she came forward
with the softest of smiles, and welcomed both gentlemen
with a gentle pressure of her little hand :—

"So kind of you to come and see me in my solitude,"
she said. " I am all alone to-day, and you knowing that
took compassion on me, Captain Adair."

There was an intonation in her voice which puzzled the
latter for a moment, but only for a moment; then he
answered :—

" I met Lisle at the door, Mrs. Herbert. Great geniuses
clash, you see; we were both bound on the same errand,
and we neither of us could consent to forego our visit.
We are fortunate in finding you in !"

And so a reproach was conveyed and an apology given
for Gerald's presence, while he (poor, unsuspecting man !)
twirled his · moustache, and tried to think of something
amusing to say to Mrs. Herbert, with whom he was very
anxious to be on good terms. But he could think of
nothing better to suggest than :

" Did you ride in the park this morning, Mrs. Herbert ?
I thought I saw you !"

"Yes," she answered, "and was much astonished to see
Damon there without his Pythias. What was Captain
Adair about ?"

She spoke of Geoffry, but never once looked at him.
Yet she saw every movement of his hand as it lifted his
watch-chain carelessly, and she knew exactly when he was
looking at her through his half-shut blue eyes.

Talk of the eloquence that lies in a look ! Let me tell
you, oh husbands ! for your‿guidance, that when your wife
carefully avoids meeting the glance of any particular man,
when her own eyes fall if they do inadvertently encounter
his—if she talks AT him rather than TO him—then be
assured that your doom is sealed, and that you are not
likely to be more fortunate than Amphitryon, Menelaus, or
any other similarly situated hero of antiquity, for there is

more danger in such avoidance than in fifty of the "becks and wreathed smiles" she may bestow on others.

Mr. Herbert was not a far-seeing man, even had he been a jealous one, so it was not probable that he should detect what even Mrs. Herbert's lady's maid had hitherto failed to discover. His wife was his property, and he believed in her even as he believed in the solidity of his well-built house, in the existence of his children, in his wife's own pleasant manners and affectionate disposition. His faith in Sophy was the result of ten years' happiness in married life. During all that time he had never had occasion to reproach her with any omission of duty. Every fresh year had made the tie stronger that bound them to each other, and unless Sophy herself were to commit some very glaring indiscretion, it was not likely that George Herbert's eyes, dimmed by long looking at his idol, should ever detect any flaw in what he held to be his faultless household deity.

Sophy was not a genius, but she was shrewd, and she possessed a good deal of that which ensures greater success than mere unsupported talent.

She had tact! tact to wound when it was required; for, like all women, she was a little spiteful at heart, especially where her own sex was concerned; and she had the tact also to make herself pleasant. She had a knack of slipping over people's "sore points" in conversation until they quite believed she had really escaped the sight of the wound she affected to ignore, and they loved her the better for it. What man forgives the woman who has seen him make an awkward step and fall down? What woman forgives the friend who banters her on a subject on which her own heart is bleeding—who makes indiscreet inquiries after "that son of yours who went to Australia, you know;" or that "dear little girl of yours I saw last year;" when the son is known to be a man who is not likely to prosper in any climate to which he may transport himself, and the "little girl" has been lying stiff and cold in her coffin for many weary months past?

Such mistakes as these Sophy Herbert never perpetrated, and as (to do her justice) she was a kind-hearted little woman, she would have been a welcome guest to every house she visited were it not for that certain nameless fascination which she employed sometimes, and which made other women nervous about their lovers, in the same way that a hen clucks uneasily when she sees her duckling offspring swim down streams which she may not fathom, but which afflict her with a sense of danger and unhappiness.

While Gerald Lisle sipped his cup of tea out of the little china cup Sophy tendered him, Captain Adair seated himself at the work-table, and with all the familiarity of an intimate acquaintance, began to dislodge and pull out all the scissors, thimbles, papers, and scraps of every description that he could find. While he is engaged at this interesting occupation, and Mrs. Herbert watches him from under her eyelids (she liked Geoffry to touch all the little things that she herself used in her daily occupations), we will give a few lines to Captain Adair's personal appearance, a point that has hitherto been too much neglected, considering the position he is bound to hold in this story. The little orphan of the Lynncourt portrait had grown very tall indeed since his baby legs had been represented in such pink flesh tints in that miniature. He was now a little under six feet in height, and had only been preserved from ungainliness of appearance by the military drill, which had thrown back the falling shoulders and expanded the broad chest to its fullest extent.

"A fine-looking fellow," men called him, but "plain in the face."

Women did not make the latter objection, and Geoffry Adair's light curly hair and blue eyes were much admired by those of the fair sex on whom he had bestowed any attention. They generously pardoned the defects that caused men to pronounce Geoffry plain. These defects, which consisted of a forehead too narrow and low, eyes too close together, and lips a little too full and red, were more than counter-balanced in their estimation by the excessive fineness of the light hair that made a rippled edge over the forehead; by the full heavy lids that generally shadowed half the eyes, giving them a somewhat indolent look; by the largeness of the auburn moustache, that concealed the over-fulness of the lips; and, above all, by the pale, clear cut character of his face, which gave him that appearance prized even more by women than actual beauty, namely, that of being "interesting-looking."

As Mrs. Herbert watched the sunbeams glance across the back of his fair well-shaped head, she felt that she would give a good deal to be able to despise all conventionality and go up and kiss the tips of those glistening curls. Had she done so, Mr. Lisle would hardly have been more scandalised than Geoffry himself, for Mrs. Herbert had not succeeded as yet in establishing any position with Geoffry, more than what might be held by any friend who brought to the aid of friendship the charm of being a young and lovely woman. At present Captain Adair believed himself to be quite as much attached to George Herbert as to his wife.

He had known Sophy before she married, when he was only a boy and she a betrothed bride. He had received great kindness from George Herbert, who himself, being then in the plenitude of his happiness, could afford to compassionate the lonely unfriended young man, who had been sent to study at a private tutor's near the residence of Sophy's father, and who had no other home in England in which to spend his holiday hours.

The attachment between Sophy and this youth was naturally looked upon as being of the most harmless character, and, as far as Geoffry was concerned, this supposition was a correct one. He was very fond of Sophy. "She was very kind and good to him," he said, "only he couldn't think what the deuce it was made her go off into such tantrums sometimes."

He was seventeen to her twenty, so in most respects she had the advantage of him; but as a blunt surface will turn the sharpest of arrows, so did her consciousness rebound off his innocence and single-mindedness.

The woman who was about to marry a plain middle-aged man for the sake of wealth and position, might look wistfully at this youth with his shapely curly head, and wonder whether some deeper passion than ambition might not one day blaze up in her heart.

But the lad whose spare hours were all given to the manly sports of riding, cricket, fishing, and shooting, whose foot was like a deer's in the race, and whose seat and nerve on a horse made him even at that early age conspicuous as "being first-rate across country," was not likely to be tenderly affected by the image of a girl whom he had known for so long, and who was already engaged to be Mrs. Herbert of Castle Herbert when Geoffry entered his seventeenth year.

Could anyone have opened the eyes of this young Adonis to the nature of Sophy's feeling towards him, I cannot swear that he would not have laid down his boar spear and paid all homage to the beauty before him; but it never occurred to him to imagine there was any design in the movements that brought Sophy so near to him when they sat under the trees, and she kindly heard him say by rote the lesson he was to repeat to his tutor the next day.

When she crouched by his side in the meadow, where he angled for fish, and finally let her head slip down on his shoulder, it never suggested itself to him that he was expected to kiss the soft cheek put so temptingly near his; he would, perhaps, entreat her "to keep still a moment, and not move," but that was because he feared to startle away his fish.

On one occasion (it was the night before Sophy's marriage) she went up to him as he stood alone in the dusk of the drawing-room, and for the first time since she had felt this passion grow up in her breast she was a little over-mastered by it.

She put her arms round his neck, and kissed him passionately; her face was wet with tears, and she looked in his eyes with a yearning tenderness, which, perhaps, it was as well for him the darkness partly concealed.

"Why, Soph, dear, what's the matter?" the lad began.

But the sound of his voice, so kindly in tone, but so unconcerned, restored her at once to self-possession.

"It's very stupid of me, Geoff," she said, "but the thoughts of leaving home, and all—all of you, seems rather to upset me."

"Well, but it isn't as if you were going away to a long distance," Geoffry said, consolingly. "Your home will always be in England; and you'll have really good hunters now," he added, his eyes brightening at the idea.

"We'll cut them all down next season—eh, Soph?"

"I don't know," she said gloomily. "Mr. Herbert may not approve of my hunting."

Geoffry suggested it was impossible that George "could be such a duffer," but Sophy shook her head; and when Geoffry had retired to dress for dinner, which he did after a cheerful admonition to Sophy not to "be low, and fret herself for nothing," that young lady picked up a blue silk handkerchief that had been round Geoffry's neck, and cast it passionately at a marble statue of Apollo that stood in a niche by the fire-place.

"I might as well fling burning coals at *you*," she cried, apostrophising the figure, "as show warmth of heart towards that smooth-faced—fool ——!"

It would be impossible to describe the expression she put into this last epithet, as she glared at the statue with a look in her beautiful eyes that was positively savage.

Nevertheless she picked up the handkerchief, and pressed it to her lips and breast before she left the room, and when she went to sleep that night it was twisted round her throat, and the ends of it lay lightly over the heart that should have been dreaming of George Herbert.

CHAPTER X.

REMINISCENCES.

"Dost think old Sylvio, and his wealth of gems,
    Could buy one moment of the keen sweet joy
    That thrilled my heart to-night, when Fabian's touch
    Sent rose-blooms from my fingers to my cheek?"

A. C. S.

EARS passed away. Mrs. Herbert visited many a
foreign town, and made many new friends, before
she met the boy again whose image had stood
between her and her husband on their wedding-
day.

Sophy had become fond of this husband. She was
touched by his tenderness, and won over by his attentions
to her comfort and pleasure. She was a selfish woman, and
felt grateful to the man who ministered so much to her
selfishness. She was of an affectionate disposition, and she
loved (after a fashion) the husband on whose breast her head
had been pillowed for ten peaceful years—years that had
never been ruffled by anger or sorrow. But, in spite of all
this—in spite of her having met with many men quite as
good-looking as Geoffry, if not handsomer men, who would
willingly have given her all the adoration which had been
wanting in him—in spite of her having seen the world,
of her mind having become expanded and her manners
formed since that evening when she wore the blue handkerchief round her neck—notwithstanding that she had

grown into a matron—that he on his part was much altered in appearance,—in spite of all these, and a thousand other good reasons why she should now regard Geoffry Adair with the same kindly indifference which he had once manifested towards her, she could not help feeling all the old fatal attraction steal over her before she had been many hours in his presence, and for some weeks after Geoffry's re-introduction into the family Mrs. Herbert was fighting a battle in which honour and the duty she owed her husband made but a poor defence against the strength of her own selfish passions.

Geoffry was seventeen when Sophy's marriage separated her from him; he was four and twenty when the Herberts, after a lengthened tour abroad, returned to England, and met him by accident at an evening party in London.

Geoffry was standing by a doorway, looking at the dancing with that gentle air of indifference which is supposed to be the especial prerogative of guardsmen, when he saw a face that for brilliancy surpassed all others near it—a face that reminded him of something or somebody he knew, but which yet was unlike the image it reminded him of.

Presently a turn of the lady's head brought the rather peculiar colour of her hair and contour of her massive throat well into view.

It flashed upon him then who it was, and, with an energy which much surprised his companions in the doorway, he exclaimed, "Sophy, by Jove!" and pushing his way through the crowd, was soon before the lady in question, shaking her hand with more than conventional warmth, and asking a hundred questions without waiting for an answer, as is the custom among friends when they have been separated a long time, and have not yet re-learnt the art of making their conversation fit into each other's groove of thought.

"Don't you remember me, Soph—Mrs. Herbert?" amended Geoffry, seized with a sudden access of shyness. "Don't you remember Geoffry Adair, to whom you and Herbert were so kind? Where do you come from, how long have you been back, and where are you living now?"

Mrs. Herbert stood looking at him for an instant, without answering his rapid questioning; then she drew a long breath, and the face that had become dulled by some strong emotion at the first sound of his voice resumed its usual brilliancy of expression.

"Dear old Geoffry," she said pleasantly, "I am so glad to meet you again! you seem to me to be very little altered since the old days; your mustache has acquired much more importance, though; and altogether you are taller, more manly-looking. Yes—I think you are improved." She said the last words slowly; she hardly liked to acknowledge that there was any alteration in what she had once thought so perfect.

Geoffry laughed, and drew her arm in his. "Come and have a comfortable talk, Sophy," he said: "you must have no end of things to tell me about; there's your children, and Herbert; and do you ride still, Sophy?"

"Did she ride still?" Mrs. Herbert felt a pang of vexation rise up within her at the question. Did he think her too old now for the accomplishment she had been so pre-eminent in when he first knew her? "Of course I do," she answered, gaily. "Do I look as if I couldn't, Geoff?"

"Oh, no! but I should think we both ride a stone or two heavier now," he answered, glancing down at the increased proportions of the shoulders and bust beneath him.

"You are as fond of hunting as ever, Geoffry?" she asked, as she sank into a low ottoman, and made him a sign to take a place by her side.

"Indeed I am," he said; "it is about the only thing I do care much about, Sophy."

She looked at him sharply. "Has had a disappointment in love," she said to herself, but another glance at his clear, untroubled eyes reassured her. "No, he is still the same," she muttered; "still the same light heart and unruffled conscience," and "still the same perfect unconsciousness of my attractions," she was obliged to add, as she perceived that his eyes, instead of resting on her, were wandering round the room in search of Herbert.

When Sophy got home that night, she told her husband of how she had seen Geoffry Adair, and how the poor dear was so altered she should have hardly known him.

This was one of the delicate touches by which she laid the groundwork of her schemes. She was no vulgar artificer, was Sophy, and she knew, perhaps better than any one, how to say an apparently careless speech, which, coming lightly from her lips, was yet meant to produce a weighty effect on the mind of the person to whom it was addressed.

George Herbert was pleased, he hardly knew why, to hear in Sophy's tone an insinuation that her boyish friend had not improved in personal appearance, and her familiar epithet of " Poor dear " served to remind him of the former intimacy that had subsisted between Sophy and young Adair.

And so Herbert said exactly what his wife meant him to say, namely, that she must be sure and ask the " poor boy " to dinner ; that he was very glad indeed that she had met him again, for he was a " nice fellow—a very nice fellow, indeed."

" Yes," observed Sophy, sweetly ; and " do you re-member, George, how Geoffry used to envy you your hand on a horse, and how he used to follow your lead to hounds, saying that you were 'the best man out, bar none ?'"

" Ah," said Herbert, with a slow smile lighting up his thin face ; " did he though ?   Yes, I think I do remember. He used to go very well, that boy did.   We must ask him down to Castle Herbert this winter, Soph, and mount him well ; be sure you ask him to dinner." '

And with these amiable words, the victim to wifely ingenuity left the room, while Sophy instantly sat down to her desk with the intention of dutifully carrying out her husband's wishes, and writing a note of invitation to " Captain Adair, Guards' Club, Pall Mall."

And so it happened that Geoffry soon became a familiar and privileged visitor in H—— Street.   If, during the two years that followed the renewal of his intimacy with Sophy it assumed a warmer nature than he was himself conscious of, it was because she flung her charms round him with so light a hand, that he became entangled in them without knowing why or wherefore.   She combined the parts of friend, sister, and flirt with excellent effect, and made her-self so agreeable to him in this triple capacity, that she obtained an influence over him superior to that of any other person.   Perhaps she was not willing to risk any decided expression of her real sentiments, fearing lest Geoffry's generous nature should take alarm at the thoughts of doing any wrong to his friend, or that friend's wife, or it might be that she was not prepared to commit herself to anything that might forfeit her her position with Herbert, should it be discovered that she had done aught to merit such forfeiture; but, whatever the reason was, it is certain that, up to that summer afternoon in which I have introduced Geoffry Adair, sitting in the drawing-room in H—— Street, Mrs. Herbert had said or done nothing that could lead him to imagine that she regarded him with any feeling but that of the tenderest friendship.

We will now return to the trio we left discussing their afternoon tea in Mrs. Herbert's drawing-room.

"I have been trying to persuade Adair to run down into X——shire for a few days," said Gerald, who, having tried for some moments in vain to catch a glimpse of himself in the mirror over the mantelpiece (the view being obscured by vases of flowers), thought he might as well plunge into conversation again.

"Captain Adair already knows X——shire very well. X——shire is *my* county," said Mrs. Herbert, carelessly fluttering a feathered screen before her eyes.

"Ah, but he doesn't know our side of the county," said Gerald, eagerly. "Castle Herbert is at least ten miles away from Lynncourt and Gardenhurst."

"And why do you want him to go down there?" asked Mrs. Herbert, curiously.

"Oh! only because I want him to know my people. My father is one of the pleasantest fellows in the world when he likes to be so; and as for my mother and sisters ——"

"Oh, you have sisters!"

Sophy said this with a sharpness uncommon to her soft, low voice, and glanced furtively at Geoffry, while she put other questions to his friend:—

"Of what age are your sisters, Mr. Lisle? and are they pretty?"

Sophy looked at Gerald spitefully as she spoke, thinking it not impossible that his sisters might be pretty; his was just the sort of baby-face that might be lovely in a woman, although it was insignificant in a man.

"Ya—as; I rather think they are," said Gerald, softly, pulling his moustache, with an air of conceit that made Sophy feel as though she would like to box his ears. "But they are mere children—children, both of them," Gerald added.

He wasn't altogether a fool, this baby-faced young man— no Lisle was. In some things he was almost as shrewd as a woman, and he already knew this much more than Geoffry did, namely, that Mrs. Herbert would not allow the latter to go to Gardenhurst if she thought he was likely to meet young and attractive women there.

"Really," said Sophy, sweetly, in answer to Gerald's last remark. "Then, if Captain Adair accepts your invitation, I hope you will allow me to send down a few *bonbons* and French toys to your little sisters. I am so fond of children (Oh, Mrs. Herbert!), that I have constant importations from Paris of all the latest inventions in wax dolls."

Gerald laughed. He could not help it. The idea of Esty as associated with wax dolls was too much for his equanimity. But the laugh was a mistake, for Mrs. Herbert heard it, and detected its motive immediately.

"You mean they are too young! But perhaps they have always lived in the country, and that keeps children rather backward—don't you think so?"

This was a "back-hander," delivered at her possible rivals, and at the same time it was calculated to draw Gerald out.

"Backward," he echoed, indignantly. "I tell you what it is, Mrs. Herbert, there are very few women who, to all the freshness of youth (Mrs. Herbert winced, though very slightly), can bring such attractions to bear as my sister Esty can boast of. She is the cleverest girl I ever met, and the most accomplished. She can sing like a nightingale, and plays as well as she sings. She speaks French and Italian like a native ——"

"Of X——shire?" interrupted Sophy, interrogatively, with a smile on her face to conceal the impertinence.

"Like a native of Paris or Florence," said Gerald, coolly. His blood was up, and he did not choose that *his* sister should be spoken of in a derogatory tone by any woman, however great his wish to please her.

"Quite an infant phenomenon," suggested Mrs. Herbert, pretending to repress a yawn.

"A phenomenon, certainly, but not an infant," said Gerald. "Esty must be at least—let me see—well, about seventeen."

And then Mr. Lisle made his bow and departed, having first made an appointment with Geoffry to meet him the next morning at Tattersall's to see a horse. He did not wish to prolong the encounter of wits with Mrs. Herbert, for he felt that he was already worsted. True, he had departed with the privilege, unusual for a man, of having had the last word; but then he suffered under that which Scrub declares to be much worse than telling a lie, namely, the consciousness of being "found out."

Sophy had found him out, and he quite understood that it was now very improbable that Geoffry should visit Gardenhurst yet awhile.

As soon as the door had closed behind Mr. Lisle, Sophy glided up to the back of Geoffry's chair.

"What are you thinking of, boy?" she said, softly. Mrs. Herbert frequently used a maternal manner and form of address towards Geoffry. It gave her excuses for touching his curls, putting her hand on his shoulder, and a thousand other of those little familiarities that seem to give inexpressible pleasure to women who love.

Geoffry looked up and patted her hand kindly.

"I was thinking of my father," he said, in rather a sad tone.

"And what made you think of him?"

With that quick tact that distinguished her, Sophy had already altered the inflexion of her voice to suit the tone of his.

"Lisle mentioned Lynncourt just now, and that reminded me of Lady Renshawe. She was a great friend of my father's; he often used to talk about her, and say he hoped I should know her. She must be a very old woman now," said the young man, meditatively poking back with his cane a flower that threatened to tumble from its vase.

"What relation was she to your father?" asked Mrs. Herbert.

"Oh, none! only a great friend of his. Sophy," he continued, "do you know, I think I should have been a much better man if my father had lived."

"Why so?"

"Because he died when I was too young to receive any bias from his influence. I've had no one to love me [here Sophy gave him a look which he did not see]; no one to direct my studies, tastes, or pursuits; I was left to drift along the world as best I could at the time when I most wanted a pilot."

"There is your stepmother, and Amelia," suggested Mrs. Herbert.

"My stepmother and Amelia," echoed the young man, scornfully. "How can I have anything in common with a big wax doll and its baby duplicate?"

"And there's Alfred."

"Alfred is a sneak!"

Alfred Cadogan was the name of Mrs. Adair's son by her first husband.

"I never see Alfred enter a room without comparing his movements to those of a sinuous black snake. ·I'm thankful that his continued residence abroad obviates the necessity of my being brought much in contact with him."

"He is a commercial genius, is he not?" asked Sophy, with a slight yawn, which she concealed by bending her face, until her lips swept the flossy fringe of Captain Adair's short curls.

"He is a great speculator, and a successful one," answered Geoffry, gravely. "It was said that his father, Cadogan, was of Greek origin; that he was beautiful in face, and treacherous of nature. He was a well-known member of the Stock Exchange, and when he died all the rumours which his wealth and daring audacity had enabled him to live down in the course of his prosperous career broke out afresh. Men at his death shook their heads when they spoke of Xerxes Cadogan—'the sharp practitioner,' they called him; 'a knowing hand; rather too knowing, perhaps.'"

"Where did General Adair meet with Mrs. Cadogan?"

"After her husband's death she went to Italy, being afflicted with anxiety as to the state of health of her blue-eyed Amelia. · [Amelia, by the way, was and is a thorough

Saxon in appearance, and takes after her mother.] She gave her 'dear Alfred,' as she called him, the option of staying at Eton, where his father had placed him, or of accompanying her."

"Of course he went with her?" suggested Sophy.

"On the contrary, the sagacious youth preferred to stay where he was; he was only fourteen at the time, but he reasoned like a man of sixty. 'I was sent here by my father,' he said, 'in order that I might form good connections. These I have to a certain extent already made, and I hope that in my future life I may find them useful to me. I mean to follow in my honoured father's footsteps by adopting his profession.'

"'You do?' said my stepmother, opening her blue eyes in astonishment at this early display of decision on her pampered favourite's part.

"'Yes, dear mamma, I do indeed. There is nothing I should so much wish as to be rich, and to be feared, as he was; and with this intention of emulating him, the first thing I must adopt is his advice, which I am sure must be good, for it was born of successful experience.'"

"Fancy a child of that age talking in that strain," interrupted Sophy; "it makes one long to box his ears."

"Aye, doesn't it?" said Geoffry, energetically; "and I did it afterwards," he added, with a pleased smile passing over his face at the remembrance, "but that was about something else."

Then he went on:

"'And what was your dear father's advice?' asked my stepmother.

"'That I should never lose anything once obtained, but spend my days in acquiring fresh gains; that I should live as much as possible in England, for that, while all the world over I should find an equal proportion of fools whom I might hope to dupe, nowhere should I find so much money for fools to waste as in this country. You start, my son,' he said, 'with advantages I never possessed. You have name, station, and a certain amount of capital; I had nothing but my genius and my handsome face. The former was useful with the men, the latter was invaluable with the women. (My stepmother must have winced at the sug-

6—2

gestive remembrances called forth by this latter part of the
departed Xerxes' counsel.) You, my son, have an ugly
face, but I hope and believe you have talent. Your want
of beauty will enhance your success with the men; besides,
a man in business who is ugly and grave obtains a double
share of confidence—he is introduced sooner to the Lares
and Penates of the Englishman's household.'

"'Indeed! And what more did your father tell you?'
demanded Mrs. Cadogan.

"'I have got it all written here,' said the wise boy, producing a note-book. 'I have taken down all my father's
axioms from time to time, as I was afraid I might forget
them, and he always told me I should never get anyone to
give me such good advice as he could.'

"'And what more does he say?'

"'He says, with regard to women, he will not presume
to lay down any laws for my guidance, as the sharpest men
have been subject to the wildest delusion about this branch
of the creation; but he assures me that the woman does
not exist who may not be won by perseverance and
audacity, the former being to the full as valuable an in-
gredient in a man's success as the latter. He further
recommends me to select the richest and best-looking
heiress of my acquaintance, and marry her. He did so,
and he found it answer. If he gets tired of her he will
not get tired of her money,'" pursued Master Alfred, consulting his note-book. "And then father ends by saying,
'Speculation, my son, is a beautiful and interesting occupation. The man who speculates, like a Chinese juggler,
spends his days in tossing up and catching golden balls
—balls from which, like the wily Asiatic, he must never
remove his gaze; but he should remember, if possible,
always to play this dazzling game with his neighbours'
tools, at least until he has acquired sufficient dexterity to
be quite sure of making no mistake in his play.'"

"And what did your stepmother say to all this?"
asked Mrs. Herbert, curiously.

"She said," answered Geoffry, laughing, "'My dear
boy, follow your own devices. I feel quite assured that
I can give you no counsel or protection but what would
be utterly superfluous. I will leave you at Eton for the

present. If you have need of more pocket-money, write to me at the post-office, Lucca, in Tuscany.'

"'Mother,' said her son bowing, 'I am glad you acquiesce in my decision. As to pocket-money, I shall not exceed my allowance, but I think it might be as well, perhaps, if I spent my holidays with you. I may find it useful to acquire the language.'"

"Then it was at Lucca Mrs. Cadogan met your father?" asked Sophy, interrogatively.

"They met at Florence," said Geoffry, with a cloud passing over his forehead. "My own mother had been dead about two years, and I believe it was more a notion of supplying her place to me, than any idea that it would conduce to his own happiness, that induced my father to marry the round-faced widow of Xerxes Cadogan. She was not a bad-hearted woman, and if my father had only been as intensely commonplace as herself, they might have been tolerably happy. As it was, their life was one continual jar, and I believe the only comfortable moment he knew during his married life, was that in which the time came for him to say good-bye to us all. I remember it as if it were yesterday," the young man said, with emotion. "I can fancy now I hear the chestnuts falling, and the brawl of the Serchio, as it rushed down the valley, beneath our windows. My father's hands were folded in prayer, until the sun fell behind the mountain; then he became a little revived by the evening air, and called for me.

"He, too, gave me some advice, but it was of a very different character to that given to my stepbrother by Xerxes Cadogan.

"He said, 'Geoffry, are you there?' I said, 'Yes, father, I am holding your hand.' I had been crying all the afternoon, for as I sat there listening to the river, and looking at the chestnut-wooded hills, it seemed so hard to think that he might never walk up those hills again— never follow the winding of the stream with me—never shoot, fish, ride, or box with me any more. He heard me sob, and he grasped my hand a little tighter. 'Don't, my son,' he said; 'I am not afraid to die—like Collingwood, I am content with the memory of my past life—it is only you I am troubled about.' Then he paused for breath, and my sense of hearing, which had been strained to catch his low-spoken words, again fell attuned to the rush of the waters and the rustle of the leaves. Presently he spoke again. ' Be good, my son,' he said; 'do your duty to God and man—be brave in all ways—physically, because you are a soldier by inheritance, and because you would not wish the memory of your father's naked sword and hard-won medals to be contrasted with a full scabbard and an unadorned breast, but be brave in being good—that's the hardest—and, above all, it's most hard for a young man who has to fight with the devil single-handed, with no father to back the right—but be good, Geoff, and remember that you had a father who was proud to live, and not afraid to die.' "

" It wasn't much," said Captain Adair, passing his hand over his eyes, " it wasn't much he said, you see, Sophy—he was ever a man of few words—but I hope I shall never forget those words. For ten years they have served me in the place of father, mother, or brother ! "

" Was Mrs. Cadogan, that is Mrs. Adair, kind to you? " asked Mrs. Herbert, her eyes devouring Geoffry with a degree of tenderness in their brown depths which made them look as if they were melting into her eyelashes.

" Not otherwise. She meant to be kind, but she was as fussy and conventional among the hills of Tuscany as if she had been living in Berkeley Square, and she was at constant war, not so much with my morals as with my manners : it horrified her to see me with sunburnt face and hands shaking down the chestnuts, scrambling up the hills in company with the donkey-boys, or fording the river with my linen trousers rolled up round my knees. One evening I was having a chase after Pietro, the farrier's son, he had cheeked me, and I pursued him to punish him ; he had scrambled from ledge to ledge with the agility of a monkey, and every time I stopped I saw his little brown legs dangling just above my reach, and his dark eyes glowing like coals, as he peeped through the branches, crying, ' Oh, little Englishman, Mother of Christ ! but you are slow.' At last he took to the river, and I followed him, laughing and halloaing as my bare feet slipped over the broken bits of rock, and splashed through the foam that eddied round them. Just as I had caught little black eyes,

and was magnanimously contenting myself with ducking
his head by way of revenge, I heard a rustle of silks by
the water's edge, and there stood my stepmother, shaking
her parasol at me, looking like an agitated hen in a cackle
of impotent wrath.

"'Come out, Geoffry, you naughty boy. Oh, what a
trial he is to me! Your brother has just arrived from
England; come out, directly, and say 'how-d'ye-do' to
him, and pray, my dear boy (this was said soothingly), do
come in and make yourself look more like a gentleman
before Alfred sees you.'

"But it was too late, for already Alfred was seen
descending, with careful, diminutive steps, the declivity
that led down to the stream from our side of the house. I
watched the little man with the greatest interest, not unmixed with curiosity: it was as though a strange animal
were visiting our wilds.

"Master Cadogan walked with deliberation beyond his
age, he seemed much disturbed by the uneven nature
of the ground he had to descend, and he extended his
hand to obtain the support of every bough that overshadowed his path. He was clad in the latest stage of
Eton fashion: his hat was diminutive, but his shirt-
collars were portentous; he wore a frock coat, made of
glossy black cloth, and a waistcoat to match; across the
latter extended the heavy links of a handsome gold chain;
he had on the tiniest of patent boots, and he held in one
hand a small gold-mounted cane.

"'Something like a gentleman,' his mother said, proudly,
as she watched him coming down the slope. 'Come out
and shake hands with your brother, Geoffry.'

"'Ho! that's my brother, is it?' said I; and then I'm
afraid I was rather rude, for I put my hands on my knees,
and laughed. 'Let him come in and shake hands with me,
if he's anxious about it,' I said.

"'For shame, Geoffry; here is General Carteret, too, an
old friend of your father's! he has kindly brought Alfred
with him from Florence.'

"I looked up and saw that behind Master Cadogan
came the figure of a tall, soldier-like looking man, whose
grizzly mustache and military bearing brought a pang to

my heart: 'A friend of your father's,' too. I was out of the water in an instant, Sophy, and pulling off my straw-hat, with a grave bow to the Etonian who had evidently thought to overawe me by the formality of his address, I advanced to General Carteret, and clasped his hand warmly.

"'I am very glad to see you, Sir,' I said; 'all who loved my father must be welcome to my mother, and his son.'

"Mrs. Adair looked extremely astonished and a little pleased. Her black-eyed boy glanced slant-wise at me with an expression in which contempt had given place to surprise; while the general returned my greeting most cordially. 'I knew Jasper Adair's son would be a gentleman,' he remarked in an undertone to my step-mother, and she bit her lips and proposed an adjournment to the house.

"The fact was, Sophy, I was determined to show them that my father's son and constant companion could exhibit as much courtesy of manner as though he had lived all his life in the most fashionable school in England, and that however much spurious politeness my step-brother had learnt to assume by associating with a large community of youths who affected good manners as 'a style,' it wasn't likely that he could surpass in refinement or innate good-breeding a boy who had spent all his days with a man so intellectual and gentle as my father. We spent a formal but rather pleasant evening. Amelia was perched up on a high chair, and her chubby white shoulders and fair curls shone resplendent from their constrast with her black dress. I had watched the greeting between the brother and sister curiously; I pictured to myself how, if I had a sister, I should rush up and kiss her and ask after a thousand old pleasures of our play-hours; how I should love, torment, and caress her.

"But Alfred's notion of fraternal affection was evidently very different from mine.

"'Here is your sister Amelia,' my step-mother announced, when that young lady sidled into the room. 'Aw-oh!' said Alfred, with a conceited intonation in his voice, that made me long to kick him; and he got up, and just touching his sister's cheek, observed languidly that she was 'really grown;' and then subsided again into the rocking chair by the window.

"Alfred was nearly two years older than I, but he was much slighter in frame, much more supple of movement, whenever he did condescend to move. After dinner we retired outside, and began to stroll down the high road leading towards Lucca.

"'This is a dreadful place!' remarked Alfred, shivering. 'Are there none but brick floors here, and do they never put carpets down?'

"I looked at him, and saw that his thin pinched lips were blue with cold. 'Let's have a run,' I suggested, cheerfully, 'up that hill; that will warm you.'

"The Etonian shuddered: 'I never run,' he said.

"'Do you box or fence?'

"'I never box. I can fence a little.'

"Then he turned round on me, 'I suppose you haven't learnt to ride in this beastly country?'

"'Can't I?' I answered, with a chuckle. 'If you go up to Rome with us this year, I'll show you some timber in the Campagna that's well worth riding at.'

"Again my brother shook his close-cropped, shiny black head. 'I never ride at timber,' he said, and then he relapsed into silence, and I began to wish that I might rejoin my little monkey-faced Pietro, who, I decided, was worth twenty of this sleek, solemn muff."

"How did it all end?" asked Sophy, sweetly.

"Well, things went on pretty smoothly," said Geoffry, flushing at the remembrance, "and then ——"

"Well, and then?"

"There was a very pretty little girl, called Carolina, Pietro's sister; a girl of about fifteen; a girl so pretty and so typical of her country that I never think of Tuscany without remembering her bright face, shadowed by her red handkerchief as she lounged at her doorway in the evening, her large dark eyes flashing with mirth and mischief, and every movement filled with a lithesome grace peculiar to the natives of her country. My admiration was harmless enough, as you may suppose, Sophy; I thought her a jolly little girl, and I delighted in trying to make sketches of the landscape,

with Carolina's hair, and Carolina's eyes enlarged to an unnatural and impossible size, in the foreground.　But Alfred,
you know, was two years older than I."

"Well?"

" Well, one day " (the young man blundered over the rest
of his story. like a horse stumbling over broken ground),
"Alfred, finding Carolina alone at her door when the men
had gone to the chestnut beating, fixed his eye-glass in his
long eye, and called out imperiously, 'Vieni qui, Bellina.'

"The girl stared at him, and made no reply, only tumbling over and round her arms a pet kitten, of which she
was fond.

" Alfred put down her silence to her not understanding
his invitation, and approached her familiarly and put his
arm round her waist.　At that moment the kitten pounced
on his bare hand, thinking, no doubt, from the abruptness
with which it had been placed in its position, that it was put
there on purpose for it to play with; the sharp hook of its
claw drew a long blue streak down Master Alfred's hand,
and, angry at the pain, he grasped the kitten by the throat,
and threw it with all his force against the opposite wall,
where it fell dead.

" It was at this moment that I came up, and Carolina in
a passion of rage and tears threw herself over to where the
kitten lay, invoking the vengeance of all the saints headed
by the Virgin Mary, on the ugly, ever-to-be-despised little
Englishman who had murdered her dearly-loved cat.

" Fired with indignation, both on Carolina's account and
that of the kitten, I pulled off my linen jacket, and invited
Alfred to 'Come on.'

" He took no notice of my proffered courtesy, but
attempted to pass out of the house, whereupon I gave my
stepbrother a vigorous thrashing."

"I daresay it did him good," remarked Mrs. Herbert,
piously.

"I doubt it," said Captain Adair.　"I don't think *anything*
would."

Mrs. Herbert laughed at the hopelessness of his tone.

" Where is he now?" she asked.

"At Munich, I believe.　He has long since embarked on
the career marked out for him by his father.　He is already

noted for his abilities among the money-shifters of the day. Whether he will ever emulate his father's daring or his 'sharp dealing' remains to be proved. I should fancy he is too cautious ever to be a great speculator."

" And your stepmother and Amelia ? "

" They are at present in Paris, but they expect to be in England next month. And now, Sophy, I will take my leave. I fear I have wearied you as it is."

Mrs. Herbert glanced kindly at him from under the deep fringe of her eyelashes. "You never weary me," she said ; " but tell me, Geoffry, what is the tie between this old Lady Renshawe and you ? Why should you wish to go and see her ? "

" Only that my father used to speak very warmly of her. It seems she was a dear friend of my mother's. They used to correspond with each other until my mother's death, and then the connection dropped ; but my father often told me that, if ever I wanted a friend in England, he was sure I should find one in Lady Renshawe."

" You do not want for friends, Geoffry, while you have me —*us*," said Mrs. Herbert, correcting herself.

Geoffry smiled a pleasant smile, that showed all the lights in his blue eyes.

"I know I do not," he said ; " but I should like to go and see the old countess soon. I should have done so long before this, only that I did not like to obtrude myself on her privacy ; now that her nephew has asked me, I have a good opportunity of making her acquaintance."

"At any rate, don't go yet," pleaded Sophy, earnestly. " I am so much alone in session time that it is a real charity to come and see me. Besides," she added, rapidly, " Herbert depends on you to assist us in our summer purchases at Tattersall's. We've got to make up our stud for next winter, you know, and—and there's no one to take me about. At least, Geoffry, promise me that you will keep the next month clear of any engagement to go to Lynncourt."

Seeing that he still hesitated, Mrs. Herbert snapped the rose in her waistband petulantly, and flung the decapitated head out of the window.

" I did not think you could be so unkind, Geoffry, as to prefer a stupid old woman to me. Since you won't do anything to oblige Herbert or myself, I suppose you must go. But you might have delayed your visit a month."

"Well, Sophy, since you really wish it," said Geoffry, puzzled by her vehemence, "and if I really can be of any use to you in town ——"

"Yes!" she said eagerly, and she placed her hand on his shoulder.

"I won't go until July," he answered; and, unconscious of her touch, he walked to the window whistling a little soft Italian air.

CHAPTER XI.

THE PARTY FROM MR. CLUTTERBUCK'S.

"A most acute juvenal; voluble and free of grace."
LOVE'S LABOUR'S LOST.

HE month Mrs. Herbert had petitioned for came and went, and still Captain Adair lingered in town, finding it almost impossible to extricate himself from the many engagements the Herberts involved him in from day to day, without seeming positively rude and ungrateful to friends to whom he owed so much. At least this was the light in which Sophy continued to make every endeavour on his part to go away from town during the season appear to him.

It might seem singular that Mrs. Herbert should fear for Geofiry a week's seclusion in the country with women of whose attractions she was not assured, rather than the constant opportunities he had in London of meeting again and again some of its fairest and most attractive denizens, but Sophy had gauged her favourite's character pretty correctly, when she said :—

"He is a romantic fool, and he is young. Love with him will have to be nursed by sentiment, and his first passion will be as fresh and pure as the early morning. Did he love only for love's sake he would have loved *me* ere this; but, no! at his age he scorns the attractions of well-dressed women and perfect manners; he thinks they are so many milliner's dolls, and sighs for the ethereal charms of some

' Egeria of his soul ; ' some floating vision who is independent of Parisian stays and Isidore's *coiffeur.* It is only the middle-aged men who appreciate the luxury of our faultless gloves and infinitesimal boots. Boys of his age," concluded Sophy, vehemently, "are either angels, puppies, or brutes : they haven't learnt how to mix their various phases of character in one agreeable whole, and so they are insupportable."

Nevertheless Mrs. Herbert contrived to waste a good deal of thought on one of the tribe she anathematized. And if Geoffry continued to be too much of an angel to please her, it certainly was not her fault.

It must be remarked, that when Mrs. Herbert made the above remarks, she made them in the strictest confidence to herself. Indeed, she rarely confided in any one else. She was a woman to whom many poured out their most secret thoughts, being lulled into security by the soft, quiet, sweet manner with which Mrs. Herbert soothed doubt and encouraged timidity ; but she never reciprocated her friend's confidence by communicating any of her own weaknesses to them.

> " Tell all your secrets into Chloe's ear,
> But none of Chloe's shall you ever hear ! "

Like the suspicious king, who never slept without his shirt of mail, Sophy was never off her guard. "All men are weak," she reasoned ; "all women treacherous. Tell your secret to Samson, and the next evening he spends with Delilah she will acquire it, as he reveals all his thoughts under the influence of the inevitable hair-cutting ; tell the same to Delilah herself, and you simplify the matter, but the result is none the more pleasant when you suddenly find yourself brought up for judgment before the High Court of Philistines."

So Mrs. Herbert let her thoughts grow in silence ; and her thoughts were none the purer or better for being cultivated in the dark corners of her mind away from the sunshine of human observation.

But in her irritation at Geoffry's want of sensibility to her own fascinations, Mrs. Herbert had permitted her vanity to mislead her a little in the judgment she had formed of his character.

Geoffry was by no means an angel. What high-couraged, warm-hearted young man of four-and-twenty ever was entirely ethereal in his aspirations? But in his very faults he was generous; in his very vices he was essentially manly. It would never occur to his broad, open nature, to deliberately mark down a woman as an object of conquest, or to regard his friend's wife as a more refined species of *lorette* to serve as an instrument of his own pleasure, and that friend's dishonour.

"I like to talk to that Adair," said a celebrated sylphide of the —— Theatre, whose charms were generally considered to be superior to her refinement; "he makes me feel as if I were a duchess."

"I like that young man, Adair," said the old Countess of Stonehenge, who lived in her antiquated mansion in Cavendish Square, but whose parties still comprised (as, indeed, they had done for upwards of half a century) all that was best of London society.

"I like that young man; he is one of the few of his class that know now-a-days how to treat a lady. More shame for us!"

And so it happened that Geoffry's instinctive delicacy of mind, which showed itself in chivalrous courtesy to women, made him as great a favourite with the fair sex as his pluck and straightforwardness did with men. Gerald Lisle, indeed, who piqued himself upon the amount of classics he had *smattered* into his mind, if I may use the expression, during his public-school life, was wont to declare supremely that, "Adair was a good fellow, but there was nothing in him—nothing!"

But Gerald was one of those people who, failing knowledge of a subject, are content to judge from their ignorance of it.

Geoffry was a somewhat reserved man, and was as chary of displaying his inmost thoughts to mere acquaintances as he was of discussing women's names in public.

He would play cricket, ride, fence, or box, against any member of the Household Brigade who cared to compete with him; but, as for seeking any sympathy from these juvenile warriors for the more intellectual phases of his character, he would as soon have thought of asking a

Chinese to admire big feet, or of discussing with Alexander the coppersmith, the claims to immortality of Alexander the Great.

Without being a genius, Geoffry was much, as far as literary attainments went, in advance of most men of his own age and position. The late General Adair had taught his little son other accomplishments besides those purely physical ones in which every Englishman desires his boys to excel. He had grounded him well in Latin and Greek, and he had added so much interest to the beauty of the country in which Geoffry's young days were passed by relations of the beautiful romances with which almost every broken column in Italy is associated, that he had planted poetry, as it were, in the boy's very heart. When Geoffry was sent over to England to complete his education for the army, he nearly burst into tears of rage and vexation at his first view of London. "It is ugly; it is black; it is detestable!" he said. And he was only comforted when he was promised that he might, if he liked, return to Florence to see his stepmother on the first favourable opportunity.

"I don't care about my stepmother," he said candidly; "but I feel stifled in this yellow fog, and I hate these ugly square houses."

He was rather comforted when he reached the country residence occupied by the private tutor who was to "coach" him in his studies. There was a river that flashed by this gentleman's house, and therein were fish to be caught; there were dogs in the kennels for those youth who were wealthy and skilful enough to choose shooting as an amusement; and, above all, there was stable-room for the two hunters with which Mrs. Adair's liberality had provided her stepson.

One winter's season in England did much to banish Geoffry's regret for the land of sun and flowers. Association with his father had taught his eye to appreciate grace, and his mind to recognise beauty of form and colour, whether it existed in art or nature; consequently, the cool, grey primness of an English life seemed at first intolerable to this youth, accustomed to revel in all the easy luxury of a southern climate; to sit down every day to dinner in a dress-coat and starched shirt, and to be served afterwards with an orange, placed formally in his plate, accompanied by a small portion of dry fruit, was very irksome to Geoffry; and he sighed as he thought of bygone summers abroad, when, with his linen trousers rolled up to his knees, he would stick his bare legs into the river, and, as it played and splashed over his feet, pull a basket of black juicy figs towards him, and tumble out half of the luscious freight into his own lap, the rest into Pietro's little brown hands.

"It was very jolly there. These English don't know how to manage a hot day!" he ejaculated, mentally, when his host sat down one burning July evening to a dinner of hot roast meat and steaming pudding.

"Oh for a bare skin and a *granita!*" groaned Geoffry, his thoughts taking a backward flight to Naples.

Still, the winter months in England brought enjoyments to the lad which soon caused the memory of Italy, with her vivid skies and smooth seas—her purple vines and crumbling palaces—to pale in his imaginations. Day by day the brilliant panorama which had delighted his childish days faded from his mind, until it only lived there like some beautiful picture dimly seen through the broken phases of a pleasant dream. After all, was he not a thorough islander at heart, and did he not rejoice in the hard blows he received and gave at football—the sharp raps that taught him caution with the single-stick—the keen practice with the oars he gained on that reach of the river that swept by his tutor's house?

There were nine other pupils who shared with Geoffry the advantages of the Rev. Mr. Clutterbuck's tuition—well-born, well-bred youths, all of them; and a boy thrown on his own resources so early in life as was Geoffry Adair could hardly have been placed better than in their companionship, and under the control of so cultivated and kind-hearted a gentleman as their master.

Geoffry did no discredit to his father's training of his mental qualities; and Mr. Clutterbuck was as much surprised as pleased to find that his new pupil could hold his own as well in Latin verse and Greek iambics as with the bat and gloves. But it must be owned that the boy's attention to his studies relaxed a good deal during his first winter season in England. It was in the month of November that the charms of an English landscape first became patent to Geoffry's eyes. At such a time, what could be more beautiful than those low, blurred lines of bare hedges that crossed and re-crossed the brown lands of O——shire, as far as eye could see, until they faded into indistinctness in the blue haze that shrouded the edge of the horizon! Those wide ditches, with rich earthy scents rising from their black depths of water and dead leaves; those woodland coverts, with bright patches of red coats dappling in and out the misty shadows; the sudden lights made through grey-hued switches by glossy-coated horses that champed their bits impatiently, or tore at the nut-boughs, to take compensation in a quiet nibble for their enforced inaction; and then how instinct with life the whole covert seemed as the hounds swarmed through its tangled labyrinth, their dewy eyes so full of eagerness, and the whole of their well-knit forms, from their keen, intent noses to their waving sterns, quivering with anxiety as they flitted with quick, restless movement from clump to clump!

It was on a soft autumnal morning that Geoffry first made his *début* in the hunting world of O——shire.

Two other pupils had received Mr. Clutterbuck's permission to accompany young Adair on this occasion; and these two youths, both fair riders and both well-mounted, watched, with no little interest and curiosity, to see how "the Italian," as they nicknamed Geoffry, would acquit himself on this his first introduction to a day's hunting in his native country.

As the three rode to covert accompanied by an experienced groom who had been sent by the tutor to keep some check over the convoy, many were the speculations indulged in by Bentham and Colburn, Geoffry's companions, as to the probable result of the day's sport as far as they were concerned.

"Hope Nora will take me steadily at her fences; sometimes (when she's fresh) she rushes like a Bedlamite, and makes me feel beastly nervous," candidly avowed Bentham, who was a boy of a lethargic disposition, and hated being hurried at anything.

Colburn on the other hand was a nervous lad, who had just courage enough to let his horse "go," provided that it *did* go without any reference to its rider.

"I like to know nothing about it until it's all over," he remarked, with a slight shiver; "and when Little John refuses I feel as if I should have a fit."

Geoffry meantime contented himself with communicating his secret sentiments to his horse.

"I don't know much about you, old boy," he said, as he swung his leg across his last-arrived hunter, a fine Irish horse, which he had christened "Orangeman," both out of compliment to its colour (a golden chestnut), and to its country. "I don't know much about you, but you've got to carry me to the 'fore to-day, somehow."

And then he joined his friends, and took a roguish pleasure in simulating such an amount of ignorance of horsemanship as made them first ridicule, and then commiserate him.

Colburn almost forgot his own sufferings in the wonderment with which Geoffry's loose seat and uneven handling filled him.

"By Jove! Bentham, *L'Italiano è Sartoio*, a tailor, by Jove! fresh from Moses, and as green as the owner of the spectacles. Whatever could have induced the governor to put him on such a fine quad? He'll fall off at his first fence—he will, indeed."

Bentham remarked, sententiously: "See what comes of bringing up a fellow on the Continent, where riding is still an early art; I say, Edwards!"

Edwards, who was the groom, moved his horse up alongside that of Mr. Bentham's at the latter's summons.

"Yes, Sir."

"You'll have to pick up the pieces there presently," indicating with his whip Geoffry, who was a few yards in advance, and who looked at every step his horse took as if he were suffering dislocation of the limbs. "Pray, keep an eye on him," pleaded Bentham, earnestly. "It would be a dreadful thing if there were any accident; it might spoil my nerve for life."

"All right, Sir; I'll take good care on him." And the groom fell back with a smile on his grim face, for he knew

Geoffry's capabilities much better than did these youths, who were new arrivals at Mr. Clutterbuck's.

"Don't you think we'd better give him a word of advice?" suggested Colburn.

"Well! what kind of advice can you give a fellow like that?" said Bentham, despairingly, as Geoffry's horse gave a slight swerve, and Geoffry, ere recovering his balance in an apparent access of alarm, flung himself on Orangeman's neck; "excepting to go home; and any fellow who rides like *that*, and who's been mad enough to come out, isn't likely to follow such good advice."

The meet was at a place called Oaklands, but a short distance from home. By this time Edwards and his charges were drawing near the scene of action, and the two commiserators of Geoffry's incapability became too much self-absorbed to think more about him. Horseman after horseman clattered by the party, and signs of increasing excitement over the country's face warned the lads that the day's work would shortly begin.

Colburn became very pale, and his lips compressed, but he held up his head and rode proudly on like a young martyr as he was.

Bentham, on the other hand, wore a sullen expression, and settled his somewhat square person down on to his saddle with determined *aplomb;* he took up his reins with a heavy grasp, and clenched his whip fiercely; but with all this display of determination his heart was nearly as heavy as the less spiritual portions of his frame.

"She's just as likely to rush and knock over the master as not, if she has a chance," was his dismal reflection, as Nora, tickled with some secret delight, squeaked and lashed out behind at poor Little John, who was trotting along with a stolid indifference to all the excitement surrounding him.

When I have said that Bentham and Colburn were "fair riders," I should have perhaps qualified the expression with the word "average."

They *were* fair average riders for lads of sixteen or thereabouts, they could sit very well on a quiet horse, and if they had a good lead they could follow their leader creditably over any ordinary sized country; but as for assuming any direct control over their horses or their mode of going, that was quite beyond either their powers or experience. With Geoffry it was different. General Adair, who had been a Leicestershire "crack" in his youth, had spared neither time nor money to render his boy an accomplished horse-man ; from the age of seven to that of fourteen Geoffry had been kept in constant practice by being mounted on almost every variety of the equine race that entered his father's stables. One day he would be luxuriating in the sea-wave kind of flow of an Arab's canter; on another he was taught to submit with a smiling face, but with inward anguish, to the rough tumbrel-like trot of a Normandy cob ; or, mounted on a well-bred English hunter, he was exercised over every variety of artificial fence—his father having erected a series of these in the large space of ground he occupied by the gardens of their Roman villa.

Here were "ditches to you and ditches from you," "doubles" to fly and doubles to leap in and out, where the horse was expected to emulate the agility and neat-footed-ness of a cat. There were banks to crawl, and banks to top with a quick parting kick to aid the impetus over the off-side ditch. One thing General Adair strongly impressed on his little son's mind, and that was the necessity of being modest with regard to this particular accomplishment.

"The more you think you know, the more you'll have to learn," he said ; "and remember, in any difficulty you may always sooner trust your horse than he can trust you."

And thus it was that, thanks to the careful training he had received to aid his natural advantages, Geoffry Adair started for his first day with the hounds in England under far more promising auspices than any other youth of his age out that day.

The only thing he felt anxious about was Orangeman's temper. The horse had been purchased for Geoffry by Mr. Clutterbuck of a London dealer, a few weeks previously;—ninety guineas had been the price paid by the master on his pupil's behalf. "Rather a large sum to give for a boy's mount," you will say, but then Mrs. Adair had ordered that want of money should be no obstacle to any of Geoffry's pursuits, whether studies or pleasures. It may be that Geoffry's stepmother wished to cast off as much as possible in the world's eye the odium that had attached to her when it was discovered that General Adair had left nearly all his fortune to his surviving widow, including even that which he had derived from Geoffry's mother, and which ought, properly speaking, to have been secured to Geoffry himself.

General Adair's first marriage was a "love match"—a match contracted in haste and secrecy, consequently no settlement of Mrs. Adair's fortune was ever made on her; during her lifetime no injustice accrued to her from this oversight, as her husband consulted her scrupulously in every outlay he made for their mutual benefit, and invariably insisted on paying into her own hands the quarterly instalments he received of her fortune. When she died, her only surviving child was naturally looked upon as being the heir to his mother's property. General Adair rather aided this impression during his lifetime by giving his boy such advantages as might be supposed to belong to the future possessor of £5000 per annum (for such was the produce of the deceased Mrs. Adair's fortune); but to the astonishment of all, excepting those who had known Xerxes Cadogan, and who imagined that his widow must have caught from him some of his acuteness with regard to money matters, it was discovered at General Adair's death that he bequeathed all he had to his widow, with the exception of a sum, which, put into Consols, was sufficient to allow Geoffry £500 a year. He "also recommended his boy to Mrs. Adair's protection and affection." "And it shall be my pleasure as well as duty," said the widow, piously lifting up her eyes to realms in which they seemed, by their rapt expression, to discern the spirit of her late husband hovering in the yellow fog that obscured her lawyer's chambers in the city, "to act by that dear boy as if I were indeed his mother."

So, as I have said, Geoffry did not feel any pecuniary deprivations from his father's death; his stepmother made him a liberal allowance, and at his age the thought, as to whether he should in future possess £500 or £5000 a year, affected him very little.

Certainly, as far as appearances went, on this particular morning at Oaklands, young Adair had every reason to be contented with his lot, for no man in the field boasted a handsomer mount than Orangeman, or one that looked more like "work."

"Who's that lad, I wonder?" said Mr. Chesham, the keen-eyed master, as Geoffry, separating himself from his friends, brought his chestnut leisurely round to the other side of the cover, "a neat seat and hand, and gad, what a handsome beast he's on—the young profligate!—Can't have cost less than a hundred guineas."

"*Ecco la Mita!*" said Geoffry, softly, to himself, as he passed the master, and the master stared all the harder.

"His tongue's Italian, but his legs are English, that I'll swear!" the latter said, following the easy, and yet assured, seat of the youth with his eyes; and then Mr. Chesham turned his attention to someone else, and for the moment forgot all about the chestnut and its rider.

CHAPTER XII.

THE HUNT.

' Th' impatient courser pants in ev'ry vein,
And, pawing, seems to beat the distant plain;
Hills, vales, and floods appear already cross'd,
And ere he starts a thousand steps are lost."

POPE.

AKLANDS was a favourite meet, and Geoffry had a good opportunity of contrasting the appearance of an English "field" of sportsmen with the motley assemblage he had been accustomed to see gathered together under the shadow of Roman ruins, to pursue the fox over the desolate wastes of the Campagna.

Geoffry felt and acknowledged to himself that for this kind of sport, the comparison was much in favour of the English landscape—the soft, tumbled-looking clouds that floated over the woodland ; the woodland itself, nay, even the stumpy trees that lined the hedgerows, and the birds that fluttered in and out thereof, whose nests made round-looking shadows in the bare thicket, they all seemed like so many friendly companions, so many landmarks to give evidence of neighbourhood. "If I lose my way in this country," thought Geoffry, "there are plenty of houses to put me on my course again;" and then he thought of a certain December evening, two years before, when the superiority of his horse carried him so far away from the rest of his companions that he lost them altogether; and, having mistaken the road, found himself some hours later staring all round the dismal, windy plains that stretched away in solemn monotony till they joined the low, yellow line of sky, striving to guess, by the only clue afforded him— namely, one or two gaunt, broken columns (that looked even drearier, from their utter disconnection with anything habitable, than the empty plains themselves)—what might be the road to take that would lead him to Rome. He remembered too, how, as the night deepened, and the winds increased their wail, he lost heart, and nearly cried, for the rush of the sea seemed to become mixed with the moan of the wind, and from his ignorance of the geography he could not tell whether he might not be moving in the darkness towards some clift's edge, and then how hard he found it to smother his tears, when he fortunately encountered a herdsman, who, with bare knees and goat-skin mantle, which accorded well with the savage nature of the scene, started up from behind a clump of grass, and volunteered, for a few baiocchi, to guide the little Inglese home to Rome.

It took Geoffry far less time to remember than me to record this episode of the past, and his attention was soon recalled to the business of the day, for the hounds were already in possession of the covert, and every man was, if I may be allowed the expression, "pricking up his ears" anxiously as he awaited the result.

For a few moments comparative silence fell on the assembly: one or two "knowing ones" strolled off quietly to "favourite points;" nearly all settled themselves in their saddles, and gathered up their reins. Even the ladies (there were three out), with feminine tact, ceased to worry their male companions with inappropriate observations; for to the nervous (and there are many such) on these occasions, what observations are there that do not come *mal àpropos* to a man who is undergoing the process of "winding himself up," often with much the same difficulty that is experienced in screwing up a stiff, obstinate guitar-string, that slips from under the hand at each effort to elevate its tone?

Dapple, dapple flapped the hounds' ears, and patter, patter, went their busy little feet through the dry leaves and creeping tangles of the underwood, when a clear, musical yelp sent a sort of electric thrill through men and horses,

Another, and then another, and the chorus is taken up quickly; there is a desperate rush towards one side of the cover, the hounds tear, scramble, and drop in and then out of the outside ditch, and are quickly over the next field, streaming down wind in a compact body, while one or two horsemen farther on have the satisfaction of seeing a handsome-looking brush bob up and over a fence with the rapidity of lightning, as the fox seems literally to fly across country, with the advantage of at least two fields between him and his pursuers.

Geoffry had made up his mind that, whatever he did, he would not put himself in a position to be taunted for any gross blunder that day. "If I killed a hound, or upset a man, or overrode the scent, or anything dreadful of that kind, I should never get over it," he said, and he attempted to turn the chestnut's head towards as lonely a line as he could pick out among the scattered groups of horsemen. The chestnut bitterly resented the interference; his temper had been working up to blazing point ever since he had heard that first quick holloa, and now he commenced kicking so violently that Geoffry had some trouble in keeping his seat. Moreover, the latter found to his horror that every time he applied spur and whip, he was answered by fresh kicks, and that so far from making any advance towards the fast receding pack, he was going back in the direction of the ditch they had just come out at.

"Oh, d—— you! get on," said the boy, in helpless despair, and then he relaxed his reins, and ceased to make any further effort with hand or heel; the ruse succeeded: Orangeman, no longer occupied in fighting, dashed forward with a plunge and a pull, and was presently settled down into an easy gallop, which showed his fine proportions to perfection, as he strode over the heavy plough with as much ease as if it were the soundest turf.

Geoffry had hardly recovered from the confusion of mind he had been thrown into by his brief but fierce contest with Orangeman, when a high brown line seemed to spring suddenly from the earth before his bewildered eyes, and with a crash, bang, slip, and up again, he found himself in another field, with a wide ditch behind him, and the hounds straight in front, but still divided from him by two fields; he could see them streaming up a bit of upland, followed by one or two scarlet coats that presently disappeared over the brow of the hill; these belonged to the fortunate few who had stationed themselves at favourable points up the country, and who had been the first to view the fox away. Geoffry was, however, in advance of the rest of the field, he having unconsciously taken a short cut, by accepting a fence where the landing on the off side was so notoriously rotten that nearly every one else had gone a quarter of a mile farther up, to a corner where three fields met, to avoid it.

Geoffry now began to enjoy himself; his eyes sparkled as the wind swept by his tingling cheeks, and every advancing stride of Orangeman brought him nearer to the pack; looking back, he saw the field dotted over by those who had escaped from their bondage, in the triangular corner in which they had been held by the press of the crowd, and who were bustling up the furrows with all the speed they could.

Among these Geoffry discerned Bentham's solid figure bobbing up and down uncomfortably under the wild, un-even bounds made by Nora, in her efforts to get forward,—efforts that were partly suppressed by the dead weight Bentham's hands were keeping down each side of her mouth. Colburn was still farther behind, applying whip and spur to Little John, in a frantic endeavour to move that leisurely animal out of the steady trot, which was all he considered necessary to keep his stable-friend and companion, Nora, in view.

Hitherto Orangeman had not relaxed his speed since the auspicious moment when he first decided to begin his gallop, but now, as Geoffry neared the last fence that separated him from the hounds, his horse slackened his pace into first a slow trot and finally a walk. Then with cat-like caution he crept up a rather high, steep bank and stared meditatively into the ditch on the other side; Geoffry had had enough of interfering with his horse, and gave him his head, but happening to glance behind him he saw that Nora had taken the law into her own hands or rather legs, and was bearing down upon him with the speed of a cannon-ball. Incautiously Geoffrey pressed his heels against the chestnut's side, and that capricious animal wheeling suddenly round began to gallop wildly up the field; Geoffry turned him by a strong effort, and the chestnut flew furiously at the bank without a vestige of his former caution, excepting that he struck his heels against it in a masterly manner as he flew over with an impetus which brought him ploughing up the ground some yards in advance on the other side. "That horse is a clipper," was the emphatic assertion made by Mr. Chesham, as he edged his pony slowly through a gap made close to a tree a little farther up, and then he followed in the chestnut's wake, and was soon out of poor Bentham's sight. Bentham, who was only relieved from the fear of becoming an involuntary homicide to find himself being bucked all over the place, for Nora, disappointed of her expected lead, had swerved suddenly round, and was relieving her excited feelings by a succession of plunges more agreeable to herself than to her rider. To add to his bitterness he saw the last wave of the chestnut's tail as it disappeared in the distance. "And that fellow is a workman, after all," he ejaculated; "and oh! do be still, you brute!"

At this juncture Little John trotted up, and after his sedate fashion, crawled through the gap; he was followed by Nora with a vehemence which showed very little consideration for her rider's leg, which was scraped cruelly against the tree.

Presently a welcome sight met Bentham's eyes, and a welcome silence fell upon the air.

" They've left off their horrible 'hark forrads,'" he said, cheerfully; "and I do believe; yes, there is a check," and then he and several others took advantage of the pause to gallop up with a recklessness which was meant to induce people to believe that they had been going as hard as any-one else during the last ten minutes, but their temporary self-assertion was doomed to be short-lived, for a sagacious old hound, who was so covered with scars that he looked as if bits had been chipped out of him with a chisel, and who was appropriately named "Ulysses," after the crafty hero of old, quickly hit off the line; with noisy joy the rest of the pack testified their coincidence with their leader's penetration, and in less than two minutes the hounds were again in full cry, making such running as threatened to distance all pursuers.

Mr. Chesham was there on his gallant little roan, but then he always managed to save his horse so well during a day's work that he could generally afford a good extra spurt when it was required. Bentham was there, for Nora was determined to show her powers in spite of him, and having out-paced Little John, she had decided to follow the chestnut.

The country was becoming very heavy, and none but light weights on good horses could be expected to hold their own much longer. Nora's coat was white with sweat, but the chestnut had only begun to look a little darker in the gold lights of his neck, and his action was as grand as when he started. The field was now reduced to seven, and consisted of the two boys (Adair and Bentham), the master, the huntsman, two other men in pink, and a lady—a lady who had been riding well in front all day, whose striking appearance would have challenged admiration, even had she not taken so successful and prominent a part in the day's sport. With a face that glowed just enough to make it look charmingly full of life, with flashing brown eyes, and coils of bright-coloured brown hair drawn tightly up under her hat, with a supple, rather full figure, that swayed in her saddle with a voluptuous grace of outline pleasant to look at, with a light hand and steady seat—such was the lady who, with the remaining few that now constituted the field, galloped down to a small fence, through which the hounds had just scrambled with unabated ardour.

"It's too good to last much longer," thought Geoffry, regretfully, as Orangeman swept over this last obstacle with a bound that would have cleared a five-barred gate.

"Never knew such a beast," the master said, as he, too, made his way through the fence. He was thinking of the fox, but ere the words were well out of his mouth he had occasion to transfer the epithet, for Nora made up her mind to follow the track of the roan, and, despite Bentham's wild cry of despair, and the desperate effort he made to turn her, she had accomplished her purpose with such indecorous haste as to cannon against the master just as the roan was lifting him gently in the air, preparatory to landing on the other side, and to knock him clean out of the saddle. Unhappy Bentham! why could not he and Nora at once jump into a gulf like Curtius, and hide in death their terrible disgrace? The master was a gentleman, and in the first shock of the surprise he had cried, "Hey, what! I beg your pardon;" being under the momentary impression that it was his own fault. But the master was a man, and as he struggled to regain his legs, he called Bentham's mother by epithets which would have startled that poor modest lady, could she have heard him.

Bentham flung himself off Nora and caught the roan, who had strayed to a bit of dewy pasture, which she fancied would be nice and refreshing after her fatigue.

"I beg ten thousand pardons," he muttered feebly, as he met the eye of the master glaring at him with a baleful expression, as the latter regained his seat in the saddle.

"Ten thousand devils!" cried that angry gentleman : and then he dashed off in pursuit of the pack, and came up to them just in time to see the last hound vanishing through an aperture in a flight of park palings.

"By Jove!" cried the master, breathless with excitement, "they've got into Lord Snelgrove's park, and it's five miles long. What's to be done now?"

"Is there no place anywhere we can get in at?" cried the lady, who seemed ready to cry with vexation.

"None whatever," answered Mr. Chesham, emphatically. "The scoundrel keeps locked gates, and mends his palings twice a year."

The lady looked lovingly at Orangeman, and lifting her eyes she met those of Geoffry.

"If I had such a horse as that, I'd take him at anything," she said, softly.

The lad laughed. The paling was about four feet six inches in height.

"I wonder whether he'll face it," he thought. Then. without a moment's delay, he wheeled the chestnut round, and took him back a few yards.

"Stop! stop, Sir! I've got a key," cried the huntsman.

"Good God, boy! what are you about?" screamed Mr. Chesham; but ere he had finished the exclamation, Orangeman was galloping towards the palings, and Mr. Chesham felt his heart in his mouth as the horse, collecting himself at about two yards from the fence, rose with a mighty jump, and cleared it in magnificent style, his hind legs only just brushing the topmost bar.

"I'll give you two hundred guineas for him," cried Mr. Chesham, enthusiastically.

And the lady's eye glistened ; and she looked as if she, too, would like to grant an adequate reward for this daring act.

By this time the huntsman had unlocked his gate, and had received a curse from the master for not having produced his key sooner. The party galloped through a shady avenue of limes, when presently a sound, or rather a chorus of sounds, that came a little from the right, made Mr. Chesham turn pale with mortification :—

"They've killed, by G—!" he cried ; and after they had cantered another quarter of a mile they came upon Geoffry, standing by his horse's head, while the hounds lay round him in various attitudes of contentment and fatigue.

"I was too late to save any of him for you," the youth said, advancing towards the owner of the brown eyes.

The latter smiled kindly at him, and then Miss Sophy Vane called to the gentleman who was in attendance on her :—

"Mr. Herbert," she said, in a low tone, "I want you to find out this boy's name, and to be civil to him."

"Certainly, dearest," was the acquiescent reply.

And this was how Geoffry first made Sophy Herbert's acquaintance.

CHAPTER XIII.

"Nurse, cherish, never cavil away the wholesome horror of *debt*. Personal liberty is the paramount essential to human dignity and human happiness. Man hazards the condition, and loses the virtues, of freeman, in proportion as he accustoms his thoughts to view without anguish or shame his lapse into the bondage of debtor."

E. B. LYTTON.

T has been hinted in a former chapter how Mrs. Herbert, *née* Miss Vane, "improved the occasion," afforded her by her acquaintance with Mr. Clutterbuck's handsome pupil. True, he was as she said "a mere lad," but he gave the impression of being older than he was, an impression confirmed by his foreign ease of manner.

Miss Vane admired "pluck" above all things in a man, and, next to pluck she admired beauty; both of these Geoffry had already shown himself possessed of in a remarkable degree; yet for a long while Miss Vane did not cease to regard him as otherwise than a kind of handsome, agreeable toy, which she was to pet and patronise, much in the same fashion as she used to treat her dolls, in her earlier years, until that evening when, four years after their first meeting, she discovered that the image of this "boy" had crept into her heart, much to the detriment of him who was that heart's lawful owner. Sophy Vane had been engaged to plain, middle-aged, wealthy Mr. Herbert ever since she was fifteen, still, had this "boy" chosen to return her kiss in the spirit in which it was offered on that evening before her marriage, I think she would have willingly thrown over Mr. Herbert, of Castle Herbert, for the sake of sharing with this disinherited youth his £500 a year and his little villa in Tuscany. But we have made a long digression, or rather retrogression, from the chapter where we described Captain Adair as being detained in town by Sophy's manœuvres, and we will now return to that drawing-room in H—— Street, wherein Mrs. Herbert contrived that Geoffry should spend so much of his time.

The month, as we said, which Sophy had petitioned for, had elapsed, and another four weeks might have slipped by in the same way, had not Mrs. Herbert herself been un-expectedly summoned from town. Her eldest child, a little girl who was living at a fashionable school at Brighton, was suddenly taken ill with an infectious dis-order which had also attacked some of her companions. Her schoolmistress, in writing to acquaint Mrs. Herbert with this fact, suggested that it would be as well if the latter could remove dear Mabel to her (Mrs. Herbert's) own house at —— Marine Parade, as the number of cases made it difficult for the schoolmistress to attend equally well to all.

We have said that Mrs. Herbert was fond of her children, and we do her but justice in affirming that the receipt of this intelligence made her really unhappy, but she was selfish enough to feel very keenly the prospect of leaving town at the height of the season, to hide her brilliant eyes in the darkness of a sick-room at what was now a lonely, glaring watering-place. She thought of her little dinner parties, all light, wit, and sparkle; of her pleasant evenings at the opera; when leaning back in her box she would dream herself away into the music, carrying her own and Geoffry's image into every love scene—every passionate duo that was sung in garden bower or shadowed chamber.

"Oh dear! what a nuisance it is," she sighed; but when George Herbert said, "Of course you will go directly, dear?" she answered promptly, "Oh! of course." George kissed her, and said she was "an angel," and Mrs.

Herbert accepted the compliment with a conscious air of modest merit.

"I must go," she said to herself. "If Mabel died, I should never forgive myself. I should always have it on my mind.".

By this it will be seen that Sophy's selfishness was actuating her even when she seemed generous. It was not so much love for her little daughter that took the mother to the sick-bed; it was the fear of future self-accusation assailing her in case she omitted to do her duty, that determined her to make the sacrifice of leaving London for Brighton.

It was this selfish species of good-nature, this conscientious kind of love for those who lived with her, that made Sophy's life a constant war to herself. She was sufficiently fond of George Herbert to be careful never to vex him by an unkind word, or by any action done against his expressed wishes; but she did not love him enough to keep herself pure at heart for his sake; she did not regard his wishes with sufficient reverence to prevent her doing things privately, which would have broken his heart had he even dreamt of their existence. She gave him lip-service and eye-service, and after having made any slight personal sacrifice to please her husband, she felt entitled to grant herself a comfortable absolution for the next sin against him she felt inclined to commit. It was much the same with her children: she endured at odd times more trouble from them than people gave her credit for, simply because she knew that moments would come when, in her occupation with Geoffry, and the amusements in which he shared, these innocents must inevitably suffer a good deal of neglect at her hands, and she loved them, these little bits of flesh of her flesh, and they held a certain authority over her, so she indulged them to their hearts' content, at those seasons when chance or necessity severed her from Captain Adair, that she might feel the easier when, in her re-union with *him*, she allowed herself to forget *them;* still it was certainly a great effort to leave him at this juncture, and once having made up her mind to the sacrifice and started by an express train for Brighton, she allowed herself to luxuriate in irritation, and snubbed her husband in a manner quite unusual to her, but then she was doing a virtuous action much against the grain, and felt she might accord herself such small privileges. Meanwhile, having heard nothing of Gerald Lisle for some time, and excepting that he was absent from town, she hoped that Geoffry might not at least yet awhile find an opportunity of availing himself of Gerald's invitation of nearly two months ago— and so she went. And London seemed so dull without her, and the closed windows in H—— Street so blank and forbidding to Geoffry as he passed them daily on his road to the club, that he declared he would leave town himself; where he would go he could not yet determine, but he thought of taking a month's leave and revisiting some of his boyish haunts in Italy.

"I wonder what has become of Pietro," he said, with a yawn, as he stared out of the window of his lodgings.

An old woman crouched at the corner of the street, with a stall of dust-dimmed oranges before her, and the young man thought longingly of their golden yellow he had seen peeping in and out of the dark-green leaves in the groves round Genoa. "I'll go," he said, "but first I'll go to Lucca. The very sound of that river brawling down the rocks would make me feel young and cool again."

Meanwhile, what had become of Gerald Lisle, that he was absent from London during the gayest part of the season? Why had he deserted the Bond Street tailor, at whose shrine he was so meek and subservient a follower? The opera, he affected to criticise; the beauties of the ballet, whom he avowed he adored, and all the thousand other enjoyments of town-life, the participation in which induces so many young men of Gerald's calibre to believe that they thereby entitle themselves to the designation of "men of the world." Gerald had disappeared from London shortly after that interview he had with Mrs. Herbert in H—— Street. His absence from his usual haunts at first caused no little surprise to his friends, and no small alarm to his creditors, but the friendship which is composed of such little coincidences as meeting the same man three or four times a day in the same club, ball-room, or playhouse, is not made of very strong links; Gerald's creditors were more tenacious of memory, but the most importunate of these were quieted by the information given them, in confidence, by Gerald's valet, " that master was gone into the country to see his father." The very word " father " breathes hope and comfort into the minds of the most anxious tradesman, and the extravagant youth who can boast of a "father living in the country" will have at least twelve months longer credit given him than he could procure were he an orphan.

Gerald's friends were not more surprised by his absence from town than were the Lisles at his unexpected arrival at Gardenhurst.

Colonel Lisle was enjoying his evening cigar on the ragged lawn, whereon the daisies had already shut themselves up for the night, when he was aroused from the contemplation of his paper by the sound of carriage wheels.

"Who the dev—why, it's Gerald!" began and ended the colonel in the same breath, and in his astonishment he departed from the usual stately regularity of his pace, and almost ran towards the front door, at which his son was descending slowly, being somewhat embarrassed by the paraphernalia of sealskin rug and great-coat, etc., which the delicate youth had thought it necessary to adopt for protection from the night air.

" How are you, gov?" Gerald inquired, in an amiable voice, as soon as he had divested himself of his wraps, while his father answered the greeting with suspicious civility, much as one dog answers the advances of another when both are smelling a bone in the air. Gerald entered the house, and embraced his mother and Christine with a graceful condescension peculiarly his own.

" I hope I find you well, mother," he said, sweetly. Then, without waiting for an answer, he turned to Christine with " Christy, dear, will you see that my portmanteau is taken up to my room carefully, very carefully, if you please, as there are some bottles of scent in it ; and, oh, Christine, will you have some hot water taken to my room, and will you see about some dinner for me. I am afraid I'm too late for yours," he added, consulting his little gold watch.

Christine looked up rebelliously. In her heart she said, " Carry up your own portmanteau. You know we keep no men-servants. Fetch your own hot water, and go without your dinner, as you've chosen to arrive so late." But she reflected that as he had only just arrived he was for the moment on the footing of a guest. So she conquered the uncivil impulse, and only remarked, drily, "Dolly and I will carry up your portmanteau. I will take up the hot water, and I will broil you a chop and make you an omelette as soon as I can get a clear fire, for cook is out."

I think that Christine had laid a slight emphasis on the pronoun "I," in the faint hope that the little reproach conveyed therein might strike home to Gerald's conscience. If so, the poor child was disappointed, for her brother, catching her eye as she left the room, merely said, approvingly, "Do dear; thank you."

"Lor, what does Mr. Gerald want to come worriting here for at this time of night?" was old Dolly's peevish remark, as she had to upraise her bones just as they had settled into comfortable stiffness in her arm-chair, to get out sheets for the spare bed, and to re-make the fire, which had long since died away, in the kitchen grate.

"That's just what I think," said Christine; then she added, pensively, "I wonder when he is going away?"

And when she awoke the next morning the same thought recurred to her mind, for she had to arise early (and Christine was not very fond of early rising) to assist Dolly in the preparations for Gerald's breakfast.

"Young people take a deal of washing, now-a-days," said Dolly, as she rolled a washing-tub towards Gerald's room, and deposited it with a vicious bang at his door. "And I 'spose they think themselves mighty clean when they pour a pailful o' cold water over their heads, as if it didn't run off 'em as it would off a duck's back."

Gerald was, as usual, quite unconscious of any inconvenience caused by the constant occupation he provided for every member of his mother's limited household.

He strolled about the house in the morning, resplendent in a richly flowered dressing-gown, and slippers to match. And in the evening he gave a certain air of formal magnificence to the unpretending meal, which answered to the name of dinner, by arraying himself in the glossiest of dress coats, and the most spotless of finely-worked shirts.

These dinners, formerly so cheerful and unconstrained, seemed to grow quite solemn under the influence of Gerald's irreproachable costume, and the kindly patronage of his manner.

The one sole that lay on the dish, which, by a tacit understanding between Mrs. Lisle and her daughter, was left for the consumption of the gentlemen, was discussed in solemn silence by father and son; the former, who ate the faster, would sometimes take advantage of his having first regained the power of speech, to fling some little snarl across the table at his son.

"I see you young men all wear those turn-down collars now-a-days, like what poor Byron used to wear. Ah, well! HE could afford it, for *he* had a beautiful throat." And the colonel glanced slightly at the somewhat "picked bird" aspect of his son's neck.

"Ah, yes," said the latter, pleasantly, "I've always understood that stiff, high chokers were invented to cover some deformity of throat that disfigured George the Fourth. What an unpleasant idea it makes them convey, doesn't it, Sir."

"Not necessarily," growled the colonel, moving his head uneasily in his neckcloth; and then the little spar being over, silence fell on the group again until Christine and her mother withdrew, and then Gerald would draw his chair nearer to his father, and endeavour to turn the conversation into some channel that would interest or amuse the older man.

He was not without tact and shrewdness, this selfish young Sybarite, and on this occasion, as he had an object to gain, he made his little selfishnesses pander to his great ones by taking the trouble to converse on subjects utterly uninteresting to himself, with the view of pleasing his father; he even made what was to his indulged taste the greater sacrifice of foregoing his usual allowance of claret, and permitted the colonel to finish the bottle by himself, which the latter did, with an irritating affectation of abstraction.

"I say, Sir," observed Gerald, watching wistfully the dark line of the wine as it got lower and lower down the bottle, "that this present age, with all its hot-press system of education, cannot produce such officers as did the old Peninsula campaigns."

"You are quite right, my boy, perfectly right," and the colonel helped himself cordially to another glass. "But the fact is, Sir, you start on a mistaken principle altogether in imagining that you can force soldiers as you can cucumber beds. A really good soldier, Sir, is as rare as an aloe bloom. Scholarship will not make him, nor want of scholarship prevent his military abilities, if he have any, exhibiting themselves. Look at the Duke. I wonder what number of 'marks' he could have gained at a competitive examination. Certainly not many in French, and I should think he was shady in the classics; but in the field, Sir—ah, that was the time to see him!" And—

> "Something that spoke of other days,
> When the keen eyes could firmly gaze,
> Through battle's crimson glare,"

lighted up the colonel's wrinkled face. It was the memory of an old excitement, of a great glory which he had shared in when his hair was brown and his cheek red.

"Ah!" he continued, enthusiastically, "there were giants in those days; it will be long ere the present age can show such men as commanded us in the Peninsula. There were real soldiers then, soldiers to the manner born, and born, also of experience. That's one of the principal ingredients that go towards making a good officer. We give our boys the tuition of learned dons to coach them for examination where other learned dons will test their abilities; but we can't give them what would be really useful, a hot day with an enemy's fire in front! Theoretically, Sir, you combine, or endeavour to do, the soldier, mathematician, classic, philosopher, chemist, linguist, geologist, etc., in one; and yet I don't believe that you," added the colonel, looking viciously at his son, "would know how to command your troops in action, not only if your mens' lives, but your own, depended on it."

"Yes, I should," said the young man, placidly; "my sergeant-major would tell me what to do!"

"And supposing he should be shot first, Sir?"

That was a contingency which had not occurred to

Gerald, but he answered, readily, " Oh, there are plenty of
very clever fellows in my troop. I daresay I should get on
somehow; but we have fallen upon peaceful days, you
know, and the great military abilities which adorned your
time would be thrown away now. If your age nourished
good practical soldiers, we at least have some very fine
theorists."

"True," answered his father. "But if war *did* arise, I'd
rather raise a handful of the practical men that have dissolved into dust under the Belgian corn-fields than have all
the members of the Staff College under my command. A
soldier should be quick-eyed, quick-eared, active in mind as
body, clear of comprehension, bold in enterprise and
prudent in its completion, ready, yet cautious, self-assured,
yet not conceited. Such, Sir, was he who commanded me
on the last day I ever drew a sword:

> ' He, in the shock of charging hosts, unmoved,
> Amidst confusion, horror, and despair,
> Examin'd all the dreadful scenes of war ;
> In peaceful thought the field of death surveyed,
> To fainting squadrons sent the timely aid,
> Inspir'd repulsed battalions to engage,
> And taught the doubtful battle where to rage,' "

quoted the colonel, in a fine sonorous voice. "And, now,
Gerald," he added kindly, for he was pleased at having
heard the sound of his own voice for so long, "let us drink
to the immortal memory of Arthur, Duke of Wellington,"
and he emptied his glass, apparently unconscious that the
fact of Gerald's being empty debarred the latter from taking
part in the toast.

Gerald bestowed nearly equal pains on his endeavours to
conciliate the other members of the household; he had
been to the Royal Academy of the year, and he had brought
down with him to Gardenhurst a catalogue, wherein he had
marked as his especial favourites those pictures on which
public opinion had already pronounced favourable judgment.
Mrs. Lisle would glance eagerly down the list of artists,
seeking (generally in vain) to recognise in the names of
those most celebrated, some of the companions of her old
artist life.

"Millais, Frith, Faed, Elmore, who are these?" she

asked, impatiently; " I know nothing of these people. It was Etty who used to stand over my easel when I was young ; John Moore picked out his masterly folds of white satin by my side (he died young, poor fellow) ; Maclise was *our* rising man ; his brother artists used to wonder what line he would adopt when his genius further developed. There was 'Vinegar' Uwins, with his sour face and balmy colouring ; there was poor Dick Brown, who made such clever designs, and sold them in a lot for fourteen shillings to an impostor, who, passing them off to the Brothers Finden as his own, received forty pounds for them. Finden detected the fraud by presenting some proofs to the would-be artist to touch up, which, of course, the latter failed to do. Finden found out the real Simon Pure, but too late to be of any assistance to him, he was dying of starvation in an attic."

" Shocking," said Gerald, gently, as he twirled his whiskers round his finger, and then asked, with feigned interest, what Etty had thought of such and such a picture which she had painted ? What was the subject which she was painting now ? Oh, Clarissa Harlowe and the two courtesans bidding her welcome to Mrs. Sinclair. " And who was Clarissa ? What a funny dress. She has a look of Christine. Done from Christine. Oh, that accounts for it ; and the flower-pot in the window ; so like life ! "

" He means well, poor dear," Mrs. Lisle said kindly, when Christine dissected her brother's art-criticisms, with a quiet satire all her own. " He wishes to give me pleasure, and it is not his fault if he doesn't know that I'd rather have my Clarissa's face appreciated than Mrs. Sinclair's flower-pot."

" I wonder what his object is in coming ? " Christine observed, suspiciously.

This astute young lady had not been in the least beguiled by Gerald's efforts at propitiation. It may have been that he took less trouble, or showed less tact when he came in contact with her. Certainly, such observations as :

" Christine, the way you do your hair is positively savage. You really must allow me to send you some prints of the French style of coiffure ; I know one that would suit you exactly."

Or:

" Christy, why don't Lady Renshawe dress you and Esty properly? really it's a shame that you should be so disfigured ; " were not calculated to please the rising vanity of sixteen.

Moreover, the young are so quick to penetrate and stern to judge. Mrs. Lisle was Gerald's mother, and her estimate of that ambrosial youth was softened by her affection and her own unselfish nature ; but Christine, less unselfish, and less prejudiced, saw through her brother's "humbug," as she designated his unusual efforts to make himself agreeable, so clearly as to make her presence a continual bug-bear to him ; he would pause uncomfortably in the midst of his most honeyed phrases, when he saw his young sister's blue eyes fixed on him with an expression half inquiring, half ridicule, and at last he decided to himself that " he had had enough of this, and it was time to come to the point." So, after a few more days' sojourn, at Gardenhurst, he announced one morning that business re-called him to town, and that he must leave home that evening.

Mrs. Lisle looked grieved. The plausible youth of the last week, the Gerald who was kindly, courteous, and affectionate, had so twined himself round her heart that she had been able to put away the memory of the Gerald who had been conceited, selfish, and disagreeable. In the last few days he had seemed to be her own again—as much her own as when he was a flaxen-headed babe, holding her guiding hand in his dimpled fingers.

" Must you go, my son ? " she asked, tenderly.

" No help for it, mother—not a matter of choice, I assure you ; if it were, do you think I would leave home ? Father, can I speak a word or two with you presently ? "

" After breakfast, in the library," said the colonel, with dignity.

Poor gentleman ! he had been so influenced by the flattery his son had speciously administered to him lately, that, far from anticipating any unpleasant communication, he actually fancied that Gerald was going to consult him— to ask his advice about some regimental subject—some little disagreement with his colonel, perhaps—or some entanglement of a tenderer kind. " Who should a boy come to but his father?" the colonel said, complacently, as he settled his head in his shirt-collars while waiting the impending interview.

When Gerald entered the library, he sank negligently in a chair, and for the first few minutes said nothing, and only played with a paper which lay on his father's table.

"Please put that down, unless you want to use it," said the colonel, who hated to have any article in his room displaced.

Gerald, deprived of that resource, took to twirling his moustache, and, as he did so, it might have been observed that the lips, disclosed by this restless movement, were growing paler every moment.

"Father," he said at last, speaking with a difficulty rare to his fluent tongue—"Colonel! could you oblige me— would it be very inconvenient to you—can you accommodate —me—with—an advance?"

"With a what—oh—h—h?" was all the colonel could say, his blue eyes flashing at the force of the blow that had fallen on him. His face fell to a lugubrious length, and then he answered, with military brevity: "No! I can't!" And he took up the newspaper, with a sign that he concluded the subject finished; but curiosity conquered, and he laid it down to ask a few questions:

"What have you been about, Sir?"

"Backing bills, running race-horses, entertaining friends, and buying bouquets—in fact, gov., I'm sorry to say that I've been during these last twelve months living at the rate of five thousand a year."

"And your allowance is, I think ——"

"Five hundred pounds," answered Gerald, promptly.

"I suppose you are not mad enough to think I can clear you. What about your commission—have you mortgaged that?"

"Yes, gov."

"Have you," and here the old man's face assumed a pained expression—"have you been raising post-obits on my life?"

"No, father! no!" the young man said, indignantly.

"A man who is involved will do any dirty action," observed the colonel, sententiously. "But why do you come to *me*?" he continued.

"Because I am nearly ruined, and thoug· that you might help me."

"How, pray?"

"Couldn't you" (and here Gerald began to hesitate again)—"couldn't *you* raise a little money for me as the next heir by entail to my grand-aunt—to Lady Renshawe's property?"

The young man leant forward in his chair, and looked anxiously at his father. No one but his poor, worried, debt-haunted self could estimate the importance of the answer to his question.

Colonel Lisle looked agitated. He rose from his seat, and walked quickly up and down the room, and consulted his snuff-box rapidly.

"I am afraid that what I have to say will be unpleasant news to you," he said at last.

"Yes, father!"

Gerald spoke resignedly. He had been used to receive unpleasant intelligence of late.

"The entail is—in fact—there is no entail! Of course I shall (and you after me, my dear boy) inherit Lynncourt —that is a matter of course; but the fact is, the entail is cut off."

· "WHAT!"

Gerald showed no resignation now. He started from his chair, and his face turned deadly white, while his eyes seemed to blaze out of his head.

"Don't be violent; it can't be helped," said his father. "The fact is, you know, when I was a young man I was something like you, Gerald—an extravagant, good-for-nothing scamp. By a peculiar wording of the late Lord Renshawe's will, his daughter was enabled, in conjunction with the next heir, to cut off the entail. The next heir, getting deucedly hard up, and being then of opinion, as he is now, that Lady Renshawe would live for ever, agreed to sell his birthright for a mess of pottage, and, for the sum of fifty thousand pounds, gave his grand-aunt permission to choose the next heir for herself."

"Is this true?" Gerald asked, laying his hand on his father's arm.

"Of course it is," said the other, testily. "Why the

deuce should I invent a cock and a bull story only to worry you?"

"And why was I never told of this?"

"Why should you have been? I am not bound to be a self-accusing Noah, and hold up my faults to the derision of my sons. But for your own selfish extravagance you would never have found it out at all."

"I should have found it out quickly enough if the countess died leaving her property to a stranger, and so would my creditors,—I can tell you. Nothing but the presumption that I should one day inherit Lynncourt has kept them at bay so long. Oh! it's too bad,—too bad!" groaned the young man, burying his head in his hands.

"Not at all," said his father; "you were quite ready just now to have entered into any arrangement to help yourself at this juncture, regardless of the future injury it might entail on your children; you would smother Lynncourt with mortgages, if you could by so doing meet the present exigencies of your position. That's just what I felt at your age. Like you, I indulged too much in the luxury of 'backing bills, running horses, buying bouquets, et cetera,' and my entanglements at last grew so serious that my being the next heir to Lynncourt availed me nothing, and I was obliged to turn the empty honour of prospective heirship into substantial cash. Unfortunately, my poor boy, my having done so prevents your reaping any immediate advantage from the estate in *your* hour of need, beyond that which you have enjoyed, namely, the reputation of being the future possessor of it."

"It's just that which has ruined me," Gerald said, moodily. "I was brought up to believe that I should one day succeed to a large property, and I wake from a fool's dream to find that I have been living on prospects that don't exist; I have been cruelly deceived, and what a cursed fate is mine!"

"Stuff and nonsense!" the colonel said, with an irritated slap of his snuff-box lid, which nearly immolated his own thumb. "You always had a talent for involving yourself, Gerald; as a boy of ten you ran deeply in debt to a toffey vendor; at sixteen you had proposed to marry a baker's daughter, a pretty girl, though somewhat floury, and nothing but her own prior attachment to the butcher's boy saved you from perpetrating that act of insanity; your propensities, my boy, all point towards entanglements, and as for putting the faults of your disposition on 'fate or deception,' that is folly."

"You can't even let me have a few hundreds, father, to stave off my butcher and baker with?"

"Utterly impossible! Gerald, you must be mad to ask it; my income only just suffices to pay our way, even in this dull country-place, I never have more than a couple of pounds in my pocket when the week's bills are paid. We pay them weekly now," the colonel said, with a look of virtuous pride, and he added, "thank Heaven, Gerald, I don't owe a shilling in the world."

He did not, however, think it necessary to explain that Lady Renshawe had made this punctuality in paying his debts a *sine quâ non* with the Lisles as long as they should choose to reside in her county, and as long as they accepted of pecuniary aid from herself.

"I am sorry for you, Gerald, very! You are reaping the fruits of your own imprudence, and I daresay you find them to be berries hard to swallow and bitter to digest; but I must leave you now, I am going out for my constitutional; God bless you, my boy." And Colonel Lisle resumed his newspaper, and, lighting his cigar, stepped out briskly on to the lawn, where he walked up and down as evenly as if his blessing had done everything that was necessary to alleviate his son's distress. That young man sat in his chair staring at a sunbeam which stretched from the fringe of rose leaves outside the window across the carpet till it rested tremblingly on his feet. He had regained possession of the paper-cutter, and restlessly balanced it in his hand, until, happening to catch sight of his father as the latter passed the window, he sent the paper-knife spinning across the table, and rose from his seat with an emphatic—

"Oh, damn it!"

Which exclamation was surely (under the circumstances) excusable.

CHAPTER XIV.

GERALD AND THE JEW.

"The needy man, properly so called, is commonly well-clothed and suffers from no lack of food. . . . Not that the needy man in general would perpetrate an act of downright dishonesty; but his wants, whether fancied or real, and the urgency of his desire to gratify them, combine to blunt delicacy of feeling and sense of honour."— *Modern Characteristics.*

GERALD departed for town that evening, and Colonel Lisle bade him farewell more cordially than he had given him welcome. Not but that he felt a little sorry for the young man who was going to meet his duns with a pocket, which like that of the improvident Lucy Locket, " Had ne'er a farthing of money in it;" but the colonel was never very easy under the society of his sons. He was dictatorial and selfish, and his sons resembled him in these points. The older man clung to his ease with all the petulance of advancing age. The younger men asserted theirs in all the loud-voiced confidence of youth. I do not know whether a cuckoo ever has been known to hatch its own offspring, if so, I can fancy the indignation with which the parent bird would witness the efforts made by its offspring to repeat that trick of its own youth when it edged its little brown foster-mother out of her nest.

Colonel Lisle's own self-indulgence was wounded by that of his son's ; he saw with irritation his favourite easy-chair usurped by Gerald's languid form, and his buttered toast recklessly consumed by that unconscionable youth, and his newspaper was left out of its place. Mrs. Lisle and Christine never did these things; they respected the sanctity of his arm-chair, and they always ate bread-and-butter.

Do not laugh, O reader! When a man has outlived love, ambition, and youth, the remaining little comforts that life can offer him become greatly magnified in his sight, and buttered toast, newspapers, and easy-chairs had assumed proportions in the colonel's dimmed eyes not inferior to those which love for women and desire of distinction had once occupied there.

If "two stars cannot shine in the one hemisphere," assuredly two selfish men cannot live happily in the same house. In fact, Colonel Lisle would candidly avow that Gardenhurst, large and roomy as it was, was only sufficiently commodious to entertain HIM!

After all, is there not in the heart of every man, however civilised he be, something of the spirit of the autocratic cock, who admits no rival near the throne where cluck his brood of hens. If "every woman is at heart a rake," is not every man a sultan by instinct?

Gerald went back to town to the manifest relief of every-one excepting Mrs. Lisle; and her tender mother's heart was torn with doubt and anxiety when she learnt from her husband the harrassed state of her boy's mind, and the empty condition of his purse.

Of course she subtracted five pounds from the little hoard she was scraping together for a rainy day, and despatched it to her prodigal by the very next post. And when he received the tiny donation, he smiled sadly, thinking how inadequately this little note represented the hundreds he owed. Still he would not vex his mother by refusing the gift; and, happening to stroll into Truefitt's that very day (where he had not an account), he spent by far the greater part of it in purchasing some new scents and pomades for the hair.

He came out, with his fair curls more than usually radiant, and calling a hansom, ordered the cabman to drive towards the City. He flung a shilling to the sweeper at the corner of the street, and drove off, cigar in mouth, looking the perfection of dandyism.

The crossing-sweeper sighed a sigh of envy as he returned to his work: "Lord, to be like *that*," he said; "I wonder what it feels like!"

But had the broom-owner known that this brilliant creature, whose lips seemed born to confer patronage, and who was so beautifully dressed, was driving about London with the kind permission, as it were, of tradesmen, who had confided their hats, shirts, studs, etc., in trust to Mr. Lisle's charge, the sweeper would have lifted up his hands and blessed the limited liability he held with respect to that broom which he had gone shares in with another partner.

Who that knew all the circumstances would have envied poor Gerald, as, with terrible anxiety in his breast, well masked by a careless air of ease, he drove up to the dingy little house that stood in a back street near the river, where resided Mr. S——, a well-known money-lender.

Gerald opened the campaign gallantly. "He *must* have the money," he said; but the Jew was quick at reading faces, especially those that had distress lurking behind their assumed cheerfulness. Besides, he had been feeling uneasy about Mr. Lisle for some time past. Some unpleasant rumours had come to his ears with respect to that very estate on the credit of which Gerald was subsisting.

"I've let you have a good deal already," he said, with a slight touch of insolence ruffling the oiliness of his voice, "on very insufficient security."

"There's Lynncourt," began Gerald; but the lie stuck in his throat, and the Jew saw that it did so.

The most domestic of cats is savage in defence of her kittens, and the mildest dispositioned of Hebrews will turn upon a creditor whose security is found to be less good than was anticipated. Mr. S—— became yellow with rage and apprehension. "Not another penny do you get, unless you get some very substantial name to back your bill of this date, payable a month hence."

"If he has any friend worth knowing, I won't break with him yet," thought Mr. S——.

"Who the devil of my friends *has* got a substantial name?" said poor Gerald to himself. And he ran over a

9

list of noble titles, all of which Mr. S—— rejected with a derisive smile.

There was a pause.

The patrician tapped his cane against his boot with an expression of worry and vexation sharpening his delicate features, while the Jew, with one dirty hand resting on the table, looked at his victim with much of the expression of a Mephistopheles, whose Faust has got, without leave, into a scrape from which the tempter has no idea of delivering him.

"Well, Sir!" the Jew said at last.

Gerald, lifting his head desperately, was just about to relieve his mind by damning the inexorable Israelite heartily, when the door opened, and a dark, elegant-looking young man put his head in.

"You are busy, S——; no matter, I'll call another time."

"Pray don't go, Sir; stop, Sir, pray!" and Mr. S—— stepped hastily to the door, where he remained for a few moments conversing in a low tone of voice.

"What name, Lisle, did you say? Any relation to ——?"

Gerald heard this much of the conversation, and then he walked to the farther end of the room that he might hear no more, and looked pensively out at the express penny boats that passed up and down the river.

Presently Mr. S—— re-entered and, much to Gerald's wonder, he who (to reverse the old saying about March) went out like a lion, came in like a lamb.

"There is a gentleman here," he said, with all his old suavity of manner, "who will be very happy to back your bill, if you will permit him, to any amount not exceeding £1000, and I shall be delighted to accept his security."

Gerald stared hard at the Jew in astonishment; then with a vivid flush rising over his young face, he said haughtily :

"You must be mad, S——; it is impossible for me to accept such accommodation from a mere stranger."

"Pray do not say that," said a sweet low voice at his elbow.

And Gerald turning round sharply found himself confronted with the man who had been in conversation with S—— outside the door—a man of apparently his own station, and not many years older than himself.

"Your family and mine knew each other years ago," the stranger continued. "Are you not a friend of Geoffry Adair's?"

"Yes," said Gerald, still eyeing his interlocutor doubtfully.

"I am his half-brother, and I am here in his absence from home; he would be much grieved if I did not do any trifling act in my power to oblige one of your family; pray consider his name to be a sufficient introduction for my own."

"And that is ——?"

"Alfred Cadogan," said the dark youth; and Geoffry, flushing more and more, allowed himself to be persuaded to accept the proffered accomodation; and, when they parted, Gerald gave his new acquaintance a cordial grip of the hand, and went home feeling rather ashamed and very much confused, but still with the delicious consciousness of being worth £500 more than when he left his lodgings in the morning.

Mr. Cadogan smiled sweetly as he saw the young man's dandy-bred air as he rattled away in his cab.

"It's a reprieve from hanging," he said; and then he added, thoughtfully, "I *can't* lose it; I am certain to squeeze it out of them somehow; besides, it was worth venturing a great deal to make their acquaintance, especially in such a manner. No; the estate is not entailed now; mamma ascertained that in those old letters of the countess's written to Mrs. Adair, and she may leave it where she will; and she has two nieces, one of whom lives with her. This silly fool, this Lisle, shall introduce me there, and the devil's in it if I don't manage one of the women!"

And Mr. Cadogan smiled one of those slow, conceited smiles which made his fellow-men long to knock him over the head whenever they saw him indulge in it.

CHAPTER XV.

AT BRIGHTON.

"Behold the sport of Love; when he's imperious,
Behold the slave of Love!"

BEAUMONT AND FLETCHER.

EANWHILE Mrs. Herbert was still detained at Brighton by her child's illness; her life was very irksome to her in the long, dull days she was forced to spend in this lonely, glaring town. The only thing that consoled her for her absence from London was the reflection that Geoffry was no longer there.

All day long, while the sun beat fiercely down the white line of houses on the Parade, Sophy remained in seclusion within doors; seated by her little girl's bed, she read mechanically a few fairy legends out of gaily illustrated books, but was so distracted by little odds and ends of memory, which kept bringing Geoffry's eyes and Geoffry's hair between her gaze and the page containing the adventures of "Prince Glorious," that she gave but small attention to the story, and was constantly corrected by her little daughter for inaccuracies both of plot and language.

"Prince Glorious didn't marry Marcella, the bad girl; he married Rosecleer, the good princess," cried little Miss Herbert, indignantly; and then she told her father how silly mamma had been not to know who Prince Glorious really married. So Mr. Herbert would sit down and read the tale himself; the love he felt for the child shining out

under his grizzled eye-brows, and speaking in the tenderness
of voice with which, fully entering into her eager interest, he
recited correctly the adventures of her favourite prince.

Mr. Herbert came to Brighton as often as his parlia-
mentary duties permitted; he would willingly have come
oftener, for his whole heart was in the soft gloom of the
chamber where his little daughter lay; but the Session was
a busy one, and as there was no longer any positive danger
attached to the child's case, he did not like to shirk his
work in the House at a time when the faces of his fellow-
legislators were growing sharper, and their hair greyer,
every anxious night they debated.

Mrs. Herbert was not in the least annoyed at the child's
want of appreciation of her mother's little efforts to amuse
her.

"She likes to have you with her best, George," Sophy
would say candidly. "I don't think I know how to get on
with children."

She continued to do what she thought was her duty; and
if dreaming away hours in the sick chamber while the child
slept, occasionally bathing her temples with eau de cologne
when she woke, and flitting in and out of the room with
restless steps and pre-occupied mind at all hours of the day,
was Sophy's duty, she certainly did it to perfection.

In the evening Mrs. Herbert would stroll down to the
sea, and dip her white fingers languidly into the dark wet
meshes of sea-weed flung up on the strand, or gaze with a
yearning, wistful look in her brown eyes at the rosy flush
that suffused not only the western clouds, but the dark
waters that lay under them, and the grey line of distant
houses that curved round the shore. There was no one
to interrupt Mrs. Herbert's meditations as she reclined
on the shingle on those summer evenings, her fine arm
resting in the folds of a soft cashmere shawl, and her head
bent over the pages of a French novel. The cliff was
deserted by all save a few foot-passengers, or an occasional
invalid chair, whose occupant was trolled slowly up and
down the parade, seeking to imbibe health and strength
from the salt sea winds. The shore itself was even more
solitary. Here and there a boat pushed up out of reach of
the tide, caught on its sea-worn sides, like the wave, as

transient glory from some golden rift of cloud that floated
over it. A shrimp-fisher breasting the water, and an old
sailor peering his glass at some vanishing sail—these were
the only companions of Sophy's solitude.

One evening Mrs. Herbert was lounging in her usual
attitude on a raised mound of shingle, lying on her side, her
head resting on one hand, and the other inserted within her
book to restrain the fluttering of the leaves. The day had
been sultry, and the air was still mild and oppressive,
although a slight breeze was coming from the sea ; so Mrs.
Herbert made no effort to repossess herself of the protection
of her light shawl, which was partly dragged by her position,
and partly lifted by the wind away from her shoulders, until
the rounded voluptuous outline of her figure was fully
revealed.

She wore one of her favourite soft, grey silk dresses—a dress
which, fitting close from the hip to the knee, lay in crumpled
folds round her feet. Her hat had fallen from her head, so
that the luxuriance of her rippled hair was unfettered by
pressure, and Sophy had buried one white hand in its
opulent meshes just above the pink ear and its gold
pendant. She was not reading, nor yet thinking. She was
satisfied for awhile to bask in the balminess of the twilight
hour without mixing definite thought with that golden haze
in the west, the light run of those rippling waves, and the
warm air that filled her with such a sense of content.

Drowsiness came upon her at last, and the lids drooped
lower, until the fused lines of the eyelashes threw a spattered
shadow under them ; the head rested more heavily on the
upraised arm, and the rounded bosom sank against a ridge
of stones, cautiously as a bird sinks its breast on a doubtful
perch.

Mrs. Herbert being thus oblivious, did not notice that
within the last half hour the beach had become tenanted by
other visitors than the customary shrimp-boy and the ob-
servant tar. Ere she had slept ten minutes two gentlemen
had begun to descend the cliff above where she reclined,
and were coming towards her. They did not, however,
catch sight of the fair sleeper until by a turn of the cliff
they were brought so suddenly near her that the foremost
one nearly trod on the silken hem of her dress.

The young blush with facility, and Gerald Lisle, who was the first to arrest his footsteps, crimsoned over with excess of astonishment. "By Jove, it's ——," he began, but his companion checked his expression of surprise by drawing him softly backwards.

"Let's look at her," he said. And accordingly, for a few moments, while Gerald was framing some speech with which to judiciously awaken the sleeping beauty, Alfred Cadogan feasted his eyes on what was even to his experienced gaze the most beautiful object he had ever seen.

The very imperfections of her form—the too great breadth of throat and bust—were attractions to this man, whose Eastern origin sometimes would assert itself in spite of his Christian education, and his trained intellect. The one had taught him to conceal, the other to control, the savage nature of the passions he had inherited by virtue of descent, but the quietest of volcanoes may occasionally send up a flash to warn people of the nature of the green heights on which they build their habitations, and those who knew Alfred Cadogan best were apt to suspect (only to suspect, for he was wealthy, and wealth always carries such an air of virtue on the face of it) that he was not the man they would like their pretty wives or young daughters to associate much with.

Xerxes Cadogan was unjust when he called his son "plain." At any rate, had he lived to see that son grow to manhood, he must have retracted that unfavourable opinion, or at least have qualified it.

Alfred, the son, was not so regularly handsome as had been Xerxes, the father; his features were not so delicately correct in outline, nor his eyes so large, as those of the deceased Greek; but Alfred's face was not without its attractions, his eyes were very dark, nearly black, they were shrouded by heavy almond-shaped lids, and they were surmounted by the most delicate pair of arched eyebrows; his nose was straight and fine, but the lips were heavy and colourless; these, however, were partly concealed by the black mustache that lay over them. In person he was slight, too slight, in truth, for manly beauty, but his tailor had done somewhat to hide these defects by the judicious amount of padding he had applied to

Mr. Cadogan's coat at the termination of the latter's falling shoulders. The complexion had a yellow, solid tinge about it, like that of old marble; it was only under the influence of very strong emotion that any colour ever came into Alfred's face, and then it was a little faint pink tinge, like that which blushes on the smooth sides of a Jenneting apple.

In dress and in manner he was as quiet and as faultless now as in those days when he first made the acquaintance of his half-brother, and was so shocked at the appearance presented by that sunburnt youth, as the latter kicked his legs in the foam of the river, and grinned his red lips from ear to ear, at the care with which Alfred moved his little feet from ledge to ledge; only that the self-contained manner, and the foppishness in dress, sat far better on his twenty-eight years than they had done on his boyhood of sixteen. Altogether Mr. Cadogan was decidedly attractive, and women who were not penetrating enough to observe (or who, if they did observe, did not dislike) the cunning that sometimes lurked in his narrow, dark eyes, and the conceited smile that occasionally played round his curled mustache, were wont to think that Mr. Cadogan was a charming man, and had "oh, such a beautiful, low, soft voice."

His voice *was* very low-toned, and pleasant in ordinary conversation, but it was thin in quality, and if anything caused him to raise his tones, they became harsh and shrill. Like Mrs. Herbert, Mr. Cadogan was not in the habit of displaying much emotion in public, accordingly this defect was rarely noticed. When he looked at Sophy, lying asleep as we have described, the faint, pink tinge rose to his cheek, and when Gerald Lisle made a forward move, to awaken the sleeper, Mr. Cadogan restrained him. "No," he whispered. "Let us go;" and, taking the unwilling Gerald by the arm, he withdrew him softly, only turning once as they neared the curve of the cliff, to take another glance at the recumbent form on the beach.

"Why didn't you let me wake her?" asked Gerald. "It is Mrs. Herbert, you know, that handsome woman I spoke to you about,—I would have introduced you to her."

"It is much better that you should do that in her own

drawing-room," answered his wiser friend. "Women of the world don't like to be seen *en déshabille.* It's all very well for very youthful Musidoras to unconsciously reveal their perfections to their peeping adorers, but modern beauties like to be conscious to an inch of the loveliness they unveil. Mrs. Herbert would probably have been startled and provoked at our intruding on her at a moment when she was 'off guard,' and although *I* thought her lovely in that unstudied attitude, she would probably fancy she had been caught at a disadvantage, and that idea would have made her angry, not with herself, but with us."

" But she will catch cold if she sleeps there any longer," objected Gerald.

"We will call at her house now," his friend said; "and finding her not at home, you shall beseech the servant to seek for her at her usual haunt at this hour; your request shall be backed by two half-crowns, you shall pay one and I the other."

" No," said Gerald, true to his instinct of speculation, "let's toss who shall pay both."

" As you like," said Mr. Cadogan, "but I shall win; I almost always do win chances."

Win he did; and when Mrs. Herbert's servant received the little bribe which came out of Gerald's hand, he asked them civilly to walk up and sit down while the under-foot-man went to look for his mistress.

Mr. Cadogan had not turned over many leaves of the photograph book that rested on Mrs. Herbert's writing-desk, when the servant returned with a message from Mrs. Herbert to the effect that she would be in shortly, and begged that Mr. Lisle would await her return.

"Who is this fair-haired young giant?" asked Mr. Cadogan of Gerald, as he continued to inspect some half-dozen portraits that bore a strong resemblance to each other. These portraits represented a broad-shouldered young man, whose close-cropped curls rippled beneath the edge of a forage cap, and who wore the undress frock-coat of an officer in the Guards.

"Don't you know?" said Mr. Lisle in great surprise; "why that is Geoffry—Geoffry Adair."

"Not at all like him," said Alfred, decidedly, and not in

the least losing his presence of mind. "At any rate if they are, he must be much altered since I saw him."

"How long is that ago?" asked Gerald, with a little curiosity in his voice.

When Mr. Cadogan had rendered his new friend that important service about a fortnight back, he had insinuated that he was acting as a kind of proxy for Geoffry, and Mr. Lisle had been too grateful for the timely assistance to cavil much at the terms on which it was offered, more especially as his new acquaintance further intimated that he should be willing to renew his assistance until Gerald should be "in funds again;" but it certainly did seem odd to the latter that he could never remember to have heard Adair speak of his half-brother.

Geoffry was on the Continent, so he could not be appealed to; however, as Gerald nobly observed, "'Tisn't as if the fellow had done *me* out of money, you know," so he resigned himself to the fascination of Cadogan's society, and was even now beginning to like him so well that he had almost forgotten (as Cadogan intended he should) to inquire whether or not his new acquaintance was accredited by Geoffry's friendship.

Mr. Cadogan's incautious remark had recalled the question, but Gerald's inquiry remained unanswered, for even as he asked it the door opened, and Mrs. Herbert entered the room.

She had made but a slight alteration in her dress, as she wished to convey the impression that she had come straight from the beach; but her cheeks had a somewhat warmer tinge on them (possibly due to the exercise of walking), and while the shawl and hat were hung over one arm, there was the addition of a white boa round her neck, the fleecy framework of which was eminently becoming to the brilliant face that shone out above it.

"I am very glad to see you again, Mr. Lisle," she said graciously. Gerald introduced his friend, whose name Sophy did not quite hear; and all three fell into easy conversation,—Gerald explaining that he had come to Brighton for a couple of days to see a brother officer, who was ill there, and that his friend had kindly borne him company to alleviate the dullness of such a journey taken alone.

"Had I known how little Lisle could require the consolation of my presence here, I should not have accompanied him, and I should thus have missed the pleasure
of being introduced to you," said Alfred Cadogan, in that
sweet, low voice which accorded so well with the dimness
of the twilight hour.

"Am I to infer that you regret or congratulate yourself
that you acceded to Mr. Lisle's request?" said Sophy,
languidly.

"I don't know," he answered, shortly; and for once Mr.
Cadogan spoke truth; he did *not* know whether to be glad
or sorry that he had put himself in the way of this woman's
fascinations, which already affected him with the sort of
dreamy, giddy sensation that assails one's brain on the first
inhalation of chloroform.

"You are looking at my photograph book," Mrs. Herbert
said, rather astonished at the abruptness of his last observation; "do you find anyone you know there?"

"Oh yes, several," he answered; then, with a furtive look
at her from under his heavy lids, he added: "My half-
brother, Geoffry Adair, ought to be much flattered, Mrs.
Herbert. I see you possess no less than—let me see—one,
two, four, six, different portraits of him!"

He observed how, at the mention of his brother's name
Sophy's face flushed, and then that the flush faded away
from her mellow cheeks only to be succeeded by excessive
pallor; he drew his deductions, and cursed Geoffry accordingly.

"So it is he, is it?" he said to himself; while Mrs. Herbert, half rising from her seat, said eagerly:—

"Your brother—Geoffry. What, then, are you ——?"

"My name is Cadogan," he said. "I'm afraid, Lisle,
you could not have been very distinct in your form of introduction."

"Oh, how very stupid of me!" cried Mrs. Herbert, taking
the blame to herself. "I heard, but I did not quite understand. And so you are really Alfred Cadogan, are you?
Geoffry's half-brother?"

"I hope," he said, softly, "that when you have known
me a little longer, Mrs. Herbert, you will recognise in me
other claims to your consideration, independent of my re-
lationship to Geoffry, as you call him,"

"I call him Geoffry," answered Mrs. Herbert, coldly, "because I have known him ever since he was a boy. He is one of my—and Mr. Herbert's—most intimate friends."

She laid a slight emphasis on Mr. Herbert's name while uttering the above, but she did not in the least deceive her listener. She could impose on Gerald Lisle and other men of his type so successfully that the very inflexion of her voice would lead them astray as to her feelings concerning Captain Adair, or any other person concerning whom she wished to conceal her real feelings ; but with Geoffry's half-brother she had to deal with one as quick and wily as herself.

He said to himself, "of course he is Mr. Herbert's most intimate friend. The very first thing a clever woman does when she embarks in an affair of this kind is to make her husband partly responsible for it. But," he answered aloud, "that he had no doubt but that his brother fully justified the confidence Mr.—(he made a slight pause here)—and Mrs. Herbert reposed in him."

He fancied that this little bit of satire would "go home," and so it did, but not for the reason he imagined. Mrs. Herbert looked for a moment as if some one had struck her across the face ; but it was not the thought of her treachery towards her husband which thus agitated her, it was the angry pang with which she recalled the fact that Captain Adair had in truth been, if anything, over faithful to Mr. Herbert's trust in him.

The evening closed in very pleasantly on the trio in Sophy's drawing-room, and just when the pier-lights began to sparkle through the grey-coloured gloom of sky and sea, Mr. Herbert came home (it was Wednesday, and this was one of his visiting days to Brighton), in time to cordially in-dorse his wife's invitation to the two gentlemen to come and dine with them that night.

"This is one of the few evenings that I can ask for the pleasure of your company," said Mrs. Herbert, looking fondly at her husband, "as I never entertain even the oldest friends at dinner without George's co-operation."

George was pleased at this proper little speech. He liked that Sophy should put forward his claims to attention, and to herself, and he said :—

"Yes, to be sure; this is almost the only night I spend at home, I hope you will come, Lisle, and your friend too!"

Mr. Cadogan smiled when he got outside the door (they had accepted the invitation, and were now going to their hotel to dress), and said, speaking to himself: "As if a woman who can spend two or three hours of twilight in the dusky gloom of an unlighted boudoir, unchaperoned by any-one but her lovely self, wasn't fifty times more dangerous than when she smiles behind cut-glass and silver épergnes, with monsieur her husband opposite, and messieurs the foot-men behind her!"

"Hey! what are you talking about, Cadogan?" said Gerald, cheerfully. He had been lighting a cigar during Alfred's commentary on Mrs. Herbert's "little bit of pro-priety," and so had missed hearing it.

"Nothing," answered Alfred. And the walk was finished in silence; but when the latter gentleman reached his comfortable dressing-room at the Old Ship, he lingered for a few moments by the fire, which blazed in the grate by Alfred's orders (he hated cold, and the nights were apt to be chilly in that fresh wind-blown town), and thought of the woman he had just left. "She shall be mine," he said; and then he continued his toilette, and parted his dark crisp hair in a rippled line down the middle of his head. "Am I handsome?" he asked himself, as he saw the reflection of that pale, dark-looking face in the mirror. Already Sophy's influence was sufficient to make him feel a doubt where his vanity had never before admitted of one. He could not answer that question quite satisfactorily, but he did not doubt his ultimate success with this beautiful woman.

The wealthy Mr. Cadogan had had occasion once or twice to recall his father's cynical axiom, "that every woman was to be won;" and he was fully imbued with the truth of the doctrine. Whether he would succeed on an occasion like this, where money could hardly be offered or accepted as an inducement to temptation, remained to be seen.

They passed a pleasant evening, Mr. Herbert and his guests. Mrs. Herbert sat at the head of her table, looking even handsomer, Mr. Cadogan thought, than when he first saw her. Every glance from her velvety eyes, every rise and fall of the black lace that was flung over the creamy whiteness of her bust and shoulders added to his infatuation.

"Oh !" he said to himself, with a sort of groan, "how I could love that woman !" Then he exerted himself to talk, fearing that his admiration for his hostess was becoming too evident ; and in that effort he quite won the heart of his host, who was delighted with the great amount of information his guest displayed on almost every subject of interest. It was impossible that a man who had travelled and seen so much of the world as had Alfred Cadogan should fail to be very entertaining when he chose so to be. He could tell of bargains made with the wary Tartar tribes that take six days to complete, so cautious and slow of dealing are the northern savages ; of sharp transactions done on the French Bourse in times of war. Bearded Turks and sharp-faced Greeks, plausible Italians, and shrewd Frenchmen—he had anecdotes to give of all, and of the countries of each. In a few well-chosen sentences he could convey the scenes of his stories so completely to the eyes of his listeners that, as Mrs. Herbert said, she could see the long, low tracts of Eastern sand, and the hot film through which the camels moved dark against the blue sky, as clearly as she could imagine the vineyards that rippled along the sides of the Tuscan hills that figured in his narratives.

Mrs. Herbert, woman-like, only thought of the scenery and the quaint costumes Cadogan's vivid word-painting brought before her, but Gerald Lisle and Mr. Herbert were more struck by the practical portion of some of Alfred's narrations.

"A sharp customer he must be," thought Gerald, looking a little askance at his new friend; "I wonder *why* he backed my bill?"

Mr. Herbert, delighted as he was by his guest's brilliant flow of conversation, was left with a little perplexed feeling in his mind, that somehow (he did not know how) it seemed as though some of Mr. Cadogan's clever transactions were a little on the "off-side" of honesty.

Still the evening, as I have said, was a remarkably pleasant one, and when dinner was over it happened somehow, through the agency of Mrs. Herbert, that Gerald Lisle and her husband became entangled in conversation in the front drawing-room, then the hostess sank into an easy chair by the fire in the inner room, and while the flame flared up on her glowing face and snowy throat, she was receiving from Alfred Cadogan looks which Mr. Herbert would hardly have approved of had his eyes been able to penetrate through the red folds of the damask curtain that was wholly concealing Mrs. Herbert and partly Mr. Cadogan from view.

Mrs. Herbert sat and listened to the sighs breathed on her shoulder in a more softened mood than usual; she was thinking very much of Geoffry this evening; and there was something of sweetness in the fact that Geoffry's brother was so quickly feeling the thraldom which Geoffry himself never even seemed to understand the existence of. So she gave glances back to those fiery ones of Alfred which nearly maddened him. She allowed him to babble broken words into her ear, conventional words, it is true; but words agitated by a ring of passion in them. And when the clatter of cups in the next room warned her that their *tête-à-tête* would soon terminate, she made no sign of displeasure at the soft touch of a pair of lips which she suddenly felt descend on her shoulder. Perhaps she thought it best not to notice the insolence. At all events, she merely moved gently in her seat, and rose to go; but when she caught sight of the trembling line that hovered round Alfred's mouth, the almost convulsive look of passion that swept over his face—his face which seemed to have turned blue in that moment—she felt a little alarmed at the storm she had evoked, and began to doubt the wisdom of the resolution she had formed to play with this man until she had made him a malleable tool in her soft fingers.

"When he may be useful to me," she had murmured; but after catching sight of all the devilry she had roused in his face, she was a little scared.

"What if he masters me!" she thought; but she laughed off the feeling of weakness ere Mr. Cadogan left the house.

"What man ever could cope with me?" she reasoned proudly. Clever as Mrs. Herbert was, she little knew what would be the strength of the Frankenstein she was about to create, nor had she ever yet met a man so fit to overmaster her by passion, determination, and deceit, as was her new acquaintance.

CHAPTER XVI.

TEMPUS FUGIT.

"And one, an English home, grey twilight pour'd
On dewy pastures, dewy trees,
Softer than sleep, all things in order stored,
A haunt of ancient peace."

TENNYSON.

THE summer days at Lynncourt always seemed to be of quite a different order from those passed elsewhere. There appeared to be a species of glamour over the place, partly engendered by the rich, moist air that steamed up from the marshes, and held and condensed in its weight all the luscious scents that exhaled from fruit and flower.

The wind rarely seemed to have any freshness in it. Even when it blew up from the river it was seldom strong enough to do more than just stir the creamy blossoms on the lime-boughs. To those who understood the laws and proportions of architecture, the house itself was rather a rambling, irrational sort of building. The manor of Lynncourt had existed since the days when Thomas de Lynncourt had gone to fight by Richard Cœur de Lion's side in the Holy Land. He was away ten years, and perhaps it was more a circumstance to be deplored than wondered at, that he found on his return that his Lady de Lynncourt had grown tired of waiting for him, and had married again —a neighbouring baron. Thomas de Lynncourt took that course which, if adopted by modern husbands, would save the divorce court a world of trouble—he cut off the heads of both wife and lover, married again, and (untaught by experience) joined the next Crusade.

The only relic that survived at Lynncourt of this grim warrior's presence, was an old, lightning-blasted oak, to this day called "Lord Lynncourt's Oak," which he was said to have planted.

Peace be to him! His dust has, hundreds of years since, been incorporated with the sands of Palestine ; but his monument exists in the Lynncourt Chapel, and he lies there in a perpetual state of prayer, his hands clasped, and the tip of his marble nose turned upward in supplication. If all that is reported of his wild life be true, he cannot pray too long or too fervently.

The manor of Lynncourt passed through strange changes in the years that followed its founder's death. One successor would be a wasteful reprobate, and let the whole place tumble down into ruinous disorder; another would rebuild, and improve, and spend his fortune in repairing the evil work of his forefather. It was like the German story of the nose which lengthened or contracted, according to the different bites its owner took of apple or pear. Between friend and foe, poor old Lynncourt came down to the present generation in rather a patched, and, as I have said, a rambling condition. One side of it (the oldest surviving portion of the house) had been built in the Tudor style by an unfortunate young lord of the manor, who had been mixed up in an affray with the keepers of one of the royal parks, and was accordingly hanged by his Majesty King Henry the Eighth, who had cast a covetous eye on the fair lands of Lynncourt, and who accordingly appropriated them on the owner's death.* The portrait of this ill-starred nobleman, painted by Holbein, hangs in one of the oak panels of the Lynncourt dining-room. He wears a melancholy expression of countenance, as though anticipating his fate,

---

* Thomas Ffynes, Lord Dacre, a lineal ancestor of the present Sir Thomas Barrett Lennard, Bart., suffered in the manner and for the cause above described.

and his rather weak-looking blue eyes have a wistful gaze in them, as though to invite compassion from the future generations that might stare at him long after his poor neck was wrung, and his fate forgotten.

His widow recovered the estates and title for her son by a well-timed petition to the Queen (Elizabeth).

She is depicted in a very carefully painted portrait by Lucas de Heere. Her black satin sleeves, the lace on her stiff collar, her fingers, her ring, all the adjuncts around her, are depicted with extraordinary skill and minuteness. This lady's son's son held the estate with credit and profit to himself, and neither was the building suffered to decay, nor did the blue blood of the Lynncourts become tainted by *mésalliance,* until the corruption of Charles the Second's court spread through the land, and the then Lord Renshawe (he had tacked that name on to the noble one of Lynncourt in consideration of some property that had been left with it), not only ruined himself at faro, but espoused a natural daughter of the king, born to the monarch by that splendid beauty and abandoned courtesan, Barbara Villiers, Duchess of Cleveland.

If her immoral Grace did nothing else for the family of Renshawe, she imparted some of her beauty to it. Her heavy-lidded, lovely grey eyes came out afterwards in many of her descendants, though, if truth be told, the long upper lip of Charles Stuart generally appeared to neutralise the effect. By her father's death the little grand-daughter of the duchess became sole heiress of these great estates, now somewhat damaged by Lord Renshawe's gaming propensities. This lady inherited a good deal of her grandmother's beauty, only it was of a less imperious description than is generally ascribed to King Charles's lovely mistress. She married and died young, and it was her only son who was Lord Renshawe, the father of the old countess.

The present Lady Renshawe was apt to speak somewhat scornfully of her ancestral honours. Her father, the late earl, had been rather proud of his left-handed connection with royalty. King Charles's little daughter had brought with her a patent entitling her to quarter royal arms with those of Renshawe. She had also imported to Lynncourt two very lovely portraits, by Lely, of her mother, some equally good ones of her royal father, and a soft, brown curl of King Charles the First's hair, clasped by a little gold crown, and resting in a red velvet case.

Little Esty Lisle, when a child, used to regard it as a great privilege when she was allowed to unlock the glass case where the curl was preserved, and to pass her tiny fingers over its silky threads.

"It is like a woman's hair, so soft! Oh, aunt, are you not proud of possessing such a relic of the royal martyr!"

"Royal fiddlestick!" her aunt would say, prosaically. "He wasn't half such a martyr, child, as that other poor ancestor of mine who was hanged because a king wanted his lands. I suppose Charles the Second thought that as an ancestor of his had taken a life from our family he was bound to pay us back our pound of flesh by giving us his daughter. A nice lot those women were!" added the countess, looking up grimly at the portraits of her fair but frail ancestresses, for scandal had ascribed to Barbara Villiers's daughter some of the vices that disgraced Barbara Villiers herself.

"Why, aunt," said Esty, looking lovingly at the beautiful grey eyes and heavy down-cast lids of the duchess, "I'm sure that lady looks as if ——"

"As if butter wouldn't melt in her mouth," interrupted her aunt, sharply; "but it would, though; and don't let us talk about her any more, my dear. I'll tell you about the good Dorcas, if you like."

But the history of the "good Dorcas," who was a virtuous lady of the House of Lynncourt, and who, indeed, could have had little time for dissipation of any kind, judging by the immense quantity of tapestry which covered the walls, all said to be the work of her diligent hands, did not interest Esty nearly so much as this dark-eyed, dreamy-faced beauty, with dishevelled hair falling round her oval face, and a necklace of pearls clasping her round throat.

Her Grace of Cleveland seemed to have been attached to this string of pearls. They adorned her fair neck in no less than three different portraits that hung on the Lynncourt walls. Esty often wondered what had become of those pearls. Who knows?—even now they might be lying in some faint-scented drawer secreted in some lurking place in one of those old oak cabinets.

It was autumn at Lynncourt. Faint perfumes came from sandal-wood cabinets, and the pot-pourri vases full of dead rose-leaves that stood by the open doors. Old-fashioned scents they were, breathing of decay; and it was quite a relief to Esty to be greeted by the fresher odour of the flowers she had placed in the china jars, as she passed from room to room.

These untenanted rooms, with their polished oak floors, and their deep window-recesses, had great charms for Esty. She liked to see the sunbeams striking through the coloured panes and throwing quaint hues of red, blue, and yellow, on the gleaming edges of the picture-frames, on the carved backs of the oak chairs, and on the curious flowers traced in faded patterns on the tapestry cushions: the delicate rims of the little china cups caught strange radiance from these variegated hues, and even the damask roses in them became tinted with a misty glory of blue and purple. Outside all looked equally old-fashioned and peaceful: the once deep red of the walls had been toned down by the grey hues of age, and softened by the blurred edges of lichen; there was no footstep to sound on the broad gravel walks, the Lynncourt gardeners had always done the greater part of their work by eight in the morning; and when Lady Renshawe and Esty took their evening walk, they seldom heard anything but the tinkling of the sheep bells as the flocks strayed over the broad pastures, or the tapping of the deers' feet as they trotted now in slow lines, now with a rush and a gallop across the paths that intersected the grass.

It was evening, and Lady Renshawe had drawn her morocco chair to the window, that she might more easily see whereabouts to draw up the loops of red wool she held on her knitting pins. A bird was trilling outside, and pleasant scents from the heliotrope and mignonette beds came through the open windows, but the old countess's senses were becoming rather dulled; she could not hear the bird, and she drew her woollen shawl over her shoulders at every faint gust of the flower scented air.

She worked quickly for some time, and then when a

darker shade came over the landscape, she missed a stitch, the work got entangled, other stitches became complicated, and with an impatient jerk her fingers unravelled the whole of her previous labour. The countess laid down her knitting pins with a tear of helpless irritation in her eye.

"Is it come to this?" she thought, sadly. "Has proud, self-contained Annabella Renshawe lived to see her fine intellect and masculine powers dwindle down into second childhood?"

She looked out on her broad territories, the meadows over which the dying rays of the sun were streaming, the flocks of sheep that bleated to each other under the golden chestnuts, the deer that had stolen up to the house, and were gazing at her with alert ears and startled eyes.

"I cannot take these with me," she thought, discontentedly. "And yet I don't like leaving them behind. Helpless and old," she continued, looking sadly at her wrinkled hands. "Grey hairs and feeble fingers, and the hours roll on as blithely as when I used to watch them with bright eyes and a joyful heart; even my legs refuse to do their office without the assistance of this wooden prop," touching her gold-headed cane. "This stick will outlast Annabella Renshawe—this piece of oak which can neither reason, think, nor feel, is so far superor to my sentient self that it will endure when I am a handful of white dust! They'll put you away in an attic, and you'll live a dull life among spiders and cobwebs after stumping about with me so long, poor old thing!" she said, apostrophising her stick, and then her meditations were broken in upon; for a bright face peeped in at the window, and Esty's fresh, sweet-toned voice asked—

"Aunt, are you coming to walk to-night?"

The countess, glad of the diversion to her thoughts, said, "Yes, she thought she would;" and she put on her walking things and stumped down the marble steps with an activity which proved that she had somewhat over-estimated her infirmities.

"Esty," she said, passing her shoe over the edge of the velvety lawn. "This has not been properly mown this morning! remind me to speak about it to-morrow."

The countess had recovered her spirits with the exertion

of exercise, and she needed the assistance of her walking-stick less than usual to-night, as she passed from her flower-beds to the conservatory, from conservatory to orchard, finding fault with various arrangements with as much liveliness and asperity as if she numbered only forty instead of seventy summers.

"Lord bless her!" said her old coachman, admiringly, as he watched her quick movements, and listened to the vehemence of her reproof to some hapless fellow-servant. "What a spirity old 'oss it is! She'll die in harness, she will; when she do drop down, 'twill be on the road."

When the countess had finished her tour of inspection, she settled herself at one of her favourite rose-beds, where her black satin bonnet, rounded in shape, and shiny in texture, looked somewhat like a huge blackbeetle hovering above the damask beauties. Esty was commissioned to pluck off the dead blossoms of the scarlet geraniums that were planted in the vases on the terrace, and armed with a pair of garden scissors and a wicker basket, that young lady betook herself to the task.

CHAPTER XVII.

"O'ER AGAIN."

"She had a nosegay in her bosom, but a look so pure and fresh-coloured you'd have taken her for one of the seasons."—*The Accomplish'd Fools.*

"Ipse Amor, puer Dionæ, rure natus dicitur."

HE dying sunbeams that slanted across the grey stonework of the balustrade cast pleasant golden glimmers on Esty's brown hair, as she stood, with uncovered head, near the geraniums, her little hands moving busily among the scarlet blossoms, the petals of which fell in profusion over the light folds of her blue muslin dress. When she had snipped off the last withered stalk she looked round to see what had become of her aunt, but the countess was out of sight, so the girl, dropping her scissors idly into the basket, rested her arms on the balustrade and looked out into as much of the future as that boundary of distant blue hills would permit to her imagination.

"She would like to have wings," she thought, "and fly away over those hills."

Then she wondered what kind of a place the swallows found the world beyond those hills to be, whether they ever got chilled and wearied in their flight over the seas, and wished themselves back in the withered nests that hung under the eaves.

"I wish something would happen!" she murmured. "Nothing ever *does* happen here: always the same routine,

the same stillness ! It would be something it one lived in a
farm-house, and could hear dogs bark and hens cluck. That
would be life—life that gives and receives interest; but here
all is as dead, silent, beautiful, and indifferent as death;"
and she looked a little weariedly at the blue hills, the
indistinct ridges of which were becoming irksome to her.
She looked and dreamed until the dying sun, the shadows
that lay on the paths, the cawing of the distant rooks,
became mixed up in a host of fancies, which at last resolved
themselves in a sort of vague romance of which she was
the heroine, associated with some indefinite hero—a hero who
was as yet scarcely more than an idea. She had not even
imagined the colour of his eyes; he was as shadowy as the
scenes she pictured of those foreign lands where she was to
meet him.

Visions of orange groves, rich-scented flowers, hot suns,
blue seas, and shadowed coves passed before her thought-
enrapt eyes, and in one of these bays her boat should be
moored, while she sat by *his* side, listening first to the soft
drip of the water as it ran down the rugged channels of the
sea-washed rock, and then to the deep, low tones of his
voice as he read aloud to her.

"What should he read to her?" The visioned picture
became broken up by the disturbance this query raised in
her mind.

She thought of "O'Connor's Child," but that was not
appropriate; "Gertrude of Wyoming," "Parisina," "The
Corsair." She declined them all, and at last decided
on—

> " We two will rise, and sit, and walk together,
> Under the roof of blue Ionian weather,
> And wander in the meadows, or ascend
> The mossy mountains, where the blue heavens bend
> With lightest winds to touch their paramour;
> Or linger where the pebble-paven shore,
> Under the faint quick kisses of the sea,
> Trembles and sparkles as with ecstacy ;—
> Possessing and possest by all that is
> Within that calm circumference of bliss,
> And by each other, till to love and live
> Be one."

"Till to love and live be one," repeated Esty, softly, her

voice taking the intonation of tenderness suitable to the imagined occasion.

While the unconscious Esty was enacting her little drama —scenery, words, and characters all supplied by her own vivid imagination—while she sought to evoke from the dreams of the future the image of her "fate," Fate stood nearer to her than she had any conception of, and Fate, in the shape of a handsome young man, who carried a carpet-bag in one hand and a great-coat over his arm, said, half audibly:

"By Jove! what a pretty girl!"

> "We two will rise, and sit, and walk together
> Under the roof of blue Ionian weather,"

reiterated Esty, softly.

"Ahem! I have the honour of speaking to ——" Captain Adair began in a low voice, but if he had fired a cannon off in Miss Lisle's ears he could hardly have startled her more. She turned round abruptly at the sound that had broken in upon her reverie, and the reality before her completely scattered away the whole "baseless fabric of her visions." She blushed vividly a quick, hot blush, that flew from forehead to throat, and then faded, leaving her as pale as the urn against which she leaned.

"How very genuine she is!" thought Geoffry, and then, taking off his hat, he apologised for his abrupt arrival.

"I fear I startled you," he said. "I suppose you could not hear me come across the grass?"

"N—no," stammered Esty. Then, recovering her composure a little, she said, "But what—but who ——?"

"My name is Adair," he said, anticipating her question. "I am the son of an old friend of Lady Renshawe, and I was taught at a very early age to believe that I should not be otherwise than a welcome guest here; but the difficulty is, you see, that I should not know Lady Renshawe if I saw her. I might make some dreadful mistake. You are not the countess, are you?" he said, with a smile, which put Esty more at her ease than the whole of his explanation.

"No," said Esty, answering his smile. "I am Miss Lisle. There is my aunt, coming there."

She indicated with her hand a vista of the shrubbery, through which a glimpse could be obtained of Lady Renshawe's bonnet.

Captain Adair lingered a moment, as if he expected the young lady would accompany him up to her aunt, but, finding that she had returned to her occupation of cutting off stalks (or, rather, was pretending to do so, for in her confusion she decapitated blooming and withered blossoms indiscriminately), he bowed, and stepped quickly across the grass to meet the countess.

There was still sun enough to throw bright lights on his fair, close-cropped curls and gold-hued mustache, and, with his small head, broad chest, and lithe, easy gait, he looked a perfect embodiment of Saxon beauty. Lady Renshawe's wonder was not unmixed with admiration as she fixed her spectacles on her nose, and stared hard at her unexpected visitor.

Meanwhile, Esty had caught up her basket, and, without venturing to look round at the meeting of her aunt and the stranger, sped away with the swiftness of a lapwing to the house. She retreated to her little room, and sat down on the window-seat, her face crimsoning when she thought how childish and how *gauche* she must have appeared to Captain Adair. So this was Captain Adair, was it?—the grown-up original of the little miniature that hung in the breakfast-room. On the whole, Esty thought she was disappointed. He was not at all what she had expected he would be. She had fashioned a bright-eyed, hectic-looking youth out of that delicate baby-face of the portrait, and lo! here was a young Hercules, whose broad chest left no possible opening for consumption.

"I suppose he will stay here to-night. I wonder if aunt will ask him. Of course she will, though. I wonder what Christine will say!" and then Esty went to the glass and looked at herself. "Oh, dear! how ugly I'm looking!" she said, discontentedly, and she seized a brush and swept the long floats of her hair, until it shone in its waves like brown silk. · Then she twisted it up in a glossy coil at the back of her head, and began to seek for some further adornment to her person. To her dress she could do nothing; it was a plain blue muslin, and nothing could have been more suitable to wear on that sultry autumn evening, to say nothing of its being eminently becoming to her graceful, pliant figure; but, in its simplicity and plainness, poor Esty felt it to be quite unworthy of the gorgeous apparition she had encountered on the lawn. However, she stuck a red rose in the waistband of her little black silk apron, and thought after all, "she didn't look so bad." Perhaps "he would not notice either her or her dress." Then she walked slowly down the great stairs. She paused on the way longer than usual, feeling, for the first time, that the oak-griffins that flung such long shadows down the corner steps were protections not to be wantonly deserted. She was shy and nervous, and it was a relief to meet Lady Renshawe suddenly face to face.

The old countess's face wore a softened expression; a smile agitated the wrinkles round her mouth, and her eyes had a light in them which made Esty look at them with wonder.

"I have been much pleased, my dear!" the elder lady said. "The son of a very dear old friend has come to see me, and in his kind eyes and cordial voice I seem to have called back a taste of youth to my dried-up old heart. I seem to have reached out my hand to that of Geoffry Adair's dear dead mother once again. I have seen her glance in his—heard her voice, with the same inflexions that graced it when she and I were young, my dear—young, aye, and beautiful too, though 'Wha would think it to see me now?' as the 'Auld Wife' sang!" Even as Lady Renshawe spoke, the light of animation faded from her withered face, and a look of fatigue usurped its place. "I'm tired," she said, wearily, "I think I'll go and lie down for a while. Go and make yourself agreeable to my friend, Esty. But, my dear," she added, with a spice of her old malice, "if you keep your head stuck on one side in that fashion, you'll look like one of those wooden dolls that has a string running up from its heels to its head, and whose head hangs over when the string isn't pulled;" with this Parthian shaft the old lady hobbled up-stairs, while her grand-niece descended to the breakfast-room, where she found Captain Adair swinging a flower in his hand, and looking out rather wistfully at the blue mists that were beginning to rise from the valley.

Lady Renshawe not only gave her guest a cordial invitation to stay that night at Lynncourt, but she begged him to extend his visit over as many days and nights as possible.

"The only quarrel I have with you," she said, "is, that you should have been in England so long without coming to see me before."

Geoffry explained how near he had been to coming to X——shire, on Gerald's invitation.

"'Near' isn't 'quite,'" the old lady said, snappishly; "besides, your mother's son need scarcely have waited for an invitation to my house. However," she continued, graciously, "now you are here, it must be my business to prove to you how welcome your presence is; and the first thing I beg of you is, that you will not withdraw it sooner than you can help. I am such an old woman, and Esty is such a chit," she continued, "that I fear you will be very dull here; but you must make yourself quite at home, and that will compensate for many deficiencies."

Geoffry smiled, as his eyes met those of the niece, and he assured the aunt that he should not be in the least dull: he was certain of that. He walked over with Esty to make the acquaintance of her family, and he was introduced to Colonel and Mrs. Lisle, Christine, and Toby. The colonel put on his grandest company air to receive the young man.

"I knew your father, Sir," he said, "a most gallant and distinguished officer. What is your regiment? The —— Guards, you say! That is not the kind of regiment in which I should have expected to find your father's son."

This was rather spiteful of the colonel, but then he was feeling spiteful on this particular day, for he had found a button off his shirt that morning, and had been compelled to fasten his collar with a pin, and every man knows what an irritating, scratchy sensation at one's throat such a proceeding entails.

"You are quite right, Colonel Lisle," the young man answered good-humouredly. "It is not the regiment for a man desirous of being something better than a carpet knight, and I've got so sick of it that I have during this last month arranged an exchange to the —— Lancers. They are likely to be under orders for India or China at any moment, and although I don't imagine the barbarians will give us any brilliant opportunity of distinguishing ourselves, yet it will be something to have a chance."

"Young men's chances of that sort are not what they were in my day," said the colonel; "any profession now brings more honour than a soldier's."

"Do not say that," Captain Adair answered, his blue eyes flashing. "I would not change my profession for any in the world; it is true that war rarely blows its hot breath our way, now-a-days, but whenever it does so, think what a privilege it is to be among those who have to face it! Supposing that a European war broke out now, who would change places with a lawyer, poring over dusty books in city chambers, or the clergyman, treading down daisies in country lanes, when there's telegram after telegram pouring in news of hard-fought battles, or dearly-won victories? Fancy being contented to read in men's faces, to hear from men's mouths, rumour of cannons roaring and comrades dying, when one could be in the thick of the smoke oneself! You, Sir, I am sure, could never sleep at home in peace under such circumstances; you'd fancy you heard the word of command in every branch that beat against your window-pane; you'd be startled by sounds of artillery in every gust of wind that woke you from your slumbers; at last, able to bear it no longer, you would hasten to London and beg the commander-in-chief to let you air your old uniform in an element congenial to a garment that became blood-spotted, torn, and dun-coloured in the dust our men made in that desperate defence of the Chateau of Hougomont, on the 18th of June, 1815;" and the young man raised his hat to the veteran whose gallantry had been conspicuous on that memorable occasion.

"By God, I would, Sir!" replied Colonel Lisle, his eyes glistening with excitement; "and you talk like a gentleman and a soldier, Captain Adair, and, by Jove! you're very different from that puppy of mine, Gerald, not but what his heart's in the right place, and if he were placed in the front of the enemy I feel sure he would walk up to them as coolly as if they were a room full of pretty women; but he 'haw-haws' and 'yaw-yaws' as if it were a duty he owes his caste to repress all natural and manly emotion; as if a pretty woman or a gallant enemy weren't objects to make any gentleman's eye grow bright and heart beat high. I wouldn't give *that*," continued Colonel Lisle, with an energetic snap of his fingers, "for such cold-blooded affectation !"

" I believe that I am rather too voluble," Geoffry said, smiling ; "but I must claim my excuse in the fact that my father taught me when I was a boy to feel very enthusiastic about his profession : I think, too, he allowed me to talk too much, and there's no language like the Italian for running one's tongue into unreasonable fluency."

"Don't be ashamed of your enthusiasm, it's uncommonly refreshing," Colonel Lisle said, kindly, and then, encouraged by the interest his visitor took in that (which, it was the old man's opinion, the world had too easily forgotten), namely, the glory which attended the Iron Duke's last and greatest battle, he entered into many details which, though familiar to his family, were new and interesting to Captain Adair. He told him how he and General Adair were side by side when the English line was ordered to advance and attack the reserve battalions of the Imperial Guard.

" I shall never forget that moment," Colonel Lisle said ; "never forget the grim desperate faces of those grand old savages who met us. They had been ordered there to die. They knew that. It was their business to stand and be cut down to favour the retreat of those shattered remnants that fled behind them. Their foreheads were scarred and wrinkled as withered leaves, and many of them had hair as white as mine is now. They fought hard for the eagles, which in twenty years' warfare had never been wrenched from their hands. They fought like rats at bay, Sir, and as the ground got heaped with their bodies, the rest formed closer, and fought harder, but our superior numbers soaked them down, and mixed with the death-sobs that came from under our feet, came also, in disjointed phrases, the motto of their regiment, 'We die, but we surrender not,' as fine an amen as a soldier could breathe his way out of this world with, I call it !" And the old man took snuff hastily.

"I remember," he added, "there were some rather good lines written by Danson of ours, about the charge of the French cuirassiers—poor fellow, he died young !" and the colonel looked sentimental.

"From the effect of his wounds, papa?" asked Christine. "No, my dear, from delirium tremens; but the lines are good ones for all that;" and going to an escritoire on which stood his battered despatch-box, Colonel Lisle extracted from its interior some faded yellow scraps of paper, and in a voice, now sonorous, now quavering (for the voice of age, like that of youth, is uncertain and wayward in its modulation), he read as follows :—

"'CHARGE OF THE FRENCH CUIRASSIERS:

"'JUNE 18, 1815.

"'When we trampled the vineyards round Hougomont's walls,
  Through the smoke and the blaze of that turbulent hour,
Our heads held erect midst the whirr of their balls,
  Till we fell like ripe fruit that is swept by a shower.

"'When their cuirassiers charged us, twelve thousand in mass,
  With the furious speed of a cataract's flow,
We met them in square, not a horseman could pass
  The bright line that bristled to welcome the foe.

"'They had scattered our cavalry, swept through the play
  Of the cannon that roared its full charge at their breast;
With haughty defiance they kept on their way
  Till the points of our bayonets held them in rest.

"'Then they wheeled and re-formed, and they galloped again
  On the spear-points that never had faltered a jot,
Till riderless horses rushed back through the slain,
  And many bold spirits that had been, were not!

"'With their line rent and torn, yet once more they re-formed,
  With their forces condensed to give weight to the shock,
Swept by our first line through the cross-fire that stormed,
  To the second, who met the wild charge like a rock.

"'One body of horsemen, in mocking despair,
  With a "Vive l'Empereur!" met the Englishmen's cheer!
Trotted up at a foot's pace—then cut in the air,
  And slowly returned through hot fire to the rear.

"'We were worthy their swords—they as worthy did prove :
  Peace be to the fallen! whether foeman or friend,
For next to the grasp of a friend, what I love
  Is the grasp of a foe who is staunch to the end.'"

There was a pause for some moments after the colonel
had rolled out the last line in a voice that would have been
solemn had it not also been rather choked. Christine's eyes
glistened; while Esty, glancing askance at Captain Adair,
pictured to herself how grand *he* would look charging
with his troop; then she thought of the fair head bowed
by some deadly stroke from its place in the line, and
shuddered.

Colonel Lisle walked up to the window, and looked out
without seeing the roses that grew against the pane, or the
clematis that overshadowed it; the old-fashioned room filled
with the quiet atmosphere of home—the sunshine, his
daughters' faces, all had faded before the stirring images the
conversation had evoked: his eyes were blinded with
smoke, his ears filled with the din of battle—he felt himself
once more carried onwards in a line, where friends dropped
away and were succeeded by others with startling rapidity—
he remembered the thrill that went through him as he
waited for the shock of those thundering hoof-treads; the
flash of a Frenchman's sabre, who nearly swept over his
bayonet's-point; the crash and the thud as a man and horse
fell, doubled up in mortal agony before him—the wild
struggles of the charger—the dull insensibility of the rider,
who lay there equally unconscious of the trampling feet and
the additional thrust given by the next bayonet, to "make
all sure." Colónel Lisle was a tender-hearted ensign then,
and he remembered that he could not help wishing, when
he saw the rest of the troop gallop back, that *his* man could
rise and go with the rest.

The old man was recalled from his meditations by
Captain Adair's walking up to him.

"Thank you, Colonel, for reading those lines," the latter
said. "I seemed to see the men that charged and the line
that received them 'like a rock,' as you say; that mighty
rush of cavalry had no more success in unsteadying our
squares than had the poor Mamelukes when they charged
the French line in Egypt."

Then the young soldier and the old one plunged into
an eager disquisition as to the comparative merits of
French and English cavalry; and Esty, pleased to see
her father so well disposed towards the new acquaintance,

11

for whom she felt in some degree responsible, retired with Christine.

"Don't you think he's very nice, Chrissy?" she asked, shyly, as she and her sister walked round the ragged flower-beds, and Christine answered "Yes, very!" adding emphatically :—

"He's not a bit like Gerald!"

CHAPTER XVIII.

"you look such ——"

> " Love's sooner felt than seen, his substance thin
>   Betwixt those snowy mounts in ambush lies;
> He therefore soonest wins that fastest flies:
> Fly thence, my dear, fly fast my Thomaline;
> Who him encounters once, for ever dies.
> But if he lurks between the ruddy lips,
> Unhappy soul that thence his nectar sips,
> While down into his heart the sugar'd poison slips.

> * * * * *

> Oft in a voice he creeps down through the ear,
> Oft from a blushing cheek he lights his fire,
> Oft shrouds his golden flame in likest hair,
> Oft in a soft, smooth skin doth close retire,
> Oft in a smile—oft in a silent tear."

P. FLETCHER.

T is extraordinary how different everything at Lynncourt looked in Esty's eyes after Captain Adair had prolonged his stay there a few weeks. The figures that waved on the tapestry, the Mandarins that nodded their heads in shadowy corners of the oak-chambers, the very books that stood in ponderous rows on the shelves, seemed to lose their sense of old acquaintanceship and to assume an air of novelty in the glamour his presence shed over them. She quite neglected all her old friends now; the ghost in the " Old English Baron " might clank his bones all night along the "windy corridors"

—his footstep had ceased to echo in Esty's ear as she lay awake listening to the snatch of a song or a careless whistle that was wont to attend Geoffry's progress when his light step passed along the passage that led to his room. Harriet Byron might have as many hair-breadth escapes of abduction, and glorify herself in tedious epistles to her friends, as much as she liked—Esty no longer felt any sympathy with her; nor did she give one thought to the distresses of that virtuous maiden, Pamela, who endured so much and who loved so little! Heroes and heroines, evil magicians and good fairies, kings, warriors, and poets —all the ideal shapes that had tenanted the unoccupied chambers of her mind for the last ten years, were ruthlessly swept away, to give place to the image of one pair of shining blue eyes and a head of crisp yellow curls.

It was as though all the beautiful shapes and glittering intricacies in an ice cavern were suddenly exposed to the rays of the sun, and real flowers had sprung up in the place of scentless phantasms of ice and snow.

True, Esty would voluntarily spend hours away from Geoffry's society. If she heard his step coming to the chamber where she sat, she would remove herself to a more distant one, and search with apparent interest for some book or paper, of which she tried to persuade herself she was in want; or she would sit down with her work in the recess of some old window and listen vaguely to the bubble of the fountain in the garden, or the soft wail of the Æolian harp, which was always placed in the corridor-window in fine weather; then she wondered whether Geoffry would be likely to pass by the window, and her heart beat high and her cheek flushed as she saw by the shadow thrown on the gravel path, that he *was* coming; and then she applied herself to her work with such reckless industry that she generally ended by snipping off the head of the silken flower she was embroidering for Lady Renshawe's sofa pillow.

It was a golden age for them both—both so young and so happy—both so inexperienced that their hearts did not even dream of foreshadowing evil or prophesying sorrow : their lips only breathed one thought—one doubt.

Hers was : " Does he care for me ? "

His : "Does she love me ? "

And if neither of them had hitherto put that thought into actual sound, it was more owing to the instinctive modesty that clings to a first true passion, than from any real doubt each felt of the other's answer.

" Do you ride, Miss Lisle ? " Geoffry asked, shortly after his arrival at Lynncourt. Esty's face lighted up as she remembered her youthful exploits on the Shetland pony, and she said " that she used to ride as a child, but she had now no opportunity of doing so."

"But should you like ·to ride ? " persisted Geoffry, and Miss Lisle's eyes sparkled as she admitted she should like it extremely : but "there are a good many things I should like," she added, philosophically, "which I shan't get."

"Such as what ? "

" Oh, I should like to have a great deal of money."

"And what would you do with it ? "

" I should go to W——" (the county town) "and buy mamma a fresh set of oil paints ; and Christine a beautiful work-box, fitted up with satin, you know, and everything ; and I'd buy papa a large case of the very best cigars ; and Dolly a cap ; and, oh ! don't let's talk about it any more ! " and Esty came to a sudden check, feeling rather ashamed of her enthusiasm.

"What would you get for yourself ? " asked Captain Adair, his blue eyes shining down ineffable love on the little face beside him.

"Oh ! I don't know," she said, indifferently ; " I don't think I want anything of that sort. I sometimes fancy that if it wasn't for leaving aunt, and mamma, and Chrissy, I should like to travel very much."

"And where would you go ? " said Geoffry, secretly determining that every wish she had hitherto expressed should be fulfilled, and, with a faint hope in his heart (a hope so sweet that for an instant it made his cheek flush and his voice tremble) that he might one day accomplish even this last-named aspiration.

" I am not quite sure where I should like to go first," she said, dreamily ; " I have sat on the big staircase, studying the map for hours, fancying myself wandering over different parts of the globe ; but I think I long most to see

Italy ;" then she plied Geoffry with question after question about the towns, cities, and scenery he had lately revisited. "Have you really seen Keats' grave?" she asked, solemnly. Captain Adair smiled at her eagerness, as he answered " Yes," he had stood by Keats' grave a month since; "it looked ragged and desolate compared to the cool, shadowed corner where Shelley's heart rested in a bed of violets in the inner cemetery. Keats' grave was in the outer cemetery, and it was overrun with wild weeds and grasses, there was not the same cool glooms from cypress trees, and fragrance from the roses, as there was on the other side of the grounds."

Then Geoffry produced his sketch-book, and Esty was charmed into expression of delight at the little vivid bits of colouring and the boldness of touch with which he had represented some of his favourite nooks and corners. Here was the green framework of a Venetian window,—a window ensconced in fretted marble-work, and overlooking dim waters; and out of the window leant a boy in his shirt-sleeves, with a laugh in his elfish-looking black eyes, and a red cap on his head. " 'A sketch in Venice,' " said Geoffry. But when Esty asked him to describe Venice he shook his head.

" I cannot," he answered, " it is indescribable. Charles Dickens gives you the best idea, when he speaks of it as 'a strange dream upon the water.' The city resembles a beautiful woman in death. It oppresses you alike with a sense of magnificence and decay. The marble palaces that stretch away in tender-hued masses down the waters, the crowds that glide through wave-enclosed streets, no clamour attending their floating progress—nothing, at least, but the dip of the oars and the ripple of the water; the bells that clang out from the churches when the rosy twilight has deepened into night; the lights of the city that then sparkle out in that dismal waste of skies and waters ; all is dream-like, airy, and strange : you can never realise it, Miss Lisle, until you see it and feel it for yourself."

He showed her sketches of Roman ruins, with their once noble length of column buried in long grasses, where the pink tints of the monthly roses that clustered over them made a pleasant contrast to the cold grey hue of the broken bits of marble. Of fountains in old Roman gardens, that gushed out volumes of spray over the tangled margin of flowers and weeds that had clambered over their scarred sides, and dropped their ripe petals into the green depths beneath.

Then there was a bay of sleepy-looking blue sea, with a bit of garden wall leaning over its narrow strip of beach, and the twisted branches of an olive tree, and the red edges of some carnations, in pots, peeped over the crumbled summit of the wall. " This was at St. Remo," Captain Adair said: he hoped that when Miss Lisle made that excursion into Italy she talked of, that she would travel on the Corniche road, and spend on that strip of beach, as he had done, some of the balmiest hours possible to imagine.

" Who is that ?" asked Esty, suddenly cutting short Captain Adair's reminiscences of blue seas and purple hills, as her quick eye detected the portrait of a woman in the recesses of the portfolio.

Geoffry drew it out, and disclosed the rich brown eyes, abundant hair, and thick throat of Mrs. Herbert.

" Oh, that's Sophy," he said, carelessly. And then he told Esty all about his friendship with the Herberts, how kind they had been to him, how he had known them since he was a boy; and, above all, how he hoped that Miss Lisle would make their acquaintance when they came to stay at Castle Herbert, as he hoped and trusted they would do ere long.

Miss Lisle looked long and earnestly at the face depicted upon the piece of paper before her, and then she replaced it in the portfolio.

" The forehead is too low," she observed, presently. Geoffry answered lightly, " Oh, was it? he daresay it was ; " but the fact was, he had know Sophy so long, he never thought of observing her looks at all.

" A friend like her is not the same as a woman one loves," he said, musingly. " Such a friend resembles the scenery of a beautiful familiar road. One passes it often, one is to a certain extent grateful for its sunshine and flowers ; above all, for the smoothness of its pathway, but it does not strike the imagination with the freshness of novelty, and so, at last, one forgets to notice whether it be lovely or not,"

Esty made no further allusion to Mrs. Herbert at the time; probably she was re-assured by the utter indifference of Captain Adair's voice when speaking of the possessor of those big brown eyes, but they came before her sometimes, in the grey hours, between night and dawn, ere her thoughts had settled into any definite channel, and filled her with a vague sense of uneasiness. Inexperienced as she was, instinct supplied her imagination with doubts as to what kind of attachment a woman so young and lovely as Mrs. Herbert was likely to feel for a man of Captain Adair's age and appearance.

Meanwhile the latter had been taking means to provide Esty with some of the treasures she had said .she coveted. He ordered down a paint-box from London, a work-box lined with red satin, and some of the best cigars Bond Street could produce; then came the consideration of the cap for Dolly — this rather puzzled the young man. After much deliberation he decided on sending for ten yards of the broadest and best ribbon that could be purchased.

"It must be dark-coloured," he said; "it was to be made up into a lady's cap."

And the shopman at Swan and Edgar's (not the handsome, amiable young creature who bows at the doors of that establishment, acting as a kind of decoy to persuade weak-minded ducks to enter those portals where "all hope is abandoned" by their pocket-suffering drakes, but another youth who serves behind the counter, and who received Captain Adair's orders) wondered exceedingly as to what kind of a cap and what kind of a woman those ten yards of ribbon were going to adorn.

There was something else which Esty had not mentioned in her list of unattainable wishes which Geoffry ordered from London; but about this he resolved to say nothing until circumstances should determine whether or not the gift would be welcome to the person for whom it was designed —namely, Esty herself.

He had also sent for his horses, and he established these in the village inn stables, preferring to run the chance of exposing valuable animals to the risk of strange company to trespassing further on Lady Renshawe's hospitality. But that venerable lady became most indignant when she heard of this arrangement.

"A pack of stuff and nonsense !" she said, energetically ; "send for them directly, Geoffry" (she always called her guest by his Christian name now, and seemed to take pleasure in doing so) ; "my horses only occupy two stalls, and there are at least eight in my stables."

The young man accepted her hospitality gratefully ; he much preferred having his horses within such distance that he could stroll in the first thing before breakfast and the last thing before dinner, to pass his hand over their legs, and judge how much or how little additional exercise the owners of them required.

Like all men much accustomed to horses, Geoffry was very careful over them, and he had frequently irritated Mrs. Herbert by the strenuous objections he raised against cantering on any road that had not a "bit of soft" by its side. During some riding party in which she would attempt by out-riding the rest of her friends to secure him in a *tête-à-tête*, frequently Mrs. Herbert had feigned inability to hold in her horse, and, after galloping forward some yards, had looked back intensely disgusted at seeing Captain Adair a long way behind her, leisurely picking his way among the stones, and only lifting up his voice to remonstrate with her on her inhumanity.

"You're going as hard as if you were on the Downs, Sophy ; do remember that your horse's legs are not made of cast-iron."

And Sophy would turn with a vicious twitch of her bridle, and ride back sullenly, thinking that all the inhumanity was not on her side.

Captain Adair had no such rebellion to encounter from Esty ; her delight was unbounded when she found what was the purpose of his bringing his horses to Lynncourt, and she expressed so much pleasure to her aunt on the subject that the countess could not find it in her heart to object to what she secretly stigmatised as "dangerous tomfoolery." She was further mollified by the anxious inquiries her niece made as to *her* mode of riding in the days of her youth.

"I feel so stupid about it, aunt ; it is so long since I was on horseback," Esty said.

Lady Renshawe gave her so many intricate directions, to
keep her eyes always looking out between her horse's ears,
to sit upright—yet by no means to sit stiffly—to hold her horse
well in hand, but on no account to give him his head, that her
niece felt more bewildered than ever, and was quite relieved
when her aunt finished the lecture and went to her clothes-
press, in the drawers of which reposed the petticoat Esty
was to assume for her ride.

The countess looked tenderly at the green faded skirt,
which, guarded by camphor bags from moths, had lain
undisturbed for the last eight and forty years.

" I shouldn't wonder if it wanted a little airing," she said,
musingly, as she unfolded it ; and then her thoughts strayed
back to a certain ride she had taken with that child's grand-
father on the afternoon of the very day his attachment to
Lady Clara had been discovered, not as yet by herself, but
by her father.

Frederic Lisle's manner had been unusually tender that
day, either because he felt remorse towards, or covetous of,
the prize he had *not* chosen ; and so the elder sister breathed
in a fool's paradise until the evening came, bringing with it
news that turned her bright, imperious youth into hard-
minded, cold, middle age.

" Habit-skirts were worn shorter in my day, my dear,"
the countess said, startled from her meditations by feeling
Esty's fingers touch her shoulder, " and I don't think you
can wear the top at all anywhere out of the park ; but, I
daresay, you won't wish to extend your rides farther than
Lynncourt for a day or two. And, my dear, old John must
go with you, you know ; he can follow you on one of my
horses ; it wouldn't look well for you only to have that boy
Geoffry with you ! "

" The top " the countess had referred to was a jacket,
such as might have been worn by Die Vernon, or any other
amazon of her period ; it was a green jacket, laid back over
the breast in flappets, like a man's coat, and it was heavily
trimmed with what was now tarnished silver lace.

When Esty entered the room habited in this quaint, old-
fashioned costume, her aunt started to see how much of
grace and freshness still seemed to belong to the faded
green-cloth and its tawdry splendour ; she pulled the comb

from Esty's head, and let the long coils of hair unravel and tumble down in soft profusion over the girl's shoulder.

"Now, if you only had a hat and feather you would look just as I did eight and forty years ago," the countess said. Captain Adair, who entered the room during this observation, thought in his heart that, if what she said was correct, Lady Renshawe must have been a very lovely young lady—much more so than her present appearance seemed to indicate.

"You look such ——" "a darling," it was on Geoffry's lips to say, when he lifted Esty on to her horse ; but he checked himself, and tagged his sentence with—"such a quaint, old-fashioned little fairy ;" but I think that in the break of his speech Esty read the first epithet in his eyes, and rather preferred that silent mode of expressing his sentiments. As soon as Lady Renshawe had provided her niece with a modern habit, the rides, which had at first been confined to circles round the house, became extended to the green lanes outside the estate ; and Geoffry declared that he had never met before with so apt a pupil as his present one. As far as her seat was concerned, Esty had nothing to learn ; she had had too much practice as a child, and was too naturally graceful not to fall involuntarily into her right place on her horse's back ; in every other respect she was docile and intelligent. Could Mrs. Herbert have guessed how much tenderness Captain Adair felt towards the creature whose accomplishment he was perfecting, and what pleasure he experienced in guiding Esty's ignorance into proficiency, I think Sophy would have cursed her own competency, and wish her hand had been less expert in its management of a bridle when she first knew Geoffry.

The days had never appeared to pass so swiftly to the latter as now. It seemed pleasanter to him to wander with this girl in country lanes, to stain his fingers with dewberries in her service, and to gather handsful of hedge-flowers and wild ferns for her pleasure, than to be on the top of a drag escorting gaudy actresses down to Richmond, whose conversation was as tawdry as the false bloom on their cheeks, or to be on a visit to some country-house where London fashions and London tone are imported into

"Verdurous glooms and winding mossy ways."

Those quiet dinners, where the two sat in the cool shadows of Lady Renshawe's dining-room, and ate and drank out of old-fashioned chased silver and pure-looking goblets of cut-glass—where the glowing sides of the peaches rested between layers of green leaves and crystal lumps of ice, and where the epergne of flowers shed perfume over the whole table—was not all this far pleasanter than crowded dinner-parties, where the room feels stifling from the oppression of its numbers, and a ceaseless babble of conversation is considered necessary to keep up an appearance of enjoyment? Geoffry thought so, and he expressed his opinion to Lady Renshawe, who was short-sighted enough to appropriate to herself all the compliment of the enjoyment he evinced.

CHAPTER XIX.

A KISS.

"Oh, that joy so soon should waste,
        Or so sweet a bliss—
        As a kiss—
Might not for ever last:

So sugar'd, so melting, so soft, so delicious;
        The dew that lies on roses,
        When the morn herself discloses,
Is not so precious."

BEN JONSON.

"HERE is Mrs. Herbert now?" Esty asked Captain Adair one morning, and he flushed guiltily, and said, "By Jove! yes! What a brute I have been!"

"Why so?"

"Because I ought—I intended—to have written to her immediately I returned to England, and here I have been at home for nearly three weeks, and have never let them know it. I will write this very afternoon."

When the afternoon came, Geoffry retreated to the library, and, sitting down before an escritoire, took up his pen, with the full intention of writing a full account to Sophy of all he had seen or done since the date of his last letter to her. Somehow his thoughts would not arrange themselves in proper order; his memories of Rome and Naples had grown indistinct since he had passed those three last weeks at Lynncourt—and Lynncourt was a subject which as yet he did not care to discuss. He was feeling a sort of breathless happiness at the near approach of this new joy—this love, the consciousness of which was beginning to steal over his heart. He watched the progress of the novel but delicious sensation with the same kind of half hope, half fear with which a mariner might hail the first faint dawn of day in a foreign island on which he had been thrown over night by the waves.

"My dear Mrs. Herbert," Geoffry began, fluently enough. Then he stroked with his pen a vase filled with flowers that stood near him, and presently commenced again : "Since I wrote to you at Rome, I ——" There was another break, and Geoffry's restless fingers were occupied during the next two minutes in strewing his note-paper with rose leaves.

"I wonder where she is?" he said presently. (This observation did not refer to Mrs. Herbert.) "Since I was at Rome "—" Oh, what a lovely day it is! too hot to write, really. I'll go out into the shrubbery," and he flung down the pen, snatched up his hat, and went in the direction where he had seen the flutter of Esty's dress disappear half an hour before.

Esty had betaken herself to a favourite seat of hers, the trunk of a fallen beech, which the dark shadows, thrown by the birch and cypress overhead, kept impervious to the noontide heat. The lower air was filled with buzzing of innumerable insects, while the soft cooing of a wood-dove came at intervals through the long range of covert. The sun, which streamed through the lighter foliage of the lilac boughs that over-arched the path, played in flickered gleams over the moss-grown gravel, and on the edge of the red gold leaves of the dying beech, on which Esty was sitting. She had come to this retreat when Geoffry vanished into the library to write, as he said, to Mrs. Herbert, and there was still a pout on her lips, and a discontented expression in her blue eyes, at the thought that Captain Adair might as well have postponed his letter-writing until that time in the afternoon when Esty would necessarily be occupied in reading to her aunt.

By degrees the pout vanished, and the frown died away, as her mind became attuned to the soft calm of the summer

day. There was a pond on the other side of her seat, and
she sat and watched the quick flash made on its dark
surface by the dive of the water-rat and the leaps of the
small pike.

"I wonder if he has finished his letter," she said to herself, and then she dropped a clump of pebbles and grass
into the pool at her feet; and in the splash and the whirr of
the water she did not hear the sound of footsteps coming
behind her.

She had clasped her hands before her, and looked
musingly into the water, when presently she felt her heart
stand still. "Esty!" a voice said at her ear. "My Esty!"
and a hand and arm stole round her waist.

She felt as if she were in a dream; her breath came and
went quickly, and all the scenery before her, the pond, and
the willow that leant over it, seemed to be going round.

"Esty," said the voice again, and this time it trembled
with a thrill of half-repressed, half-expressed passion—"my
child! my darling!" Encouraged by her silence, or led
away by an impulse impossible to resist, her lover moved
his lips from the little ear where they had first rested, and
pressed them timorously on her mouth. A rose leaf blown
against her lips could not have caressed them more gently;
but Esty started up as if she had been scorched by a fire-
brand.

"You had no right—how dare you!" she began, passionately; then she burst into tears, and, flinging aside
Geoffry's proffered hand, rushed impetuously past him, and
fled towards the house.

The young man pulled his mustache with a troubled expression. "Now, I did not in the least intend to do that
when I came out," he said; "but I don't know how it was,
I couldn't help it! Is she really angry? She seemed so;
and if she is angry, it is because she doesn't love me; and
I've made a fool of myself." Captain Adair finished his
cigar alone in the shrubbery, looking disconsolately at the
wavering reflection of his face in the pond, and disturbing
the quiet inhabitants of that sheltered pool by kicking in
every stone, stick, or clod of earth that came within reach
of his foot. "I will go and see if she won't forgive me;"
and then he arose and began to walk slowly towards the

house, feeling extraordinarily shy and nervous as he drew near the doors.

But when he got within, Esty was nowhere to be seen. He might "importune" all the "alcoves" in the house, but she was not in any of them, and he wandered nervously from room to room, and at last took refuge with Lady Renshawe, who had just aroused herself for tea.

"And where is Esty got to, I should like to know?" the old lady said, cheerfully.

Geoffry looked guilty, and said, "he was sure he couldn't tell."

Esty was lying on her bed, her face buried in her hands, and her heart beating with a strange mixture of joy and anger. She had shed tears of rage during that run from the shrubbery.

"He insults me," she said, passionately; "he does not love me—he cannot respect me;" but as she lay there, her eyelashes wet and her cheeks still crimson, one feeling rose above all the rest, and that was the knowledge that she could never forget that kiss—never while she had life. She could feel it on her lips now. While she compelled herself to feel angry at the giver, her heart thrilled with ineffable delight at the sweet memory of that caress. "I had never thought of this!" she said, in her foolish bewilderment, and she said truly; for first love in the young is as pure and vague as the clouds on an alpine height.

She had united herself to Geoffry in dreamland, and in dreamland there had been no clasping of hands or touching of lips; and now, at the first breaking of the bubble, she stood confounded, red with shame and anger, and yet touched by a secret joy which would probably never again accompany a similar caress.

When the servant came to summon Miss Esty to tea, that young lady swept into the room where Geoffry and her aunt were sitting, and took no notice of the penitent glance the humbled warrior shot at her underneath his thick lids, or of the dewy suffusion which after awhile began to dim the brightness of his eyes.

Miss Lisle felt her heart to be in a softened and pervious state, so she erected a buckler of haughty defiance before her in case the enemy should discover the weakness of the country, and she determined for the next three or four days to treat the man whom she had just discovered she loved with marked coldness and disdain.

When Captain Adair retired to his room that night, he carried up with him the letter he had commenced to Mrs. Herbert in the morning, and wrote that lady a long and effusive epistle.

It was some comfort to him, now that he felt unhappy, to pour out all his feelings to Sophy. He felt sure of her sympathy, and could not resist the impulse to call upon her for it, now that he felt uncomfortable and perplexed in mind.

CHAPTER XX.

"YOU KNOW I DO!"

"Sweet, silent rhetoric of persuading eyes."

DAVENANT.

"When least I seemed concern'd, I took
    No pleasure or no rest,
And when I feign'd an angry look,
    Alas! I loved you best."

PARNELL.

"WILL you come out this morning, Miss Lisle?" asked Captain Adair, meekly, as he stood outside the breakfast-room window the next morning, the half-smoked cigar withdrawn from his mouth, and his straw hat casting a soft shadow over the pleading expression of his eyes.

Esty leant out of the window, and pretended to be absorbed in the beauty of the roses that bloomed round the framework.

"I will come presently," she answered, temporising with her consciousness.

"Esty," he said, softly, drawing a little nearer to the pretty head that hovered above him, "do say you forgive me! On my honour I didn't intend it. If I had any notion that it would have offended you so much I wouldn't have done it for the world. Esty, I really—now do, do forgive me. I'll never do it again, if you bid me not."

"It was very wrong of you," she answered, sternly; for with the perverseness of her sex, the more she was moved the more she was resolved to keep up the appearance of anger.

Geoffry looked dejected.

Had he not been in love he would have said, "Hang it, what a fuss about a trifle!" Being in love, he felt really unhappy at having incurred the displeasure of his goddess.

"You won't forgive me?" he asked, twirling round the straw hat nervously in his fingers.

"No," she said, decidedly; and Geoffry, with the variableness of a lover, changed his mood, and with a muttered "d—— it!" flung his cigar into the cool recesses of a laurel bush, and walked away.

Esty felt blank. She was not prepared for this counter check to her anger.

A slight chill fell on her heart, and for a moment the sun lost its brightness and the roses their scent. She watched him until his hasty steps had traversed the length of the gravel path, and his figure had disappeared in the soft gloom of the distant avenue; then she withdrew her head from the window; and when Lady Renshawe sailed into the room in all the majesty of black satin and Spanish lace, her little grand-niece was seated demurely on a hassock, hemming a pocket handkerchief with more rapidity than regularity of stitch.

The old lady twitched the work out of Esty's fingers and scrutinised it closely.

"Crooked as a ram's horn," she said. "I'll finish it myself;" and she settled herself in her morocco chair, casting glances of defiance at Esty, as her wrinkled hand unravelled the misshapen stitches the young heedless fingers had formed.

"Don't sit mooning there, child," the old lady said presently, perceiving that her niece had found no better occupation than that of staring wistfully out of window and plucking to pieces the petals of the rose that had fallen from her belt.

"Put on your things and walk over to Gardenhurst, and ask your mother if she will bring your father and Christine to spend the day here to-morrow."

12—2

It was remarkable, that while Lady Renshawe accorded to Mrs. Lisle all the full privileges and dignities of womanhood, she always seemed to regard her nephew in the light of an unpleasant little boy who was still to be coerced by strong means, as in those days when his youthful exuberance of spirits made him the terror and pest of Lynncourt.

"I shall send the carriage for them," she called out, as Esty prepared to leave the room. "And tell James that he is not to—I mean," she added, correcting herself, "ask your father not to smoke in it."

When she was left alone, Lady Renshawe nodded sapiently over her work, and said to herself:

"Just as well to get Esty out of the way for a bit. Who knows, those two young fools might be falling in love with each other!"

And while the sunbeams moved westward round the panels of the room, the old lady continued her work in silence, unbroken save by the whirr of a passing bird and the hum of bees in the flower-beds, quite unconscious that the two young fools had already fulfilled their destiny.

Meanwhile Esty passed rapidly down the meadow path that was to take her by a short cut to Gardenhurst, her feeling of disappointment at being put out of the way of seeing Geoffry for some hours being considerably softened by the reflection that he would suffer as much if not more than herself at her temporary absence.

Cheered by this idea, she walked quickly through the thick sward, her restless hand taking wanton toll from the heads of gaudy poppies as she passed by the side of the ripening wheat; and soon the dim, vague sense of happiness which had attended her lonely walk was exchanged for the practical pleasure of kissing Christine's blooming cheek, and feeling Toby's rough paws patter round her ankles in a helpless ecstacy of delight—helpless, because the growing obesity of his body prevented its adopting the same lively method of showing his pleasure as was displayed in his agitated tail.

Esty was greeted warmly by her mother. Mrs. Lisle's pale face would flush, and her dim eyes sparkle, when she gazed on the growing beauties of her young daughter.

Had Esty's skin been freckled, and her features contorted, she would doubtlessly have been regarded by Mrs. Lisle with equal tenderness, if not with equal pride; for such is the beautiful elasticity of a mother's love, that it ac-comodates itself to the nature of its recipient, and contracts with tenderness over an object whose weakness requires additional shelter of affection as easily as it can expand with pride over the perfections which all acknowledge and admire. But no one can deny that the last is the more pleasurable feeling. It is a divine kind of vanity which makes a mother rejoice to see a beauty—once, perhaps, her own—glow out with renovated lustre in the face and form of her offspring; and the most cynical could not sneer at the complacency with which Mrs. Lisle would stroke Esty's bright brown hair, and hold the dimpled hand within her own, saying : " Your hair is exactly like what mine was at your age, child; and so is your hand. My hand was considered very beautiful when I was a girl. The artists at Florence used to swear by it. You see, sculptors do not care for thin, bony hands ; they rejoice in rounded fingers, that terminate in pink tips and almond-shaped nails." And the mother would fondly caress the tiny duplicates that rested within her palms.

Colonel Lisle received Esty with mingled dignity and complaisance. In his heart he was pleased that the flower he had planted at Lynncourt should have taken such strong root into that ancient soil, but this pleasure was mixed with a little jealousy that Esty should have found favour which he had never attained in his aunt's eyes. He put aside his paper as Esty entered on this particular morning, and lifted his eyebrows with an affectation of surprise.

" Oh, here you are ! " he said, carelessly ; then perceiving that Esty after kissing him was about to leave the room, he commenced to put a few leading questions : "Well, Esty, how's the old cat to-day ? " "The old cat" was the irreverent appellation which Colonel Lisle invariably gave his aunt, when speaking familiarly in the bosom of his family. Esty having assured him that Lady Renshawe was "never better" (an assurance which the colonel received with a discontented "humph"), he proceeded with his cross-examination : "And how does she get on with that

young puppy, Gerald's friend? What's his name —
Hare?"

Colonel Lisle knew perfectly well (none better) the correct name of his aunt's guest, but it seemed more dignified
to feign ignorance of it; besides, he had an instinctive con-
viction that his witting mistake would irritate Esther.

"Aunt gets on beautifully with Captain Adair," retorted
Esty, with equal dignity. "She finds him a charming
companion."

"Tut, tut! I'm sure he must be as dull as death. What
on earth can he find to do all day in such an out-of-the-way
place? *I* can't think what can induce him to stay so long,
unless he expects to get something out of the old girl. Do
you think that *I'd* stay mouldering down here if I had his
years and opportunities in life?"

By which it will be seen that, with the denseness of age
and its selfishness, Colonel Lisle had quite forgotten that
there was a time when even he would have left the most
brilliant society in Florence to stroll by moonlight, in a
garden steeped in rich scent of tuberose and heliotrope,
with his arm round Elinor Morley's waist; and that in those
days of youthful folly, solitude, thronged with a thousand
sweet vague memories of pleasures past, and enriched with
anticipations of pleasures to come, was very different from
the loneliness which was oppressing Colonel Lisle now that
all the bloom was gone from his life, and only the dry stalks
left in his hand—now that his feet had no longer any upward path to tread, and the "shadow feared of man" sat
waiting for him at the bottom of the slope.

Esty looked rather conscious at her father's surmises as
to what on earth the young man could find to amuse him at
Lynncourt, and she was glad to get away with Christine to
the undisturbed privacy afforded by a thick-leaved mulberry
tree, where the sisters exchanged confidences as they sat in
the shadow—their fair fingers dabbling red berries into their
mouths at every break in the conversation.

"Oh, Christine, he is beautiful!" was Esty's emphatic
commencement; and her sympathising sister, with her face
aglow with interest, asked :—

"What is he like?"

Next to the pleasure of guarding such a secret as Esty

now for the first time possessed, what could equal the
delicious thrill of satisfaction with which she recalled the
events of the last few days, to make her sister a participator
in all the mingled sensations of hope, doubt, and fear—all
the varying emotions that had lately thrown such brilliant
colour into the pure region of her "unstained thoughts?"
I am bound to confess that the young girl was not altogether
candid in her revelations to her sister; for, although she
told of walks taken together, of thoughts exchanged, and of
many other symptoms denoting the interest she and her
lover had vested in each other, she never mentioned the
little quarrel that was now dividing them, nor its cause.
Something in her heart withheld her from making that kiss
a subject of conversation even with Christine.   Indeed, she
flushed even now down to her finger-tips whenever the remembrance of it crossed her mind.   Still, she revealed
enough to make her sister suggest meekly :—

"Ought he not to ask aunt's leave, or papa's, if he means
to go on like this?"

"Oh, Christine!" Esty cried, with the utmost distress in
her voice. "Pray don't talk like that; perhaps he don't
mean anything at all, and it's all my foolish mistake. I
am sure nothing has passed that makes it necessary for
him to speak to anybody, and I would not have told you
anything if I had thought you meant to turn round like
this."

Esty talked so fast and warmly that Christine withdrew
her little suggestions, and felt quite ashamed of herself for
having made it; but she was right, nevertheless, and Esty
would have acknowledged this had the case been applied to
any other person.   But now she was swayed by the growing
intoxication of a first love; and love is such a thief, so instinctively opposed to all lawful authority, that its devotees
shrink from observation as naturally as a schoolboy out of
bounds avoids the eye of his master.

Esty, observing that a slight cloud of trouble still obscured
Christine's usually clear face, skilfully turned her attention
to another subject by telling her sister of the invitation she
had brought from Lady Renshawe.

Christine looked delighted. "I shall see him again," she
said, enthusiastically; "and I shall see the parrot, and the

gold fish, and the last new books, and have as many peaches as I can eat."

Esty smiled superior; the sublimer interests of love were beginning to dispossess such minor pleasures as had hitherto been held of account in her existence.

Christine, now that Esty had exhausted all the glowing rhapsodies born of Captain Adair's presence at Lynncourt, began slowly and methodically to unfold her little budget of news :

"Miss Jennings was here yesterday, looking more like a peacock than ever; her voice as harsh, and her attire as splendid. There is a passage about natural history in my Lemmi's Italian Grammar, which says that Il pavone goes about pavoneggiando 'peacocking himself;' that just describes Phœbe. She hoped you were well, in a shrill vicious voice, which seemed to contradict the wish, and she inquired how long Captain Adair was going to stay at Lynncourt. She called him 'Geff Adair.'"

"What impertinence !" said Esty, loftily.

"She says that she has often heard of him from some intimate friends of his, the Herberts; and that the Herberts are coming to stay at Herbert Castle for the winter."

"How does she come to know the Herberts?" asked Esty.

The notion she had formed of Mrs. Herbert was the reverse of what she would expect a frend of Phœbe Jennings' to be.

"Mr. Herbert is M.P.," said the astute Christine; "he has to know and keep well with all sorts of people."

"What makes them think of coming here, I wonder?" mused Esty.

"Perhaps they think it is time to reassert their influence in the county; they have been abroad so long, you know."

Then Christine proceeded to confide to her sister many other bits of intelligence of a domestic nature. She feared that Gerald was giving trouble, she said. Mamma was getting to have quite her old, worn, worried look, and papa was more satirical than ever at breakfast when the letters came; as for Dolly, she was more like her own old scrubbing-brush than anything else, always rubbing people's temper the wrong way with the most brutal pertinacity.

"And oh, Esty," said her sister piteously, " I do wish that you could marry a prince, or some rich nobleman, and live in a house like Lynncourt, only more beautiful, and then we need never hear anything more of worrying bills, and mamma and papa could be peaceful and happy at the close of their lives, and Dolly should have a little house of her own to nag in ! Oh dear !" she said, interrupting herself wearily, " I must go in and make papa's omelette for lunch."

"I'll come and help you," said Esty. And the two walked arm-in-arm over the broken clumps of what had once been cultivated garden beds, their young heads bowed close to each other, as they still continued to exchange their girlish confidences.

Mrs. Lisle, looking out from a window where she sat making calculations of a far less pleasurable nature, smiled as she saw them pass. " I have two very lovely daughters," she thought.

When Esty returned to Lynncourt that evening, the sun was getting low, and was sending burning shafts of gold along the boles of the old oak trees. She paused when she came to the last meadow that separated her from the grounds, and rested her arms over the top bar of the little rustic stile she was about to cross. She paused with a sensation in her heart of intense happiness, not unmixed with awe. Her earthly Eden lay before her in the realm of those majestic groups of sun-tipped trees ; those golden ranges of gravel walks ; those grey urns, whose graceful forms were beginning to lose their distinctness in the soft films of the evening mist ; those flowers whose bright petals, cooled by dew, were exhaling even more fragrance than the noon-day sun had evoked ;—all breathed but of one idea and one image. She was, perhaps, hardly conscious herself of how much the charm of this sleeping landscape was owing to the touch of bright living passion that had sprung up in her heart. She did not know how dull that setting sun and how scentless the flowers would have appeared to her could she suddenly have learnt that the shrine had lost its jewel, and that the young lover, whose presence was throwing such a magic radiance over all nature, had left her and Lynncourt,

As it was, the girl lingered in a leisurely manner at the threshold of her enchanted palace, plucking off the heads of the wild grasses that grew in the hedge, and staring into the flush of sky in the west, as though she would read there the end of all the wild sweet hopes that were filling her breast.

Presently, with a long slow sigh—a sigh of pleasure that seemed to drink in all the balmy odours of the evening air, all the music of the one thrush that sat carolling in the hedge beside her—she arose; and then her cheeks reddened and her heart beat, for she saw standing in the shadow of the avenue before her the object of her thoughts.

Geoffry was resting against the low bending branch of an elm; he seemed to be awaiting Esty's approach. Yet he did not make one step towards her, and assumed (such are the puerile affectations of love) to be totally unconscious of her presence, although for an hour past he had nearly stared his eyes out in endeavours to see down the whole length of those misty undulations of distant meadow tracks, in the hopes of seeing the little figure which now he pretended not to perceive.

The young man felt indignant and low-spirited; he was feeling the more indignant against Esty, because he had just received an unpleasant piece of intelligence—intelligence which, he felt inwardly convinced, would be as unwelcome to Esty as it had been to him. But he felt no pity for her possible distress. She had been unkind to him. "She does not love, or she would have forgiven me by this time," he argued, and he looked at Esty with an appearance of sullen indifference, as she advanced nearer to him.

"I hope you have enjoyed the afternoon, Miss Lisle," he said, gloomily. "I didn't, I know, for you are cursed with an afternoon post here, and I have received letters by it which bring the reverse of pleasant news."

All the little flutter and consciousness with which the girl had approached him died out of her manner; she stopped short. "What is it?" she asked.

"Oh, nothing that will interest you;" and he walked on, switching away obtrusive boughs with his cane.

"What is it?" she repeated, laying her little hand on his arm.

Geoffry's tone softened imperceptibly as he answered :—

" I am under orders ! It seems there is some chance of the regiment's going abroad, so they have recalled my leave, and I shall have to go back to-morrow."

" To-morrow ! "

Esty repeated the word mechanically, but she felt as though an iron bar were pressed down on her heart; her eyes burnt and her pulse throbbed with what seemed to be, for a moment, intolerable suffering.

The increasing gloom prevented Geoffry seeing the stricken look that had come over her face, and while he wondered at her silence, she had time to recover herself a little.

" I should like to go over and say ' Good-bye' to your people," he said, ruefully. " Perhaps you will take me over there to-morrow morning ? "

Esty having assented with a faint " Oh yes ! " the pair passed through the massive door of the house ; and, while Esty stole away through the shadow of the corridors to hide her face from the keen glance of her grand-aunt, whose stick was heard coming, with loud taps, down the front stairs, Geoffry sought his bed-room ; and, going up to his open window, rested his face on his hand with a sickening feeling of disappointment. He watched the wavering flight of a grey owl as it circled round the oaks in front of him, and thought sadly that by to-morrow at that time he should be far away from these soft-plumed woods and sylvan sounds, with nothing pleasanter to look at than a straight range of white houses and blackened chimney-pots. He thought of his friend Sophy, but only to turn from the thought with impatience. Sophy, with her worldly wisdom, her bright smiles, and brilliant toilette, had never reached the depths in his nature which this girl had.

" I love her !—oh, my God, how I love her ! " and he turned, with a heavy sigh, from the window.

Presently he was startled by hearing a step outside the door.

" Who is it ? " he said; but, as the sound was not repeated, he took no further notice, until he had put out the wax candles that stood in the old-fashioned griffins' heads each side of the table ; then he felt his way to the door, and, flinging it open, said again, "Who is it?" speaking more mechanically than if he expected any one to answer him.

He was answered, however, by a faint sigh and the sound of a repressed sob.

His heart stopped, and he trembled from head to foot.

"I am so sorry—I was—I didn't intend to—I hope you'll be happy when you're away; I have brought you a flower, Captain Adair, and dinner is ready." And the sentence, begun so brokenly, ended in a firm conventional tone.

But Geoffry, although he might be a fool (and had not that experienced judge, Mrs. Herbert, said he was one?), could not miss such an opportunity as this.

He drew the white-robed figure from the dark corner into which she had shrunk into the recess of the window in the corridor, where the light of the rising moon shone down on her pale tear-stained face. He held her tight in his caress for a moment, unable to speak.

"She loves me!" he muttered, hoarsely. "She does love me after all!" and, still holding her to his breast, he turned his blue eyes up, with a light and expression in them which had something of ecstacy in it. "I am too happy," he murmured. Then the red lips descended and showered passionate kisses on the shrinking face and averted throat. "I will make you pay for that kiss you so grudged me," he whispered, and again she felt the warm touches from his lips fall rapidly on her hair, cheeks, and shoulders. Suddenly he ceased.

"Do you love me?" he cried.

She paused.

She had come to him swayed by a feeling which, if strong, had still all the timidity of a woman's first passion in it; and she was feeling terrified and crushed by the violence of the storm she had evoked.

"You will not answer me!" and he flung away the hand he had been holding, and turned to go.

He was determined to have a direct avowal from her own lips. He had suffered so much from doubt and anxiety that he swore to himself that he would not suffer more—at least, not on that score. From the moment he felt her heart palpitating against his own—at the first touch of her clinging arms—he felt autocratic, and his passion blazed forth in its full glory of power, intensity, and selfishness.

"I *will* know!" he repeated; and the young girl, reeling forth in the moonlight, stretched out two warm round arms towards his neck.

"You know I do!" she cried; and Geoffry caught her to his breast once more.

There, with the young head thrown back to meet his kiss —with the gleaming arms round his neck—the rounded bosom throbbing such wild pulsation on his breast, Geoffry felt, and felt truly, that to him in this world the acme of earthly happiness had arrived, and that time could bring no future to surpass the sweetness of this moment.

The tapestry waved in the rising wind, and the grotesque figures embroidered on it, by fingers long since dust, nodded grimly by the side of these living pictures of youth and beauty. The moonlight flung cold gleams on the rusty breastplates and battle-axes that adorned the walls; and if the dark-visaged ancestor of Lady Renshawe, whom Holbein had immortalised in the panel above the fireplace, could have spoken, he must have owned that of all the specimens of life that had shown an utter disrespect to and disregard of his presence for the last four centuries, none had ever formed a more lovely group than this boy and girl who stood in the window babbling of love that was to live for ever—of passion that would survive all earthly changes, and that would even extend to the memory of the one who should be called first by death from the other's side.

CHAPTER XXI.

A MAD PASSION.

"Continual burning—yet no fire or fuel,
 Chill icy frosts in midst of summers frying,
 A hell most pleasing, and a heaven most cruel;
 A death still living, and a life still dying,
 And whatsoever pains poor heart can prove,
 I feel and utter in one word—I love."

P. FLETCHER.

"If it be love to wake out all the night,
 And watchful eyes drive out in dewy moans,
 And when the sun brings to the world his light,
 To waste the day in tears and bitter groans;
 If it be love to dim weak reason's beam
 With clouds of strange desire—and make the mind
 In hellish agonies a heav'n to dream,
 Still seeking comforts where but griefs we find."

DRUMMOND.

NCE more the clocks were ticking gaily in the drawing-room in H—— Street; the parrot swung himself slowly backwards and forwards in his ring, rejoicing in the hot sun, and giving out, in a choked voice, sleepy invitations to some unknown person to "come along," and not "be shy."

This little drawing-room, with its abundance of down cushions and yielding ottomans, presented somewhat the appearance of a comfortable fluffy nest. And Sophy, who sat ensconced in the softest cushions of the softest chair, with her face sullenly drooped on her full white breast, her brown eyes giving out restless intermittent light, and her hair shining a burnished brown, like the hues of a pheasant's wing, rather resembled a dejected bird buried in ruffled plumage than a prosperous matron, happy in the possession of wealth, station, a good husband, fine children, and an excellent digestion.

"Fool! fool!" she was murmuring to herself in a voice that had a ring of acute anguish in it. "Why did I not prevent his going? Why did I not take him with me to Brighton?"

She took up and re-read an opened letter that lay by her side on the sofa. It was a letter in which Geoffry had poured out, with passionate egotism, all the hopes and fears that had agitated him during the last few days of his sojourn at Lynncourt. "Sometimes I cannot help thinking that she loves me." 'Poor fool, of course she does!' interpolated Mrs. Herbert, savagely. "There comes such a beautiful rosy flush on her cheek if I address her suddenly"—Sophy looked involuntarily at the reflection of her own pale olive-tinted skin in the glass before her—"but I think that it may arise from shyness"—'Shyness! stuff and nonsense'—"and then I am all down again. Forgive me, Sophy, if I bore you; but I know the kindly interest you have always taken in me, and how disinterested your affection for me is. —'What fools men are!' again interrupted Mrs. Herbert, grimly, 'to imagine that one ever takes a "kindly interest" in them for *nothing!*'—I have no one but yourself to confide in, no one but yourself to fill the part of a sister to me. I fear that you will think me a fool, but if you could only see her—see how much more lovely, more clever she is than any woman I have ever met, you would cease to wonder at my infatuation."

"Should I?" murmured Geoffry's confidant, as she tore the letter into a thousand little bits. "*Should I?*" and then she got up out of her cushions, and walked quickly up and down the room. Presently she flung herself down again, and began to piece together the bits of the letter she had just destroyed; but she could glean no comfort, no consolation from those torn remnants of Geoffry's confidences. Her hot eyes stared blankly at such disjointed sentences as "ran away like a wounded bird; soft lips; so modest and pure."

Words which indicated that Geoffry's sense of delicacy had not been so keen as Esty's, since he had evidently not preserved the same reticence as she had done in the matter of that little episode of the beech tree.

Sophy crushed the torn sheet in her hand with such violence that the inside of her fingers were indented and bruised by the rings that encircled them.

"He writes this puling nonsense to me—to *me*—who am dying for him!" And the unhappy woman clenched her fingers in the soft meshes of her hair. "I have been loving him, yearning for him all these years. I was the first woman to love him. I had at least that prior claim. My heart has been taken from my duties, and has gone forth wandering after him ever since I first saw his boy's face. What have the days been to me?" she continued, passionately, as her hands pulled at the golden pendants that drooped from her ears. "What have the days been to me since my heart has been burnt up with love for him? the moments passed away from him have been as leaden and cold as those breathed by dying men; those spent with him so feverish and restless that I yearn even for the pain of his absence to be free of such terrible disquiet. If he could but love me; if I could but live to see once his eyes and lips turn towards mine with passion in them, I would be content to die—to die at that moment in the plenitude of my youth, beauty, and happiness." Her voice sank into a low sob as she spoke that last word.

Happiness could never come to this woman, who had allowed ungoverned irregular passions to storm her life until they had made a broken wreck of it.

The harbour might lie smiling and peaceful beyond her, but she must be carried for ever on advancing and receding waves, without sufficient force to reach that calm shelter.

While Geoffry had been indifferent to other women, she had been able to bear the wound of that indifference when displayed towards herself. She had nourished her passion on the kindly looks and words which their intimacy had naturally evoked from him. As a starving man snatches at broken scraps and morsels of food, and, from the relief afforded to his hunger, rates them as highly as a gourmand does the most delicately-flavoured dish, so had Sophy fed her hopes on the most trivial proofs of interest evinced towards her by Geoffry, until she had nearly fallen into the delusion of believing that such proofs were all that any woman could ever win from him; that his light-hearted unconsciousness of manner indicated a want of depth, an absence of feeling, which would render him as impervious to the charms of others as he had been to those she had so lavishly displayed to him.

She was now suffering the cruellest mortification it is possible for a woman to experience. Wounded alike in her vanity and in a love which at once comprised all the best and worst feelings of her nature, she was completely crushed by the unexpected blow. She felt inclined to doubt the power of her own attractions; she looked at herself in the mirror, and laughed a little, bitter, hard laugh as she scanned the eyes, hair, and figure which all other men but the one man whom she loved had found so irresistible. She was like the unhappy enchantress who found that her beautiful shepherd had at last awakened to love, but to love not her.

Mrs. Herbert had lived such a peaceful life—a life so unbroken by any sorrow or reverse—that she was utterly unconscious of how far it was in her nature to feel deeply should any occasion arise to call out the full force of her passions.

Since the night when her tearful eyes pleaded to Geoffry with an emotion that met with no response, she had experienced no stronger sensation than that of a mild affection towards her husband, a somewhat stronger feeling for her children, and an overwhelming regard for herself. She loved herself; she loved the placid sensuous warmth of her nature, which enabled her to appreciate so thoroughly all the good things of this life. She loved her satin, sleek skin, and would delight in stroking the rounded arms, and in contemplating the little feet, not less rounded and dimpled. She liked to pass her hands through the thick masses of silky, warm-coloured hair, which would have put to shame, with its soft luxuriance, all the hard artificial knobs which modern fashion has ordained shall disfigure English-

13

women's shapely heads. She revelled in the abundant nature of her beauty, and she would watch in the mirror all the undulating charms of her figure as she moved across her room with something of the satisfaction, it is supposed, the peacock experiences when he expands his brilliant plumage in the sun. This self-satisfaction of Sophy's was far removed from any of the ordinary flutters that attend conceit. Indeed, her admiration of herself was so genuine and deep-seated, that it rarely showed itself in any outward gesture; but when accident brought any of her personal graces to her mind, she certainly rejoiced in their possession. She rejoiced, too, in the serenity of temper which enabled her to dash away small troubles from her mind with that facility ascribed to ducks of flinging off water-drops. She rejoiced in her husband's adoration, wherein she perceived so clearly the potency of her own charms, and until now she had confided in the belief of her imperviousness to any acute form of suffering.

She had misjudged her own strength. She did not dream how she had nourished her love for this boy, until it had wound itself round and round her heart, to sting like a serpent, when its poisonous nature was once provoked.

Sensual, selfish, narrow-minded as she was, she was still a woman. What there was in her of good as well as of evil had gone to feed this huge furnace of misapplied devotion.

She had even prayed for him—and murmured her otherwise somewhat rare orisons with a feeling not so incongruous as might have been imagined, since she only begged for that which was good for him, without any reference to her own feelings—feelings which even she did not dare to think of under such circumstances. She was a lyre on which his hand might have played at will, had it cared to do so; but he did not care, and so the music was wild, wayward and fanciful, coming out in fitful exultations, or wailing monotones, as was natural, seeing it was governed by woman's ill, and not by man's control.

It was four o'clock; and as the gold chimes on the mantelpiece announced the hour, Mrs. Herbert rose, and almost mechanically began to shake out her dress and smooth her hair.

She was very miserable—but that was no reason why she

should be less lovely than usual. Presently she heard Geoffry's step on the stair; and, as she stood there—her red lips apart, to admit of her quicker breathing—her colour coming and going under her clear skin—her feet still, as though frozen to the ground, but her bosom heaving rapidly under the soft lace that lent a subdued charm to its beauty, —it would have been a very fastidious eye that would not have been gratified with such a picture of ripe, womanly perfection. Surely no one but a pre-occupied lover could have been blind to its merits.

But such was the man who came bounding up the stairs now, and who greeted Mrs. Herbert with such warm cordiality of manner that she seemed to feel herself shrink and wither before the blighting sincerity of his unconcern.

Geoffry had that light in his eyes and gladness in his tone which rarely bless a man more than once in his life. It is thus with him when he is conscious of possessing a secret treasure, of hoarding a joy too deep for words, but yet which he will endeavour to put into broken, incoherent language, from the necessity felt by his soul to send the delight that is within out to the world, that all who will may take reflected pleasure from his.

Sophy thought that he looked handsomer than ever, as he stood leaning over her chair, with a high-bred grace of manner peculiar to him.

"Well, Sophy," he said, with a cheerfulness that was positively irritating to the woman who had spent the last few hours in such torture of spirit.

"How are Herbert and the children?"

Without waiting for an answer, he went on.

"It's quite a godsend finding you in town; I didn't think I should see a soul I knew, nor did I until I came here. What on earth brought you up?" then, dropping his voice involuntarily into an inflexion so tender that it made his auditor grind her little pearl-like teeth, he continued:

"I've told you my secret, Sophy."

There was a pause. Mrs. Herbert watched mechanically the motes that danced in the sunbeam, and paid particular attention to the proceedings of an over-weighted and perplexed spider, which had not constructed a web

13—2

s...iciently strong enough to bear the combined weight of himself and his captive fly.

Then she steadied her voice into what was after all a hoarse, unnatural sound, and answered :

"I suppose I am to congratulate you." She gathered strength and composure with the effort of speaking, and continued, more fluently :

"How is it, Geoffry, that you, who have passed scathless through the perils of London seasons, should have fallen captive to a little rustic like this Miss Lisle? It's like the princess, who, rejecting all the straight, fair sticks, was obliged to put up with the crooked one at last."

The tone of her voice was hardly congratulatory as she said this.

"I don't know," said Geoffry, simply, "I am sure, how it happened; but as for London seasons, Sophy, I don't think I could ever fancy a woman for my wife who had run the gauntlet of *them*. Such women are all very well to flirt, talk, and dance with, but a woman to be attractive to me must have the bloom and freshness of youth on her mind as well as her person."

Sophy winced.

"True," she answered, softly. "Your feeling is one which is natural for a man to possess before marriage, and while his feelings only are under discussion ; but when he is married, and his wife becomes a practical, and not an ideal, portion of his life, I think he generally wishes her to glide pleasantly into her place in society : and if she cannot do so —if the nature of his little daisy's previous life makes her unfit to herd with hot-house flowers—he is the first to be annoyed at the failure of his transplanting."

"Why," said Geoffry, with a laugh, and his blue eyes sparkling kindly at her, "you talk as if I had picked up a female Orson in the woods. You do not know that one of Esty's principal charms to me is the richly-cultivated intellect she possesses. All the hours of her young life have been spent, not in the close atmosphere of London *salons*, but in serious studies and simple pleasures. You and I, my dear Sophy, have spent two wearisome years in being bored by every variety of the human fool that society has turned loose on us; but my little Esty has suffered no such interruption to the poetry of her youth. She has had trees, flowers, and sky for her out-of-door companions ; she has not yet learnt to appreciate the advantages afforded by a secluded woodland corner for picnic and flirtation, but she can find keen delight in watching nature's changes as they spread slowly over the face of her favourite trees, and sit motionless for hours in the summer sun watching all the varied specimens of insect existence flashing into life and motion under its genial influence. Confess, Sophy," he added, laughing, "that your interest in a butterfly would begin and end in this."

He lifted up a little case adorned with dry moss, wherein butterflies of many hues disported themselves (according to the fancy of the arranger of them) on gold pins.

" I didn't do those," said Mrs. Herbert, shortly. "I am not cruel."

"Nor is Esty," said the unconscionable egotist, enthusiastically:

" ' Her feet spare little things that creep.'

Oh, Sophy, she has such lovely feet!"

"Prettier than mine?" said Mrs. Herbert, with a faint smile ; showing a wee pair of French boots pressing lightly on the footstool before her.

" I don't know quite," he said, candidly; "but I think they are."

He put down his hand, and spanned the silken shod instep, which Sophy had tipped gracefully over the other.

A "thousand little shafts of flame" seemed to burn up in her at the light pressure of his hand. Her lip quivered, and her face worked convulsively.

" Leave it alone," she said, petulantly, withdrawing her foot. "Of course it cannot be compared to that of your paragon." There was a pause; and then with a great effort, she recovered some of her usual cheerfulness of manner.

" I wish you every success, Geoffry, and I shall love your *fiancée* like a sister of my own."

" Yes ; but look here, Sophy, I know it is in your power to do me a great favour."

" What is it ? "

" Well, you must know that I came away from Lynn-court in such a hurry that I had not an opportunity of speaking to Miss Lisle's father, or her grand-aunt. I told my darling that I should write by to-night's post ; but since I have been in London I have ascertained that we are actually under orders for India. Now, how on earth am I to write to Colonel Lisle, and speak of my wish to marry his daughter and my going abroad in the same sentence ? "

" Why not ? "

" Why, Sophy, you must see ! " the young man exclaimed, emphatically. " I have little enough to offer as it is, Heaven knows ! I cannot settle much more on my wife than the worth of my commission, and if, in addition to these disadvantages, I give her the option of going to India, or a long engagement, cannot you imagine what her parents' answer will be ? "

" What is it that you want, Geoffry ? "

" I want time—more time in England—that I may spend it in trying to soften any prejudices that I may have to contend with on their part. Lady Renshawe loves me so well for my father's sake that I think I could win her over to my side if I could see a little more of her."

" And what good can she do you ? "

" She is wealthy, and, consequently, powerful in the family. Moreover, Esty has been her favourite companion and relation for years past, and is considered to be her grand-aunt's peculiar charge. If the latter favours my suit, I don't think I should have much difficulty with the rest of the family."

" And what can I do for you ? "

" You have great influence with General S——, and if you would exert that influence to obtain me two months' leave, you will be doing all that I require of you. Two months would be quite sufficient for me to ascertain the nature of my future prospects. Only fancy," he continued, dreamily, "in eight short weeks I might be holding my darling to my breast as I looked back on old England with not a regret in leaving it, if I took such a treasure of happiness with me."

"Oh, Geoffry, Geoffry!" cried Mrs. Herbert, with a cry of pain. "I cannot bear it. I ——" Then she checked herself, and said, more soberly, "You are selfish, Geoffry, and are forgetting that we, at least, should feel regret at your departure—we, who are such old friends."

"Forgive me, Mrs. Herbert—Sophy, dear, forgive me!" Geoffry cried, impulsively. "I am horribly selfish, I know; but I am so bewildered by the novel sensation of my happiness, so troubled as to the means of carrying it out, that I am not responsible for my actions to-day, and I must look to your old and tried friendship to pardon my extravagances. Please forgive me that thoughtless speech; you know that I did not mean it. You must know how sorry I shall be to lose your society. Say you forgive me, Sophy?"

And the young man who, in the plenitude of his happiness, was loth to think that anyone near him should be annoyed or vexed, tried to raise Sophy's head from the dejected attitude into which it had drooped, as he gently pulled it towards him by a tress of her hair. She looked up, and for the first time since this interview, met his eyes.

She had not dared to seek to meet them before, fearing lest the trouble of her soul should find too much expression in her glance. As it was, the look she gave was a terrible one—such a one as a wild animal, suffocating with rage and pain, might cast towards the hand that is descending to deal its death.

For one moment Mrs. Herbert felt as if further concealment of her feelings was impossible. She longed with inexpressible longing to throw her arms round his throat and cry,—

"Pity, forgive, and love me a little, for I am loving you to madness!"

But ere the tumult in her heart could rise to her lips, Geoffry had released his hold of her hair, and was looking eagerly round the room as though in quest of something.

"What is it?" she asked, faintly.

"I am looking for writing things. Will you give me some, Sophy, and then I can write my letters here?"

"It will seem more natural to write to her here than in

that noisy club," he said, looking complacently at the waving white curtains and the bright array of flowers in the window that threw a faint fragrance over the pleasant soft-hued room.

He walked up to a heliotrope, and picking a blossom, smiled sweetly, as he inhaled its perfume; his face wore a far away look for some minutes after, as he lazily caressed the parrot that stood watching him with furtive eye and crooked claw.

Sophy arose, and with somewhat unsteady footstep walked to her escritoir. "Here are pens, paper, and ink," she said in a tired voice. "You can write here, Geoffry."

"And you'll do that for me, about General S——?" the young man pleaded, turning round his radiant face on her.

"I will do all I can," she answered hesitatingly.

"Oh, you can do it well enough if you'd only try, Sophy; or Herbert can do it, he and you have influence which a poor, penniless fellow like myself could never possess had he twenty times such gallant fathers in the service as mine was. But of this you may be sure, Sophy, that General Adair's son will never ask for anything unbecoming a soldier to grant: if it were active as well as foreign service I was ordered on, I should not hesitate for a moment. Now, Sophy, you will help me all you can, won't you?"

"Yes," she said, "I will do all I can;" then she seated herself at a little distance from him, and stared again at the sunbeam, seeming to hear from a great distance off the hurried scratching of his pen along the paper, as he rapidly covered sheet after sheet with rough, eager sentences.

Nearly an hour elapsed in this fashion, and then Geoffry got up, and, thrusting his letters into his coat-pocket, advanced towards Sophy with an apology for ·having remained thus cccupied so long in her society.

She started at the sound of his voice; and, as she looked up, a less careless observer than Geoffry would have noticed what dark rings had deepened round her eyes, and how grey the tints about her mouth had become.

"Where are you going?" she asked.

"To post my letters," he said. "I have written to her father and to Lady Renshawe to explain matters, and to ask their consent; but these I shall not send until I hear the result of your mission to General S——."

"And the other?"

"The other is to *her*," he said, flushing; "I suppose I ought not to send it before the others can go, but I cannot let a day pass without communicating with her, besides, I must explain to her the reason of my delaying to send the other letters."

"At any rate do not go now, Geoffry," said Mrs. Herbert, sweetly; "considering the length of your visit here to-day, you must own that I have seen very little of you; the first hour you occupied in conjuring up Miss Lisle's image to your mind; the second in writing to her. Now, do stay and have a cup of tea with me as in the old times, and talk to me a little about yourself."

What man ever resisted such an invitation as this last? Geoffry hesitated, and finally succumbed to the fascinations of Mrs. Herbert's easy chair, only stipulating that his letter should be sent at once to the post-office that it might be in time for the country-post.

Mrs. Herbert rang the bell.

"Francis," she said, as her quiet well-trained servant answered her summons, "Take these letters at once to the post," (she had added a heap of her own to Geoffry's one), "and be sure they are in time ——"

"Stop!" she continued, as the servant was withdrawing; "go up into your master's dressing-room, there are some there which I have addressed to be forwarded to him."

"So Herbert isn't in town, then," asked Geoffry, for the first time awaking to the fact that he had spent a two hours' *tête-à-tête* with Sophy without interruption from her husband.

"No;" she said, under her breath; inwardly she was saying to herself, "It all hangs upon a chance."

"I have got a new picture to show you," she said, presently, and she glided out of the room, leaving Geoffry occupied in pouring out her tea.

She was back again almost directly, but when Geoffry asked what the picture was, she seemed perplexed as though she had forgotten all about it; however, she speedily turned his attention to some other subject, and exerted herself so successfully to please him that the next half hour passed as pleasantly as was possible under the circumstances.

"You will not forget, Sophy, dear, to write to the general," he said, when he at last took leave of her; " I have no doubt of your success, but if you should fail —— !"

"Yes?"

"You must let me know as soon as possible, that I may have a chance of running down to Lynncourt before I go, to set matters as straight as I can. Good-bye, Sophy, I shall never forget your kindness to me—never!" so saying, he pressed her hand affectionately, and passed with light footsteps down the stairs and out of the house.

Sophy went to the window and watched him walk swiftly down the street; as he turned the corner he looked round and waved his hand gaily. When he had quite disappeared she drew a deep, long breath, and came back again to her former seat; then she let her hand slip gently down the folds of her silk dress until it reached her pocket, from which she extracted the massive-looking epistle which Captain Adair had confided to her servant's care an hour since.

Her hand shook and her eyelids quivered as she looked at the envelope, and she felt a sickening oppression over her heart as she broke the seal, not because of the dishonour and treachery of the thing she was doing, but because she shrank from seeing those expressions of tenderness directed towards another, which she would have given world to have had addressed to herself.

For a moment she thought she would burn the letter without perusing it, but then the miserable curiosity which causes those who love to pry into the inmost heart of the object of their affection, even when they are conscious that such knowledge will be fraught with the keenest pain to themselves, conquered her first impulse, and she tore the letter open, and read as follows.

CHAPTER XXII.

TREACHERY'S NEMESIS.

"Slow are his steps that leave a heart behind."

GRÆME.

M Y OWN,

"Do you know what a world of pleasure lies in those two words? That you *are* my own, and that you allow me to call you so, comprises all the joy of my existence; you cannot imagine how blank everything seemed to me when I left you yesterday,—the whole world was lying behind me in that garden, and I was going out to nonentity and oblivion.

"Once or twice, I felt as though I *must* turn my feet back. I longed so desperately to hear again the sound of your voice; you have in a brief space become such a part of me that I wonder how I could have lived so many years without you.

"One thing is certain—and that is, I can now think of no future in which you are not. If it were not for the deep joy with which your love has filled my heart, I could not face the sorrow and annoyance of that which I have to tell you; but I am treading on air, and trouble—even the trouble of parting from you, which is the heaviest I can suffer, seems far off and trivial.

"My dear love, I find that I am under orders to sail with my troop sooner than I expected. It is possible that,

through the interest of a friend, I may get it put off for two
months longer; if so, I shall spend the greater part of
those two months at Lynncourt striving to win your
people's sanction to our love. If my application for leave
fail, I do not know what on earth I can do. I fear under
the circumstances that I should be utterly rejected by your
parents. I could not bear to ask you to act in defiance of
them—still less could I bear to give you up. That would
be too terrible. Remember! whatever happens, we must
never give each other up. Should I be obliged to go, I
shall still have time to run down and bid you good-bye,
and then we will concert our measures together. But I
hope and believe that I shall gain the extra two months,—
and who knows what will happen! I may, perhaps, gain
first your grand-aunt's approval, and then my own darling
for a wife. I have been alone all my life till now, but
could I win you for my own, I should feel as though all the
sweetest ties in life were concentrated in the one that
bound us together. Good-bye, my treasure; the touch of
your lips is thrilling me now; should I live to be a very old
man, I shall never forget that June day I first found out
how dear you were to me.

"Once more, good-bye, my first and only love.'

"Yours,

"GEOFFRY ADAIR."

Mrs. Herbert read this letter rapidly, and yet every word
seemed to sink into her mind, as though they had been
conveyed to her with the slow distinctness of a sermon.

"And I thought this man could not feel," she muttered,
as her hand involuntarily clenched the paper into a
crumpled ball. Then she smoothed out the folds and
applied a lighted match to their thick, creamy edge—she
watched the flame first curl slowly round Geoffry's signature,
then ascend in a wild leap, consuming his name with its
progress. She watched, until all that was left of his
passionate outpourings to his distant love lay in a few grey
ashes that smouldered in the grate at her feet; but long
after the paper was dust, she saw one sentence as vivid as
ever before her eyes: "My first and only love." She could
not escape from it—it haunted her sleeping and her waking

hours; she had amply reaped her punishment in the base breach of trust she had committed, for those words were doomed to cling to her tortured memory for many a long day to come. Did no thought of others cross the selfish passion that aimed but at its own gratification? Did she feel no compunction knowing that she might bring life-long sorrow and trouble to the man whose love she coveted? No pity for the poor little heart, that was throbbing with restless anxiety down amidst the dew-laden woods of Lynn-court, far away, and utterly unconscious of the treachery that was being perpetrated against her; but praying for the morning light which she expected would bring to her her lover's greeting? No! — it was not likely that Sophy should pity her rival when she could not even control the cruelty of her passion for Geoffry's sake; she had been wrought to such a pitch of unexampled anguish in that interview with him, that she had but one thought left, one hope, one determination: and this was, that the time might come when Geoffry should sue for that which he now could not even perceive; and that, come what might, he should never be happy with another woman. "She would rather he died," she thought, with a sullen gleam in her brown eyes. After she had stared in silence for some time at the ashes of his letter, she went to bed, and as she heard the wind, which had risen with the night, howl round the roof, she clung to her lonely pillow with a kind of terror, and even wished for the shelter of her husband's arms.

CHAPTER XXIII.

THE GOOD-BYE.

"Lo stral voto; ma con lo stral, un voto,
Subito uscì, che vaola il copo a voto."

TASSO.

"On her whom all my sufferings cannot move,
What pray'd I rashly for?—my maddening prayer
Ye winds disperse unratified in air!'

GRAINGER'S TIBULLUS.

HEN Mrs. Herbert descended to her boudoir the next morning, she found two letters on the breakfast table—one was in George Herbert's handwriting, a handwriting firm and precise, thoroughly suggestive of the writer; the other was Geoffry's impulsive-looking scrawl.

Mrs. Herbert had hardly recovered her nerve yet, and her pale cheek turned paler, as she eyed the letters askance, while the servant hovered round her with the breakfast things.

These little motionless squares of paper that lie so quietly amidst glittering tea-cups and fresh-baked rolls—how much of our destiny they may convey in their innocent looking, travel-worn envelopes! Sophy waited until she was alone, and then she opened first her husband's letter : it was sensible and short.

"All was well," it said ; "the children sent their love and

would be glad to see her again ; he himself should come up
to fetch her that afternoon, and, with best love, he was ever
hers,—G.H."

"I have only just time, then," said Mrs. Herbert, as she
consigned George's note to her pocket ; then she turned her
attention to the other one.

It merely contained a few hurried lines, from Geoffry, entreating her to lose no time in applying for his leave, since,
unless it was given at once from head-quarters, he must
that very night go down to Gravesend to join his men.

"I do not ask you now to try for the two months' exten-
sion," he said ; "it would be almost impossible to obtain it
at so late a moment, but for Heaven's sake do try and get
me the two days' grace, that I may see my love's face once
more before I go."

Sophy smiled.

"Is it likely !" she thought. Then she ordered her
brougham, and drove to General S——'s house, which stood
in one of the quiet, shady streets leading out of Piccadilly.

The hour was still so early that there was no one likely
to notice her as she passed swiftly through the streets, en-
folded in voluminous pure-looking draperies, with her mellow
face glowing like a faint-coloured autumn peach. No one,
indeed, excepting a meditative butcher-boy, who was
shouldering his tray close to General S——'s area-gate, and
who ejaculated as Sophy drove up : "Blest if here ain't a
five o'clock turning out at ten by mistake !"

"Ask the General to be so very kind as to come and
speak to me for a few moments," said Mrs. Herbert, as the
door was answered by a highly respectable-looking butler.
Presently the General appeared on the threshold, radiant in
shiniest of boots and black satin stocks, his face bright and
clean-shaven, and his white moustache glistening like a
clump of snow, with the sun on it.

"My dear Madam," he said, with old-fashioned courtesy,
"you do me much honour by this visit. It is the first time,"
he continued gallantly, "that the sun has ever penetrated
so early into my windows."

"General," interrupted Sophy, abruptly, "you remember
what I told you the other day about that young friend of
mine, Captain Adair ?"

" Yes, yes ! sad case, very ! I remember : poor fellow got into some low entanglement—going out to India. Best place for him. Not that India is the best place for a man disposed to run those risks," added the General, correcting himself.

" When does the troop of the —— Lancers sail ? "

" Really, my dear lady, I forget. If I had my papers here, or Janson, my clerk, I could tell you immediately."

Sophy groaned inwardly. " His memory is like a sieve," she muttered. " I will take you down to Whitehall, General, if you will allow me," she said, with her sweetest smile; "and then I shall enjoy the double advantage, first, of your society on the way ; secondly, of getting the information I require when we arrive there."

The General, nothing loth, called for his hat, and got into the brougham ; and Sophy, with her usual tact, made the drive so pleasant to him that he rode along with a misty idea that he was a young man again, diffusing as much pleasure by his attentions as he felt in receiving them.

" Wait here, my dear," he said, when they arrived at the door of his office. While he disappeared up-stairs, Mrs. Herbert sat watching the handsome giants that sat motionless in the archways, and wondering who was ever going to make up to them for all the lost time their big bodies, and what amount of intellect they possessed, had wasted in their mimic vedette.

Presently General S—— reappeared. His usually serene face seemed much troubled as he put his head in at the carriage-window, and said, in a low voice :

" Your young friend is now under orders to be at Gravesend, and the troops will embark to-night."

" I suppose," said Sophy, " that if he were to attempt to gain a few hours' delay, he could not do so now, could he ? Supposing he were to wish to meet that—that person ? " (and Sophy looked down with an air of embarrassment, which touched the old man immensely : he worshipped modesty in a woman). " And to do so, risk disobeying his orders —— ? "

" He would risk his commission ! " the General said, sternly. " What little time he has will be fully occupied in getting the troops on board. To say the truth, my dear,"

lowering his voice still more, "we are accelerating the des-
patch of troops as much as we can. There are ugly rumours
about."

"What, what are they?" said Mrs. Herbert, in a sharp,
quick voice.

"There is bad news from India," the old soldier replied,
sadly. "I fear we may have heavy trouble there. The
morning papers will tell you as much as I know," he added
reservedly. "But, as for your young *protégé*, if I'm not mistaken, he'll have such man's work cut out for him in the
next year as will put all women out of his head; for as soon
as he lands he will be sent where the disaffection exists most.
Good-morning, my dear lady; I have so much to do. You
will excuse my leaving you. Where shall I tell them to
drive?"

"Home," she said, in a low, suffocating voice.

And home she went accordingly. She felt it difficult to
breathe as she passed swiftly through the sweet morning air,
and all surrounding objects of houses, people, shops, seemed
blended in one hideous phantasmagoria that danced wildly
before her eyes. "Oh God! oh God! if I have sent him
to his death?" she said. What have I done to you, my
darling! Oh, my darling, my darling!" With the passion
of the appeal that rose from heart to lips, her eyes seemed
to get loosened from the hot bands over them, and she wept
fast scalding tears. She had never calculated on this. The
worst her selfishness had allowed her to anticipate for
Geoffry was that he should be exiled, perhaps only for a year,
and that at the end of that time she would secure his return
home. "He should come back cured of his boyish passion,"
she thought, "when his eyes would be opened to her riper
charms." At any rate, he should have the opportunity of
forgetting this folly. For the bitter heartache he might feel
she had no sympathy, but she was all but maddened by the
idea of any personal danger touching him. When she got
into her own drawing-room again, she felt scorched by the
bright rays that shone through the west window. She loathed
the cheerfulness of the flaunting flowers, and the irrepressible
trill of the canary, and she flung her head down on the table
with wild self-abasement, crying out for her "love, the man
she loved, and whom her love might murder." She soon

14

rose to her feet. While Geoffry was still within reach, it was not likely that her grief should lose its restless impetuosity; besides, there was yet more to be done, and Sophy was not a person to let her hand "grow faint to its work," when she had once undertaken it. "I must see him," she thought; "I must see him to dissuade him from writing again to Lynncourt." Inwardly her heart told her that, come what might, she *could* not let Geoffry go without seeing him once more. She ordered her carriage again, and drove to Captain Adair's club. She sent up her card, and sat with bloodless lips, and with hands twitching nervously at her ermine muff, until he came running down the steps. His face was white with excitement.

"It's of no use, Sophy," he said, hastily. "I'm off directly; and even if you could have got me those two months, I could not have accepted them, dear. Don't be vexed about it," he added, kindly, fearing Mrs. Herbert might reproach herself with her ill-success.

"Why not?" she gasped; anticipating, yet dreading his answer.

"You haven't seen this morning's paper?" he said. "If you read the telegrams you will understand that any man with a spark of man-like feeling in him must be mad to get out there as soon as he can!"

"When are you going?" Mrs. Herbert asked, with a stiff look in her face, which was with her a symptom of intense mental pain.

"Almost directly. I must save the 12.50 train to Gravesend. It was very kind of you to come, Sophy; I am so glad to have seen you again."

A softer gleam came into Mrs. Herbert's eyes, but it passed away as he continued:

"I did so want to consult with you about Esty. I fear she will be—be—" and there came a break and a gulp in the young man's voice, "very much upset at not having seen me before I went. The only comfort is to think that she will have got my letter this morning, which will have prepared her in some degree for the blow."

Sophy said nothing; but her hand twitched out a large piece of fur from the muff she was twisting round on her wrist. He went on eagerly :—

"Are you and Herbert going to stay in X——shire this autumn?"

"Yes; Herbert wishes it, and I have no objection."

"Then you will only be some eight or ten miles from Lynncourt. Sophy! will you indeed act the part of a true, kind sister to me, and look after my interests when I am gone? Will you make my future wife's acquaintance, and take every opportunity of letting me know all about her? How she bears my absence, and how the family seem inclined towards me?"

"Yes," said Mrs. Herbert; "I will be sure and make her acquaintance."

"Not acquaintance only, Sophy; you must be a friend to her—as good a friend as you have always been to me. You are older than my little girl, and there are a thousand ways in which you can be useful to her. You are sure to like her for her own sake, Sophy; she is so pretty and clever!"

Which last supposition of Geoffry's proved that he was a very young man indeed.

Mrs. Herbert looked at her watch, and her breath came and went quickly, as she saw how little time there was left before he must leave her. "Oh, Geoffry!" she said, "Oh, Geoffry!" and she laid her hand on the arm that was leaning inside the carriage window.

"You will do what I ask, dear, won't you?" he responded, looking down on her with his blue eyes a little dimmed.

She withdrew her hand as if she had been stung.

He did not attend to the movement, but went on talking hurriedly: "It's an awful blow to me, not being able to say good-bye to her; but I shall write again to her to-night."

"Do you think that will be wise?" asked Sophy, anxiously.

"Why not? One letter cannot make much difference, and I haven't said good-bye to her yet. I will not write again after this once, if you think I ought not."

"Certainly you ought not," Mrs. Herbert said. "Reflect on what you are doing, Geoffry; either you must write to her parents and obtain their sanction to your engagement with Miss Lisle, or you must give up all communication with her until you are in a position to claim her; what will they think of you if they find you have taken such advantage of Lady Renshawe's kindness?"

"That's what troubles me," the young man said, flushing. "I cannot bear that her people should think I've acted meanly. I have written to Lady Renshawe."

"You have?" said Sophy, sharply.

"Yes; here is the letter. I have told her everything, and begged for her interest with Esty's father and mother. I have entreated her to advise me what to do, and I shall be guided by her answer. If she says, 'Speak out like a man,' Heaven knows how glad I shall be to do it. If, on the other hand, she counsels me to wait until I have better prospects to offer, I will accept my lot with patience; anyhow, I could not take Esty out with me now."

"Give me that letter," said Sophy, speaking as though under the influence of a sudden impulse, "I will take it myself to Lady Renshawe. Herbert used to know her a little, and she liked him, and will not look unkindly on his wife, and your ambassadress. I shall be able to judge what will be the best opportunity of giving her your confession, and, as of course you will keep me *au courant* with your movements, I shall be able to give you the first intelligence of how things are going on. Trust me, Geoffry," she added, with an earnestness not altogether assumed, only she was actuated by a very different motive to that which Geoffry imagined was sending fire to her eyes and voice. "Leave it all to me, and you will see that I shall manage infinitely better for you than you would even do yourself."

Geoffry shook his head; he had very little knowledge of human nature as yet, but passion sometimes, with its instinctive truthfulness, supplies the place of acquired wisdom.

"It is best to go straight to the point in a subject like this," he said; "so, if you don't mind the office, Sophy, I should be very grateful to you; but you must communicate with Lady Renshawe at once."

"I will do so at once," said Mrs. Herbert, eagerly; "and now, Geoffry, is there nothing I can say for you to Miss Lisle? no little token you can send to her through me as a proof of my intimacy with you, and my desire to aid her?"

"Oh, thank you a thousand times, Sophy; how kind and thoughtful you are! Give her this," taking a pin containing a small antique from his scarf: "she knows it well. Give it to her from me. Since you are to see her, I will not write again to her until I hear that all is right. Plead my cause as though I were your brother, Sophy. And now, good-bye; it is time for me to be off."

"I will take you down to the station," Mrs. Herbert said, in a subdued voice.

So Geoffry despatched his luggage, and then jumped into the brougham, not sorry to have friendly companionship during that long, weary drive to Fenchurch Street.

On arriving there he bade her an affectionate farewell, thanking her earnestly for all she had ever done, and was about to do for him, and then he disappeared up the stairs, and Sophy, with a heavy weight on her heart, said, "He is gone!"

But love, ever tentative, all-enduring love, rarely leaves a hope ungrasped by which he can climb to the summit of his desires, and her next thought was, "I will see him again."

When Geoffry turned from the adjustment of his small luggage in the otherwise empty carriage he occupied, Sophy's face, peach-like no longer, but of a dull paleness, with black rims round her eyes, making them look like those shadow-swept orbs Lawrence delighted to paint, appeared at the window.

"Good-bye, Geoffry!" she said, gaily. Heaven knows what it cost her to speak thus, but she felt that this last movement of hers required some subterfuge of easy manner to cover its singularity. "And oh!—well, there is nothing else I can do for you?"

The whistle sounded. Mrs. Herbert hastily put her head a little more into the shadow of the window.

"Kiss me, Geoffry!" she said, piteously. "God knows when we shall meet again!"

He leant forward and kissed her with a cold affection, which made his kiss fall like an ice-drop on her hot, tortured heart.

"You will write to me, Sophy, and let me know directly you have seen her?"

"Oh, yes!" she said, vaguely. She felt as if she should lose consciousness, and she grasped one of the railings on the station to prevent herself falling.

The train moved slowly on like a great, black, torpid serpent waking from apathy to sullen life; the faces that appeared in the carriages began to get misty and blurred before her straining eyes. She saw only one thing distinctly, and that was the bright bare head of short curls that still kept its station at the window.

"Sophy!" he called, and she was at the window with a speed which nothing but intense mental excitement could have lent her footsteps.

"What is it, Geoffry—*my* Geoffry?" she muttered.

"Be sure and say 'good-bye' to Herbert for me. I shall write to him on the first opportunity. Good-bye!"

The train increased its speed, and he was really gone. Mrs. Herbert crept down to her carriage, and was speedily conveyed to what her husband imagined was an abode of domestic bliss—her own home.

"Oh! that I could have gone with him!" she cried, when she reached the privacy of her bed-room, and threw her arms out wildly on the bed as she lay there stunned by the force of her own emotions. "Oh! that I could die for him!"

But yet she did not once feel that she would choose as an alternative that Geoffry should have stayed in England secure from danger of his life, and been happy in the love of Esther Lisle.

"Curse her!" said Sophy, vindictively, as she laid her cheek on her pillow that night.

She had returned to Brighton with her husband, and had been wrought almost to frenzy by the irritation his *mal àpropos* questions and calm placidity of manner had occasioned her. If, like herself, he had been crushed by some great sorrow or agitated by strong anger, it would have better suited the stormy nature of her feelings. As she lay motionless on her pillow, her brown-red eyes staring like coals of fire from the masses of snowy drapery that surrounded them, she could see light streaming through the open door of the dressing-room, where two of the children slept, and hear her husband's voice, accompanied by a childish treble, as he repeated, "And forgive us our trespasses, as we forgive them that trespass against us." To most women such a sound would have been an inexpressibly sweet and soothing one to have sunk to rest on; but Sophy turned round impatiently :—

"I wonder if George would forgive me my trespasses if he knew all!" she said.

CHAPTER XXIV.

" Send me some token that my hope may live,
  Or that my easeless thoughts may rest and sleep."

T was the evening after Geoffry's departure, and
Esty walked under the shadow of the limes
where she and her lover had so frequently trodden
down the dewy rifts of grass together, and wondered whether she was most happy or most miserable.

The memory of his parting kiss was very sweet to her.
When she thought of his love, she felt as if her world of
gardens, trees and flowers was all too small to hold the ex-
ultance of her happiness. But there was bitter mixed with
the sweet. He was absent; and, as the shadows grew
deeper on the land, and it became time for her to return to
the house, she loathed the solitude he had left behind him.

Where was he now? Walking the deck, perhaps, and
looking at the first dim star that was peeping out above the
fir-trees, whistling some snatch of song her voice had made
dear to him, or recalling to his mind those words yet
dearer which she spoke when her arms were round his
neck in that last embrace, her eyes corroborating the oath
which her tongue swore, " to be true to him for ever—to
be one with him in heart, even though their feet should be
hundreds of miles apart."

" We love each other, and what can separate us now?"

she said simply, in answer to the look of anxiety that clouded his eyes as he bade her " Good-bye ! "

" No man feels happy in leaving a newly acquired treasure unguarded. How do I know some other fellow won't be falling in love with you ? "

" I don't think I could even see any other while you were in my thoughts," she said, in a low voice, and the doubt cleared away from his eyes, and he believed her— believed her as man ever does believe during that hour of delirium when he is pillowed on Delilah's breast, and has not yet felt the click of the scissors amidst his hair.

The box from London had come to Geoffry's hand two days before he left Lynncourt, and it was pleasant to see the quiver of delight with which Christine had inspected the beauties of her work-box, lifting the satin lid as reverently as though each recess contained saintly relics, and finally carrying off her treasure with a glance in her blue eyes which spoke eloquent thanks to the donor of it.

Next Captain Adair unrolled Dolly's ribbon, and that venerable woman received it with a scrutinising glance, which seemed to read the quality of the silk through and through.

" It's none of your three-halfpenny a yard," she murmured, complacently, as she curtseyed her acknowledgments.

Colonel and Mrs. Lisle were scarcely less pleased with the young man's courteous remembrances of them.

" Very pretty of him, really," the colonel said, eyeing the fragrant bundle of cigars with the anticipatory look of enjoyment which beams on the visage of a dog that smells a bone coming his way.

The presents were not sufficiently valuable to cause any discomfort in the mind of the receivers, while they were so suited to each person's taste as to be peculiarly welcome to all.

Mrs. Lisle felt the tip of her paint-brushes tenderly with her fingers ; her own brushes had been worn to the stump for some years past, and it was pleasant to think that she could paint her next picture without being irritated by the adhesion of numberless camel's hairs to the wet surface of her canvas. But to Esty came the greatest delight from the recesses of that deal box; her present was enclosed in a small morocco case, and it was given to her by Captain Adair in a dusky corner of the Lynncourt shrubbery, with a whisper that sent the warm blood running up to the little ear that hearkened to it. She never showed this present to anyone, and, when asked what Captain Adair had given to *her*, was hypocrite enough to produce a roll of new music which he had procured for her some days previously.

It had been agreed, as may have been gathered from Geoffry's revelations to Mrs. Herbert, that he should either return or else write immediately to Esty's parents to ask their sanction to an engagement between him and their daughter. Neither he nor Esty doubted the result of this application. Love is so sublimely insensate that it walks blindly over pitfalls and sloughs which more rational people discreetly avoid. What man who suffers from the mingled embarrassment of a large family, and an overdrawn account at his banker's, can recall without a shudder the insane resolution he and his wife took many years past, to link themselves together to eternal discomfort? And what lovers like these two, smitten with their first madness, could be expected to appreciate the objections parents might raise to a union in which love and hope were the chief ingredients?

Geoffry's own modest income had always seemed sufficient for himself, and looking at it through the generous magnifying glass of love, it appeared to expand into actual wealth when he talked to Esty of her sharing it with him; removed from the charm of her presence, and when about to bring his proposals before her parents, his means seemed to shrink to their more natural proportions; but even this shadow of a doubt never crossed the girl's mind; "the fated fairy prince" had come to her at last and set her heart afire with the touch of his lips; henceforward she viewed him through that glamoured veil Love casts over the eyes of all his devotees; her prince's robes were genuine purple, and his ermine truly royal.

If anyone had suggested that a long course of privation — in which dunning tax-collectors, imperious landlords, scanty meals, and threadbare habiliments were disagreeable but inevitable incidents—might weary their affection, she would have laughed them to scorn; with the scorn that sits so richly on the lips of youth—when youth has strengthened itself with that sublime selfishness called love for another.

On the evening I have mentioned, Esty paused several times during her lonely walk under the limes to pull out and regard stealthily the little oval of ivory whereon was the "counterfeit presentment" of her lover's face. It was pretty to see the wariness she exercised during these stolen glimpses at the interior of that cherished little case; but she need scarcely have troubled herself, for, excepting the sleepy caw of a benighted rook, or the sudden drop of an acorn at her feet, there was no sound to disturb these darkening glades, no foot but her own to crush those wind-drifted heaps of dead leaves.

When she returned to the house it was tea-time, and her grand-aunt was already seated at the table. Lady Renshawe checked Esty's impending apology :—

"Don't mention it, my dear," she said, kindly; "I know it's a way girls have got when they are deprived of the society of an admirer. They invariably take to damp arbours, lonely strolls, dead leaves, and wet feet, as naturally as their lovers adopt less innocent forms of distraction. Men are not generally so reckless of health as women are under these circumstances. They become pensive over cigars, and look sentimental at their glasses of cold brandy-and-water; but they rarely omit to put on their great-coats in the night air, and never forget their meals."

Esty looked grave under this badinage : other men might attend to these trivialities, but she felt convinced that *her* "Prince" would gallop over any road that led to her,—whether golden or stony, with the same reckless indifference to self.

After tea aunt and niece sat round the fire : the latter as usual reading aloud, while the former dozed slightly, awaking with a start whenever the reader's voice seemed to relax its efforts. At last the dozes lengthened in duration; and Esty, gently laying down her book, gave herself up to meditation. She was staring into the fire, and had just succeded in discerning in its embers a lovely *Château en Espagne*, where she and Geoffry stood hand-in-hand on a lofty turret, looking down over a wide expanse of foaming seas, purple plains, hills, valleys, and cities, sparkling amidst all like "grains of salt," when her fancies suddenly died away in the blaze before her as she felt her aunt's hand touch her shoulder, and the wrinkled face peered kindly into her eyes as the countess said significantly :—

"He has spoken, has he?"

The girl looked up for an instant, and then hid her face in the folds of the elder lady's silk dress.

"Oh, aunt, how could you guess?" she cried in a tremor.

The countess looked at her tenderly.

"I am not so old that I have forgotten all the signs and symptoms of youth," she said. "Do you think he loves you, child?"

"Yes."

"And you love him?"

"Yes."

Again there was silence in the room for awhile. The younger woman's eyes were all dazed by the beaming glory of the future; she sighed with pleasure, and felt inclined to weep for joy. The countess, with her feet on the brink of an unknown world, shrank alike from contemplation of the past or future; there was something that agitated her once as this girl was agitated now, but it had died away in that wrinkled breast years and years ago, and left bitter in place of sweet.

"When is he to speak to your parents?"

"In a day or two;—he is coming back here to ask you all;—only he may have to go to India, and then he will write. Oh, aunt, do let me tell you all about it!" And Esty lifted up her face, all flushed and eager, yet with a shy look in her eyes as she poured out her confession, glad of an excuse to recall every detail of that beautiful dream of the last few weeks. "He may come back for a couple of days; but, at all events, he is sure to write; I am to hear from him to-morrow," she said, in conclusion; "I wonder what they will say at home; they *can* have no objection to him; can they, aunt?"

In her heart Lady Renshawe thought it improbable that the lovers would meet with any opposition from Colonel and Mrs. Lisle. Geoffry had, probably, inherited a large portion of his deceased mother's fortune, and what exception could be taken to his person, manners, or morals? All that they had ever heard of his good qualities from Gerald Lisle had been confirmed by personal observation.

"He seems good, brave, and frank, and I imagine his income won't be less than £5,000 a year," the countess thought. "What could we wish better for our Esty?"

But it was a duty she owed to her age and experience not to encourage her niece by being sanguine; so she shook her head gravely, and said—

"We will hope for the best, my dear; but now let us go to bed, for it is getting late. It gives me great pleasure, child, that you trust and confide in your old aunt; but when you are my age you will find yourself prone to sleep through the most interesting of love-tales. Go to bed and dream of your letter."

"I quite forgot to say that Geoffry is not rich," Esty thought, as she lay in bed that night, with a flood of moonlight streaming over her white draperies and virginal face; "but of course that will make no difference."

The next morning she sang as she ran down-stairs to the breakfast-room, and sang still louder as she stood on the front door-steps waiting for the letters. The fresh, sweet air of the morning and the glitter on flower and leaf seemed to harmonise pleasantly with the hope in her heart. She plucked off a bit of scarlet geranium that grew in the vase on the steps, and placed it in her belt.

"Surely he must be coming now," she said.

But only the cattle passed through the morning mist that hung over the meadow path by which the postman was expected; and Esty had to return to the house, for the breakfast bell rang, and she knew her aunt and the servants were assembled for prayers.

When the prayers were concluded she looked eagerly over the breakfast-table to see if the expected letter was there. One glance sufficed to prove her disappointment. There were several letters for the countess, but none for Miss Lisle; Esty sat with a tightening over her heart striving to swallow her breakfast as unconcernedly as possible, and looking very straight at an elm-branch that waved before the opposite window.

"At my age and with my property one only gets begging-letters," the countess said, with a cursory glance at her own packet. "Thousands of destitute orphans recommend themselves to my care ; clergymen seem to propagate large families for the express purpose of throwing them on my hands; while there are churches and asylums unlimited that threaten to fall down or collapse entirely unless supported by my charity. How fortunate you are, Esty, only to expect one letter, and that ——"

Lady Renshawe paused suddenly, for Esty's empty hands and pained face told the story of her disappointment, and her aunt felt grieved that she had made so untoward a remark.

" I wonder if it is accident, or whether he is like all the rest of them," the countess muttered. She said, aloud—

" I daresay there has been some delay in the post with your letter, Esty. Meanwhile, read one of mine."

Lady Renshawe tossed over a little cream-coloured note, the contents of which were more interesting to Esty than her aunt was aware of.

Miss Lisle flushed when she read the signature to this note, "Sophia Herbert." So this was Geoffry's female friend,—the original of that bold, massive head and dark-brown eyes. She was coming down to Castle Herbert, and she hoped that she might be allowed to renew an acquaintance which she and her husband had so much valued in bygone days.

" Did you know her, aunt ? " Esty asked, gloomily.

She had been expecting to grasp a rose all the morning, and lo ! her hand seemed filled with nettles. Something that was neither jealousy nor suspicion, but a vague compound of both, passed over her heart when she found that this "friend" of Geoffry's was coming into her neighbourhood.

" What does she want with us? why does she come here ? " she thought. Then she reproached herself for the doubt. " May he not have firm friends in women as well as men ? " But her mind recurred again to the brown eyes and sensual mouth, and she sighed involuntarily.

" I knew her very slightly," the countess said, in answer to Esty's first query. " Him I knew for many years before his marriage. A kind, good, true man is George Herbert. He brought his wife to call on me on the occasion of their first visit to Castle Herbert, and since then I have not seen her."

"What was she like? Did you admire her?" Esty asked eagerly.

"Hum! I don't know. She was handsome, certainly, but not attractive to any old woman who likes to see fresh, young, spring-like faces. This woman might have sat for a representation of autumn, she was such a brown, full-bloom sort of beauty. I don't know what her object is in renewing her acquaintance with me. There are rumours of a dissolution of parliament. Perhaps George Herbert feels uncertain about his seat, and wishes to secure my interest with my tenantry on his behalf."

"And, perhaps," Esty whispered to herself, "it is in some way connected with Geoffry."

The countess guessed the purport of Esty's murmur.

"I see we are ascribing different motives to the same action," she said. "The difference in our years is so great that this is not to be wondered at. Fancy two travellers arguing from different points of a hill, one tottering on the summit, the other looking upward from the base. If their voices could reach one another what a diversity of opinion would be expressed, the former breathing of cold and caution, the latter extolling the warmth that seems to shine on the far-off peaks! *You* fancy that this little attention of Mrs. Herbert's is connected in some way with Captain Adair. It is a part of love's mania to believe that every one else is in some way touched with the same disease. I am convinced that prudence lies at the origin of this little note. What a goose you are, Esty! What can Captain Adair know of Mrs. Herbert?"

Esty was silent. She was ashamed that her uneasiness should have been detected; and the countess, when she sent a gracious answer to Mrs. Herbert, was quite unconscious that Geoffry was even acquainted with the "full-bloom beauty" whom she promised to welcome to Lynncourt whenever the latter would honour her with a visit.

The rest of that day lagged very wearily to Esty. She was glad when the rooks began to caw good-night in the elms, and the sun sank behind the black gloom of the firs.

"So many more hours to post-time," she thought; by the time night came, hope was fresh again in her mind.

"To morrow! I shall hear to-morrow," she said, as she heard a distant clock tolling away the hours; but when the morrow came, her face was even sadder than before, and helpless anger filled her heart as it rebelled against the weight of her disappointment.

"He promised he would write or come. Why does he not write? but, perhaps, he will come yet."

But although she watched the park-gates until her eyes ached almost as her heart, she never could discern any form more interesting than that of some working man slouching home at the end of the day's labour, or the village children, who were permitted to pass through the park on their way to school, and who made Esty's heart throb many a time in vain as she heard the click of the distant gate when occupied in reading to her grand-aunt. Day succeeded day; autumn faded away into winter's bleak winds and dark skies, and yet Esty neither heard from nor saw her lover. Colonel Lisle had read to her from a newspaper that the ship had sailed in which Captain Adair and his regiment had embarked. And Esty was left to solve by herself the miserable riddle that haunted her night and day. "Why did he not write? had he ceased to love her?" The countess, who had been watching with secret concern the unhappy look in the young face that was so dear to her, at last thought it "her duty to speak."

"You have not heard from him, child?"

"No."

Such a piteous "No" it was, that the countess was unable to speak for a few moments. When she did raise her voice again, it sounded older and more trembling than ever.

"Then he is a scound——!"

"Hush, aunt, I won't have him spoken against!" Esty cried, in a sharp tone. So the countess finished her anathema under her breath.

"Have you told your parents, or Christine?"

"Must I?" the girl faltered. "I had not yet, you know,

because he said he would write to them himself, and that would have been so much nĭcer. I had told Christy, just a little bit before, when I was so happy, and now it seems so hard, oh so hard!" and she bit her lips nearly through in her effort to keep down the sob that was rising in her throat

"They ought to be told," the countess said; then, seeing how Esty shrank from the idea of laying bare her unhealed wound, she added, "but, if you like, my dear, I will tell them all myself, and arrange that you shall not be troubled by having the subject mentioned to you again—will that do?"

Esty kissed her aunt tenderly. "You are very kind," she murmured; and then she ran away to her room, and sobbed as though one dear to her were dead.

"Oh, Geoffry, Geoffry! you cannot mean it! Surely you did love me; and if you *did*, how can you have changed in so short a time? It is so hard to understand," she moaned; when she heard the carriage wheels drawing up to the front door, she sobbed afresh, for she knew that the countess was departing on her mission to Gardenhurst.

"I should have been so proud to have told mamma, had it been otherwise; and now they will think hard things of him, and call him what aunt did."

Struck by a sudden thought, she jumped up and ran down-stairs, all tear-smeared as she was, just in time to put her head in at the carriage-window ere the countess gave the order to depart.

"Auntie!"

"Yes, child."

"Don't let them judge him too harshly, he may come back, you know!"

The countess shook her head.

"If a woman values her peace of mind, she should let her first doubt be her last," she said, sadly; "however, I will do my best."

As the carriage rolled away, Esty gave one more wistful glance at those park-gates through which she had so long and vainly expected the advent of some token from her absent lover. A man on a horse was advancing towards the house, and for a moment her heart beat wildly with a vague hope, as she walked down the path to meet him, but

15

the horseman proved to be a servant in livery, who brought a note for Lady Renshawe, directed in a hand-writing Esty had learnt to recognise as Mrs. Herbert's.

"I wonder if *she* has heard anything of him," Esty thought. When the countess, on her return, informed her niece that an invitation had been received at Gardenhurst for Colonel and Mrs. Lisle to dine at Castle Herbert, and that a similar invitation was given to "Lady Renshawe and Miss Lisle" in the note the servant had brought over that day, the elder lady was astonished to find that her niece's face expressed a faint gleam of satisfaction.

"You don't mean to say you would like to go?" the countess said.

"Yes, aunt, I think I should."

"Then, my dear, you shall go with your father, and I will get you down a new dress for the occasion."

"Oh, thank you, very, very much," the girl said, gratefully; and the countess looked pleased, and congratulated herself on having so rapidly encouraged her niece's wish.

"Do her all the good in the world—give her an opportunity, perhaps, of seeing some fresh face, that makes the old love seem still farther off than he is. I would do anything to see her look her own bright self again for half-an-hour!"

So the countess wrote one note to Colonel Lisle, announcing her wish that Esty should accompany her father to Castle Herbert (Mrs. Lisle had declined going on the plea of ill health), another to Mrs. Herbert to announce her acceptance, in her niece's behalf, of their kind invitation, and a third to Madame E——, requesting her to send down from London a dressmaker to measure Miss Lisle for an evening dress.

"White silk and tulle, lilies of the valley and pearls—that will do," the countess said, musingly, as she sealed up the last of these communications. "That wicked young poet with the Welsh name talks about 'one nail' driving out 'another;' if Esty finds a new nail at the Herbert's, I only hope the old one will feel every tap of his successor through the head. I hear there is a large party staying at the Herberts'."

Meantime Esty was seated at her bed-room window, her

eyes looking wistfully down over the leaf-strewn path. " If I could but see you for five minutes," she thought, " even though it were to hear you say that all the past is as nothing to you, and that you did not really love me ; but to sit here through these sickening hours, in ignorance of what it is that is dividing us—this is what is so hard to bear. It is as though you were shut up in a dungeon near me, and you kept silence so that I did not know whether you were alive or dead."

The evening arrived on which the Lisles had been invited to dine at Castle Herbert, and Mrs. Herbert sat before the looking-glass, smiling a little smile of pleasure at the beauty reflected in the glass opposite to her.

She had paid more than ordinary attention to her toilette to-day. Not for worlds would she have appeared but at her beauty's height on this night, when she was to meet her rival. A red rose peeped out from the folds of her bronze-coloured hair; a slight touch of rouge heightened the rich light in her eyes, and diamonds trembled brilliantly at every movement of her head and throat.

Mrs. Herbert scorned the notion of not adorning herself with jewels when she played the part of hostess. Diamonds became her, and she rarely allowed etiquette to interfere with the most favourable display of her personal charms.

There was still an hour to elapse before her guests for the evening would arrive ; Mrs. Herbert put on a cashmere dress, and dismissed her maid, bidding the latter to return in half-an-hour, in time to put the finishing touches to her mistress's toilette.

The maid had barely quitted the room when Sophy's attention was attracted by the sounds of footsteps outside the window. She put her head out, and her gaze fell on the figure of Mr. Cadogan, who was walking up and down the gravel path, cigar in mouth, and seemingly absorbed in the perusal of a newspaper.

" ' Dark faces pale against the rosy flame,' "

quoted Mrs. Herbert, dropping a rose-bud at his feet as he passed under the window : " What a mild-eyed, melancholy lotus-eater you look, Mr. Cadogan."

15—2

He glanced up quickly at the sound of her voice, his face no longer deserving the epithet of pale, for that rare pink tinge rose to his cheeks as he looked at the beautiful head leaning out above him, with bright lights striking across the rippled hair and over the white breadth of bust, somewhat liberally displayed between the uneven folds of her wrapper.

"Come down," he said, in a low voice. "I want to speak to you."

Mrs. Herbert nodded her head. "In the boudoir," she said; and then she walked swiftly from the window, and entered her husband's dressing-room.

George Herbert was seated in an easy chair, by a comfortable cosy fire, his head thrown back, and his eyes closed in slumber. His wife looked at him for a few minutes, to assure herself that he really slept, and then she gently placed a newspaper by his side.

"He will never be able to resist the *Times*, if he does awake before I return," she argued, as she left the room, and ran quickly down the little flight of stairs that led to her boudoir.

It was a pleasant little room at all times, but never did the chamber Sophy reserved for her own especial use appear to so great an advantage as in dusky twilight hours like these. Dead leaves might flutter past the window-pane, winds might mutter in the elm branches, and rain-drops thicken on the leaves, but the outside desolation only enhanced the charm of this sleepy-cosy little Paradise within. There were easy chairs that would have tempted the most wakeful anchorite to slumber; there was a marble statuette of Love, with his finger to his lips, turning an exquisitely dimpled chin away from the fire, as though he shrank from the genial light that played on his polished neck and close-curled head. Highly-finished French photographs were scattered over the room, picture-frames gleamed from the dimness of the walls, and sweet scents came from a stand of hot-house plants that stood in a recess by the window.

"I like this room," Mr. Cadogan was saying, half aloud, when Sophy entered the door. On seeing her he got up, and went forward, eagerly, to meet her. "Shut the door," he said, imperiously. "You must," he added, seeing that she hesitated. "I particularly wish to speak to you without interruption."

She closed the door, and walked slowly across the room, apparently unconscious of the ardent look with which he followed her every movement; but, in reality, not a single symptom of his state of mind escaped her. She sat down on a low cushion by the fire, and, taking up a sandal-wood fan, fluttered its pleasant odours backwards and forwards before her face, while she quickly revolved her position in her mind :

"The game is nearly played out," she thought. "The brute will fondle his chain no longer, and in the acme of his passion will find strength to snap it."

She decided, if possible, to avoid perceiving the climax, which she felt was at hand. Many a time she had diverted a restive horse from battling with her by affecting unconsciousness of its design. Mr. Cadogan was showing "temper," but by bowing her head the storm might pass away over her, and spend its rage in air. While she meditated in what manner to speak to him, he was standing near her, his arm resting on the mantelpiece—his impassioned eyes drinking in the full measure of her beauty.

"What is it you wish to say ?" she began, in a soft voice. "It is getting late, and Herbert will expect me back to finish dressing."

"D—— Herbert !"

"You can d—— Herbert as much as you like in solitude, and thus avoid offending the good taste of his wife. Let me go now; I will return later."

Be it observed that when a woman pleads to be "let go" from the society of a man, the very plea proves that she has lost the right of enforcing it; so it may be conjectured that Sophy's intimacy with Mr. Cadogan had made considerable progress since that hour when he stole a kiss off her shoulder, and she forgot to rebuke him for it.

Her wounded vanity had been consoled by his adoration; but now that a tone of menace was mixed with his passion, she rebelled inwardly against her self-inflicted bonds, and almost loathed the gaoler whom she herself had set to watch at her heart's door; but if her disgust at this man was

great, her love for another was greater; and, when her
jealous fancy pictured Esty and Geoffry Adair as being
re-united, she vowed that she would deem no self-sacrifice
too great that would tend to separate them. She had risen
to go as she uttered that last speech, but he seized her wrist,
and forced her back to her seat.

"No!" he said, in a determined tone; "you have played
with me long enough; it is time to be serious."

"What do you mean?" she faltered; but the slight tinge
of alarm in her tone was affected to gain time. In all
matters, save where her own especial madness was concerned, her self-possession never deserted her.

"What do I mean?" he said, bitterly. "I mean that you
have made a plaything of my love. You have made me
mad about you—so mad that in your presence I have no
control over my eyes, lips, or heart. My eyes bless you,
but my lips curse you; my heart is torn in two between
anger and adoration. I know that I am as nothing to you in
comparison. I pray all day for a look of love in your eyes,
and I see nothing but indifference. In my fondness I try
to think that it is caution that represses the sigh I crave
for; but reason tells me that real love would peep from out
the thickest veil that caution ever swathed it in. I seek
your hand when you are near, and your fingers never know
that mine close on them. I detect your voice among a
dozen others, and you fail to hear me even when I address
you. Don't imagine, Mrs. Herbert, that because I love, I
am utterly blind! My very passion sharpens my perceptions.
By all that I feel I know what you lack. I am a slave
where I had hoped to be master; but the most faithful of
slaves would throw down the implements of labour if he
knew there was to be no termination to—no appreciation of
—his life-spent toil. I will leave you, Sophy, since you
cannot love me. I will go to-morrow, and you shall never
see me again to be the trouble of my days, the torment of
my nights."

His face was set in such a sharp look of pain that Sophy
felt almost penitent as she looked at him.

"Must you go?" she said, softly, inclining her head a
little nearer to the hand that hung over the back of her
chair.

He took up a tress of her hair that had fallen loosened from the burnished mass behind her ear.

He stroked it gently, and the contact lent fresh agitation to his manner; he bent his head down and passed the lock before his lips.

" Oh ! " he whispered, more to himself than her.   " If I could but win her love ! "

She turned round and looked earnestly at him, and he returned the glance with such a world of passionate entreaty shining in his eyes that her own fell involuntarily.

" What would you do to gain it ? " she murmured.

He knelt by her side and put his arm round her waist.

"I would give up the love of father, or mother, or child, to gain yours ; I would sacrifice wealth, name, and position ; I would consent to be a leper, loathed and loathsome for the rest of my life, if, while I was yet sound, I had been blessed one short month with your love.   Oh, Sophy," he added, his voice dying away in a sob, "don't ask me what I would do ; rather tell me what there is I would *not* do to gain that for which I thirst as men withered by drought pant to hear the bubble of water.   Oh, Sophy, my love, my love ! I die for you.   I am starved for the want of you ! "

Mrs. Herbert looked at him with wonder.   She had not thought he could have expressed his love in such eloquent fashion ; she did not put much faith in his offers of self-sacrifice, she took a tolerably correct estimate of them when she judged them to proceed from the excitement rather than the solidity of his affection.

" It is now or never," she thought.   " To-night he will do all I ask—to-morrow the chance will have passed away ;" yet she hesitated, for hardened as she was, it was difficult to her to say that which was in her mind.

" What could I do for you ? " he murmured, his lips still caressing the detached tress of hair ; "how could I serve you ? "

Something in her face had awakened a hope in his mind, and he looked wistfully at her while he awaited her answer.

It came at last, although with evident reluctance.   She had been less than human if such a proposition could have come trippingly from her tongue.

"Would you," she said, looking at him askance; "do anything to please me?"

"If you loved me—yes!"

"Would you marry another woman?"

Cadogan opened his long eyes very wide.

"Marry another woman!" he repeated, slowly. "What can you mean?"

"I mean what I say; if you love me really—if you would be content to be loathsome and despised for my sake, surely you could make the lesser sacrifice of marrying a young and pretty woman."

"But I do not see how! Are you in earnest, Sophy?"

"So much in earnest, Alfred, that I would bless you for the rest of your days—I would love the sound of your name if you would do me this service. Listen to me, it is not so impossible as you might imagine; there is a girl coming here to-night."

"*The* girl?"

"Yes; she is young and attractive, well-born, and rich in prospect."

"Prospect!" Mr. Cadogan repeated, in a meditative voice.

"It is Miss Lisle, the sister of that Gerald Lisle who owes you ——"

"£4000 10*s.* 6½*d.*," Alfred said promptly; the tremulous langour of his tone quite merged in the quick business-like accents with which he recalled the extent of Gerald's obligation to him.

Mrs. Herbert smiled. "I wonder which passion is strongest in his mind," she thought; "avarice, or that which he dignifies by the name of love."

Then walking to the door, she listened for a few moments to be certain there was no voice calling her amongst the murmurs the wind was making round the house; she could hear the patter of her children's feet overhead, and remembered that it was nearly time for her to go and give them her good-night kiss.

"I have yet ten minutes or so," she said, consulting her watch, and she returned to her place by Alfred Cadogan's side.

I need not enter into the details of their conversation; it is sufficient to say that this woman, whose character stood so fair before the world and whose heart before God was so black, added yet a deeper stain to her soul that night, for she used the loveliness He had given her to persuade Alfred Cadogan to grievously wrong an innocent girl, pledging herself at the same time to do her good-hearted husband a still deeper injury, since her own rare beauty was the devil's bait by which her accomplice was to be lured into fulfilling her designs.

Mr. Cadogan perfectly comprehended the motive of her desire that he should marry Miss Lisle; he felt rather than knew that this woman was making a sacrifice of herself to him because of her love of another man, and in his heart he almost hated her for the concession thus made.

"She will do anything rather than let my milk-faced brother come near the woman she is anxious I should marry," was his bitter reflection. But it consoled him to think of the anguish that brother would feel if Alfred succeeded in this scheme, and still greater was his satisfaction when he meditated on the noble estate to which Miss Lisle would probably succeed on the demise of her grand-aunt.

He took care, however, not to acquaint Sophy how much his own plans had coincided with her wishes; she knew of the money lent to Gerald Lisle, but she did not know that Lynncourt was not entailed, and that Mr. Cadogan would never have perilled so large a loan to Gerald had he not some ulterior object in view.

Mrs. Herbert, shrewd and subtle as she was, was outwitted, since she was furthering Alfred's own designs when she proposed to make him acquainted with Esty Lisle, and the supplementary temptation she offered him was in reality unnecessary for the accomplishment of her scheme, at least, in so far as he was concerned. He did not tell her of all this; he was a man who, if his tradesman had accidentally underrated a charge, would have taken instantaneous advantage of the omission. It was not likely that he should throw away the additional boon Sophy was disposed to grant him. He sighed and looked miserable; he kissed her hand passionately, as if tempted beyond control by the prospect opened out to him of winning her love, or rather, of winning the semblance of it; and then he sighed again as though he found it impossible to make the self-sacrifice she advocated, even with such a prize in view.

Woman-like, she grew more eager as he appeared to waver. It is an attribute of her sex to be tenacious of purpose, and the tenacity grows in strength with every fresh instance of opposition. Before their interview was closed Mrs. Herbert was pleading earnestly for that which she had found it so difficult to propose half an hour previously.

Were this an age of miracles, surely the innocent lips of her children that night would recoil before the poison that had just polluted her own; as it was, she embraced them calmly, and after finishing her toilette, descended the stairs arm in arm with her husband, and with him entered the drawing-room to welcome her guests.

The room was tenanted by visitors who were staying at the house, and while Mrs. Herbert waits the arrival of the rest of her party we will briefly describe the group already collected round her. The most noticeable in person is Colonel Jasper Macpherson—notorious alike for gallantry and gallantries; foremost in the battle-field, and first in the boudoir, his success in both has been unequivocal. While other stars arise and set in the glory of London seasons his has been a constant shining luminary; albeit, he one day gave a severe shock to his worshippers by unwittingly permitting a lady to marry him; why he did it was an enigma. The clubs could not solve it; at Poodles and at Noodles there were oracular shakes of the head over this episode in Colonel Macpherson's life; and henceforward he was always spoken of as " Poor Jas." His lady admirers were at first incredulous, then frantic, and finally, despairing; but as years went on, and Mrs. Macpherson proved too well-bred to obtrude her claims to her husband's attentions, they agreed to consider Jasper's marriage in the light of one of his habitual acts of gallantry—a thing to be passed over in silence and not to be regarded in any way as an obstacle to fresh flirtations.

He is bending down now to speak to his hostess, and his hair shines like a nimbus round his head; he is celebrated for the beauty of his hair and beard, which are of an extraordinary hue, resembling the effect of gold sunlight shining on snow. He is brave, courteous, and kind, but there is one defect in his character which can scarcely contribute to his happiness, namely, his deep-rooted incredulity in the existence of woman's virtue. If he were reasoned with on the subject by some enthusiastic youth, whose chivalry was not yet choked up by the ill weeds that grow in the soil of capitals, he would laugh and gently stroke his silvery mustache, as he said : " I daresay you are right, my dear boy, but the sex has always been kind to me, and why should I bother myself by thinking of hypothetical resistance which I never encountered ? "

Close behind Colonel Macpherson is the graceful figure and bent head of Sir Charlton Desmond : his manners are fascinating in the extreme, their apparent simplicity being the very perfection of art ; and he looks better in the saddle, and rides straighter to hounds, than any other officer in her Majesty's army. He has an illusion that he is romantic ; if he were not a courtier, a man of the world who appreciates thoroughly all the world's luxuries, he fancies he would like to be a Spanish scaler of balconies, serenading under his mistress's window, or engaging in impromptu affrays for the love of a pair of black eyes ; and this is the impression he gives those young ladies who delight to listen to his chivalrous aspirations.

Practically, nothing would induce him to relinquish his ride in the row, his tailor in Bond Street, his daily papers, and his well-arranged dinners. Theoretically, he is a lover of deserted prairies ; of angry seas ; of Italian fastnesses, where the brigands play bo-peep behind the vines, and pontifical gendarmes fraternise with *vi et armis* inheritors of the traveller's watch and chain ; for the rest, he is generous-hearted, manly, and brave, and although many envy him his indefinable charm of manner, few can successfully imitate it.

He is bending his head now to address a young lady who sits on a sofa near him ; she is an X——shire belle, her name, Amelia Dayrell, and her exceeding beauty has inspired Sir Charlton with a desire to ingratiate himself with her. The girl, for all her loveliness, has an ill-tempered expression of face ; report says, that she is "a character," and if a "character" implies leading a cat-and-dog life with her parents, and heaping unlimited oppression on the little heads of her brothers and sisters, she certainly justifies the epithet. Nature has given all the elements of refinement in those star-like eyes, those delicate features, and that well shaped head —it is an exquisite shell, but it is void of the soul that should have shone through such a surface. The mouth is marred by a petulant twitch, and the eyes reflect nothing but sullen dullness.

"Do you not envy Mr. Moens?" Sir Charlton asked as he bent tenderly over his fair companion.

"What?"

"Do you not envy the al-fresco sort of life Moens passed with the brigands?" he repeated.

"They seemed to have been much troubled by fleas," the girl said, shortly, and Sir Charlton turned away with a sigh. He could worship beauty, but he could not tolerate vulgarity; and he transferred his attentions to a young lady whose fat round face and snub nose did not prevent her from possessing far more elevated sentiments than she of the big eyes and perfect features.

Mrs. Herbert's other guests were now arriving in quick succession, and she looked eagerly towards the door at each fresh announcement. Mr. Cadogan also waited with some anxiety to hear the name of Lisle.

"I hope she will be good-looking," he murmured to Sophy. "I do so hate an ugly woman."

The words had barely left his lips when he noticed that Mrs. Herbert's cheeks turned pale under the roseate tinge that lay so delicately on them, and that she made a sudden start forward, and then as suddenly checked herself. Her ears had been quicker than his to hear the name of the woman she longed and yet loathed to see.

"Colonel and Miss Lisle," was being echoed by the servants from staircase to ante-chamber, and when Alfred removed his eyes from Mrs. Herbert, the last announcement of their names was sounding at the opposite door.

For a moment Sophy felt blinded by the rage that took possession of her. The consciousness that the woman Geoffry so much loved was near her, seemed to sting her heart with venom.

She prayed that she might find some deficiency of person or manner to prove the folly of his adoration, and then she

looked up, and her eyes were scorched by the fairness of the
face she saw before her. Miss Lisle was never more Miss
Lisle, and less " Esty," than she was at this moment, as she
came down the room on her father's arm, in a "shimmer of
satin and gleam of pearls," her graceful, high-bred looking
head unadorned, except by one wax-like hothouse flower,
that was fastened by a gold hair-pin in the twisted coils of
her hair. "Every inch a Lisle," the Colonel had said
proudly, when he beheld his daughter dressed that night,
for the first time, in a manner befitting her rank. And
"Every inch a lady," Sir Charlton whispered to Colonel
Macpherson, as he noted the delicate arch of the satin-shod
feet that peeped out from under those voluminous tulle
draperies, and the turn of the little hand that carried Esty's
bouquet of flowers, white, like her dress. "Who is she?
Oh, a Lisle; grand-daughter of the old countess at Lynncourt.
Blood shows in the hands and feet, eh, Jasper?"

Colonel Macpherson shrugged his shoulders indifferently.
"Not my style," he said, and he turned to Miss Dayrell,
who was looking at Esty with all her eyes.

"What do *you* think of the new arrival, eh, Miss
Dayrell?"

" Madame Elise," said Miss Dayrell, laconically; and the
colonel was mystified for a moment, until, following Miss
Dayrell's glance, he perceived that it rested, not on Miss
Lisle, but on Miss Lisle's skirts; and then he dimly conjectured that Madame Elise must in some way be connected
with those sheeny folds of satin, puckered so artistically
under the weight of the Lynncourt pearls.

" You must wear the duchess's pearls," the countess had
said, when she superintended Esty's toilette; "maybe it
will purify them a bit to rest on your neck and shoulders."

And so the fair young breast was circled round by jewels
that had, nearly two hundred years ago, been dangled in the
fingers of his most sacred and most lascivious majesty, King
Charles the Second.

The pearls and the white draperies harmonised well
with the pure colouring of the young girl's white neck and
cheeks,

" Rose-tinted, like the inside of a shell."

The sorrow that had clouded her face for so many days past could not take away the youthful lines that made up the grace of her features.

"There's nothing like youth, after all; our fair hostess can never 'make up' into that appearance," thought Sir Charlton, and he determined to take the first opportunity of being introduced to the new comer.

"Allow me to present my daughter, to whom you have so kindly given this opportunity of making your acquaintance," said Colonel Lisle, bowing to his hostess.

Mrs. Herbert held out the tips of her fingers, and murmured something about "being very happy," although, if she had seen an asp settling that moment on Esty's breast, she would not have raised her hand to brush the worm away.

Could she have spoken her thoughts she would have said, " I hate you for being loved by my lover ; I hate you for being pretty; for having small hands and feet; for your soft voice and long eye-lashes ; and I should like to scatter your white dress into shreds, and pull your hair down, and tear it up by the roots."

Had the two been alone on a desert island, Sophy would undoubtedly have expressed these sentiments ; but being in society where savage instincts are subdued by *convenance*, she merely wreathed her lips into a false smile, saying, " I did not know that you had a daughter so old as this ; really, Miss Lisle is quite 'grown up.'" The tone was patronising, and Esty felt the "putting down" it was meant to convey; her young blood fired up, and she answered for her father in a voice to the full as nonchalant as that of her rival.

"It is not unpleasant to have many years of youth still to look forward to," she said, smiling.

Her tone was so gentle that none but a woman (or a man as shrewd as a woman) would have appreciated the sting of her remark ; the sting lay in those wrinkles that had begun to mar the smoothness of Sophy's forehead. Alfred Cadogan, who was standing near, caught a side glance of one of these, as Mrs. Herbert turned her profile to the light, and he laughed a low, amused laugh, when he heard Esty's apparently artless retort.

"What creatures women are " he thought, "they take to

worrying each other as naturally as well-bred terriers gripe rats, only that rats are less venomous and dogs less savage than these gentle-looking darlings."

"She is very lovely, certainly," he whispered to Mrs. Herbert, as Esty and her father retired into the general circle; he enjoyed the baleful glance with which Sophy answered his observation. Much as he loved her, and he loved her intensely after his own fashion, he rejoiced in her misery, guessing, as he did, what caused it. "Won't you introduce me?" he whispered.

Mrs. Herbert, with more abruptness than usually characterised her gentle manners, went through the formula of introduction, and requested Mr. Cadogan to take Miss Lisle down to dinner.

Dinner had already been announced, and in a few seconds Esty found herself seated between her companion and Sir Charlton Desmond. The latter was delighted with his position, and addressed Miss Lisle with that easy grace peculiar to him.

"I am an old friend of your father's, Miss Lisle," he said, blandly, "so I may be excused for claiming acquaintance with his daughter. I served under him when I was quite a lad; we were in Spain together. Ah! what days they were! Black eyes peeping from behind the lattices; bright swords flashing in dangerous juxtaposition with one's head; a constant flutter of handkerchiefs and whiz of bullets; a kiss and blow, you never knew which the hour might bring you; scanty rations and chestnut leaves for a feather bed: what a glorious life it was!" And Sir Charlton sighed, and seemed as if Esty's presence alone prevented his instant return to the land of olives.

Esty looked at him with interest; then, observing that he seemed plunged in meditation, she hesitated to speak, fearing lest she might be disturbing some cherished reminiscence of the past. Sir Charlton himself broke the silence.

"I don't like it at all," he said, shaking his head.

"Like what?" Esty asked, rather mystified.

"This dinner *à la Russe* system. A man doesn't marry a wife or buy a horse unless he can have a good look at either of the desired objects, and yet one is expected to insult a delicate palate by eating recklessly of dishes of the composition of which we are profoundly ignorant. I like to study my dinner, Miss Lisle, before I consume it. If it be turbot, I like to see his beautiful sheeny sides as he lies in state on his silver bier, white damask for his shroud, and parsley for his grave-flowers. If it be wildfowl, I equally prefer beholding the delicate morsel in its entire perfection to having it presented to me in a state of *disjecta membra*. The only dishes that are set before us are those which contain fruit—objects that one need have no hesitation in partaking of—that is to say, if they agree with you. A melon is a melon, and we have confidence in its internal structure, but it would require a necromancer to penetrate into the mysteries of a French dish concocted by an English cook."

Esty laughed. She had thought that Sir Charlton's fancy had strayed back in search of some of those eyes that haunted the dusky olive groves in Spain, and lo! he was deep in a sybaritic disquisition on eating. She looked up from her plate to make some trifling answer, when her eyes accidentally fell on an antique pin, which held together at the breast a delicate lace shawl Mrs. Herbert wore round her shoulders.

The gentleman who looked up to recognise on his butler's finger a ring which had once belonged to a murdered friend, could hardly have felt more sick at heart than Esty did at this moment. Surely it was the pin Geoffry had worn up to the very day he had left her. On it was a Medusa's head, beautifully cut; and the dull red snake that curled round the throat was broken at the tip of its tongue. There might be other pins similar in most respects to this one, but the blemish was peculiar, and the closer she looked, the more certain she was of the justice of her first suspicion.

"What does she do with it? When did she see him last?" she asked herself.

She sat with trouble in her heart for the rest of dinner, and felt glad when the signal came for the ladies to rise from table.

"She will do," Alfred said to himself, as he watched her disappear through the door, "She's too slight for my taste, but she's undeniably good-looking. I will send Lisle a reminder to-morrow morning."

When he met Miss Lisle again in the drawing-room, he told her of his name, which had escaped her when Mrs. Herbert introduced him, and of his connection with "her friend, Geoffry Adair." He had the mortification to find that the indifferent expression of her face gave way to one of earnest animation, as, with her eyes all sparkling, she questioned him for news of his brother.

"He had none or little to give," he said, "excepting that, from a letter Adair had written to Mrs. Herbert, she imagined he was becoming attached to some lady who had accompanied him out."

Mr. Cadogan was not altogether inhuman, and he turned his face away from Esty as he inflicted this little stab. Miss Lisle's pain gave him no pleasure. He did not love her, and so had no hate to bestow on her.

"She will soon be consoled," he said, with a twirl of his mustache, as he caught sight of his dark face reflected in an opposite mirror. "There can't be two such fools as Sophy in the world."

"Do you sing, Miss Lisle?" he asked presently.

Esty answered abruptly "Yes," and then turned her face again towards the gloom of the fir trees outside the window near to where they stood.

"Miss Lisle sings, does she?" said Sir Charlton Desmond, coming up to them. "Pray let us have some music, Mrs. Herbert. You sing divinely yourself, I know. Perhaps you will set a good example." He offered his arm to his hostess to conduct her to the piano, but she repulsed him gently.

"We must persuade Miss Lisle to honour us first," she said, looking straight into Esty's face.

She could read nothing there of the effect of the wound she had dealt her enemy. The girl's face was as cold and haughty, if not as insolent, as her own, and she answered with perfect composure that she should "be very happy."

"Shall you require anyone to play your accompaniment?" Mrs. Herbert asked shortly.

"No, thank you," Miss Lisle said; "I play my own." And she walked up to the instrument. "What shall I sing?" (turning to Sir Charlton.)

"Anything you prefer. I myself should choose some
16

old-fashioned melody more familiar to my ears than the wild anguish of the modern Italian school."

Esty paused for a moment, and then struck a few chords of the introduction to " Bid me discourse."

Sir Charlton looked delighted.

" Pray continue," he said. " If your singing is equal to your touch, I shall enjoy a rich musical treat."

In a few seconds the girl's voice had burst out in a rich volume of song, and the murmur of conversation in the room ceased like a storm subdued by an enchanter's wand. Rarely had such sweet thrilling notes filled Mrs. Herbert's drawing-room. The charm of the voice lay, not so much in the marvellous execution, which kept the ears of the audience in "a constant feeling of sweet surprise," nor in the bird-like trills she executed with such brilliancy in the upper scale, nor in the full melodiousness of her lower notes, as in the sympathetic thrill her tones excited in the breasts of her hearers. They held their breath as the last stroke warbled away into silence, and then Colonel Lisle had the pleasure of listening to such a deafening burst of applause as rarely greets the conclusion of an amateur's song.

Sir Charlton looked at Esty, his eyes glistening with pleasure.

" Your voice reminds me of some lines in Crashaw's conflict of the ' Nightingale and the Pipe,' " he said :—

> " ' Straightway she
> Carves out her dainty voice as readily
> Into a thousand sweet distinguished tones,
> And reckons up in soft divisions
> Quick volumes of wild note.' "

" The simile ends there, as I have not expired with my vocal effort," Esty answered, smiling. " Now I hope that Mrs. Herbert will favour us."

But Mrs. Herbert waived the subject of singing for the present. She never put herself in a position to appear less than other women. She was conscious that her tones after Esty's would have sounded husky and meagre. Hers was a voice pleasant enough to hear in the quiet gloom of a summer evening, when her eyes would gleam out from the dusk with an expression that doubled the charm of aught

she sung; but here, in a brilliant glare of light, and
with people's ears still haunted by those musical shakes on
the high A and B flat in which Esty had luxuriated, she felt
she would perform under a disadvantage.

" Perhaps Miss Dayrell would play something ? "

The sulky beauty rose from her chair, and sitting down
to the piano, played with immense rapidity a *Tarentelle*, the
gay liveliness of which formed a strong contrast to her stolid
expression of face.

" Very fine—very brilliantly played, indeed," Mrs. Herbert said at its conclusion.

" It's Kuhe's," Miss Dayrell muttered, with her usual
abruptness, and she returned to her seat, paying no heed to
the compliments which Mrs. Herbert showered on her.

Sophy, like many other fair tacticians, hoped by excessive
praise of " Lydia's air and feature," to throw a reflection on
her sister performer as being an "ugly creature "—that is, by
eulogy of Miss Dayrell's performance to lessen the merit of
Esty's.

Miss Lisle retired quietly into the background, meeting
all the advances that were made her with a quiet dignity
which surprised her father, who had not · expected that the
unruly, unkempt little girl of six years back would ever have
developed into anything like this.

" A very successful evening indeed, my dear," he said in a
gratified tone, as he and Esty returned home in the Lynncourt chariot. " I have had some most interesting conversation with Desmond—he and I served together under
Lord Fitzmore Seymour. Oh, what a charming fellow he
was ! Dear ! dear ! he's dead now ; so are most of the
gallant fellows who turned their young faces towards the
enemy's fire on the glorious 18th of June. It makes me feel
like the last withered leaf on the tree—likely to be shaken
off at any moment. And you have been looking very nice
indeed, Esty ; I had no idea you could sing so well. Desmond was quite charmed with you—he was really, now."

" I am very glad, papa," his daughter said gently ; and if
the colonel was a little surprised at her lack of enthusiasm,
he was quite contented with the delight Mrs. Lisle and
Christine expressed, when they heard of the great success
the party had been to their father and sister.

Colonel Lisle was set down at his own door, and then Esty went on alone to Lynncourt.

Relieved of the necessity of responding to her father's remarks, she leant her head against the side of the old-fashioned carriage window, and wept bitterly. As she passed the dark hedgerows through which the rain was pattering, she thought of the summer that was gone, when she had sauntered in those lanes, pulling at the tendrils of honeysuckle, and inhaling the warm scents that came over the clover fields.

" I shall never walk there again with him," she said pas· sionately. "He never loved me ; I was a new toy to him, just something to play with for an hour, and now he forgets that such a trifle existed. He is intimate with that dark woman, and she wears his token ; he has been looking love at some other since he left me, and I have been imagining that his heart ached in absence from me, as much as mine has done."

" Wake me up when you return," the countess had said; so Esty went straight to her aunt's room, and kissed tenderly the withered cheek that lay on the pillow before her.

The countess awoke with a start.

" I'm so glad you've come, Esty. I've had such dreadful dreams. I thought that Barbara Villiers came out of her picture and demanded her pearls, and said she would catch her death of cold without them. I told her that you had gone to the Herberts' with them, and she said she would go after you. I suggested it would be dirty walking, and she laughed; she shouldn't touch the ground, she said; and she went with a rustle of her indecent draperies, which seemed to wake me up : no doubt it was the movement of your dress that did so. How has it been with you, my dear? have you been happy?"

The countess lifted herself on her elbows, and looked anxiously into her niece's face.

" They tried to make me show my pain, aunt. That woman, that friend of Geoffry's, paraded signs of her intimacy with him, and then she watched to see if she could detect the wound in my face. All the evening my heart seemed dying within me ; but I would not show it. I talked and laughed and sang my best; I swore that her cruel eyes should not know pleasure in my pain. But oh, auntie! I don't think he will ever come back; they say he already loves another, and, oh me! I am so miserable!" She knelt down and hid her face in her aunt's pillow.

The withered hand of the countess stroked the bowed head by her side, and her old heart beat high with pity and resentment.

"You mustn't believe all you hear, child," she said with a faint attempt at consolation. "Lovers are so credulous they throw their whole hearts into their illusions, and they are equally unreasonable in their sudden disenchantments. How do you know that story about a new love is true?"

"Why didn't he write to me? Oh! why doesn't he write to me?" the girl cried, looking up with hungry eyes into the sympathising countenance before her.

And the countess was dumb, only stroking the brown head the faster.

CHAPTER XXV.

"NO TIME TO BE LOST."

"If I have erred, there was no joy in error,
  But pain, and insult, and unrest, and terror;
  I have not, as some do, bought penitence
With pleasure, and a dark yet sweet offence."
                                    SHELLEY.

MRS. HERBERT did not sleep well the night of her party; she closed her ears and eyes to all outward sounds and sights, but she was haunted by the slender form of her rival and cursed by the remembrance of those marvellous tones. When the morning dawned, she was still lying awake, staring at the streaks of light in the east, and as soon as these were expanded into broad daylight, she jumped out of bed and walked up to a large swing mirror and looked at herself. How she despised the luxuriant style of beauty which constituted her chief attraction!

"I should like to be slim, slender, and eighteen," she thought. "Ah me! why can't I be so as he would love me?"

She did not bestow much pity on the girl whom she had promised Geoffry she would befriend. A woman despised in her own love has rarely any soft place in her heart for a successful rival.

Mr. Herbert had a rough time of it that morning, when

his wife decided that her bust was too expansive, her arms too massive, for true loveliness. He was glad when the breakfast was over, and he could retire to his library, leaving Cadogan to bear the brunt of Sophy's stormy brow and laconic speeches.

" What progress did you make ? " she said shortly to Alfred, when they were left alone together.

" Hum ! pretty well, I think," that gentleman answered complacently. " I told her I should accompany you when you called at Lynncourt, and she seemed pleased. I shall write to Gerald Lisle to-day."

" I suppose you are in difficulties," Sophy said, significantly.

" Yes ; there is an inexorable creditor whose claims I cannot meet, and I am in immediate want of £4,000 5s. 6½d.," Alfred said gravely; " Lisle has paid no interest, so the sum has accumulated ; it will be very useful to me, if I *do* get paid."

" And if you do not ? "

" I would marry a Hottentot if it would please you."

Alfred said nothing of the fine estate which he hoped his future wife would inherit. Sophy, in common with the rest of the world, believed Lynncourt to be entailed on James Lisle, and Mr. Cadogan had no wish to undeceive her.

" It will lessen in her eyes the effort I make to win her," he thought.

So when he accompanied Mrs. Herbert to call on Lady Renshawe that afternoon, he looked so pensive and ill at ease that Sophy, in pity for the lover who sacrificed so much for love's sake, allowed him to press her hand rather more warmly than was consistent with strict propriety as they sat side by side in her barouche, covered up to the chin with fur rugs, their faces looking with an innocent, blank expression on the gaping rustics they passed on the road, and their ears happily oblivious of the remarks made by one of these sons of the soil to a fellow-labourer.

" That be Squire Herbert's wife, been't it a driving with the strange gentleman who stays oop at th' house ? "

" Ayes it be."

" Well, I'm glad my wife ain't got a carriage ! "

" Whoy, surely ? "

" 'Cos I shouldn't loike to see her a muddled up like that wi' another man."

Miss Lisle contrived at first to evade seeing her aunt's visitors that day, and they were received alone by the countess, who was sitting up in state, her most valuable lace mittens on her arms, and a royal flow of drapery at her feet.

"Her niece was out in the grounds," she said, and she looked pleased when Mr. Cadogan took advantage of a pause in the conversation to say he would go and seek Miss Lisle, suiting the action to the word by stepping through the window on to the lawn.

"He is handsome, though rather sly-looking," the countess thought; but on her making some observation concerning Alfred to Mrs. Herbert, the latter responded by such a warm eulogium on that gentleman, such an eloquent panegyric on his manifold virtues, that the countess felt herself stirred by a secret delight when she saw the young couple emerge together from one of the shrubbery walks.

She longed desperately to avenge her niece's wrong on that fair-faced, black-hearted man, who had made so bad a use of the hospitality proffered him for his dead mother's sake.

When Mr. Cadogan re-entered the room he was accompanied by Esty, who acknowledged Mrs. Herbert's presence with as much ease and composure as she had shown on the previous night.

"She does it well; the girl has pluck," Sophy thought, looking at her slender adversary with a sort of unwilling admiration. "I wonder how she will bear the last blow when it comes?"

Mrs. Herbert carried back with her to Castle Herbert a cordial invitation from the countess for herself and Mr. Herbert to dine at Lynncourt in the ensuing week.

"If Mr. Cadogan will accompany you," said Lady Renshawe, bowing to that gentleman with old-fashioned courtesy, "I shall be much honoured."

Sophy declined on her own and her husband's behalf. "Our house is so crowded with people, that it is impossible for us to leave them," she said; "but it will be a real charity if you will allow Cadogan to come to you now and then ; he gets so bored always seeing the same faces round my table, and he loves music so much, he will thoroughly appreciate Miss Lisle's singing."

" Pray come as often as you like," said the countess, in a cordial tone, turning to Alfred.

The latter murmured something about "not being slow to take advantage of such a tempting offer ; " and then the callers withdrew, and the countess and Esty resumed their usual occupations. ·

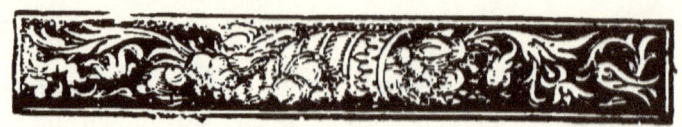

CHAPTER XXVI.

COMMENCING OPERATIONS.

"Who in want a hollow friend doth try,
Directly seasons him an enemy."
KING HENRY III.

"Creditors ! devils."
TITUS ANDRONICUS.

EANWHILE Gerald Lisle had been thrown into the utmost consternation by Cadogan's unexpected demand on him. "How am I ever to meet it—how tell my mother?" he asked himself in an agony. He was even ungrateful enough to curse Cadogan for having granted him the loan; but then what man ever does feel obliged to the friend who lends him money, and who exacts its return at a time when such a demand is as inconvenient to meet as was the embarrassment from which he relieved you?

"From frying-pan to fire," grumbled Gerald; "and the fire is a d——d deal worse than the fry. There's an air about Cadogan's note which in a tradesman would be impertinent; from him it's positively offensive."

Gerald was down at Gardenhurst at the time he received this communication, and it caused him to go about the house with a worried look in his eyes, and a nervous irritability of manner that made his mother's heart ache.

"Some fresh difficulty," she moaned to herself. "Are we never to know the comfort of easy circumstances?"

As yet she said nothing to Gerald on the subject; his manner did not invite confidence; but she sat in terror every time he opened his lips, not knowing how much misfortune his words might bring to her.

She had a painful keen-sightedness in such matters, and she could read unpaid bill on her son's face as clearly as a drunkard's wife detects the first flush of intoxication.

Mrs. Lisle had felt very sad for Esty when she heard from the countess of Captain Adair's behaviour; she entreated, however, that Colonel Lisle and the boys should not be made cognisant of what had passed.

"They are so hot-headed, and Egbert is at the same station with that man's regiment; pray let us have no further mischief to increase poor Esty's unhappiness."

So the secret rested between aunt and niece; and, with the exception of Mrs. Herbert and Mr. Cadogan, no one suspected the nature of the pain that had made Miss Lisle's face wear such a wistful expression for the last two months.

Winter was succeeded by spring, and still the Herberts lingered in X——shire. Mr. Cadogan came constantly to Castle Herbert, often prolonging his stay to a fortnight or three weeks, and generally contriving to spend at least half that period in Miss Lisle's society. He attended Esty in her walks, and listened at the piano when she sang; he brought her presents of new books, prints, and magazines, and paid her a thousand little attentions in so delicate and kindly a manner that Esty insensibly began to feel his society a pleasure and a relief.

The black thought in her heart weighed less heavily on her when she could converse with Cadogan on the subject of Geoffry's early days—that far-off time when he resembled the fair faced miniature that still hung in the breakfast-room.

Geoffry had never told her how little he liked his half-brother, and Alfred quickly ascertained and took advantage of Esty's ignorance on this point. He invented a great number of anecdotes connected with his and Geoffry's boyhood, which proved that they had lived together on terms of warm affection. Esty felt quite a love for the dark face before her when she heard how many and how dire were the blows his constant love for and defence of Geoffry had exposed it to in those bygone days.

Mrs. Herbert, to the great astonishment of her X——shire neighbours, did not even go to town this fine season. George Herbert went up for the session, but Sophy remained at the Castle with her children, and with occasional visitors to relieve the tedium of her solitude.

It need hardly be said that Sophy never fulfilled the trust Geoffry had reposed in her with regard to his letter to Lady Renshawe ; it had long since shrivelled away into ashes, and all the letters she herself had received from him since his departure shared the same fate. These last were filled with such tenderness for his absent love that Sophy felt her hate of her unconscious rival deepen at every fresh line she read. Nevertheless, she wrote encouraging answers to Geoffry, bidding him hope for the best, and to trust always to her friendship and Esty's affection. Latterly she had infused an air of constraint and doubt in her replies ; but still she would not directly avow that she suspected Esty's allegiance to be wavering. She feared such news might hasten his return to England, and she did not want him home yet awhile.

One morning Mrs. Herbert received a letter by the Indian mail which materially accelerated her plans.

In it Geoffry told her that he had obtained six months' leave, and was coming home as speedily as possible to plead his cause in person with Esty's parents. "I have come into a little more money by the death of a cousin of my father's," he wrote ; "I am positively a 'well-to-do' man, and now nothing need keep me from speaking out any longer." He also informed her that he had made the acquaintance of Egbert Lisle, who was in Peel's Naval Brigade at Cawnpore. "Lisle got badly wounded some time ago, and I rather think he will return home about the same time as I do. He is a noble fellow, and has covered himself with distinction. What a pleasure the return of us both will be to Esty !" The letter concluded with a request that Mrs. Herbert "would give the enclosed" to Miss Lisle.

"It will keep hope fresh in her heart till I come. My kindest regards to Herbert,

"P.S.—I thought the last message you sent me from Esty seemed rather cold. She should remember what kind of a punishment it would be to a starving man to receive a bit of bread no bigger than a pea, and how my soul yearns for every little token of her. A line with her name in it is dearer to me than folios from other people. So write always of her—not that you will be troubled to send me many more letters, as I hope to be home in October.—Yours, G. ADAIR."

"No time to be lost!" muttered Mrs. Herbert, as she dropped Geoffry's "enclosure" into the fire. "I will go over to Lynncourt to-day."

CHAPTER XXVII.

THE LAST STRAW.

> "Be sure
> You credit anything the light gives light to
> Before a man; rather believe the sea
> Weeps for the ruin'd merchant when he roars;
> Rather, the wind courts but the pregnant sails
> When the strong cordage cracks; rather the sun
> Comes but to kiss the fruit in wealthy autumn,
> When all falls blasted. If you needs must love
> (Forc'd by ill fate), take to your maiden bosoms
> Two dead-cold aspicks, and of them make lovers;
> They cannot flatter nor forswear; one kiss
> Makes a long peace for all!"
>
> MAID'S TRAGEDY.

MEANWHILE Mr. Cadogan had a long interview with Gerald Lisle, and decided that he could wait for his money a little while longer. When Esty next went home her brother's eyes followed her with a wistful expression in them which she could not comprehend. Before many weeks were over, she understood only too well the pathos of those entreaties that "did not speak," but "looked her in the face," until, like the hapless betrothed in the Scotch song, "her heart was like to break." "I would do anything for him but *that*," she thought, but ere long Gerald was at pains to explain to her that there was nothing else she could do. Her heart had never sickened so much for news of her absent lover as it did at this juncture. She prayed so earnestly for him to come back to her that she at last, from the very intensity of her entreaties, began to have a vague hope they might be answered.

"Only to have some kind of news of him. That would be better than nothing. This silence is so dreadful to bear."

It came at last—the intelligence of the name she craved to hear—but in such fashion that she would have given worlds to have been able to go back to the old uncertainty, the old sorrow, in which at times a thread of hope still shone silver-bright.

Mrs. Herbert accompanied Mr. Cadogan to Lynncourt the very day she received her last packet of Indian letters, and after conversing for some little time on indifferent subjects, she, as though by accident, introduced Captain Adair's name.

"You knew him, I think?" she said, addressing the countess.

The elder lady answered stiffly she had had that honour, and Esty looked out of the window to conceal the flush that rose to her cheeks, and toyed with a hot-house rose that stood in a flower-pot on the sill.

"Then you will be interested to hear that he is married."

"Married!" the countess said, and there was dead silence for a few moments. Alfred was the first to speak.

"You have torn your hand, Miss Lisle, with those thorns; pray let me extract them for you."

"Thank you," the girl said sweetly. "How do you know of Captain Adair's marriage?" she added, turning to Mrs. Herbert.

"From this paper;" and Sophy handed her a copy of the *Overland Mail.*

Sure enough there were some letters staring her in the face—letters horribly large and distorted that seemed to shape the name of Adair.

" *Captain G. Adair, to Frances, only daughter of the late J. Maxwell, Esq.*" Thus the announcement ran.

"Thank you," Miss Lisle said, returning the paper to Sophy with a steady hand. "I suppose there is no mistake?"

"Oh, no!" Mrs. Herbert replied, with a slight touch of insolence in her tone. "I should think not; why should there be? Young men generally marry when they go out to India: they find it dull, you know, Miss Lisle."

"True," assented Esty; and the carriage being announced she bowed out her visitors with the same quiet ease that had characterised her manner during the whole interview. The door had closed, and the sound of their wheels had died away in the distance before Esty turned her face to her aunt.

"Don't be afraid, darling," she cried, in a harsh, unnatural voice. "I can bear it. I shan't die; but I can never have faith in anything again. I have lost all—all. Pray God to soften my heart so that I may live to believe once more in his goodness!"

"How did you manage the newspaper?" Alfred asked, admiringly, of his coadjutor, as they drove home together.

"Very simply; I sent the announcement, through a friend in Calcutta some time ago, to the paper, with the proper fee for its entrance; it will be contradicted in the next number, but she won't see it. Meanwhile, it is your turn, Alfred; the Lisles are as poor as rats; the old lady is already prejudiced in your favour. You are a greater fool than I took you for if you can't follow up your advantages."

Alfred smiled. "Kiss me," he said: and Mrs. Herbert, glancing first out of one window and then another, to be sure there was no spectator in those lonely roads to witness her, kindly assented to his demand.

When Esty next went home, she found trouble and consternation in the faces dear to her.

Mrs. Lisle had been stricken down by a nervous fever, and Gerald watched by the sick bed in an agony of remorse and apprehension.

"It's the worry and anxiety that's knocked her down," he said. "Cadogan is so d——d importunate, and she knows I can't meet his claims. Oh, Esty, you might help us if you would!"

CHAPTER XXVIII.

THE POWER OF SYMPATHY.

"He chid the billows that their course delay'd
His heart that swifter sped than waves could flow;
The ship was laden with his hopes and fears;
Joy laughed in every breeze that fair did blow,
While adverse winds were filled with lovers' tears."

A. C. STEELE.

"E shall sight land to-morrow, you say?"
"Yes, Sir."
The seaman who had answered Captain Adair's interrogation whistled a low tune of content as he ran up the shrouds with even more than usual activity.

Great animation prevailed on board the Queen of the Isles. Faces that looked ill-favoured, thin, and weary, during their long captivity on the waters, became quite radiant with comeliness; peevish women forgot to murmur complaints as their hearts fluttered at the notion of the near approach of home, and the re-union of ties so long dissevered by absence—so long, indeed, that in some cases little nervous doubts clung to high-wrought anticipations; and one of the ladies, a withered woman of forty, who had left England a blooming bride twenty years before, candidly avowed that "the links had been so long broken, she should not in the least know where to hook on *her* chain again."

17

But these depressing forebodings only existed in exceptional cases; the majority of the ship's passengers were in a state of feverish happiness.

"I seem to smell flowers already," said one.

"I am quite sure I saw something white just then, which looked like a bit of cliff."

"Do tell me," pleaded another, "isn't that the shore?" and then there would come a rush of eager faces to the side of the deck, to catch a glimpse of that which had only loomed in the hopeful imagination of the speaker.

The hot plains, the vivid skies, the dark faces he had left behind him, faded very quickly from Captain Adair's mind; the past year seemed to be blotted from his memory. His thoughts flew back over that chasm to an evening which appeared to him but as yesterday. Once more he stood at the garden gate at Lynncourt, with the soft veil of the morning mist hanging like a silver shroud over the meadows; he could almost fancy he heard the gate move on its hinges, as Esty came through it, and he felt the clinging pressure of her arms round his neck, as she sobbed her farewell words on his breast.

"I will be true, Geoffry; come what may, I will be true to you."

"I know she has kept her word," he murmured. And he lifted up his head and turned a beaming face towards a light bank of clouds that lay in the west. "England is behind them," he thought,—"England and Esty;" and then he vented his restlessness by walking quickly up and down the deck.

"How the hours will lag to-night!" he said, half aloud.

A middle-aged, rough-looking man, who stood looking out at the side, with his hands thrust into the pockets of his pea-jacket, turned round at the exclamation.

"You'll be glad to get on shore again, Sir?" he said, interrogatively. "Maybe you've been away a long time from England?"

"Only a year," Captain Adair said, feeling rather ashamed of the short period of exile, "but it seemed a hundred," he ˡᵈᵉᵈ candidly. "And you?"

" 'I've been away these twelve years."

"ᵒ. ᵇˡᵃᵈ to come back?" Captain Adair

asked, looking absently at the gleam made by a porpoise's back, as it bobbed up between the clefts of a wave. He spoke more from courtesy than interest, for joy makes people selfish, and his ears were still troubled by the sound of that garden gate.

"Ay, Sir, truly I shall; I've sweated away twelve of the best years of my life in a shipping office at Calcutta, that I might earn enough to keep my wife and the babes from want; and I've worked double tides to get the chance of this one holiday. I couldn't have kept going all this weary time if it hadn't been for the hope of having one year in cool, shady England, with my wife at my side, and my children by my knee. Lord, Sir, I've lain in my hot, stifling bed at night, with those mosquitoes playing the devil's own delight round my curtains, until I've almost cried to think of the mulberry bough flapping against the window at home, and my wife, dear soul, resting her little head on her pillow, with nothing to torment her but a few harmless gnats, and, maybe, the thought that I was pining to death for her and the children."

"I suppose they were very young when you left them?" Geoffry said, kindly.

"A boy and a girl—one two, the other one year old. Oh, dear! they were fat-legged, toddling darlings then, with just a wisp of yellow hair on their round heads, and now they'll be too big to take on my knee, and the father that begot them will be like a stranger to them."

It was the speaker's turn to look absently into the waves, which he did, with a sigh and a smile, while Geoffry took advantage of the pause to take another hasty turn up the deck. Then he came down again to the spot where the steerage passenger was still standing.

"We shall see land to-morrow morning, they say," Geoffry observed, repeating the information the seaman had given him an hour before.

His companion turned round with a deep glow on his sunburnt face. "Yes, Sir," he said, "I heard so." Then with a gleam in his eyes which made his scarred, wrinkled visage look almost beautiful, he looked up at the sky: "I thank Him from my heart; I thank Him that He has brought me thus far towards them. Praise be to Him!"

"Amen," said Captain Adair, softly; and, bidding his companion good-night, he returned to his old place on deck.

"This is the last evening we shall spend together," said one of the passengers, an old Anglo-Indian officer, as they sat at dinner that afternoon. "Let us drink, first, the captain's health, and many thanks to him, for he's ——" The veteran paused for an appropriate epithet.

"A regular brick," suggested a youth from a distant corner. And amidst much laughter this sentiment was taken up and cordially endorsed by the company.

Many other toasts were drunk, champagne glasses clinked rapidly against one another, and stiffness and constraint melted away under the genial feeling of happiness that pervaded the whole company.

"We've had a fair voyage and prosperous weather," the captain said modestly, in answer to the compliments showered upon him. "No thanks are due to me; but don't forget, ladies and gentlemen, when you take your last night's rest in the ship's berths to-night, to render thanks where thanks are due. And now for our parting pledge: 'Here's to the Queen of the Isles, and those who are waiting for her at home.'"

Amidst uproarious cheers, waving of handkerchiefs, and general shaking of hands, the dinner came to an end, and Captain Adair, flushed and happy, ran up on deck to enjoy the calm of the coming night alone with his cigar.

The moon had risen, and all the line of ocean under her beams shimmered like liquid silver. The black hull, the spars, the cordage, and the tapering mast of the Queen of the Isles, threw long shadows over the waves, that trembled round her as she passed through the moonlight, her sails flapping idly in the soft peacefulness of the summer night. The waves parted gently before her queenly bow, and then fretted and bubbled at her wake as she swept on, leaving her trace in a long troubled line behind her.

Geoffry was aroused alike from his meditations and from his cigar by hearing the sound of low sobs coming from what seemed to be a diminutive bundle of clothes huddled up in the corner of a seat to his right. He walked up to the object in question, and found it to be a little girl known to him by the name of Norah Moore, an orphan, who was being conveyed to England in the charge of an ayah. The child, who was about eight years old, had not been a favourite with the passengers; her pale pinched face, as well as her depressed and apparently sullen manner, had militated against her claims to popularity. There were plenty of pink-cheeked, blue-eyed cherubs on board, whose mothers were present to appreciate the compliments paid them; but this pale, dark-eyed little girl had nobody— nobody, at least, but her ayah, Marian, of whom she was afraid, and a pet canary, on which she doated. It was the loss of her favourite which was causing the bitter sobs Geoffry heard as he approached her.

"What is it? Who is it?" he said at first; but when he got up to her he knelt at her side, and pulled the tear-stained face into the moonlight. "Why, dear, what is the matter? what has hurt you?" the young man asked, tenderly.

The child, melted alike by sorrow and his tone of sympathy, threw her little thin arms round his neck and sobbed still more.

"Do tell me what it is; I can't help you if you don't. Is it because your nurse has left you? Shall I go and find her?"

"No, no, *no!*"

"What is it, then? Stop, you will catch cold; let me wrap your shawl round you. Now I'll take you for a walk, and then you shall tell me all about it."

And, hoisting her on his shoulders, Geoffry carried his self-imposed charge rapidly up and down the deck, having a vague idea that all children were soothed from tears to sleep in that manner.

"Do you know we shall be in England to-morrow? Sha'n't you be glad to see the flowers and the trees again? Sha'n't you be glad to get home?" Captain Adair suggested presently.

"I haven't got a home," the little girl said, with fresh tears gathering in her dismal black eyes.

"What do you mean? I heard that you were to go to

your aunt, and of course she will love you and take care of you."

"But it won't be like home," the child answered, piteously. "Papa and mamma won't be there, and now I haven't even got Lulu to take with me."

"And who was Lulu?"

"My poor little canary. He would whistle all day, and sit on my finger; and he was always gay when everyone else was cross; and he'd say 'sweet' to me, and drink from my hand; and now he's dead, and his dear little feet are all twisted and stiff; his eyes are dull—and oh, I wish I were dead with him, I do!"

"Hush, hush!" Geoffry said, gently. "Where is he? Show him to me." Setting the child down, he followed her to the seat from whence he had taken her. There, under the bench, was the cage containing the dead bird, and Norah drew the latter forth from its now useless wicker prison with as much care and tenderness of touch as though her tiny friend were still able to ruffle his plumage on her friendly finger.

"Poor little fellow!" said Geoffry, kindly. "What killed him?"

"I do not know."

"Well, what can I do? Would you like to bury him?" The child's eyes brightened a little.

"Yes," she said; "she would like to bury him herself."

So Captain Adair went in search of an old cigar-box, which he brought back filled with cotton wool; and the hand which only a few months before was clenched tight on the hilt of a sabre doing good work at the head of the —— Horse, emulated the gentleness of the child's touch as it assisted her to inter Lulu in its impromptu coffin.

"There, now; let me fling over the cage too; it will only remind you of him."

Norah, with a sigh and a gulp, listened to the double splash in the water, and then wept again, but not so bitterly as before; for Geoffry had given her what all human beings yearn for, whether old or young—sympathy; and "he was really sorry," she thought, "not making believe." So she held up her face to her new friend with a half-choked "Thank you," and "Good-night," for a dusky face appeared behind her, and the ayah summoned her long-neglected charge to "come to bed."

Geoffry bent down and kissed the little pale face.

"I will see you again," he said, "and I will buy you another little bird, a bullfinch, for you won't care about another canary after Lulu."

The child nodded and whispered, "I will pray for you and Lulu to-night."

Her little figure disappeared, and Geoffry walked to the side to have a parting look at the moonlit sea before he "turned in " himself.

"Poor little soul!" he said, his thoughts reverting to his late *protégée.* "What a sad thing for her to be so alone in the world! 'Ocean, thou mighty monster,' accept the last end of the last cigar I shall smoke on you for many a day to come;" and tossing the calcined bit of tobacco overboard, Geoffry turned on his heel and went down to his berth, humming a verse of a rough sort of duet he had heard both soldiers and sailors singing in chorus when the Naval Brigade were on shore at Cawnpore:—

"Sailor (*Solo*).

"There are soldiers and sailors and lieutenants also,
     And there's captains and admirals, as we all very well do know,
     And they fill their insides at th' expense of poor men :
     May the d——l ram-jam and hammer them !
     Said the soldier, 'Amen.'"

The duet purported to be between representatives of both professions. Whatever the sailor said the soldier affirmed with "Amen," and *vice versâ.* In chorus the amens sounded very imposing; and the natives, when they heard it, used to fancy that the infidels were singing a hymn over their rations. The song goes on loyally to commend our "good Queen" for the contribution she has made to the ranks of both services, and concludes with a blessing on her, and the reverse to those commanders who were personally unpopular.

"And the next thing I'll pray for is the good of all men,
     And whatever I do pray for, you must answer, 'Amen!'"

With the last "Amen" Geoffry's head disappeared below stairs, and the deck was left untenanted by all save the watch.

Meanwhile a cloud no bigger than a man's hand passed over the moon, and the wind began to freshen. By the time Captain Adair was in his "first sleep" it had veered round to E.N.E.

CHAPTER XXIX.

AN AWFUL SCENE.

"Beneath thy tide, ah! silent now they roll,
   Or strew with mangled limbs thy sandy shore ;
The trumpet's call no more awakes their soul ;
   The battle's voice they now shall hear no more.
In vain the constant wife and feeble sire,
   Expectant, wish their lov'd return to see ;
In vain their infants' lisping tongues inquire,
   And wait the story on their father's knee."

PENROSE.

"His wearied feet no more his will obey ;
His arms hang useless, and forget to play ;
Borne by the surge, supine and void of breath,
He drinks the briny wave, and draws in death."

COOKE'S MUSÆUS.

CAPTAIN ADAIR slept soundly and sweetly for the first two hours of the night, and then his slumbers were disturbed by a dream. He dreamed that he was somewhere under the sea, in a place where all was shadow ; and through the shadow he saw the forms of men, women, and children walking together hand in hand. He went up to address a group of them. They never turned their heads, but glided on, seemingly unconscious of his appeal. Then a youth passed him who had died on board shortly after the vessel left Calcutta, and on his finger he held Norah's canary. He nodded gaily to Geoffry. "I'm glad you're coming," he seemed to say.

" We've got to walk here for hundreds of years, and we are
always glad of fresh company." Geoffry turned and essayed
to fly, but stumbled over a heap of lead which the phantoms
had cast from their feet, and then he fell with a sob and a
splash, and awoke—awoke with sweat on his forehead to the
sound of great commotion on deck, mixed with the rush of
a strong wind and angry waves. Geoffry's first exclamation
was :—

" Where the d—— are my pistols and boots ? " Then,
as his brain became clearer, he understood that there was a
mightier enemy at the gates than sword or pistol could
rebut, and, hastily putting on a few clothes, he rushed up on
deck.

" What is it ? " he asked of a sailor, who hurried by him
with marks of agitation in his face.

" It's blowing a gale, Sir, and we haven't made any way
for this last half hour ; she's driving up tide to the
shore."

" Good God ! " muttered Geoffry, and he made his way
up to the captain, who, surrounded by crowds of white
eager faces, was endeavouring to make his voice heard
through the howl of the tempest. Her engines had ceased
to have any effect on the Queen of the Isles ; the wind
rushed through her cordage with increasing violence every
minute, and her timbers seemed to start with the violence of
the strain put upon her.

" Lower the maintop-sail." The order was obeyed with
great difficulty, but the vessel still drifted ; and ere the
hands could be got above to furl the sail again, there came
a mighty rush of wind—and it fluttered away in shreds.

The port and starboard anchors were let go, and all the
port-chain paid out, for they yet hoped to bring up the
ship ; but the cable snapped, and she drove on as though
the fury of the blast meant to give her no respite from quick
and certain destruction. They were now not more than
half a mile from the land, for the sight of which they had
so pined in the morning—the touch of which was to bring
them death to-night.

Wild cries rose up amidst the uproar of the elements ;
wails of human beings brought unexpectedly, in the full tide
of health and hope, to face the agonies of violent death.

"The rocks   the rocks—we are driving on the rocks! Oh, captain, is there no hope?"

The captain turned round: "I have done; I will do to the last all I can, but they who have offended God had best make their peace with *Him*, while there is yet time."

The scene on board now became one of indescribable confusion; through the darkness voice called to voice for succour, rarely to obtain an answer. The seas broke over the decks with terrific fury; some clambered frantically over the obstacles on the slippery decks, others descended to the saloon, where a clergyman was breathing a few earnest prayers to his terror-stricken congregation, who cowered round him in various attitudes of despair. Parents embraced their children with the desperate anguish of those who fear each kiss may be the last. The old Anglo-Indian who had toasted the captain so cheerily at dinner-time stood with his arm round his daughter, smoothing her hair with a helpless, piteous movement of his hand, and looking up to Heaven with unutterable pleading in his eyes.

> "Death in the foughten field
> He oft had met;"

but death, amidst shrieks of women and children, with his own daughter by his side—he had never dreamt of such a termination to his honoured career as this. The girl looked up in his face with a sort of ecstacy in hers. "We are together, dear," she said, simply; and the old man clasped her hand tight, though he did not dare to meet her eyes.

The ship swept on her fatal course, battered by shrieking wind and raging sea, like some beautiful soul perverted and driven to destruction by a relentless demon. They were now so near the rocks that the surf which rebounded from them swept over the ship's sides.

"*It's coming,*" said Geoffry to himself; then he stepped up to the captain: "Can I do nothing?"

"Nothing; excepting that if by any chance you survive this night, bear witness to the efforts my crew have made to save the ship."

"And you?"

"I must perish, of course. Good-bye! God bless you!"

"God bless you, Sir!" and Geoffry wrung his friend's hand warmly, and then ran down-stairs to the saloon. In a moment his quick eye singled out his little friend of the afternoon; her ayah was lying by her side convulsed with abject terror; the child looked more puzzled than alarmed, but she smiled when she saw Geoffry.

He caught her up in his arms, and rapidly ascended on deck again. "Listen, dear," he said earnestly: "I am going to try and save you and myself, but you must do everything I tell you—or we shall both die."

"I promise," Norah said; and Geoffry now began to consider how he was best to seize a last chance for dear life.

He was so young, so full of hope—he could not bear to think of the sudden end of it all. His love was waiting for him at home; how would she bear to be told of his death? He could not, would not die; but when he saw how near the rocks were, his heart sank within him. He lifted up his head: "Oh, God, in Thee do I put my trust!"

"Aye; we thanked him a little too soon!"

Geoffry, turning, saw the steerage passenger in an attitude of deep dejection, leaning on a cask. "Cheer up, mate!" said Geoffry, "we're not dead yet: while there's life there's hope."

"Is it not hard," the man cried, flinging up his arms, and apparently not attending to Geoffry's words, "to have given me the life of a dog all these years, and now to murder me in very sight of shore—with my hand almost touching my home—with my wife listening to every step that comes with a heart that's beating and longing for me—for me, who by to-morrow morning will be—dead?" And with this last word the man's voice sank into a wail, and he buried his head again in his arms.

Every now and then the boom of a minute-gun pealed out the ship's distress, but it found no echoing on shore, and the doomed company in the saloon sat looking at each other with the fear of death in their eyes.

Nothing could surpass the order and regularity with which the captain's commands had been carried out; the men worked with the quiet precision of a *fête* day. It is under circumstances like these that the British sailor proves that he has not degenerated one whit since the old heroic days of Nelson and Collingwood.

In times of darkness and of storm, when timid hearts fail and the noblest courage quails before the uproar of elements that seem to shriek destruction in the ears of their victims, our blue jacket rises superior to the horror of the hour. Calm, resolute, and devoted, he puts forth all his strength to confront the peril—braving death with a chivalry that renders the manner of it an example for all time—to all men.

" Mates," cried the captain, as the vessel drove yet nearer to the rocks, "you've worked like good sailors and gallant men. One cheer, lads!" and cheer they actually did — three such earnest hurrahs as had never before rung through broken masts and falling shrouds. Ere the sound died away the ponderous hull of the ship was dashed through the seething foam of the next wave as though it were a plank. There was a pause, followed by a wild shout of mingled groans, prayers, shrieks, and execrations, and the Queen of the Isles struck on a reef of rocks. Ere many minutes were over, she had parted amidships, and her maddened occupants were clinging on to her sides — to spars — to every bit of plank that seemed to promise a momentary refuge from the boiling sea beneath them.

As the ship snapped asunder, Geoffry was tightening the silk scarf with which he had bound his little charge to his back. He seized a rope, and was about to spring over the lee-side of the parting wreck, when he felt someone pull his arm. He turned impatiently, and recognised a fellow-passenger—a lady who during the voyage had been chiefly remarkable for an affectation of helplessness and fine "ladyism." Poor soul! there was no false colour in the livid tinge of her cheeks now. Her eyes nearly started out of her head as she flung herself at Geoffry's feet.

" Take my child, for God's sake, Captain Adair! Save my child ! "

A boy clung round her neck—a beautiful child of two years old, who was sobbing piteously, wailing out his weak treble among the other cries that ascended in vain to Heaven that night :—

"Mamma, mamma, take me away! I so cold, I so frightened!"

"You hear him!" the mother cried, in a hoarse voice. "Oh man, man! what can I do? Must my boy die—my own babe? must he be swallowed up *there?*"

The woman groaned as she saw a large column of wave rise up over a group of wretches struggling amidst the broken spars round the ship, sucking them down as it broke.

"I must first do what I can *here*," Geoffry said pointing to his burthen. "This poor orphan has no one but me. God has given her a father in her need, and nothing but death shall separate us. But if you will wait here—if you have presence of mind to keep where you are till I come back—I swear that if I live I *will* come back and do my best for you."

He seized the rope, and jumped—a big jump—to get clear of the people who still crowded the shore-side of the wreck. The mother looked after him, helplessly.

"He can never come back," she thought, "and my boy will die. Hush, Arthur! oh hush, darling!" and she sat herself down to the task of sheltering and soothing the child as if, poor soul! he were safe in his crib at home. "If I could only get him to sleep," she thought. "*It* might come without his knowing." And with Spartan self-control she tried to attune her husky voice to a sort of lullaby, to which the child was accustomed to be persuaded into slumber.

Meanwhile Geoffry had found his powers as a swimmer chiefly useful in enabling him to dodge the broken pieces of spars which kept threatening to crush him. He was so fearful of Norah's getting hurt in this manner, and he wasted some strength in turning from right to left, instead of making straight for the rocks, as he wished to have done.

The cries of the drowning were getting fainter in his ears now; the roar of waters blinded and deafened him; and he was seized with a terror lest he should lose his senses, and die unconscious. Presently a bit of raft drifted near him, and, feeling his limbs getting stiff, he clutched at this frail support with the faint hope that it might wash him towards the rocks. It did so, and in another instant he was in the white foam of the sea's recoil, in the very grasp and clinch of death. He struggled madly to catch hold of the sea-weed, but felt it slipping from his grasp, when a light flashed out above his head, and just as the advance of the next wave swept him off his feet, friendly hands clutched hold of his arms and shoulders, and caught him up beyond reach of his enemy. For a second or two the young man lay breathless where they landed him; then he struggled up again :—

"Take care of the child," he said. "Some of you lash a rope round me; I must go back to the wreck."

"No, no, no!" cried a dozen voices. "You're half dead now; you're saved by a miracle. Don't tempt Providence again."

"I *must* go back," he reiterated. "Here, steady this rope for me, and take care of the child if I don't return."

He did not dare wait another minute, lest the wreck should be sucked in under the waters before he could get to it, and his promise to the mother and child have been made in vain. He had nothing on but his linen trousers and shirt, which latter, lying open on his chest, displayed its noble proportions as he ran back a few paces to take his next "header."

"What a fine fellow!" a woman said. "What a pity ——" And then her observation was lost in the cheer which followed Geoffry as he plunged once more into the surf.

He never recollected very clearly what passed during the next twenty minutes. He swam until his arms fell lax by his side, and a deadly faintness came over him. A violent blow on the temple from a spar made the blood flow, and he fancied the pain restored him to consciousness. Once more he struggled on, sometimes swimming, sometimes holding to bits of raft and floating. Once his hand went to his throat in search of a gold chain and locket that hung there. The touch of this trinket inspired him with fresh energy. Surely there was something black before him. Was it the hull of the perishing vessel? Yes; and there was the white fold of a woman's dress fluttering above. Geoffry flung up his arms :

"I am come," he cried; "but I ——" His head sank on his breast, and the water sucked in the remainder of his speech. "Father!" the drowning man called. "Esty!" and then he lost all consciousness. He did not hear the cry of hope that broke from the survivors still clinging to the rafts—the return-gun that now boomed from the shore. He could not see the eager eyes in the woman above, who continued to rock her child in her arms while she watched the speck of white that was advancing rapidly towards the dismantled ruins of the Queen of the Isles, and which was greeted with voices which had yet a thrill of hope in them, as they shouted, "The life-boat! the life-boat!"

When the next morning dawned, the gale had blown itself out. A pleasant breeze just ruffled the edge of those health-smelling waves, and had it not been for the dark rugged splinters of rafts and spars, which could now and then be seen undulating between sand and sea, as the latter first cast them from and then lapped them back into its depths, and the groups of men who stood here and there along the beach, forming ominous circles round some prostrate object—but for these symptoms no one could have guessed, from the aspect of that peaceful ocean, those filmy cloudlets that drifted under the blue sky, what a tragedy of horror, what heart-rending prayers and miserable partings, had chronicled the hours of the past night.

It was, indeed, a glorious morning! At Lynncourt the sun shone brightly on the ivy-crusted walls of the old chapel; and as early as eight o'clock the village school children were rehearsing their part in the day's ceremony by dropping daisies around the feet of their tallest companion, who for the occasion represented the bride elect.

And while Geoffry lay on a pallet in a fisherman's hut, wandering in delirium, with hands that never ceased to clutch the locket that rested on his heart, and with lips which, among many incoherent sentences, always ended by blending with them the name of Esty Lisle—while with eyes which had no consciousness in them, but which seemed to be fixed on some far-away object, he called for Esty to come to him—to hold his hand—to take away the band that weighed down his forehead—she was standing under the shadow of the Crusaders' monument that towered by the side of the altar in Lynncourt chapel. Amidst the clang of bells and murmur of congratulations, she was passing up under the yew avenue that lined the churchyard path, her arm linked in that of Alfred Cadogan, and her heart wishing with all its power that it could stay at rest under one of those grey headstones that lay beyond the trees, and never beat again to vex her by its perpetual self-reproach.

CHAPTER XXX.

SOPHY'S SILENT AGONY.

"Then round her heart a beamy gladness plays."
P. FLETCHER.

"When one news straight came huddling on another
Of death and death and death, still I danc'd forward;
But it struck home, and here, and in an instant.
     *   *   *   *   *
They are the silent griefs that cut the heart-strings;
Let me die smiling."
BROKEN HEART.

"Nothing speaks our grief so well as *to speak nothing*."
CRASHAW.

MRS. HERBERT and her husband left for town immediately after Esty's marriage, and it was edifying to see the air of satisfaction with which Sophy arranged her rugs round her, and otherwise prepared herself to undergo as comfortably as possible the railway journey from W—— to London.

Honest George Herbert, immersed in the columns of the *Times*, did not notice the triumphant sparkle in his wife's eyes as she brooded over the past events of the day, nor could he understand the fervency with which she muttered, "Thank Heaven, that's over!" when she descended at her own door that evening.

"Well, it *is* a long journey for you, my dear," Mr. Herbert said; and when they got inside the house, he despatched his wife to her bed-room, with a tender injunction "to lie down and rest until it was time to dress for dinner." Sophy followed his advice, for she felt tired mentally and bodily, and after she had drunk a cup of tea, she buried her head among her pillows, and desiring her maid to call her in an hour's time, fell into a pleasant little doze, undisturbed by any disagreeable dreams or reflections. When she awoke it was with a sense of triumph that made her eyes flash, and her heart beat. She remembered it all at once; the game was her own now. Esther Lisle was eternally separated from Geoffry — he might suffer at first, but would he not come to her for pity and consolation? and, with his heart softened and his pride awakened, might he not give some response at last to the eyes that had looked love at him so long?

Sophy paled and reddened alternately as she stood at her mirror that evening, and her hands trembled as she fastened her bracelets on her arm—trembled with the sensation of hope that was beginning to dawn in her heart; for a while she felt as timid and fretful as a girl of sixteen swayed by the agitation of a first passion. "Oh," she murmured, "when shall I see his face again?" Then she counted on her fingers the number of days that would probably elapse before the Queen of the Isles could come into harbour. She was interrupted in this occupation by her maid's suggestion that it was getting late. So she proceeded to finish her toilette, and when her husband came to her dressing-room to announce that dinner was ready, he was struck by the surpassingly brilliant appearance she presented. Diamonds flashed from her arms and neck —danced in her ears, and quivered on the bunches of wheat, which were represented by delicate straw-work, and disposed tastefully over the cloud-like folds of tulle that surrounded her. Madame Elise had called this *chef d'œuvre* of her art, "wheat after rain," and the rain-drops were represented by small, but effective brilliants.

Mr. Herbert felt proud of his wife that night, as he watched her moving through the crowded salons at the French Embassy, acknowledged by the admiration of the

18—2

men, and envy of the women, to be not only one of the most beautiful, but one of the best dressed women there.

Sophy moved through the adoration which surrounded her with a dreamy light in her beautiful eyes : she enjoyed thoroughly the luxury of the hour, the lighted rooms, the melodious clangour of the music, the rare exotics which filled the atmosphere with faint suspicions of southern climes; but, above all, did she enjoy the homage paid her by the eyes of her partner, a young, handsome, and distinguished man. It seemed like a good omen for her hopes, the fascination she was exercising over all around her to-night.

She was dancing the Lancers, and had arrived at that portion of the figure where, like

> "A fine, sweet earthquake, gently moved
> By the soft wind of whispering silks," *

the ladies advanced in line amidst a crush of draperies and an entanglement of gloved fingers to meet their partners.

Sophy was just returning to her place, when her ears caught the words, " Queen of the Isles," uttered by some one behind her.

Her heart beat fast for an instant. " What! could the ship be in harbour already!" she thought. " Was Geoffry in England?" Then she had to advance again, and lost the next sentence.

The concluding figure was being danced, and the orchestra was speeding along the feet of the dancers with their most inspiriting strains, when chance brought her once more near to the person who had spoken of the vessel, which she, with the selfishness of love, thought of only as " Geoffry's ship."

" What a shocking thing ! Do you really think it can be true?"

" I fear there is no doubt of it. It's telegraphed up to all the evening papers. They were caught in a violent gale last night on the Welsh coast; she went to pieces on the rocks, and ——"

" You have made a wrong turn, Mrs. Herbert," said the bland voice of her partner. The dance was not finished

---

* Decker.

yet ; Sophy had yet one more revolution to make before the final clash of the music. She went on bravely : she danced on through a devouring pain in her heart with the courage of a Red Indian, who keeps his face calm while his entrails are consumed by fire ; her footsteps moved in perfect time with the music, and when the dance ceased she bowed with her usual grace to her companion—although her smile was so vague, and her dark eyes so meaningless in expression, as to suggest the recollection of one of those vacant-looking faces where the mind has taken leave for ever of its poor, helpless hostage,—the body.

"What were you saying, Mr. Merivale, about the Queen of the Isles ? " she asked in a dry, hard voice, of one of the gentlemen standing near.

" She has gone to pieces on the Welsh coast : a dreadful thing, isn't it ? "

" Very."

There was a pause. At last she spoke again, but the delicate handle of the fan which she fluttered before her face fell to crumbled fragments in the fingers which grasped it.

" Are all hands lost ? " she asked.

" All ! "

" *Then it's too late,*" Mrs. Herbert muttered to herself. She began to move away, but she could not have seen where she was going, for she struck her forehead against a decorated statue of Hope, that stood by the side of the wall, with such violence as to force blood from the bruise.

She looked up, seemingly more amazed than hurt by the blow.

" Dear me, how very stupid ! " she said, putting her hand to her head with a vague smile.

Disregarding the exclamations and expressions of condolence that fell from her partner's lips, she turned once more to Mr. Merivale.

" Are you quite sure all lives are lost ? "

" The particulars are not known yet," he said, gravely. " A few may have been picked up after the wreck, but there is no doubt as to the loss of life being very great."

" Thank you—and now I will go in search of Herbert, and release you from your charge," said Sophy, smiling sweetly at, but without meeting the eyes of, her admirer. He murmured something complimentary which she did not hear; and then seeing her husband in the distance she signed to him, and saying she was tired, requested to be taken home.

She told him, when in their carriage, the news of the Queen of the Isles' disaster, and of Geoffry's too probable fate, without any tremor in her voice; only to herself her accents sounded hollow and unnatural. Perhaps she found George Herbert's torrent of lamenting exclamation, and conjectures, more difficult to bear than the indifference of the crowd she had just left, for she tottered and nearly fell when she got out in H—— Street. "Take care, darling, you nearly caught your foot over that stone," George said. He added, "I shall go down to L—— to-morrow by the first train."

Sophy looked round without speaking, but there was interrogation in her eyes, and he answered it.

"To hear what I can of our poor friend. He may have been saved, after all; a strong, healthy fellow of six and twenty doesn't give up life without a struggle; at any rate I'll go, and see and hear for myself. As I shall leave by the first train, when you will be asleep, I'll bid you good-bye now. I will telegraph up any news I hear," he added, as he kissed his wife's cheek.

The latter nodded her head, and then went up-stairs to her bed-room, where she remained alone for some minutes before summoning her maid.

She sat down before the looking-glass, and stared at the pale, set face reflected there. The brilliants that quivered in her hair became multiplied by hundreds in her dazed eyes.

Her mind was too deadened by its weight of misery to permit her thoughts to regulate themselves in any definite shape. She did not endeavour, as one suffering lesser grief might have done, to dissect the cause and manner of the misfortune that had come to her. She felt as one stricken suddenly deaf and dumb. While her maid's nimble fingers disengaged the jewels from her mistress's hair, she took up a book that lay on the dressing-table, more because she was desirous of avoiding the eyes of her attendant in the opposite mirror, than from any real wish to scan its pages. The book was in "In Memoriam," and the first two lines her glance lighted on were,

> " And hands so often clasp'd in mine
> Should toss with tangle and with shells."

It was the last drop that overflowed the cup. As the meaning of the words sank into Sophy's brain, she gave a faint sigh, and then she swayed heavily on her seat, and was caught by her attendant just in time to prevent her delicate forehead from receiving fresh injury against the carved arm of the chair.

"It was the first time I ever saw missus in a dead faint," was the abigail's remark when narrating in the housekeeper's room all *she* had suffered at the shock of witnessing her mistress's indisposition.

CHAPTER XXXI.

ESTY'S DECLARATION.

"Phillis is mine for many days;
I wone her with a girdle of gelt,
Emboss'd with bugle about the belt."

SPENSER.

T had been agreed that, as Lady Renshawe depended so much on her niece's society for all the comforts of her now fast-declining days, Esty and her husband should depart from the ordinary custom of leaving home for a month after their marriage, and content themselves with living in strict seclusion at Lynncourt during that period.

Mr. Cadogan was very well satisfied with this arrangement, which, while it saved him expense, would enable him to cast his covetous eye over every nook and corner of the noble domain which he fondly imagined he might one day call his own. Besides, Lynncourt was at a less distance from Sophy and London than any other residence they were likely to have selected, unless, indeed, they had migrated to Lady Renshawe's town house; but the countess had not offered them this choice. "Why need Esty leave Lynncourt yet?" she said. "The place was secluded enough for a dozen married couples to live there without running up against each other." And Esty assented gladly, giving a furtive look at her affianced, who offered no opposition to the plan.

The wedding-breakfast had been a very quiet affair, the members of Esty's own family being the only guests present—always excepting the Rev. Mr. Jennings (who performed the ceremony), and his daughter Phœbe. It was for the benefit of these two, and perhaps, also, for that of the hoary-headed butler, that Colonel Lisle made an affecting speech over the wedding-cake; declaring that next to the love he had always borne his daughter Esther, was the esteem he felt for the "chosen of her heart:" he trusted that she might contribute as much to her husband's happiness as she had enhanced that of her parents. A faint smile dawned over Esty's pale lips as visions of the lost paper-cutters, mislaid ink-stands, misplaced books, and other little iniquities, which had made her for many years past a constant thorn in her father's side, rose up in her mind.

Christine caught her eye, and smiled, but her's was a faint smile, too, for her sister's trouble of heart was reflected in Christine's kindly face, and the latter would have liked to have boxed her new brother-in-law's ears, when he returned thanks for Colonel Lisle's "*too* favourable opinion of him," with a smile that manifestly implied that nothing *could* be too good for him.

His manner to Gerald was kind, but patronising, and that youth chafed sorely under the yoke he had put about his neck.

If a Lisle of Lynncourt thought it a *mésalliance* for his sister to marry the son of the Greek merchant, Cadogan plainly showed that he, in his turn, considered his accepting Miss Lisle in place of his four thousand pounds, as a decided equivalent for any advantages he might gain by the connection. So Gerald sat and looked uneasy when he felt Cadogan's snake-like eye fixed on him, as the latter returned thanks in answer to Colonel Lisle's speech, with a slight hint at the "mutual benefit" to be derived by the alliance of the houses of Lisle and Cadogan.

"House of Cadogan, indeed!" muttered Gerald, indignantly. "House of business, I should think he means, d—— his impudence!" When the latter sauntered up to Esty to bid her farewell, he felt quite sorry to think that she should have allied herself with such "bad form," and said, good-naturedly, that he really thought she had made a mistake and taken the wrong brother.

"Between you and me, Esty," he whispered, "Adair was a very much better style of fellow; but I don't think he had much coin, and so, perhaps, it's better as it is." And as far as the interests of Gerald and his tradesmen were concerned, certainly it was better for them and him as it was.

After the breakfast was over, Christine and Esty withdrew quietly, and stole away over the fields to Gardenhurst. Mrs. Lisle had been too ill to join the wedding-party; but had enjoined Christine to return to her as soon as possible, to report how all had gone off. The sick woman was sitting up in bed, looking wistfully out of the window at her side, and trying to catch the sound of the returning carriage wheels. The hours had passed very slowly to the invalid, who, too weak to occupy herself in any way, was compelled to lie still and listen to the ticking of the clock, or the purring of the cat which crouched in the sun. Perhaps her vagrant fancy wandered back to the old days at Florence, when she, too, stood a bride at the altar, with her lips vowing fealty to James Lisle, and her heart slightly troubled by the memory of a handsome Italian boy who had turned the sombre glory of his black eyes from the picture he was copying in the Uffzzi gallery, rather too often for her peace of mind, on the fair face of the English girl-student. Ah, well! she never allowed those eyes to come between her and her duty afterwards. So she may be forgiven for the sentimental reminiscence she indulged in, now that her face and form, reproduced on a smaller scale in her daughter, stood again before the priest, her finger being encircled by the gold link which consigned her to Alfred Cadogan's keeping, to "have and to hold" from that day forth.

"I hope she may be happy—my poor, little darling! I am sure she has every reason to be so." But, despite the confidence of Mrs. Lisle's tone, she looked uneasily at the door every now and then, waiting to be re-assured, by an account of Esty's manner at the ceremony, as to the amount of self-content her daughter was feeling. Her surprise was only equalled by her delight when both the girls entered together.

"You didn't think I could let this day go over without

being kissed and blessed by you, did you, mamma?" Esty said, in answer to Mrs. Lisle's exclamations; her mother drew the little head fondly to her breast, and whispered :—

"God bless you, my dear, and remember when you love your husband for your own sake to be grateful to him for mine : his kindness to Gerald will save my life."

Esty smiled bravely, and felt for a while that in her mother's pleasure she gained full reward for the self-sacrifice she had made.

Mrs. Lisle would not, however, allow herself the luxury of Esty's presence for long that morning.

"The party will be back soon," she said, "and fancy how scandalised they will be to find that the little bride has so soon eloped from her husband. Go my dear, and take Dolly with you." For Mrs. Lisle had a vague idea that Esty Cadogan should not be allowed, now that she had arrived at the dignity of wifehood, to tread the same path unattended which, for years, Esty Lisle had traversed alone in perfect safety.

Esty smiled, and declined the proffered escort, but she took Dolly a large piece of cake, and received a kiss from the wrinkled chin of that venerable woman, who "hoped that Miss Esty would know how to behave herself, now she was married, and wouldn't go climbing no more trees!"— a warning not altogether unnecessary, as Esty had been discovered, at a very late date, seated on the elevated branch of an apple-tree, making a clear space of the fruit all round her, like a silkworm nibbling a clean circle in its mulberry leaf. Christine accompanied her sister to the end of the first field, and then returned, thoughtful and melancholy.

"What are you thinking about, Miss?" said Dolly, sharply, who encountered her near the front door. "I suppose *you'll* be after marrying next, and leaving us all alone. The sight of Miss Esty's happiness will make you jealous, I suppose?"

"I don't think Esty is very happy," Christine said, musingly.

"Well, and why not, I should like to know? What young man could have behaved handsomer than Mr. Cadogan, giving me such a handsome gownd, too?" Dolly gave a little conscious glance at the brown silk, which she had put on in honour of Miss Esty's wedding-day, and which Esty

had given her as being a conjoined present from Alfred and
herself, thinking thus best to please the old servant.

"Well, I'm sure, Captain Adair gave you a nice present,"
observed Christine, her mind reverting affectionately to her
satin-quilted work-box—still the joy of her leisure hours.

"Aye ! but that was only a cap-ribbon ! " Dolly answered,
disdainfully ; and Christine went up-stairs, still thinking to
herself that Esty was unhappy ; "for," said that astute young
lady, "she has the composure of misery in her manner."
But she did not divulge her suspicions to her mother, who
was more than ordinarily well and cheerful that day.

Esty pursued her way very composedly along the narrow
field-paths until she was about half-way to Lynncourt, and
then she could stifle back no longer the flood of recollection
evoked by every phase of the hedgerow, every grey bit of
hill that loomed in the distance.   It was on an afternoon
like this she had walked to Lynncourt, with the dawn of a
first love rising in her heart, with the memory of a first kiss
thrilling on her lips.   Every bird that twittered in the bush
sung joy in her ears that day ; every gate of which her hand
lifted the latch seemed to open into fresh regions of hope,
since Geoffry might be concealed by any turn of the far-on
path.   And now she could not conceal from herself that she
felt sorrow and distrust of the tie which awaited her, of the
hand which she must clasp in hers, without sufficient love on
either side to render the pressure a warm one.   She did not
feel that Cadogan loved her, but she knew that she must
endeavour to make him do so, if any good was to come out
of their future lives together.   "I will try : I will be a good
wife to him if he is kind to me," she thought ; but her
opinion as to his indifference about her was confirmed when
she got back to the house, and found that he had not yet
detected her absence, having retired to the library to read the
papers and enjoy his cigar, and there fallen asleep on the sofa.

Lady Renshawe had missed her, for she said irritably,
when her niece re-entered the room :

"Where on earth have you been all this time, Esty ? I
have been wanting you to help me in my accounts for this
last hour.   I can't get the butcher's book and his meat
tickets to tally."

The young bride seated herself at her grand-aunt's side

and was soon engaged in calculating how much was owing for twenty-eight pounds of beef, at sevenpence halfpenny the pound.

Meanwhile, the clouds which had been threatening all the morning burst with fury over the house and park. For some hours the rain poured down steadily and unceasingly; it ran in streams against the escutcheoned windows; it hung in heavy drops on the peony blossoms; and it gathered in sullen-looking gutters by the sides of the saturated gravel-paths. The lawn shone the brighter and greener for the refreshment of the showers, but the delicate-leaved roses were swept to the ground, and their tender hues bespattered with mud.

The dinner was a dreary ceremony that evening. Lady Renshawe nodded her head in a half-doze over the table, excepting when she was aroused by the sound of an un-usually loud burst of rain against the window. Cadogan sat silent and meditative. He did not care for Esty, but he did care for the valuable old pictures that hung on the walls; and he thought what a price some of them would fetch at Christie's if he sent them up for sale, when that withered lady sleeping opposite should be under the clay, and the younger one, ductile as wax, in his hands. "She will never give me much trouble," he said, contemptuously glancing at her delicately-moulded figure.

He estimated his ideal of feminine power by Sophy's massive bust and determined-looking *pose*. He little knew how much strength might exist concealed under his wife's child-like face and pliant form. The silver wire strung on the guitar, to which Alfred sometimes sang his little foreign "romances," was as slender in appearance, but he would have found its ligaments difficult of dissection. When dinner was over, the two ladies withdrew: the younger one supporting the elder with her arm until they reached the drawing-room, when Lady Renshawe retired "feeling ill," she said, "and tired with the excitement of the day."

Esty, left to her own resources, sat and looked into the fire embers heaped high in the stove. The countess always had fires lit on rainy evenings, and Esty felt grateful to the bright coals for the sense of comfort and warmth they conveyed.

When tea was served, her husband came up, and, as she put a cup down by the easy-chair in which he had seated himself, he turned round languidly and thanked her.

"If you'll stoop down, I'll give you a kiss," he said, sweetly.

Esty laughed, and declined the invitation, but secretly she resented the tone of condescension it which it had been offered. Presently she stole out of the room, but her husband's voice called after her :—

"Come back again soon."

She nodded acquiescence. He had a right to order her about now. She did not dream of contesting his commands, but she felt oppressed ; her heart seemed ready to break. She wandered down into the front hall to seek air and solitude. Two tapers winked feebly in the stone griffins on the centre oak table; the embers of the wood fire were dying out in the vast grate ; there was only life enough left in the ashes to cast a red glow over the leopard's skin, that served as a rug ; the rich, decayed silk of the banners flapped their dusty sides, slowly swayed by the wind, which penetrated through every crevice of the old house. Some of these that hung on the mantelpiece caught a faint reflex of the fire-glow on the tarnished gold of their embroidered crests and mottos ; but the rest of the hall was in utter darkness, and, as Esty prolonged her reverie by the fireside, the shadows grew deeper on the ceiling, and the outline of the walls faded away into utter indistinctness. The wind howled and rattled the chain at the door, and the rain dashed in wild gusts at the windows, but yet Esty did not hasten to join her husband up-stairs ; nor did he descend below to seek for his bride. As she sat there, with the sound of the storm in her ears, she fancied she heard something agitate the door, which was more than the mere accident of blast or hail. She lifted her head suspiciously.

"Pshaw ! it's only fancy !" she thought, but, nevertheless, she rose from her seat, and moved nearer the door, although half afraid of breaking the silence by her movement. She stopped, repulsed by a fiercer blast of wind, which, piercing through the crevices of the portal, chilled her delicate throat and shoulders. She felt inclined to weep with nervousness and depression.

Her thoughts reverted to the husband of a few hours, lolling in an easy-chair by the fire up-stairs, indifferent alike to her society or its absence. "Oh, Geoffry! you would never have treated me thus!" she wailed; and as the name of Geoffry passed through her mind it smote her with a bitter pang—a pang in which love, remorse, and despair seemed fused in one intolerable burthen on her self-accusing soul.

She turned to go up-stairs. Her husband's society, careless of her as he was, would be preferable to the reminiscences that crowded round her in that dreary hall. A cheerful, boisterous dining-chamber had been that vaulted hall in the old days, when the lords of Lynncourt held carouse round the long oak table, and emptied their flagons in the face of crackling fires,—when the dogs of chase, basking in the glow, lolled away their fatigue, while the torches cast ruddy light on the gleaming armour on the wall, and the walls themselves rang with the revellers' barbaric jollity. But now in silence and gloom, with dying firebrands winking in the grate, and empty suits of mail clanking against the wall, as the wind lifted them on their rusty pivots; with shadows deepening every mystery of window recesses, and heightening the weird effect of the goblin-like faces that writhed in the intricacies of the oak carving round the casements; with elfish footsteps creaking on the stairs; with sounds of wailing blowing through the distant corridors; the grand hall at Lynncourt was at this hour about as dreary a sepulchre as any sad-faced mortal could find in which to recal the memory of dead hope. Esty shivered, and determined to go; but, just as she turned her head from the doorway, she thought she heard the massive handle move, as though turned by a hand outside. She stood motionless, her breath suspended between her lips, her ears strained to their utmost. "What a fool I am," she said, half aloud; "I am afraid of shadows to-night. Perhaps some animal is pressing for shelter near the door. I will open it and look."

She let down the heavy door-chain, which swung with violent oscillation to and fro, and then she applied her delicate hand to the stiff double bolt. Was it the wind, or was it her fancy, that something from without pressed the door towards her as she slowly drew it open? She looked out, but could see nothing but the blackness of sky and earth, and hear nothing but the steady drip of the rain. The portico stood out of the quarter where the wind was raging, so she was enabled to look out steadily into the darkness. " It is nothing," she sighed, and she began to close the door again, when her excited imagination conjured up an echo of her sigh, or rather another sigh breathed close to her ear. She looked in the direction from whence it came, and there, with staring eyes and clenched hands, with her whole frame convulsed by the horror of the moment, she seemed to see Geoffry's face pass out of the shadow into the ray of light which issued from the opened door, and Geoffry's eyes met her own with such reproach in their expression that she wished for the moment she were blind or dead.

" Geoffry," she said in a husky whisper, but no answer came from the gloom without. The phantom of her imagination had passed away, and she held out her arms in vain.

" I loved you," she cried ; " believe me, I love you even now when ——" But she did not finish the sentence, for a substantial hand was laid on her shoulder, and Mr. Cadogan's voice said behind her,—

" What, in the name of Heaven, makes you such a fool as to stand at an open door this time of night? Do come in ; I shall catch cold," he added, angrily, shrinking behind the door.

For the first time, the touch of Alfred's hand and the sound of Alfred's voice were welcome to Esty.

" Let me go up with you," she said, clinging to his arm, and looking half fearfully at the still open door.

" You can go up very well by yourself," replied Mr. Cadogan, composedly. " I am on my way to the smoking-room. Indeed, I should not have known you were here, but that I felt the draught cut my shoulder as I went along the passage, and came to see if any servant had been negligent enough to leave a door or window open."

So saying, Mr. Cadogan carefully secured bolt and chain, and then betook himself to the enjoyment of his cigar in the comfortable little chamber called the housekeeper's room, while his wife crept with timorous steps up the broad oak stairs, starting at the patter of the mice that scudded along in the wainscot, shrinking from each shadowed corner of the stairs, and, above all, dreading to turn her head back in the direction where her overstrained imagination had conjured up that phantom of her past happiness, whose rebuking eyes seemed to pursue her every step she took.

CHAPTER XXXII.

"BY THE LORD HARRY, I'LL FIRE!"

"Lacking my love, I go from place to place
   Like a young fawn that late hath lost the hind,
And seek each where, where last I saw her face,
   Whose image yet I carry fresh in mind.
I seek the fields with her late footing sign'd ;
   I seek her bow'r with her.late presence deck'd ;
Yet, not in field nor bower I can her find,
   Yet field and bower are full of her aspect."

SPENSER.

AY followed day in dull sequence at Lynncourt. Esty tried hard to put the past behind her, and to occupy herself solely in endeavouring to gain Alfred Cadogan's esteem and friendship, if not his love ; but she had the mortification to find, that so far from valuing her efforts, he did not even perceive them. " I might just as well try to train a convolvulus to cling to the stone dial on the lawn," she thought, bitterly; " his coldness utterly repels affection." Still she persevered in her endeavours, accepting her failures as a part of the punishment she justly merited for having married him without love.

"Why should he care for me !" she said to herself one day, as, on entering one door of the library she rather wistfully watched her husband walking out at the other. "And why did he marry me?" she added.

Alfred could have answered the question better than she

could, for at that moment he was studying a large map of
the Lynncourt Estate, which was suspended in the corridor.
A smile of satisfaction stole over his face as he marked the
large proportions of his wife's prospective inheritance.

" It was worth the sacrifice," he said, as he caught sight
of himself in an opposite mirror; Esty, who had followed
him out, touched him on the arm.

" What were you saying ? "

" I was saying, my dear, that the best thing I ever did for
myself was in marrying you."

" Why ? " asked Esty, much surprised, but looking pleased,
nevertheless, and clasping her little hands over one another
round his arm.

" Because," replied Alfred, sweetly, with a slight glance
at the map, "you are such a darling." And he bent down
and kissed her hand, with something very like affection in
his manner; in truth, he *did* for the moment feel a thrill of
tenderness towards this "means to an end;"—this little
girl, who would some future day augment his possessions
many thousand-fold. " I suppose's it's all safe," he thought,
as he watched, with inward satisfaction, the decrepid gait of
Lady Renshawe, as she hobbled by the window a few
minutes after. " It's all sure to come to Esty, she would
never have left it elsewhere." The bare thought of such a
possibility made him look vindictively after the retreating
figure of his venerable relative. " I must find out. If I
allowed a feeling of uncertainty to keep hold of me, it would
drive me wild." And Alfred mused deeply, as he paced up
and down that corridor, but his thoughts were not exactly
in the groove which Esty imagined, as she walked by his
side, still hanging on his arm. .

" I should be glad if he really did love me. I should be
glad to compensate for ——" and the rest of Esty's muttered
thoughts ended in a sigh.

Notwithstanding the dutiful attention she paid both
husband and aunt, there were hours which Mrs. Cadogan
found herself free to dispose of as she liked, since no one
required her to render an account of these solitary aimless
moments. She would wander on the lawn, twisting off with
listless fingers the dry leaves of the decaying plants. As
the autumn gales increased in violence, the red lush of the

scarlet geraniums peered dimly through the masses of yellow
leaves that were drifted into the beds.   And a night's hurri-
cane would rend the yellow rose-trees from the walls against
which they had been carefully trained.   Esty uttered an exclamation of annoyance, when, in one of her lonely rambles
she found a large cluster of these, her favourite flowers,
hanging their bruised heads in close proximity to the ground.
She lifted the pendant branch, but found the stalk was snapt
close to the blossom.

"Let what is broken so remain,"

she quoted, sadly, and left the roses to their fate; but this
line recurred again to her memory, when she found herself
glancing wistfully towards that wood, which she could never
think of excepting as connected with Geoffry's voice, and
Geoffry's kiss.   She avoided this wood in her walks, but she
could not altogether banish the memory of it from her mind.
In her dreams she heard the ripple in the pond, and saw
the lace-work of light and shadow made by the shrubs that
overhung its margin, rising up round her like a bowery
prison from which she could not escape, save by the pang
of awaking.

  Do not the strongest of us sometimes yearn, with a
desperate sickness of sorrow, for just one touch of "that
hand," one word from "those lips," one hour of reality in
place of the broken dreams of the past that seem only to
mock with their lack of substance, and utterly fail to satisfy
our hunger for the living presence, the living bliss?

  When the face you love is hidden under the long grasses
of the churchyard, the aching blank in your heart is hard
enough to bear; but when it is made cold and dead to you
by treachery and wrong; when your falsehood has estranged
your friend's eyes from you, and altered the tone of his
voice in speaking to you, is not that the keenest mortal pang
one can sustain?   If Herod's midnight slumbers were ever
tormented by the phantom of his slain mistress, would not
his remorse-smitten conscience have caused his eyes to seek
first for the impress of his murderous rope round her ac-
cusing throat, and would not that moment exceed in pain
all that life could ever again grant him of sweetness?

Esty found no recurrence in her husband's manner of the tenderness he had shown towards her that morning in the corridor. What attention he did divert from himself was directed towards the countess. Over her, he watched with a solicitude, which (supposing it to proceed from motives of reverence and affection) was truly edifying. The deceased Xerxes Cadogan could not have failed to be satisfied had he lived to receive such marks of respect, such evidences of watchful scrutiny from his son, as the latter lavished on Lady Renshawe. Did she propose to write a letter, Alfred was all anxiety to save her that trouble; did she complain of illness, he listened with sympathising attention to the details of her case. And whenever Esty was absent he praised her merits, and spoke of her devotion to her grand-aunt with tears in his eyes. To all this the countess would listen with an amiable expression in her wrinkled visage. She accepted Alfred's delicate flattery with an approving tap on her snuff-box; and a smile, which she intended to be bland, played round her mouth as she confirmed all he could say good of her little niece.

Lady Renshawe's crumpled-looking, projecting chin, combined with the toothless row of gums which stood revealed whenever the wrinkled line of her lips parted into a smile, gave a satirical expression to all she said during these mutual laudations; but Mr. Cadogan made allowances for the physical disfigurements of age, and quite believed that he was cementing his interests with those of the Lynncourt estate as strongly as ever the old Romans joined one brick to another. Perhaps he would not have felt so confident could he have heard the wicked chuckle the old countess gave one day, as she sat and looked in the fire, after one of these interviews, when Alfred had retired from the room at her behest.

"For, my dear Cadogan," she said, kindly, "as you're so fond of your wife, I won't detain you from her any longer; you will find her in the garden." As she was watching his unwilling steps sauntering languidly on the terrace outside, she laughed again to herself. "He will be disappointed," she said, "he shall never reach Lynncourt through his wife —poor child!"

Meanwhile, Mr. Cadogan was pacing the terrace walk

with such a moody expression of face, that when he at last came up to Esty, and turned the sullen regard of his long, black eyes on her, she asked him, timidly, "if anything had vexed him?"

"No!" he said, shortly; and then he flung himself on the grass, and appeared to be looking meditatively at the house.

"Excuse me if I smoke."

"Certainly." Esty seated herself by the smoker's side, and awaited any further remark he might condescend to make.

"I wonder if *she* knows how the will is worded," Alfred thought, as he watched the light curls of vapour that ascended from his cigar. "She's such a fool," he added, with a side-long glance at his wife, who was picking off daisies' heads with an absent look in her face. "She is such a little idiot, I daresay she never even thought of trying to find out!"

Alfred knocked away the burnt end of his Cabana impatiently against the ground, and tried to think of something to say which might lead to the subject he had at heart.

"It is a beautiful old house," he observed at last, thoughtfully regarding the noble pile of building before him. "There must be a good deal of timber in its construction. How very fast it would burn if it ever caught fire!"

"Yes," said Esty, looking up rather startled at the proposition.

"Tell me, child, what would you attempt to save first from the flames, if you were ever surprised by such a calamity?"

"First aunt and then the parrot," Esty answered, promptly.

"And me?" Cadogan suggested playfully, but with rather an evil look in his eyes.

His vanity was so great that he could not bear to think that any woman with whom he had aught to do should not worship his attractions, even when he prized that woman as little as he did his bride.

"Oh! you," said Esty, rather disconcerted, "I thought you would take care of yourself."

"So I should—first," admitted Alfred, candidly. "But

your aunt, do you imagine she would think of you under such circumstances."

"I am sure of it."

"And supposing she perished first?"

"Why do you suppose such a horrible thing," cried the girl, with a thrill of indignation in her voice.

"My suppositions won't bring it about," said her husband, calmly. "What *should* you do, now; I am curious to know which of your household gods you would shoulder, as, unlike the cobbler's wife, you repudiate the idea of carrying off your husband."

"Oh, I don't know," Esty said, indifferently. "There is some paper of aunt's she keeps in the Japan cabinet in her ante-room; in case of any accident I am to take care of that, she says; but, oh! do look what a lovely sunset there is in the west."

Alfred looked at the red and orange streaks in the sky, fading down behind the masses of woodland that skirted Lynncourt Park. He was glad to turn his eyes away that his wife might not see the light that had passed into them when she mentioned that paper which the countess had commended to her care.

"It must be the will!" then he spoke aloud, "Yes; it is very beautiful! where are you going, Esty?" for she had risen and seemed about to leave him.

"I was going in to see Lady Renshawe, I am afraid you don't find me very amusing," she said, with a faint smile.

"On the contrary you have rarely appeared more charming to me," answered Mr. Cadogan, breathing his sentences between puffs at his cigar; and he pulled her towards him with that air of insolent condescension which always made Esty chafe inwardly when she was subjected to it.

"She isn't a bad looking little thing," he said half aloud, as he stroked the glossy tresses of her hair with his long white fingers. Privately he thought, "What a doll she is compared to Sophy!" but he kept that sentiment to himself.

"Come!" he added, "we will go together to seek your aunt," and the two went towards the house, Alfred carefully buttoning his coat over his chest to protect himself from the influence of the falling dew. Esty noticed the action and smiled; it may be that she recalled a different movement of Geoffry's hands, when the latter threw off his coat one autumn evening long ago, to place it round her thinly-clad form; but if so, she put the comparison from her mind, for she was unusually attentive to her husband that evening.

A shiver of repulsion had passed over her when she felt the touch of his finger's sliding down her head, and now she imposed on herself little penances to atone for that involuntary offence.

She need not have troubled herself, for Alfred never imagined but that she would be most grateful for any mark of tenderness he vouchsafed her.

When his passions were deeply roused—where he "loved," as he loved Mrs. Herbert, he was quick enough to detect the slightest chill opposed to the lava flood of devotion he poured out; did Sophy shrink from his touch or show indifference in the careless eyes she turned on him, then he suffered such torments, and showed such ferocious agony of mind, that Mrs. Herbert was obliged to wreath smiles when her heart was sad, to coin words of sweetness when unspoken curses were dwelling on her tongue, against the man whose "love" she both feared and abhorred.

But, where Mr. Cadogan's vanity only was concerned, he was as obtuse as most vain people generally are. Sophy apart, he had rather a contempt for women as a race: he viewed them rather as a vehicle for men's convenience and pleasure than as creatures entitled to any position on their own merits. A proverb says that in scratching a Russian you discover the Tartar, and despite the Christian education which had been bestowed on two generations of Cadogans, there was a good deal of the grand-fatherly leaven in Alfred Cadogan yet. His father, Xerxes, had owned a palace on the Bosphorus, where " the eyes blue languish and the golden hair " of more than one Circassian peeped out from behind the rose-wreathed lattice-work of the hanging terrace to welcome the *caïque* of the master and the lover, when, on the pretext of mercantile occupations, Xerxes would exile himself from the shrewish tongue of his Christian wife, to repose in the soft indolence of his Oriental retreat.

During Alfred's minority the palace fell into that state of ruin and desolation which is the fate of most of these

Eastern residences on the water, unless they are constantly re-decorated, and carefully repaired against the destroying effects of weather. The fair-skinned Circassian, the small-fingered Georgian, the perfect-faced Greek, found other masters; and the pendant garden over the blue waters ceased to echo the sound of zebec or guitar; heavy-headed roses fell through the broken fissures in the lattice-work, doves flew through the apertures to build their nests in the shelter of the neglected chambers within, where the rain had trailed long discoloured streaks down the frescoed walls; and long grasses forced up their way between the crevices of the marble steps.

"It would cost a fortune to repair," Alfred decided; like the worthy Mrs. Gilpin, even when bent on pleasure, Mr. Cadogan had a "frugal mind," so he purchased a much smaller residence at a little village, called by the Greeks Mirghuen (otherwise Istenia), situated on another part of the Bosphorus, and there at the summit of the hilly town he owned one of those many gabled houses coloured dull red, in obedience to the Turkish mandate, which forbids to Greeks and Armenians the more sprightly hues with which the Ottoman loves to enliven his outer walls.

Those of his male friends in England, who wondered why Cadogan was impervious to the fascination of well-known, world-worn, Circes, little suspected how attractive was the veiled loveliness secluded behind the lattice-bars of Alfred's country-house at Mirghuen.

Whenever he saw the little court of men that gathered round fair and frail European celebrities, he congratulated himself, as fancy pictured to him the graceful forms of his Georgian Leila, and his Circassian Zirma, gathering wild flowers in the forest overlooking Mirghuen, their perfections concealed from the vulgar gaze by the mists of drapery in which they were swathed; the sunny hair of Zirma (her name signified "gold thread") clouded by the folds of the yashmak, and nothing visible of Leila's exquisite person excepting the dark gleam of her eyes.

No wonder that the undivided homage accorded to Mr. Cadogan by these fair slaves had filled his cup of vanity to the utmost, and that he regarded it as a most unlikely event that the little English girl he had married should not participate in the adoration he was accustomed to receive. When she shrank from his touch, as on the lawn that evening, he ascribed the movement to tremulous pleasure on her part at the reception of such a caress from him, and he determined, while wending his way towards the house, to be "more attentive to the poor little thing in future."

Then he sighed, and wondered when he should be able to get back to that home of his on the banks of the Bosphorus.

"These Franks talk of the advantage of making intellectual companions of their women. Bah!" said Mr. Cadogan to himself that evening, as Lady Renshawe finished a disquisition on entailed property, in which she had shown more than ordinary shrewdness, and in which her bias evidently went for, rather than against, the entailing of large landed estates.

"What advantage is it to put fire-arms into the hands of children who cannot use them properly? If we want to converse as men, we can converse with men in the mart, in the club, or in the field; but by turning these creatures into second-rate men (for they are second-rate, at the best) we lose them as lovers. We lose them in the sense in which they were given to us—as pillows for our heads to rest on when weary, their hands to hold in the silence of evening, their lips to kiss when we are weary of rough-tongued men, their eyes to meet in the sweet intervals between slumber! But these Franks allow their slaves to become their masters: and here is a specimen of the result—this horrible strong-minded, strong-constitutioned old woman!"

And Alfred threw a glance of deep disgust at the unconscious countess. Nevertheless, he addressed her with all his accustomed suavity of manner when he encountered her accidentally on the stairs that evening.

"How did you came out by that entrance?" said the old lady, sharply, glancing from the direction whence Mr. Cadogan had appeared. "*That* passage leads to *my* suite of rooms."

"I took the wrong turning on leaving my room," Alfred explained, "and found myself in a beautiful apartment, which seemed to be a sort of ante-room. There were chambers beyond it, but finding out my mistake, I turned to another door, which let me out in the passage, where I had the good fortune to meet your ladyship. Allow me?" and he offered his arm to support her down-stairs.

The countess took his arm, but she looked at him with a sidelong glance of suspicion.

"It's only the devil and the coquette who trip by design, and call it accident," she said to herself. "I wonder what he was after in that ante-room?"

Meanwhile, Alfred's reflection was:

"I cannot miss my way now."

He ate his dinner in high spirits, and patted Esty on the shoulder approvingly when, later in the evening, she sang a little song of her own composition.

ESTY'S SONG.

Once in my youth I loved a sailor lad,—
　　Loved him so dearly;
His curling locks were black, his eyes were glad,
　　Shining so clearly.

Always he thought of me, and I for him
　　Watched the dark billow,
And when the winds were wild, and stars were dim,
　　Wet was my pillow.

Fresh as the curling foam that washed the shore
　　His bright-eyed beauty;
As later rolled the tides our love grew more,
　　Though against duty:

For father bid me cease to watch his boat;
　　So did my brother;
They might as well have bade the waves to float
　　One from another.

At last, when winds were high one bitter night,
　　And mad the foam,
His skiff returned not when the dawning light
　　Brought others home.

And now, great as dead emperors or kings,
　　He who did love me,
The lad my father scorned, bears angels' wings,
　　And dwells above me!

"Really, that's very pretty," the countess said, dropping

off again into a doze, from which the cessation of the music
had awoke her.

" Very pretty, indeed ! " echoed Cadogan, languidly;
then he yawned, and pulled out his watch.

"It is bed-time, is it?" said the countess, suddenly
arousing herself, as if she had seen through her closed
eyes the movement of Cadogan's hand. "Good-night,
Cadogan."

Amidst a rustling of silks, the old lady moved slowly
from her seat, and, supported by Esty's arm, hobbled to
the door. Alfred looked after her until she had disappeared, and then he went down-stairs to smoke, whistling
softly as he walked—an invariable sign with him of a pre-
occupied mind.

Some hours later, when the blackest gloom of the night
hung over Lynncourt, the figure of a man stole gently from
corridor to corridor; a man, who held his breath every
step he took, and who, guided by his deft fingers, crept
along by the lower margin of picture-frames and the rough
sides of the tapestry, until he reached the outer door leading to Lady Renshawe's suite of apartments; then Alfred
Cadogan—for it was he who, like a thief in the night,
walked thus through his noble relative's house—paused to
collect his thoughts. It never once occurred to him to
draw back ; he had a tenacity of purpose which frequently
did duty for courage ; and although he was haunted by the
idea of footsteps pursuing him, in every uncanny noise he
heard ; and although he felt uncomfortably doubtful as to
how near the ante-room, to which he was bound, was the
countess's sleeping apartment, yet it was not these things he
paused to consider when he rested his hand on the lock of
that outer door. He could not be quite certain whether
the drawer he suspected of holding the will was the right
or the left-hand one of the cabinet ; he had fancied it was
in a drawer which bulged out a little from the rest as if
filled with paper documents, and he was desirous of avoiding any unnecessary noise by attacking a wrong position.
Having made up his mind, he cautiously applied his long
fingers to the door-handle, and was presently enveloped in
the deeper gloom of a large and lofty room. He felt with

his hands all round him, but could touch nothing substantial; he moved a step farther, when, to his horror, his
arms fell round what seemed to be the body of a woman!
With a shiver and a slight moan, which, highly strung as
his nerves were, he could not wholly repress, he withdrew
his arms quickly, when he felt a heavy blow descend on his
shoulder, which apparently proceeded from an uplifted hand.

His livid face bathed with sweat, and his heart bounding
violently, Alfred fell back against the wall, and crouched
there in abject terror for some seconds before he remembered what had probably been the cause of his alarm.

He recalled to his mind a huge wooden model, a doll,
which had served Lady Renshawe in former days as the
wearer of numberless satin and velvet skirts which her
ladyship vainly essayed to reproduce on canvas. The
countess's genius did not lie that way, so she soon ceased
to attempt an art in which she could not succeed; but the
doll had been very useful to Esty, who had made many a
careful study from the draperies arranged round its waist.

Yes, Cadogan remembered it now. The inane pink
face, the staring eyes, the expressionless mouth; and he
cursed his own folly as he passed again by the wooden
hand which had swung down so heavily at the jerk he had
given the figure.

" It ought to be here," he whispered to himself as he
passed through the thick darkness of the next room to the
angle where he remembered the cabinet was placed. He
held up his hands before his face and they alighted on the
smooth surface of its japan doors. These yielded noise-
lessly to his touch, and he then ran his fingers rapidly along
the edge of the drawers, striving to detect which it was that
contained the will. It was his intention to quietly abstract
the whole of the documents, to take them to his dressing-
room, and after he had mastered their contents, as quietly
to return them to their place.

He was quite unconscious of the fact that this cabinet
formed a species of doorway behind Lady Renshawe's bed.
It filled an aperture in the wall which had originally been
used as a curtained communication with the other room,
and the drawer, now sliding out under his hand, was in a
parallel line with the countess's head.

Lady Renshawe's sense of hearing was dull, but her
sense of touch was uncommonly acute. She was not yet
asleep, and the vibration behind her jarred unpleasantly
against the nape of her neck.

She raised her head, and, quick as the movement was,
the reflection that some one was at the other side of the
cabinet came even quicker to her ready comprehension.
She felt for her ear-trumpet, which laid on a table near the
bed, and applied it to the thin board from whence the
sound or rather sensation proceeded.

"That's it!" she exclaimed, almost triumphantly, as the
sound of papers rustling came to her ear. "There's something bigger than rats there."

Then she screwed up her face to an expression of intense
attention, and listened again.

"Common thieves come for silver and gold, but my
worthy grand-nephew only seeks for the promise of it. It
is my will he is seeking, no doubt."

She meditated deeply for a few seconds.

"I should like to give him a fright," she thought; "but I
must not recognise him. If I once saw him in this
occupation to-night I should have to be blind to him ever
after: I should have to break with him, and then I should
lose my Esty."

She lifted her quivering voice, and cried in its highest
pitch, "Who's there?" The voice penetrated through the
crevices like a cracked trumpet, and the movement of the
drawer instantly ceased.

"I have a loaded pistol, and I am going to fire," the
countess screamed, and then she quickly put up her ear-
trumpet, and had the pleasure of knowing that Alfred
Cadogan must have fallen over a chair in his flight, for
there was a sound first of a scuffle, as though of a man
striving vainly to keep his legs, then came a curse and a
heavy lump on the floor.

Lady Renshawe stepped out of bed with an agility which
would have astounded her ladyship's abigail, could the
latter have witnessed it, and went to the door communicating with the next chamber. She opened it softly,
and once more uttered her malicious threat :—

"Both barrels are loaded," she cried; "and unless you

leave the room directly ; by the ——" she paused to think of an exclamation at the same time forcible and decent—"Lord Harry, I'll fire !"

A dark shadow seemed suddenly to rise up from the floor, and passed swiftly into the far-off gloom of the outer chambers, and Lady Renshawe double-locked her door and returned to bed, where she lay chuckling for the next half hour.

"How fast he went !" she thought. "But I must manage to let him know the contents of my real will, or he will be putting something into my coffee by mistake."

CHAPTER XXXIII.

"HOW CAN I TELL HIM?"

"Fairest, if time and absence can incline
Your heart to wandering thoughts no more than mine,
Then shall my hand, as changeless as my mind,
From your glad eyes a kindly welcome find."

SHEFFIELD.

R. CADOGAN entered the breakfast-room the next morning with an expression on his face like that of a demure cat that has barely escaped detection while consuming forbidden cream. He could not be quite certain as to what Lady Renshawe suspected was the origin of her nocturnal disturbance, so he contrived that Esty should accompany him when he entered the countess's presence. He did not fancy encountering unsupported the grey gleam of those sagacious eyes. He had prepared himself to meet any spoken suspicion that might be cast at him, but spoken suspicion is not always the hardest to bear; a troubled conscience is as often unhinged by a hinted doubt in the eye, a sarcastic repression of the lips, or a hardness of a one time friendly voice, as by any definite charge of foul doing. Alfred not only feared the countess's anger, as the proprietor of wealth which she might or might not will to his wife, but he dreaded to meet contempt in her shrewd, withered face, the contempt of a vigorous, straight-forward mind, which cuts through the involvements of falsehood as

decidedly as the sharp sword of Alexander clove through the puerile riddle of the Gordian knot.

When husband and wife entered the breakfast-room, Lady Renshawe greeted them with a nod and a smile.

" Good-morning, my dears," she said ; Alfred, advancing towards her respectfully, kissed her hand, and hoped that she had rested well. " Um ! pretty well. And you ! "

" Oh, I had a restless night of it," Mr. Cadogan admitted. " In the first place I sat up an hour after my usual time listening to the nightingale."

" Really ! " said his grand-aunt, drily. " I didn't know you were fond of nightingales."

" I have frequently eaten them abroad," Alfred said, with feeling ; " and I never hear one now without thinking of their delicious flavour."

He had not meant his sentiment to terminate in this way, so he changed the subject.

" Then I felt too much awake to care about going to bed, so I took up a book and attempted to read, but I seemed to hear so many strange noises about the house ——"

" What kind of noises ? " interrupted the countess.

" Oh, such noises as are common enough in old houses," Alfred said, lightly. " They are generally caused by an exodus of rats from one side of the wainscot to another, or the flapping of some loose corner of tapestry, sounds which escape unnoticed in the day-time, but which assume weird-like importance when their origin is concealed in the darkness of night."

" Well, I also heard strange noises last night," the countess observed ; " but I do not think what I heard was either rats or tapestry. It seemed more like the fall of some heavy body—of a man, for instance."

Lady Renshawe pretended to investigate the contents of her tea-pot to hide the smile which was curling round the corners of her mouth. The hot steam scalded her nose, and she withdrew it hastily.

" I really got quite alarmed," she added ; " and was forced to threaten to discharge my pistol."

" My dear lady, why did you not call me ? " Cadogan said, kindly. " No burglar would have been intimidated by such a threat from a lady. They would pre-suppose that the pistol was empty."

"*Would they?*" replied the countess, with a grim expression on her face. "Then they would suppose wrong, for both barrels are charged. But I daresay I was foolish to be scared on this occasion. I fancy what I heard was only the falling of that huge wooden doll in my outer room; I found it this morning with its head held affectedly on one side, and its draperies dislodged from its arms."

"How odd!" murmured Cadogan, as he filled his plate with *pâté.* "I wonder what knocked it over."

"I can't imagine," the countess said, demurely; and, when breakfast was over, Mr. Cadogan retired to the library, feeling as dubious as ever as to how far her ladyship's suspicions extended.

He had one consoling reflection to fall back on. Lynn-court would certainly one day be his, or Esty's, it was all the same. He had not been deterred from his purpose by the fright that malicious old woman had given him, and when he made that hasty flight back to his own apartment he had carried the coveted document with him. He spent the whole of the remaining night in perusing it, and when the grey light of morning began to break the gloom in those silent chambers, he had stolen swiftly back to the cabinet, and replaced all as he had found it.

He had caught a slight cold, and his nerves had been cruelly shaken by that little episode of the pistol; but, on the whole, the result was highly satisfactory.

Mr. Cadogan's face expressed more than usual pleasure this morning, as he lounged on the damask cushions of the sofa, lifting his cigar to his lips with a languid movement of his hand. "I wonder where Esty is," he thought, and Esty answered the surmise by appearing at the door.

"Come and read to me," Cadogan said, in an authoritative voice; and Esty, flinging down her flowers on the table, seated herself on a footstool, and took up the newspaper.

First the City intelligence, then telegraphic despatches from the Continent, then the leading articles had to be read in routine; and Esty's sweet, low voice was getting rather husky by the time she had finished the last of these.

"I should like to rest a little," she said, looking up.

Cadogan moved down his face and kissed her. "Very
well," he answered, graciously. "You may rest for a few
minutes."

Finding his sofa cushions had slipped down uncomfortably, he pillowed his head on his wife's shoulder, and with
half-closed eyes dreamed away the next ten minutes very
pleasantly. He was aroused from his reverie by the entrance of a servant bearing the morning letters on a salver.
The visions of fresh investments, enlarged speculations, and
new slaves to grace the garden of Mirghuen, faded away
from Mr. Cadogan's mind at the sight of Sophy's handwriting
on one of the envelopes. Occupied in pocketing his own
letters for future perusal, he did not, for a moment, observe
that his wife held one addressed to herself in her hand.

She tore it open without observing the direction, and the
first glimpse of the sentence that headed the page sent all
the blood from her face:

"My own darling; my little wife!" Such was the commencement.

Alfred had not shifted his position, so that he could not
see how sharp and wan the face pressed to his own had
become, but ere the spasm of pain had passed from her
heart, his eye had fallen on the paper she held.

"What is this?" he said, and he put down his hand to
grasp the letter. It fluttered down to her feet, and as he
picked it up, his eyes met hers.

"Oh-h-h, I see, I need not ask you what it is; pray
continue reading it—or, better still, let us read it together;"
and Mr. Cadogan nestled his head again on his˙ wife's
shoulder.

"I would—rather—not now," Esty said, with difficulty.

"I daresay not, but I should enjoy it." And, in a low,
monotonous tone, he commenced reading the passionate
greeting which Geoffry had sent to the woman he loved,
and addressed to the only name he as yet knew her by
"Miss E. Lisle."

"My own darling; my little wife" ("rather premature,
eh?") suggested Cadogan in parenthesis. "I am at home
again in England—near you—almost with you once more.
Can you believe it? I can hardly do so sometimes—I
pinch myself when I wake up in the night to be quite sure

20—2

that I shall see this dear old English flower-patterned wall when the morning dawns, and not the film of mosquito curtains, and the copper face of my native servant looming behind it. I could not keep away from you any longer, little girl; twelve more such months of weariness and craving for you would take all the youth from my life. Besides, I am a richer man now than when I left you last year —I can ask for you before them all; but I will tell you all about this when I come.

"When I come! My heart nearly sets my pen bumping against the paper at the ecstacy of those words. It is something to have the power of loving as I love you, if only to feel the happiness of moments like these. A thrill passes through me when I picture you: your lips to mine, your arms round my neck, your soft hair tumbling all round my fingers, as I kiss the dear little head once again. But we have never been really separated, have we, Esty? I have never doubted you for one instant. Separation doesn't lie in the compass of a few thousand miles of sea or land to accomplish. Although I had never a line or a token from you during the whole past year, I have valued your love by my own, and I know that your eyes have been meeting mine as constantly as though they were within touching distance. It would seem foolish to you if I told you how often I have put out my hand in the darkness, and woke with a sob because I could not clasp the fingers my dreams had brought before me—could not kiss the cheek which I could swear to have felt brush past my own a moment before!—My dear, I pulled myself up then, and paused for a few moments, to let my eyes glance happiness over inanimate tables and chairs, rather than reveal any more of the weakness of my passion even to you, who are both my strength and my weakness; you will have seen the account of the wreck, and I hope you were not long kept in anxiety as to my fate. As soon as I recovered my consciousness from the fever, I wrote you letter No. 1; this is No. 2. I hope not to have any occasion to write a third letter yet awhile. I shall be in London on Wednesday, if possible; let me find a letter at the club from you.

"On Friday, at the latest, I shall be at Lynncourt;—do you remember our parting by the gate? I know you have

been faithful as truth itself to that vow—faithful as I have
been, and shall be, all my life, to the oath, and the kiss that
sealed it.   Good-bye until Friday, and then, ' O soul of my
soul, I shall clasp thee again !'   If I could only make the
clocks go a little faster, I should be a very happy man.

"Yours,

"GEOFFRY ADAIR.

" P.S.—I write from the village near which I was brought
on shore.   I send you a local account of the wreck.   My
darling, I shall soon be with you."

Cadogan had glanced once or twice at his wife as he read
the letter, but he could not see her face, which was bent
down over her knees.   When he had finished, he tossed
the crumpled paper on her lap, and yawned.

" It is very long," he said, " but I had no idea that dolt
could have written such a good love-letter.   For he *is* a
dolt," he added, musingly ; "he did not find out how to
win the woman who loved him, or to keep the woman whom
he loved.   I have been more fortunate in—ahem !" he
checked himself, and put his hand under Esty's chin.

" Let me go," she cried, "you stifle me !" and she flung
away his arm with a force that surprised him.

" I suppose you are ashamed to look me in the face," he
continued in a mocking tone.   " You don't like to meet my
eyes now that I have read of your love passages with my
half-brother—damn him !"

Mr. Cadogan was astonished at his own emphasis as he
gave vent to this curse ; he had almost forgotten, in the
triumph of his successes, how hateful Geoffry was to him.

Esty did not notice either taunt or oath.   The sharp
white look on her face had passed away, her cheeks were
glowing, and her eyes swimming in tears.   Alfred shook her
by the shoulder rather roughly.   " What are you thinking
of ?" he said, irritated by her silence.

" Oh !" she cried, suddenly, turning her radiant face on
him, " he loved me—he was never false to me—he loves me
now!   Leave me alone," for Alfred strove to detain her by
the wrist as she moved away from him.   She caught hold of
the letter, and went with it to the window.

" Faithful as I have ever been," she murmured to herself,

in a sort of ecstacy. "Oh, my darling, how could I ever doubt you!"

Then she flung herself on her knees by a chair, and covered the letter with kisses and tears.

"I have been false, but not you, thank God for that! you have kept your honour and your love unstained. My heart was broken, Geoffry, when I thought you had left me, but now I am happy—quite happy." Her voice died into a wail as she uttered the last two words, for she felt, rather than saw, that Cadogan had come up close to her.

"Listen to me," he said, harshly. "I am not going to stand any more of this nonsense. You may cry your eyes out for your old lover, if you like—not in my presence, for tears bore me—especially tears that are shed for another man; but I give you notice that I will not have Adair come here."

"No," she said, quietly; "I do not wish that. I shall go to London."

"What?"

"I could not see him here," she added, with a slight shiver, as she glanced round her. "Every path, every nook and corner would join with him in denouncing my falsehood; but I must see him. I must see him myself, to tell him of what I have done!"

Cadogan thought for a few moments. This tone of authority his wife used was as unpleasant as it was new, and he could not at once decide how to answer it. On the whole he thought it best not to arouse any further spirit of resistance, more especially as Geoffry would assuredly come to Lynncourt, and "I shouldn't like to meet him myself," Alfred confessed with an inward qualm of alarm, when he reflected how the news might affect his hot-headed, strong-armed brother.

"As you will," he said, indifferently. "I am going to London myself for a few days. I shall start to-morrow; you can accompany me if you like, only you must explain matters to your aunt; we—at least you—will return to Lynncourt at the end of the week. You have my permission to meet Captain Adair this once ——"

"Thank you, Alfred."

"But you must promise never to see him again without my expressed consent."

"Do you think I would go through such a pain twice?" Esty said, bitterly. "I could not endure that he should hear of this from indifferent lips; it will be hard enough to bear when he hears it from me—me, whose heart will bleed at every word I say. If it were not for his sake, do you think I could look him in the face again? I do not inquire now," she went on with increased vehemence, "how those lies were fabricated that helped to sever me from him; the fault was mine to be so deceived; the memory of his plighted word should have weighed more with me than all the seeming proofs you brought me of his infidelity. You have broken up my life between you, but I can bear it better now that I know I may keep my faith in the man I loved; I would rather be the victim of your lies than suffer again all I suffered in doubting his loyalty; yesterday I fancied that I had neither future nor past. Now I know that I may pray God's blessing on my darling who has kept truth and honour intact, where I have failed and am sullied ——"

"Sullied!" echoed Cadogan, with a sneer; "I was not aware that in marrying me you did anything to stain your name."

"My name; no!" she interrupted, quickly, "but my nature; yes! What is a woman who marries without loving the man to whom she gives herself? How can a priest hallow the ceremony from which love stands apart?"

"All this is very immaterial to me," said Cadogan, resuming his cigar. "I did not marry you for love."

"I know it; had you done so I should have tried to make you happy."

"Thank you," Alfred continued, insolently; "but I am afraid you would not have succeeded. You are not my style," and he stepped out on the terrace, consoling his wounded vanity with the memory of this Parthian shaft.

"No woman could like that," he thought, with a chuckle, but his sarcasm had been unheeded by the girl whom he had left pressing her hands against her face as she leant on the window-seat, staring out at the flowers and sky with a sort of horror in her eyes as she repeated over and over the self-accusing question:—

"How can I tell him? How can I tell him?"

CHAPTER XXXIV.

' ———— Ah, there's many a purer and many a better,
But more loved. . . . . Oh, how few love ! "
OWEN MEREDITH.

"Oh, false poor sweet fair lips, that keep no faith."
SWINBURNE.

R. HERBERT communicated by telegraph to his wife the news of Geoffry's safety, and Sophy had flung herself down on her knees and thanked Heaven as fervently as though she believed that Geoffry had been preserved for her especial benefit. In emergencies like this her great love made her religious, but as soon as she regained her calmness her brain was busily employed in plotting things that were hardly of a nature to be associated with spiritual devotion ; one would imagine she fancied that Heaven would ignore her sins while it granted her purer wishes. The thought that the same eye which looked mercy on her worthier impulses would mete justice to her baser ones, never seemed to cross her mind.

Mr. Herbert watched over Geoffry in the Welsh village for two days, and then returned to town, the doctor having assured him that "the cerebral excitement having subsided, no relapse need be apprehended." Geoffry had not recognised his friend until late on the second day ; a contented smile passed over his pallid face as his eyes rested their first conscious glance on George Herbert: " It seems like home, old fellow," he muttered, and then turning on his side he fell into a deep sleep, which was the precursor of his recovery.

" Did you mention Miss Lisle's marriage ? " Sophy asked, with a tremble on her lip.

" Oh, no ! I did not dare say anything that would in the least degree interest him, while his mind was only just creeping back into consciousness. I talked about you, Sophy, and the children ; I tried to persuade him to remain a few days longer where he was, but he said he should leave directly he could crawl out of bed."

" You asked him to come here ? "

" Of course, but he said he must go into the country first ; we might expect him here at the beginning of next week."

A cruel little smile played round Sophy's full lips. " He will not stay long in the country, I fancy," she murmured ; then a pang smote her heart, and she added " Poor lad ! " She pitied him, but had it rested with the movement of her hand to restore things to their former position, she would have manacled those delicate wrists rather than thus exert them ; truly, the tender mercies of a woman who loves are cruel.

Geoffry's first letter to Esty, a feeble scrawl, written as soon as he could persuade his nurse to give him writing materials, did not reach its destination until after the second letter's arrival.

" Law, Sir, I quite forgot," the landlady said, in answer to Geoffry's angry interrogations, when he discovered a corner of the envelope peeping out from a china mug on the mantelpiece. Captain Adair posted the next letter himself on his way to the station, and he stuck it into the post-office with a pleasant exultation in his heart as he reflected how soon he should follow in its track to Lynncourt. He was very little altered from what he was a year back ; his face was thinned by recent illness, and his bright curls cropped closer than usual ; but the eyes were as sweet and un-troubled as ever, and the mouth, that index of the heart, was full and tremulous, bearing as yet no trace of the com-pression of mental suffering.

As he walked quickly down the village street, the sunny,

haired children, seeking diversion in the gutters, stared up awestricken at the grand stranger-gentleman, and the women lingered at the cottage doors to pay homely tributes of admiration to his " bonny face," as he smiled response to their farewell curtseys. As he passed the last cottage in the lane that led to the station, his attention was arrested by the sight of a young man who leant over the wooden palings that guarded a long straggling garden, his head buried in his hands, and his breast heaving with convulsive sobs. Captain Adair possessed one of those kindly hearts that can never bear to witness sorrow in any shape ; just now the sight of such excessive grief especially jarred against his feeling of elation, and he lingered wistfully for a moment, trying to think of some way of approaching the mourner. " I might be of use ; it may be a money difficulty," he thought, then he consulted his watch, and finding he had plenty of time to spare, determined to make the experiment. He walked up to the weeping man, and touched him gently on the arm.

" Can I be of any use to you ? " he asked, in a soft low tone of sympathy. " Can anything help you."

The man lifted up his face and showed his brown cheeks streaming with tears. It was with a look of intense anguish he met the kindly eyes turned on him.

" Oh, Sir ! " he cried. " She's dead ! "

It is impossible to describe the pathos of that brief sentence, and Geoffry, feeling that he had intruded on a sorrow it was not in human power to alleviate, turned to go, when he was checked by the man's speaking again.

" Look there ! " he said, pointing to the cottage window. " That's where she's lying, my lass that was ; she'll never come out of there again to walk with me in the evenings. There's her rose-tree I trained for her, a real white moss, a beauty ; and there's the bit of ground I dug for her ; and other lasses will wear flowers, and go laughing and talking about the lanes ; but where will my girl be ? "

" She will be where they must come to in their time," Geoffry said, gravely ; " your heart is very sore now, but if she loved you, and was true to you, you will have that thought to look back on, and you must pray God for her future."

" But she was *not* true to me !" the man cried, with a sort .
of fierce exultation. "She wur false !—false as hell ! "

" And you can grieve for her like this ?" said Captain
Adair, astonished.

" Aye ! and why not? Don't a mother love best the
babe that's ill-favoured and ugly-tempered ? Don't a wife
kiss the fist that wallops her ? and could I go and take
away my love from my girl because she was allays doing
things that broke my heart to know? They came and told
me of her," he continued, indicating the village by a hasty
movement of his hand. " They said she wur as thick with
other men as with me. I said 'twas a damned lie ; but I
went about feeling as if someone had stuck a knife in my
heart ; at last I flung it at her and asked if 'twere true. She
laughed and kissed me ; and when she kissed me I forgot
everything else. Oh ! if she could only just get up and kiss
me now, I'd forgive her if she'd twenty lovers at her
heels."

" And was it true ?" The question slipped from Captain
Adair's tongue involuntarily, but he could not help feeling a
strange interest in the answer.

"Yes ; it was true," the man said, sadly ; "I wouldn't
credit it at first ; but one day, when she sent me to the fair
to buy her things !—Oh, Nelly ! Nelly ! how could ye !" he
broke in suddenly, with his arms stretched towards the
window of the house ; "and I did so love ye and slave for
ye !—Well, Sir, I was coming home in the cool o' the evening, with my pockets full of things to make her pretty, and
kept thinking of the sweet kiss she'd give me by way of
thank ye, when taking a short cut over the fields I came
where I wasn't expected, and I saw her — saw her —
by a honeysuckle hedge, where we had plucked nuts together often and often, with another man's arm round her
waist, and another man's head resting on her breast, and I
stepped up to her and said, ' Nelly, you're killing me,' and
she didn't say a word. So I spoke up again : ' Nelly,' I
said, ' I fear you're a regular bad one.' ' So I am, Tom,'
says she, quite brazen-like, 'and you was a fool not to find
it out before.'"

" And did you forgive her ?" Geoffry asked.

" Forgive her, Sir ! when God A'mighty makes you love

a thing, he don't leave you power to do anything but love it. You can't judge it or pardon it, that's beyond you ; you can only feel what it does wicked is sweeter than other people's good actions. I tell you," said the man, lifting a face of sullen defiance towards Geoffry, and unconsciously paraphrasing the Duke of Ormond's noble speech : " I wouldn't change my dead wench for the best brought-up lass in the kingdom. I'm going in to see her dead face again now. I got faint like, in there, so they sent me out. Good-day, and thankee, Sir."

Captain Adair watched the uncouth figure as it lounged down the garden-path, hedged by rows of fruit-bushes and rose-trees, thickly ranged against one another, and then turned to resume his walk to the station. He thought a good deal of that episode as he flitted by field and hill on his way to London.

"Was this love in its noblest or lowest phase?" He could not answer the question.

CHAPTER XXXv.

A PAINFUL INTERVIEW.

> "May we not yet, though fortune have divided us,
>   And set an envious stop between our pleasures,
>   Look thus at one another?   Sigh and weep thus,
>   And read in one another's eyes the legends
>   And wonders of our old loves."
>
> BEAUMONT AND FLETCHER.

> "I am a garment worn,
>   A love unty'd, a lily trod upon,
>   A fragrant flower cropt by another hand;
>   My colour sully'd, and my odour chang'd."
>
> THE KNIGHT OF MALTA.

T was on the evening of the day Captain Adair had said he should be in London, and Esty Cadogan sat in her aunt's drawing-room in Bruton Street, waiting Geoffry's reply to the note she had despatched to his club.

In after days, she looked back with a sort of terror on the pain of those hours of expectation, and wondered to think how she could have lived through them.   Like Fatima, she marvelled that Death, who mows down so many happy heads, should have passed by one so unhappy.   Death would have been a welcome relief to her during any one of those weary moments.

"What can I say? how am I to meet him?" her white

lips went on repeating; but they could gain no answer from the bewildered chaos in which her mind was plunged.

She could only sit, her hands clenched in her dress, and her sick heart leaping and throbbing at every sound that vibrated through the house. Her eyes kept shifting their glances nervously from the floor to the mantelpiece, and back again.

Presently a suffocating leap seemed to rise from her heart to her throat as she noted that there were only five minutes more to pass before he would come, and she repeated the old wail, "Oh, my God! my God! what am I to say to him?"

She tossed her arms above her head in a wild paroxysm of dismay and anguish, and then dropped them down again by her sides, helpless.

She was not cognisant at the time of any of those minor infinitesimal details of sight and sound with which existence is fraught, but she remembered afterwards that she had counted a hundred and forty shadows pass the window blind during that last half hour; shadows cast by the fleeting figures of the foot-passengers without.

Suddenly the haze in which her more acute sensibilities were dimmed was broken in upon by the sound of a quick, rushing step on the pavement without, followed by a sharp peal of the door bell.

"He has come," she moaned, putting her hand to her side to try and subdue the convulsions of her throbbing heart. As she spoke, the door was flung open, and Geoffry stood on the threshold.

He looked eagerly before him; for the moment he could not discern Esty. The room was dark, and as the door opened she retreated instinctively into the shadow; but it was only for a moment, and then he was at her feet, kissing her hands with an emotion too great for words.

"Oh, my love! my life!" he murmured, "you don't know how I have dreamt of this moment. I have got you again, my own, my darling."

He lifted his face, wet with happy tears; he could not see the expression of hers, which still rested in the shadow; had he done so, not all the joyous blindness of love could have prevented his noticing what a ghastly countenance it was. He was content for a few moments, content to bask in the thought that she was there, that he could really see and touch her again; and then he lifted his head to seek for welcome.

"Esty, have you no word of love for me?" he cried, with a thrill in his tone which smote her to the heart, it was so tender, so assured of what it asked.

His voice, his manner, his presence, woke a thousand recollections in her lacerated mind; she strove to stand up, and struggled to compose her voice, but it was a miserable failure. She looked one moment into his eyes, and then fell on his breast in a great passion of sobs and tears.

"Esty, my own! my little love! my wife! what is it?" Geoffry put his arm round her, and tried to soothe her with every tender word he could think of, but she only shook her head piteously when he urged her to speak.

"What does it all mean, Esty? is this pleasure's sorrow? is it the sight of me that agitates you? If so, darling, think how much more bitter your tears might have been. I might have gone down in the dark waters that night of the wreck, if a merciful God had not preserved me to know what life's happiness is. We must be married soon, Esty, or——What is it?" for she shrank away from him with a half scream.

"Don't, don't!" she cried.

"What is grieving you, my own? tell me! Who has a better right to know? Is there sickness at home? No! What is it, then?"

Geoffry began to speak impatiently, a presentiment of evil was stealing over him. This excessive sorrow exceeded his comprehension. What did it all portend? Why could not Esty speak to him?

Her left hand was lying on his knee, and in taking it up to caress it, his lips fell on a round metallic substance; he dropped her hand hastily, and looked more closely at the finger thus encircled, while a sharp cry, almost unearthly in its intensity, broke from his lips.

"What is this?"

There was that in his husky tone that made her lift her head, but she dared not meet his eyes, and she sank down again, her face buried in her hands.

For a brief space there was silence. The clock went on in its placid count of minutes, minutes which to her counted as hours, and to him were clouded by strange forebodings of evil. Presently she raised her face again.

"Geoffry."

"My own."

He moved down his head to catch her whisper, and put his arm round her.

"Tell me what it is, Esty," he pleaded, in a tone in which tenderness was mixed with anxiety. "What do you mean by wearing that ring? What—whose is it? Is this a joke of any sort? if so, it is a bad one, for it has given me a sharp pain in my heart. Tell me, dear, why do you wear it?"

"Geoffry," she whispered, in a husky, unnatural voice; "don't call me your own. I am not your own now; I never can be again. Geoffry" (for she saw a look of incredulity in his eyes), "*it is true!*"

"What is true? Why do you torture me? You will drive me mad!" and with a livid pallor in his face, and a sickness creeping over his heart, he seized her by the wrists and looked into her eyes.

"What is this you are saying to me, Esty? Whom am I to call my own, if not my affianced wife, the girl whom I love, and who loves me? You do love me, don't you, Esty? you are not going to give me up?" A terrible doubt crossed his mind for an instant, but he repelled it as impossible. "I am sure you love me; I am sure you could not change in this little time. Oh, Esty, why are you speaking like this? answer me, dear!"

The tears stood in his own eyes now, although they did not fall. His recent illness, the emotion of meeting her again, and the sight of her tears, were getting too much for his composure, strong man as he was.

"Geoffry!" she called him again, nerving herself with a desperate effort to say the three words that must be said before they parted.

"Yes, my dear love."

"Geoffry, I am married!"

He stared at her with a face out of which all reason seemed to have departed, the eyes dilated, the expression one of dull stupefaction. "What are you saying?" he asked hoarsely, and then he started up, a sound between a curse and a scream came from his lips.

"Tell me, Esty, you are mad, or that I am so, that this is not true; it cannot be true. Oh, Esty, *you could not have lived to tell me so.*"

"I wish I had not," she cried, passionately, "for my heart is dead in me, and I live like one tied to a corpse. Oh, Geoffry! listen to me," she sobbed. "I am married. I have given myself away from you. I have been so weak, so worthless. Oh, Geoffry, forgive me—in Heaven's name forgive me! for the sake of our old love, forgive my weakness now. My mother was ill, and I never heard from you; they told me you were caring for some one else, that you were married, and I thought my mother would die because of her anxiety about Gerald, and Alfred came and let Gerald off; but I've written to you, Geoffry; and, oh, forgive me, or I shall die!" She caught hold of his hand and kissed it, weeping passionately the while, and continuing her prayers for pardon in broken incoherent syllables.

Geoffry did not notice the touch of her hand, or the appeal in her words; he was looking out into space, his face white and rigid; the tears in his eyes dried up by the hot brand that seemed to scorch them.

Could this be truth?

Could this be the woman of whom he had dreamt day and night, the belief in whose faith and honesty had become a sort of religion to him? Those wild, heartbroken words that were babbling at his feet—was it Esty who was speaking them? Was this a gloomy, crushing nightmare from which some sudden shock might awake him?

Again came one of those miserable pauses in which the silence was only broken by the sound of choking sighs and the muffled roll of the carriages in the street.

She lifted her tear-stained face, and pulled his coat-sleeve gently, and then his eyes fell and met hers.

They never forgot that glance, fraught as it was with the sharpest pain life could inflict on either of them. In hers was all the misery, guiltless as she was, of a trust betrayed, of a soul whose integrity had failed, of weakness that had inflicted a mortal injury on him whom of God's creatures she most loved.

There was no want of truth in his eyes—truth terrible in its reproach, and in the intensity with which they read her faltering countenance.

"Esty," he said, in a hushed, subdued tone, " on your soul, is this true ? "

"Yes."

" It is true, and it is you who tell me of this ! Oh, my God ! my God ! " and the unhappy young man arose and walked frantically up and down the room like a wild animal maddened by the injury of an unexpected captivity. Then he stopped suddenly, and turned his white miserable face towards Heaven. "Was it for this I was preserved? Was it for this Thy hand upheld me ?   What had I done to deserve such a bitter punishment as life ?   Oh, Esty ! " he wailed, coming up to her, but not looking at her.   "If I could but have died a week ago, if I could have gone down under those waves that were stunning me and suck- ing me in their depths on the night of the storm, I should have died battling with death for your sake, your eyes met me in the black face of every advancing wave. I could hear your voice above the shrieks of drowning wretches and the wild roar of the winds.   Your image never left me, and when life seemed to me to be slipping from me—when the choke was in my throat, and darkness came over my eyes—I held you in my sight with the last moment of consciousness. If God had let me die then I should have been content—I should have died blessing Him, and loving you."

His voice broke, and he concealed his face with his hands.

Esty crept up to him with weak and uncertain move- ment. Her limbs trembled, and her head was getting dizzy.

" Forgive me, for Heaven's sake ! " she said, once more clasping his arm with her two hands.

He flung her off as though her light touch scorched him.

" Don't come near me ! " he cried.   "*You* talk to me of forgiveness ! *you* ask for pity in Heaven's name. Why, you

have outraged Heaven as much as you have injured me.
Do you think that God will smile on a union made up of
treachery and broken vows? If it were not for the
memory of what you have been to me I could curse you?"

"He curse me!" she murmured, and she cowered down
by his side. Could these be Geoffry's words?—words of
malediction in place of the loving tenderness that had been
wont to haunt every tone addressed to her? She put her
hand to her head. Her powers of suffering seemed to be
failing her, but she made one more effort to obtain the
pardon she so coveted.

"Oh, Geoffry!" she cried, in a heart-rending voice; "if
you ever loved me, pity and forgive me!"

He looked at the blank face of despair she turned up to
him—at the quivering figure huddled at his feet, and felt for
the first time since he had known and loved her, the entire
fragility of the idol he had worshipped. An access of pity
swept away his resentment. He met her pleading hands
with his own—

> "And all his scorn was kill'd, and all his heart
> Gave way in that caress."

"I forgive you," he said, and he drew her to his breast,
and kissed her forehead. "Considering what we have
been to each other, you need not grudge me that much,"
he added, misconstruing her shrinking movement.

"It is not that," she murmured; "it is that I am not
worthy of your caress."

He was touched by such excessive self-abasement.

"My poor child!" he said; "do you know what it is
you are asking me to forgive? Do you know that every
thought of my mind, every feeling of my heart, has been so
bound up in you, that parting from you is worse than death
itself to me? You, Esty—you whom I loved better than
man or woman—you who brand yourself as worthless—
what can I say to you—you whose truth I would have
answered for with my life?"

"That you forgive me," she reiterated.

"Forgive you, yes! but will you ever forgive yourself!
Will not the evil consequences of your weakness and

treachery shadow all of both our lives? Shall you be happy without my love, Esty? Can you soon forget me?"

"You know I cannot."

"Then you have been as cruel to yourself as to me; but you have not told me yet who has helped you to do me this wrong."

Geoffry's face was not pleasant to see now, a dark look of anger flushing its hitherto deadly whiteness.

"I have told you all in a letter. It is here."

"Who is it?" He took the letter, but repeated the question.

"Alfred Cadogan, your half brother," she said, in a voice filled with sullen despair.

"What! have you married *him?* Is that the man you have chosen to fill my place? My brother! No! thank God, no blood of mine is in his veins! My poor, poor Esty, you have indeed avenged my wrongs on your own head."

She was alarmed by the look of menace she had seen pass over his face.

"You won't hurt him?" she cried. "Promise me you won't. It will only make matters worse."

"Are you only anxious for his safety?" Geoffry asked, in a hard voice.

"I know he couldn't hurt you," she muttered.

The chimes on the mantelpiece struck four.

"We must part now."

She dreaded lest Alfred should return home. Moreover, she felt that a prolongation of this scene would utterly prostrate her.

"Part!" he echoed. "Part! and from you! Oh, Esty, Esty! I cannot bear it! What have I done to deserve this?"

His voice was broken by tears, and the man, whose frame was like that of a young Hercules, buried his face in the sofa cushions, and sobbed like a child. She bent over him, and tried to speak words of comfort, but only murmured inarticulate moans, while the hot tears running down her cheeks mingled with his. She fancied she heard a step outside on the threshold, and she started up.

"My husband will soon return."

"God curse him!" he said, moodily. "Kiss me, Esty! kiss me once before I go! Our lips may never meet again."

She lifted her mouth to his, and he kissed her—a kiss in which all love's passion, all death's agony, seemed concentrated, and then he rose to go.

"I forgive you entirely," he said. "It may comfort you to think that in the dark days to come. Remember, I love you! If evil ever comes to you, if you are ever friendless and unloved by all others, I shall still be yours, and yours only;" and then the words of the poor rustic he had met the day before came to his mind, "When God makes you love a thing, He doesn't permit you to unlove it," he repeated sadly; "but for those who led you into this," he added, his eye kindling with sudden rage, "may they be cursed in this life and the next!"

He walked up to her as if he would have kissed her once more, but he only touched her hand with his lips—a touch cold and hopeless as that we press on the brows of our dear dead, and then the door opened and shut and—he was gone.

"Geoffry! Geoffry!" She staggered towards the door, but fell down on the sofa beside it. "Ah me!" she sighed, putting her hand to her head.

The room seemed growing dark; her head felt on fire. She walked to the window, and attempted to open it. Perhaps the notion of seeing him once more as he passed down the street had something to do with this movement—the instinct of love was still strong even in the delirium which was beginning to confuse her brain, but her hand failed her; a film came over her eyes; she clutched at empty air to support her, and fell heavily to the ground.

Meanwhile Geoffry stood under the shadow of the portico, trying to compose his features into their ordinary expression, before facing the passengers in the street; his head seemed girt with a band of hot iron, and it was a relief, with that fever in his eyes, to feel against them the cool drops of an autumn shower that was beginning to darken the air. He was descending the steps, when he stopped short on perceiving that another man was ascending them. This man wore a fashionable overcoat, buttoned to the chin to exclude the evening damp; he carried an elegant cane in his hand, to which his slight figure bore no little resemblance, and he picked his way on the steps with dainty fastidiousness, to injure as little as possible the gloss of his beautiful little boots.

Thus it was that he did not at first see the flashing eyes and ashy face of the man above him. Man! Geoffry resembled rather a wild animal, making an ominous pause before springing on its victim—animal instinct so much preponderated at that moment over aught of divine—and yet his self-command enabled him to say to himself: "I will not compromise *her* by hurting the cur. I will pass him quietly."

He would probably have kept to this resolution, although he had a cruel mind to tread under foot this snake-like man, who was going in-doors with claims to caresses from which Geoffry must evermore be exiled.

He walked quickly down the steps, assuming not to notice the scared glare of Cadogan's eyes, as the two then met.

"D—n the fellow," the latter said, *sotto voce.* "I thought he would have been gone an hour ago."

Mr. Cadogan had forgotten that lovers' clocks are quite independent of ordinary rules of horologic mechanism. Unfortunately, Mr. Cadogan decided to attempt a show of friendly ease: "How d'ye do, Adair? haven't met you for an age," he said, holding out his gloved hand.

"You cursed hound, let me pass!" was the sole response Alfred's civility met with.

In the surprise of the moment, and taken aback by the somewhat menacing movement Adair made to clear the way, Mr. Cadogan involuntarily lifted his cane in Geoffry's face. In an instant the cane was spinning its way into a distant area, and Mr. Cadogan reeled heavily against the stone pillar at the base of the steps, finally landing on his hands and knees on the pavement.

"I'm sorry I touched you," Geoffry said, contemptuously, as he passed the fallen and shrinking man. "Oh, don't be afraid, I shan't do it again; there's my address if you want it." And tossing a card down by his prostrate relative, Captain Adair walked quickly out of sight.

Mr. Cadogan got up, rubbing his knees rather ruefully, and looked vindictively after Geoffry's figure until it disappeared at a corner of the street ; then, with an expression of intense spite gleaming in his eyes, he murmured, emphatically, " BEAST ! " which was all the satisfaction he took, or ever essayed to take, for the rough handling Geoffry had accorded him that night. So it is to be hoped that the ejaculation was a comfort to him.

CHAPTER XXXVI.

FEVER.

"———— And nothing could I realise
Save a dull strangeness,—the disgrace of a stunn'd impotent surprise."
OWEN MEREDITH.

" To be mad
Is dreadful ; yet in this a softer ill,
We have no sense of the calamity."

NIGHT had come, and Esty lay in bed staring at the fantastic play of the firelight reflected on the wall opposite. Uncorked physic bottles, half-empty glasses, a few withered flowers and bruised peaches in a plate, upright tenantless chairs, all seemed set in the silence of the hour. Only the clock on the chimneypiece kept up its watchful irritation ; that and the surging in Esty's head were all the sounds she heard during the night.

"Missus was very ill," the maid had said who opened the door to Alfred Cadogan when that gentleman re-entered the house, stiff and limping after that little " accident " (as he generously called it) which befell him on the doorstep.

"The devil she is !" Alfred said, with an expression of great discontent. He wished to send his wife back to Lynn-court the next day, and this illness, if serious, would render the scheme impossible.

" Don't you think you could move, dear ?" he suggested, in his silkiest tones ; but Esty answered his look of interrogation with one so utterly blank and meaningless that Alfred groaned and turned away from the sick bed.

He hated sick beds and illness of all sort, and he saw that Esty was already very ill. "I daresay she will be there for weeks," he thought; and then he determined to send for Christine in the morning, unless Esty were much better. Meanwhile he had an engagement which would keep him out late. He told Esty's maid, a country girl who had accompanied them from Lynncourt, "to attend to her mistress, as he should not sleep in the house that night; he had an urgent engagement." She was to send the man in charge of the house for a doctor if Mrs. Cadogan got worse.

"Call hisself a man !" the girl remarked, as she closed the door after him when he took his departure for the evening, dressed in faultless evening attire, a red carnation in his button-hole, and a bright gloss on the ripples of his black curls : "I calls him a brute." And she went up-stairs and attended to Esty, to the best of her abilities.

These abilities were not very transcendent, and Esty dimly conscious that something awkward was moving about her pillow, dropping corners of lace pocket-handkerchiefs into her eyes, and splashing eau de cologne in her mouth, said "she was going to sleep," and begged her maid to retire for the night.

The latter acceded to the request gladly. A strong, healthy girl herself, she felt she "wanted her sleep," and "she daresay missus would be all right after a good night's rest." People who are well and sleepy are always so willing to believe the best of their patient's case, under these circumstances. So Esty was left in solitude, and, as the hours ebbed away, her consciousness died away with them, and mad images of fever soon took the place of all coherent thought.

Her hair lay in a soft web of tangles over the pillow, her eyes were startlingly bright, her lips parched and open. At first she counted the throbbing of her pulses in her forehead, then she left off, attracted by what sounded to her like dead leaves whirled by the window-pane.

"We shall have a hard winter," she said half aloud. She thought she heard the moaning of the sea, and fancied she was galloping as hard as she could down a cliff. Shining patches of sand, scattered boats, and mounds of grass flash by her eyes, and then the horse stops suddenly, and the fancy melts away over a long line of purple hills and red-tipped woodland. " Geoffry, is that you?" she called, suddenly, but no one answered her ; only a little mouse disturbed by her voice ran rapidly across the floor, and retired to its family under the wainscot. This seemed to Esty very funny, and she laughed a low, jarring chuckle, that broke in strangely on the silence of the night.

Meanwhile the burning pain in her head grew worse, and her throat was parched with thirst. " Oh!" she moaned, piteously, " I want Christine ; where is Christine?" Her hot hands plucked the sheets nervously as she reiterated her plaint. " Do come, Christine! you would if you only knew how I want you!" The fire flames on the wall became confused before her gaze, and her eyes themselves burnt like hot sparks of fire.

Again her thoughts wandered. " Geoffry," she said in a low earnest voice, "come back to me, come in time to save me from him. Do you remember when we stood by the river, the red sun was in my eyes as it is now? We watched the reapers sweeping down the corn, and you plucked red poppies and twisted them in my hair. There was the river winding and gleaming through meadow and meadow. We counted the brown and white sails fluttering down the sun-streaked waters, and you said, ' Life was so sweet, 'twould be good to die then.' Did you die—or I—I forget; but I think I've been dead since then. You kissed me, Geoffry, but you won't kiss me now; you run away from my shadow, and you say ' Curse you!' Oh!" she cried out in terror, for in her delirium crowds of faces seemed suddenly to press round her, and the room was filled with strange menacing voices, "take them away. Oh, Christine, come and save me; why do you keep singing so down-stairs when I am being murdered here?"

She rose from the bed and thrust her feet to the ground ; but when she stood up she staggered and fell heavily on the floor. She fancied that some unseen hand had clasped her ankles, and in the terror and pain of her fall, she fainted.

When Christine arrived the next day—Christine, who on receipt of Alfred's intelligence, had sped up by an early train, passing swiftly by dewy hedgerows and mist-silvered meadows, with heavy anxiety in her heart—her sister stared at her fixedly in the face. "Who are you?" she asked, in a cold voice of inquiry, Christine fell on her knees, and covered the thin hands with kisses and tears. "Don't you know me?" she entreated with eyes and voice, but Esty looked beyond her.

"There is an angel there," she said, disregarding Christine's question, "but he is going without me; for an infant has died next door, and they always go first."

CHAPTER XXXVII.

"IF I COULD KILL MY MEMORY."

"Our loves have been of longer growth—more rooted
Than the sharp word of one farewell can scatter."
VALENTINIAN.

"I used to sit and look at my life
As it rippled and ran, till right before
A great stone stopped it: oh, the strife
Of waves at that stone some devil threw
At my life's mid-current, thwarting God!"
R. BROWNING.

I DO not envy the man who returns to a solitary home with such a feeling of desolation in his heart as Captain Adair carried back with him to his lodgings the evening of his interview with Esty. For a few minutes after he left Bruton Street he had felt a savage exultation at the memory of Alfred Cadogan's quivering voice and prostrate limbs, but ere he reached his own door the temporary excitement of his nerves passed away, and the heaviness of the moral blow that had been dealt him began to tell in its effect. The servant who showed him in was startled by the ghastly look in the new lodger's face.

"You're ill, ain't you, Sir? shall I get you some brandy?"

"No, thank you," Geoffry answered, shortly. "Please to bring me my letters. I sha'n't want anything else until I ring."

The wound in his mind was so raw that he could not even bear the indirect approach to it by sympathy given to its effect on his face, and he sat down in the shadow to avoid further observation. He sat there in silence for some hours after his letters had been brought, and the door had closed on the servant; sat motionless amidst the clatter in the street without and the twinkle of the lamps opposite the window. There was life underneath—life, busy, rollicking, hurrying, laughing, and genial; the street-boy's light whistle that mingled with the dainty sibilations of the gaily-dressed women who crowded the pavement; the roar of wheels; the murmur of men's voices, all represented an existence to which Geoffry had at one time thought he should never return.

Now he wished with all his heart that he never had returned—wished that he had not fought so hard against the waters—that he had gone down in the rush and struggle of that stormy hour, instead of living to envy those who never reached shore again. It was harder to sit there in the dusk, looking at the wreck of his life, than it would have been to yield up "the last poor sigh" in the cleft of the waves, when he paused to touch Esty's locket and to breathe her name.

Life seemed inexpressibly dreary to him; he yearned to be a boy again, and to be years away from this bitter hour. He thought of his father with a pang of regret; the eyes of our lost dead never seem to look so tenderly at us as when we are wounded by the unkindness of the living. "I did so love her," he said, softly, as he sat there facing the blank of the future.

This woman's smiles had been the sunlight that made the day beautiful to him. In the glamour of her presence, all that was lovely, whether in art or nature, received fresh charms from its association with her image; the hope of her, the pride in her, had become entangled with every feeling of his heart.

How could he pluck out her image? Because her eyes and voice had self-convicted her of weakness and falsehood, could he displace the idol his thoughts had cherished all these months? Even now did not the thrill of her voice, as she pleaded for pardon, ring down from ear to heart, and

did not his face flush as he thought of that parting kiss?
Was that "the last," he thought; "oh, my love, my life,
was that the very last?" Then he thought of another who
had now a right to the lips that should have been his alone,
and his brow darkened and his eyes sparkled as the hell of
an intolerable and helpless jealousy raged in his breast.

His meditations were broken in upon by the servant's
entrance with candles.

"Have you seen your letters, Sir?" the latter said,
officiously.

Geoffry, taking up a few, opened them with a dreary
indifference of manner which did not escape the domestic.

"Hard-up!" he said to himself, as he left the room.

Insolvency was a malady that came oftener under that
quick-witted youth's observation than broken hearts, so he
may be pardoned the mistake. One of the letters was
directed in Mrs. Herbert's decided-looking handwriting; it
was dated the previous day.

"I cannot tell you what our feelings were at hearing of
your peril, and subsequently of your safety," it said. "Do,
my dear Geoffry, come and see us directly you get this, and
read your welcome in our eyes and hands: words cannot
express feelings like these; and an inky scrawl on paper is a
poor, weak greeting to give to such a friend as yourself, after
a separation in which we nearly lost you altogether. We
start for Brighton to-day. Follow us as soon as you can,
and believe always in the devoted friendship of—SOPHIA
HERBERT."

"Friendship! Well, I suppose I may believe in that!"
Geoffry said, dreamily; but in his heart he felt that he
believed in nothing human. "I will go to them," he
thought. "To whom else can I go? Better be at Brighton
than within half a mile of her face, and not be able to look
at it!"

He consulted a time-book, and decided to go down by
the mail train. If he found the Herberts' house shut up at
that hour, he could go to an hotel for the night. He had
no time to lose, so he ordered a cab at once, and ere
another hour was past, he was in an express-train whirling
through the darkness between Croydon and London.

Mrs. Herbert had acted wisely when she decided to

remove from London on hearing from Alfred Cadogan that the *quasi*-lovers were to have their first meeting there.

"He will long to leave the place," she calculated. "He will endeavour to get away from the sting in his heart. He will come to me—to me, who will welcome him with love, which is only more intensified every hour I breathe—with passion ripened by long scorching under restricted confines! He will come, and then !——"

It had been what sailors call a "dirty day" at Brighton. The rain drizzled down in the morning for a few dim hours, during which the vaporous mist veiled the sky and distant sea-line in one silvery obscurity ; then the rain-drops grew larger and more frequent; finally, they came down in heavy showers, washing, in long sluices, the smooth pavements and shining white houses, and driving to distraction the weary faces that were pressed against the bespattered window-panes, to watch for fairer weather.

Peace and dulness reigned in Sophy's house at No. — Marine Parade. Mr. Herbert had gone to dine with a bachelor friend at Rottingdean, and was not expected home until late. The lamps were lighted in the drawing-room, and the fire-light threw rosy gleams over the pink damask sofas and downy *fauteuils* scattered about the room.

Mrs. Herbert sat in an easy-chair before the fire, her head thrown back, her eyelids half closed in sleep, and her hand passed through the half-cut leaves of Balzac's " *Illusions Perdues.*" Probably these pages, powerful and pathetic as they were, were not interesting to Sophy, or the brown-fringed eyelids would not have fallen so low over the rich velvety orbs they concealed.

Her bosom heaved gently under the lace handkerchief twisted carelessly round her shoulders. One little foot basked in the warmth of the fire, the other was tilted over her knee. For once, the somewhat abandoned grace of her attitude was purely accidental. She was quite alone, and she was enjoying herself, in her own sleepy, sensuous fashion. The remains of a pheasant, some light jelly, and half a bottle of Mâcon, stood on a little table near her elbow. There was also a basket of wall-fruit, and every now and then she would wake up and languidly peel off the tawny skin of a peach, and consume the fruit in slow bites, between intervals of slumber.

The voluptuous beauty of the sleeper, the ruddy blaze of the fire, the almond scents from the house-flowers, formed a strange contrast to the bluster of the storm without. The shutters were closed and the curtains drawn, for Sophy hated the wail of the wind and sea on a rough night, shutting her ears determinedly to sounds that suggested labouring barques and drowning men.

"It's dreadful!" she said, with a shudder, when her maid spoke fearfully of the fate of a vessel which had seemed in distress the latter part of the day. "Send me my dinner directly, Jane, and don't talk of such things."

The heavy curtains and barred shutters deadened the howl of the tempest to her ears, and she was dozing, with a smile on her lips, and just a rose-leaf tinge of colour on her smooth cheek, when the ring of the front-door bell reverberated through the house.

"I suppose that is George," said Mrs. Herbert, half-opening her eyes; then letting them close again; "I wish he would not ring quite so loudly."

The door opened, and a voice, strange yet familiar to her, called out her name. Her heart beat wildly as she stood up with outstretched hands to welcome the speaker. Her languor vanished instantaneously. Love awoke her to all love's alertness; at the sound of that voice, "her eye, her lip, nay, her foot" spoke, as she stood there, flushing and tremulous, crying out, in words not less passionate because simple:

"Oh, Geoffry! you have come back to us! I am glad! I am so glad!"

When George Herbert returned home, his welcome, if of a different description, was not less cordial than Sophy's.

"You haven't quite got over your illness yet, I see," he said, with a kindly wish to account for Geoffry's haggard face; and the latter smiled faintly, and admitted that the attack of fever had been a sharp one. He had no doubt but that he should be all right in a day or two.

Sophy's heart stung her as she looked at the shadow of the man who left her a year ago, with health on his cheeks and hope in his voice. The eyes were inexpressibly grave and sad; the full mouth had lost its fullness, and was haunted by a tremulous look of pain; and, above all, his voice was most altered, for, in place of its old, ringing heartiness, it was deliberate, and almost harsh in tone.

Sophy sat and looked pity on every altered lineament, but she could not repent of her share in the alteration. " Better he should die than I live in hell!" she thought. " Oh, Geoffry! if you could but love me a little, I should be content!"

Mrs. Herbert did not show her usual shrewdness in this remark. No love that is great is ever content with its reciprocation; the passion that can be limited by content ceases to be great.

Geoffry'rose early the next morning, and walked down to the sands. He had watched the grey lines of coming day creep over the sea's edge in the east, until he could bear it no longer; he could not lie there and wait for the daylight that was loathsome to him. With the unrest of sorrow he walked rapidly along the shore, as though his hurried steps could carry him away from his thoughts.

The fox may escape his pursuers by virtue of fleet foot and wary eye—the wild beast may turn and rend the incautious sportsman with tooth and claw; but the unhappy human being has no refuge, excepting in death, from the evil thought that haunts him as his shadow; his eye can never evade the image of pain, his foot never carry him away from its relentless pertinacity.

" If I could only kill my memory," Geoffry said, as he stood watching the tender light the new-risen sun shed on the foam breaking over shiny patches of sand and trailing clumps of seaweed. " If I could put away all the past, I might begin life again." He put his hand to his neck and drew forth the locket he had worn so long. He looked at it earnestly. " If I were a hero of romance, I should throw you into the sea," he said; "but I love you still, and so I kiss you, and put you up again." And he suited the action to the words.

22

CHAPTER XXXVIII. •

A WOMAN'S WOOING.

"I cannot love thee.
Without the breach of faith I cannot hear ye ;
Ye hang upon my love like frost on lilies :
. . . . . . you are answered."

VALENTINIAN.

"HOME! home! let me go home!" had been Esty's constant cry during the three weeks in which she had hovered between life and death.

When the fever left her, she was so weak and helpless that Christine carried her like a child in her arms. It was a comfort that she was too feeble to think. She would lie on the sofa motionless for hours, with nothing more important to occupy her mind than the pattern of the wall opposite, or the gambols of a soft, furry kitten, which had found its way up into the drawing-room, and there spent its days in helpless involvements amidst the contents of Christine's wool basket.

Mr. Cadogan, as soon as his wife was pronounced out of danger, bade her an affectionate farewell; he was quite happy in his mind now as to her succession to Lynncourt, and felt he could afford to pay a short visit to Constantinople; he had been away too long, both for his advantage in business matters, and his pleasure as regarded his establishment at Mirghuen.

"How glad they will be to see me again, poor little souls !" he said to himself, as he twirled his mustache before the looking-glass ; "but I must give them up now ; they are so expensive, and when I possess landed estates in England, I shall have to stay here to look after them."

"Mind you take care of Esty," he said, kindly, to her sister ; "I do not expect to be away longer than two months. Be sure and get her well by the time I return."

"If you're so uneasy about her, don't you think you had better stay ?" Christine suggested, drily.

Alfred shook his head. "If my time were my own nothing would give me so much pleasure," he said, gravely ; "I have business, very important business, at Constantinople ; and in the worry of—in the pleasure of the new tie I have contracted, I have neglected my affairs too long. Kindly write to me until Mrs. Cadogan is better, and then direct her to address to me at the English post office at Galata. Good-bye !" He offered his lips to his sister-in-law, but she turned away with an impatient jerk, greatly at variance with her usual gentle way of moving.

"I would as soon kiss a snake," she said, as she watched his shadow glide by the window-blind, when he walked past the house on his way to the club.

His luggage followed him, and, after writing a few lines to Mrs. Herbert, he sat down to dinner with a friend who was to accompany him by the night mail to Paris.

"In less than twelve days I shall be drinking coffee under the maple-trees by the Bosphorus," he thought, gleefully ; "I shall first drive a bargain or two with my Greek friends at Galata, and then I shall go and pull Zirma's yellow hair under the rose terrace at Mirghuen."

His letter to Sophy was tender, but authoritative. The very insolence of its affection made Mrs. Herbert flush with anger when she read it. The chain Cadogan held her by never seemed to gird her so painfully as now, when her heart was leaping beyond its bounds towards that other man. In Geoffry's absence, the adoration lavished on her by his half-brother was soothing to her vanity, and gave her satisfaction as being part of a scheme by which she was to sever Geoffry irrevocably from Esther Lisle. But now the scheme was accomplished, and the mad worship Alfred had accorded her was succeeded by a patronising tenderness which was very hard for her to bear.

"I hate him! I loathe the memory of him!" she said, as she scattered the fragments of the offending letter to the flames. And she rejoiced to think that the writer should leave England at this juncture.

Nothing could have happened more opportunely for her hopes and wishes. She told Captain Adair that Cadogan had left for Turkey, and watched anxiously the effects of her communication. Geoffry's pale face turned even paler, as he said, quietly, "He has left his wife very soon." Sophy did not know what a fierce thrill of delight passed through his jealous heart at her words, and hoped, by the placidity of his manner, that the wound was healing.

Captain Adair had read and re-read very often the letter Esty had put into his hand the day of their last interview. He could not at all understand certain passages of it. How was it she had not received his letters? Who were the "they" who had spread a report of his marriage in India? He would inquire into these matters as soon as Esty was recovered, but it never entered his mind to suspect treachery in so kind, so old a friend as Sophy Herbert. He frequently intended to speak to the latter on the subject of the letter and its contents; but his heart failed him each time he attempted to open his lips with Esty's name on it. "When a man is hanged, it is hardly worth considering who twisted the rope," he thought, gloomily. It never occurred to him that deliberate falsehood had been employed to separate him from his love. He thought that there had been mistakes and bad management somewhere, but, however that might be, the greatest mistake of all was in Esty's own weakness of purpose.

"No one but herself could have parted us. If she had loved me as I loved her, no mistake could have come between us."

While Esty was in danger, he could not leave the place where he could most quickly obtain news of her; he was not certain that he wished her to live. Esty dead might be nearer to him than Esty living as another man's wife, the mother of another man's children. He ground his teeth in impotent rage when he thought of her thus. Yet when he imagined her to be suffering pain and sickness, his heart melted with tenderness—he forgave all, forgot all, in the desperate wish to be near her again, to comfort and nurse her.

He had begged Christine to give him sometimes intelligence of Esty's state, and soon after Alfred Cadogan's departure from England, Christine wrote from Lynncourt to say that her sister was convalescent.

"There is nothing to detain me here any longer, then," Geoffry said, half aloud, as he stood looking out at the sea by the window in Mrs. Herbert's breakfast-room.

"What do you say?" asked Sophy, sharply, who had entered the room as he spoke.

"I was thinking that I had trespassed on your hospitality long enough. A trip across there" (pointing seaward) "would do me good, and relieve you and Herbert of a useless clog,—a visitor who is as bad company to his friends as he is to himself."

"Hospitality!" she echoed, looking at him furtively. "Is that all?" and then she checked herself.

"Have I not reason to be grateful for your hospitality?" he said, taking her hand kindly. "From my boyhood, you and Herbert have been my best, my only true friends; do not think that because I am a stricken-down man I am an ungrateful one. The memory of you both will always be held dear by me, whatever I be, wherever I am!" He still held her hand, looking, not at her, but at the sails passing away over the sea's verge.

She snatched her hand away, her eye flashed, and her cheeks turned livid.

"Geoffry," she cried, in a harsh, trembling voice, "you are a fool!"

He started, and looked at her with wonder.

"Yes," she continued hurriedly, her lips whitening as she spoke.

"You are a fool—a deceived, obtuse, pitiless fool! Stop!" She checked his impending exclamation by a motion of her hand. "Do not interrupt me. I have been mad so long that I must bring it out, or I shall die. Did you think that a woman like me could feel only sisterly interest in a man like yourself? Do you remember what I

was when I first met you? A girl—young, handsome, and
warm-blooded—going to be linked with an old plain man.
Do you remember the night before I married, when I tried,
with kisses and tears, to wake that love in you which was
scorching all my own heart? You did not understand me.
You were as beautiful but as cold as the statue which I
cursed as your likeness, when you left me there to eat out
my heart in shame and anguish! You went away. I tried
to live it down, this girlish fancy, this yearning of youth
towards its like; but whenever my husband put his
withered face near mine, I hated him for the memory of
your smooth cheeks and red mouth. Stop! you *shall* hear
me!"

Geoffry, with a kind of terror in his eyes, had moved
farther from her, and now at her last words put his hands
to his ears.

"This is not earth; it is hell!" he cried. "You are
mad, Sophy, mad—quite mad!"

"I know I am; but think of all, Geoffry—all I have
suffered, and do not wonder if I can repress my insanity
no longer. Remember how long and how much I have
been tortured. You went away, and I settled down into a
life of calm stagnation. I was content, if not happy.
George was very kind to me, and if I could have but forgotten that I had known what love was, I might have
lived content with its ghost. I almost thought that I had
succeeded in crushing the feeling; but when you came back,
oh how my sick heart leapt and throbbed again at the
sound of your voice, the touch of your hand! I forgot all
my resolutions; the calm of my life died for ever; henceforth all was storm and bitterness."

The tears welled up in her eyes, and her words came
brokenly through her sighs. Hitherto she had not looked
at Geoffry to see the effect of what she said. Now she
tottered towards him with a piteous look of deprecation in
her face. She recoiled before the expression of his eyes,
and then flung herself at his knees.

"You must pity me! If you do not love me, you must
pity me—me who have never wept but once before, and
that once I was at your feet, as I am now. Think of it all,
Geoffry: how you came to me joyous and selfish, to

demand sympathy for your love for another; think how every word that glorified her slighted me; how those tender phrases you used when speaking of her cut me to the heart! Was it not hard to have the warmth of your love shining so near me, and I out in the cold shadow? You never even thought of me, Geoffry. Don't think I impute any blame to you. I know you never thought of me, and that was the hardest pang of all. Was I ugly, old, or unattractive, that your eyes should never have owned the power of mine? Oh, Geoffry, why did you never think of me? It has been in dreams, Geoffry, that I have tasted the only happy moments of my embittered life, for in dreams I have heard the whisper of kisses that might never bless me in the day, have felt the caress of hands that never moved towards me, excepting in the illusions of slumber. I am beautiful, Geoffry; I was so, at any rate, when I first knew you, and I did so love—oh, so love you!"

The passion of the moment enriched her tones as she murmured these last words.

"It might have been so," Geoffry said, gravely; "you were beautiful, and yet I never thought of love. When we first met, I was an uncouth lad, more prompt to run a footrace than to think of woman's lips. Latterly ——"

"Yes."

"Latterly you were my friend's wife; and the thought of dishonour to him would have been as strange to me as theft or murder. Oh, Sophy, tell me that this is some hideous hallucination! that you don't mean what you say! It is so hard to think that I have lost all I had in the world, and to see you suffer like this, and for such a reason. It seems incredible. You are mocking me."

The young man tried to call a smile to his wan face, and to raise Sophy from her kneeling position. He thought it possible that this might be a temporary delirium: it is so difficult to believe that things are otherwise than as one has seen them for many years past. She lifted up her face, the red-brown lights in her eyes shining subdued through a mist of tears.

"You do not believe it," she said; "and yet if I showed you a bracelet on my arm and told you I had worn it there since I had known you, you would believe that! I love you, Geoffry. I love you best of all living things. Why should you escape knowing what I have known so long?— and I would not give it up. I would not relinquish my love even when you curse me with that cold look in your eyes. Oh, Geoffry, can you not look differently at me?"

She linked her hands round his arm, and rested her wet cheek on them.

"No, I cannot," he said, quietly.

He removed her clasped hands, and placed her in a chair.

"You may think me hard, Sophy, and the world—the fashionable portion of it—would judge me a fool if they heard my answer to your wild words. I could no more take advantage of such love as this, under such circumstances, than I could go up to Herbert and stab him in the back. I know there are men who will not scruple to accept of a friend's hospitality—will eat at his table, sleep under his roof, meet him each day with all the cordial seeming of true friendship, while they take advantage of his confidence to dishonour his wife, and taint his blood. I am not of these. To be treated like a brother by George Herbert, and to commit a sort of moral incest by intriguing with his wife, would be impossible to my nature even to conceive in idea."

"If you had loved me," she muttered, "you wouldn't reason in this way."

"If I had loved you I should not have eaten Herbert's salt for these last dozen years."

"Can—you—not—love—me—a little?" she faltered. "Is it too late?"

"Woman, what are you tempting me to?" he cried, in a harsh voice. "Where is your own conscience? Do *you* owe nothing to the man who has loved and trusted you all this while? You were portionless, and he made you rich; you were unloved (she winced at this, but still devoured his face with the unholy fire of her eyes), and he loved you; his whole life, his wealth, his name, his children—all are yours! Do you feel no reflected worth from his to induce you to stifle the dishonour in your heart?"

She was silent, but she felt even then that condemnatory words from him were sweeter than silence. She anticipated, with sickening dread, the moment when his voice would cease, and he would leave her presence for ever.

"Tell me," she said, walking up to him, and staying her hand on his chair, "if it had been otherwise, if I had never married, if you had never met that other—would you have loved me?"

With cruel truthfulness, he answered, "*No.*"

"You are sure?"

"Quite sure."

He felt the words were bitterly hard ones with which to answer such a yearning face as she turned towards him; but his instincts were all truthful, and he would not lie now to save himself the pain of the present, when his so doing might prolong this woman's torture to an indefinite period. It was kinder to crush it all out at once, he thought, but his heart smote him when he saw the glassy look that came over her eyes, the quick heavings of her breast.

"Oh!" she groaned, "I cannot breathe!"

He drew her to the window and supported her in his arm as he unclasped the fastening, and admitted the fresh air to her poor, pinched face. She turned her eyes up to him with a look of intense love.

"It is the first time," she gasped, "you have held me thus. Oh, that I could die!"

He placed her gently in a chair.

"Forgive me, Sophy," he said, "the pain you have forced me to inflict on you. It has been harder to bear than my own was."

She laughed an unpleasant little laugh that jarred on his ears.

"Shall I tell you something?" she said.

"If you like, Sophy."

The kindly gentleness of his tone exasperated her more than his invectives had done. A wild fury took possession of her breast.

"You need never have lost that puny-faced girl if you had not trusted a mad woman with your secret. It is madness, isn't it, which makes a naturally kind-hearted woman diabolically false and cruel ?   I never gave your messages to Esty Lisle ; I concealed all my knowledge of you from her ; I tempted Cadogan to marry her ; he did not like her, but he worshipped me, and to win me he would have married a savage.   He consented to ally himself with that child for love of his 'glory,' as he called me, and I was glad to do anything which should put a bar between you and her.   I told her you were engaged to another woman ; I intercepted your first letter to her, that one you wrote in A——Street."

Geoffry seized her by the wrists.

" What ! " he cried, with a strange joy in his voice ; "do you mean to say Esty never heard anything of me all the time I was away ? "

" Not to my knowledge," Mrs. Herbert said, sullenly.

" Then my darling was not so much to blame after all. Tortured by my silence, conspired against by ruthless men and women, hellish voices round her to prompt doubts of my honour—oh, my Esty ! " the young man cried, with ineffable tenderness in his tone, " if I could only tell you at once that half the weight of misery is lifted off my life."

Sophy looked on him with wonder as he paced rapidly up and down the room, with a light in his eyes which she had not seen there since his return home.

Like Cadogan, she was incapable of appreciating the moral height of love like this.

"She had the hope of you ; she might have relied on that."

" But did you leave her any hope ? "

Sophy was silent.

" I know you did not," he went on, excitedly.   " When such as you and Alfred Cadogan do the devil's work between you, one may be sure you did it well.   So, Mrs. Herbert, you have not been my friend ; you have been my enemy all this while—my false, cruel, treacherous enemy. You have killed my happiness ; you have spoilt my life for me.   The news you prepared for me on my return brought wrinkles to my face and grey into my hair, and it turned my twenty years old to sixty.   Do you not expect God will damn you for this year's work ? "

" Be silent, Geoffry."

Once more she went up to him and confronted his face, all ablaze as it was with honest wrath.

"What I did was for love of you. I lied; I forfeited self-respect, even self-love, for did not your cruel indifference murder vanity? I was guilty in life, and I have to face the prospect of that hereafter which awaits the vile in heart, for I do not repent, Geoffry; I cannot repent, and slip into the hopes of heaven by means of abject recantation of my errors. All this I did for love of you. I have loved you ever since I have known you—I love you now; forgive me if you can, and let us part in peace."

The generous heart of the young man was touched.

"Let God judge you," he said. "Good-bye for ever, Mrs. Herbert. I shall leave England to-night. May your own conscience be your only punishment!"

"It is my memory that will avenge you on myself," she cried, with a ghastly look of pain. "The memory of that one word '*No*' will be quite sufficient penance for all the years that are left to me."

CHAPTER XXXIX.

THE COUNTESS'S DEATH.

" . . . . How the swallow got a wing broken
In the spring-time, and lay upon his side
Watching the rest fly off i' the red leaf time,
And broke his heart with grieving at himself,
Before the snow came."

SWINBURNE.

HE two months Mr. Cadogan had mentioned as including his term of absence from England had
nearly elapsed, but still he gave no indications in
his letters of any intention of returning home.
He made frequent and affectionate inquiries after Lady
Renshawe, much to that venerable lady's amusement, who
had reason to know how to appreciate the worth of his
kindly interest.

Esty breathed more freely after each perusal of these
cramped, formal-looking epistles. His presence had weighed
on her like a night-mare, and she looked forward with
nervous dread to the hour when those snake-like eyes, and
that cold patronising voice should reassert their influence at
Lynncourt.

"I must do all I can. I must not bring pain to them at
home; but if it had but pleased Heaven to let me die, it
might have been better for all," she thought, during the
hours of depression that attended her recovery from illness.

She divided her time between her two homes, striving to

give pleasure to all, calling up faint smiles to deceive the anxious scrutiny of Christine's loving eyes, and exerting herself more than usually to supply interest and amusement to her grand-aunt's fading life.

The latter was by far the easier task of the two. The unconsciousness of Lady Renshawe's dulled eyes, the abstraction of her wandering thoughts, were balm to the mind so wounded that it could not bear the slightest approach to its hurt even by the pitying glance of affection.

Esty had never spoken Geoffry's name since she had recovered her consciousness, and all that Christine could learn concerning the pain of that interview was its result, as shown in two or three silvery lines that rippled through the coils of her sister's brown hair, and the increased deepening of the shadows under her eyes.

"Miss Esty mopes about the house like a sick bird," Dolly said, reflectively, after a visit to Lynncourt, when her unruly charge of former days met her with a grave sweetness of manner which quite disconcerted the testy old woman. "I wish she'd tear my cap and slap my face like she used to when she was a blessed babe."

Christine smiled at the quaintness of Dolly's sentiment, but she too wished with all her heart that she could wipe away the few last years of her sister's life, and by her be pelted with acorns, or play at hide-and-seek in the mossy glooms round Gardenhurst, as in the old blithe days of their childhood.

Now Esty's chief content was to sit with her aunt in the long grey evenings motionless and silent, her hands crossed over each other, her eyes veiled by seeming thought. In reality, she did not think at all, only sometimes the flash of suddenly-remembered eyes, the echo of a tender word, would cause a keener pang to cross the monotony of her sorrow.

She rarely left the house, excepting to accompany her aunt's chair as the latter was wheeled slowly through the golden windings of the gravel paths that intersected the flower-beds. The thick-leaved shadows of the shrubbery might deepen or wane according to the colour of the changing year, but Esty's footsteps never penetrated into those dewy solitudes now. The hare sped over the speckled light of the moss walks, the squirrel flung down the empty kernels of the beech-nuts from his breezy home in the branches, but no human tread bruised the seeds of the wild grapes or scared the bird from its twig. The ghost of her past happiness would have met her at every turn of that tangled labyrinth of trees and shrubs ; she avoided even glancing at the distant masses of gold and green that marked the windings of the woodland. So moss crept over the bars of the rustic · gate that guarded the entrance to the shrubbery, its hinges stiffened in rust, and the silvery cobweb hung unbroken on its handle.

As the weeks went on, the smell of summer died out of the air, and was succeeded by such bleak winds and dank fogs that Lady Renshawe was obliged to forego her garden-drives, and content herself with watching the whirl of dead leaves from the window of that sitting-room where she had sat down to face the approach of winter for many a lonely year.

She could no longer recall those weary, loveless days of the past, for her memory had failed her, with the yearning desire she had used to feel when she heard the prattle of cottagers' children in the corn-fields, the longing for little hands to pluck at her dress, for little feet to patter over her threshold. All these aspirations belonging to life's warm blood had faded away in the chill of age. She still felt a clinging sort of affection for her niece—the affection that makes a blind, maimed dog lick the hand that heals its hurt, and seek to grope for its protector by instinct when its other faculties have perished ; but otherwise the once keen-eyed, quick-witted countess cared for little excepting her daily meals and the small comforts of life with which Esty's care provided her.

One day, towards the end of November, Lady Renshawe crept down her broad oak stairs for the last time ; she descended with quick breath and halting steps, pausing on the landing-place beneath the picture of King Charles's haughty-eyed mistress. A flickering sunbeam played over the insolent red lips of Barbara Villiers, and Esty, who followed in her grand-aunt's wake, stopped for an instant to admire the sheen of the silk drapery Lely had depicted falling off the round-ness of the mellow-tinted bust, and the tender curve of the fingers that dimpled in and out a string of pearls they held, when her attention was recalled to her aunt by the latter's sudden exclamation of distress.

"What is it, dear?" Esty asked, running to her side; but the countess only put her hand to her heart and muttered something inarticulate. Presently she appeared to recover, and signed to Esty to give her an arm into the dining-room. They sat there in silence for some minutes, and then Lady Renshawe said in her usual voice: "Ring for dinner." Esty obeyed, and did not hazard any remark respecting her aunt's apparent indisposition. The latter never cared to have such questions asked. The dinner came up. The old butler attended with his usual stateliness to the requirements of the two ladies. All went on smoothly until he handed some dessert to Lady Renshawe, and then the spoon the countess held fell out of her hand. She smiled vaguely, as the butler replaced it in her fingers.

. "Grown stupid," she said, in that low faint voice that had become habitual to her; then she rose stiffly from her seat, and leant over the table—"For what we have received may God make us grateful."

The last word of the grace had barely escaped her lips, when she fell forward heavily on the table. Esty and the servant hastened to her, and replaced her in her chair. She was quite conscious, and when she saw the alarm in the two pale faces near her, she spoke, although with difficulty:

"It must come to all!" she gasped. "It has come to me. Don't cry, Esty. Don't take me up-stairs—to my chair in the sitting-room."

They carried her to her old place by the ivied window: there she fell into a doze which continued for some little while. Esty sat and watched the withered face of the sleeper with anxious terror in her heart. She despatched a messenger to W—— for the doctor, and another to Gardenhurst, but it would be some hours before the former could arrive. Meanwhile she would not risk vexing her aunt by having a third person in the room, or by indulging in the unusual luxury of lighted candles. So she sat alone in the grey twilight, her eyes straining through the obscurity to detect the slightest alteration in the countess's face. It came at last; that fatal change of countenance when the look of humanity sharpens into clay, and it came before aid or comfort could arrive. The wrinkled fingers groped their way to Esty's head, and there rested.

Esty lifted up her face eagerly. "What is it, darling?" She had to lean her ear very close to her aunt's face to catch the answer.

"Bless you, my child! More kind than Clara was. James will succeed me—it is right so—I am going to learn the truth. Pray God, papa may meet me. It was time to go." Such an infantine word as "papa" had not escaped those shrivelled lips for fifty years past.

Again there was silence in the room, only broken by the sound of a leafless branch that beat against the window-pane, and the patter of the rain falling on through the laurels outside.

Lady Renshawe grasped Esty's hand, and her eyes distended with sudden animation.

"Hark!" she said. "Do you not hear them?" then she fell back in her chair, and her eyes turned upward. Esty never knew what sound it was that haunted the ears of the dying woman, for the latter did not speak again.

The wind swelled its wail, and the night grew darker, and still Esty sat alone, her hand resting on the knees that might never bend again at their owner's bidding. She did not yet dream of the truth, for the increased darkness had prevented her seeing the expression of her grand-aunt's face. It was not until the lights were brought that it was discovered that James Lisle was now Earl of Renshawe; and Esty buried her face, with a sorrowful cry, in the folds of the silk dress that hung round the inanimate form in the chair.

"Would to God I had gone with thee! Would that it had pleased Him to take me also into the darkness!" she cried, in the bitterness of her heart.

CHAPTER XL.

AN EASTERN SCENE.

"Does a new life, like a young sunrise, break
On the strange unrest of our night, confused
With rain and stormy flaw?"

R. BROWNING.

INTER had come and gone, and still Alfred Cadogan lingered at Mirghuen, speeding his leisure hours in the rose-trellised kiosk, where Leila, the Georgian, turned on him the sleepy languishment of her large black eyes; and Zirma, the fair-haired, stroked her golden braids with looks of sullen defiance, as she noted that her lord's glances fell more frequently on her rival than on herself.

Mr. Cadogan liked Leila very much, but he liked self aggrandisement better, and he would not have lingered abroad thus long had it not suited his interest to do so. It pleased him to exercise the subtilty of his intellect against those wily-minded Asiatics with whom his business brought him in contact; it pleased him still better to outwit them and (thanks to the native ability he inherited from his father, he not unfrequently did so), above all, it pleased him to stay away from England until such time when keeping his wife would entail added riches, and not additional expenses to himself. One day, early in January, he was lounging on the red cushions of his sofa, smoking a hookah, and listening with an indolent, amused expression of countenance to a furious war of words that was going on between the two chief aspirants to his favour. The birds that hung in gilded cages from the lattice-bars chattered the louder to drown the shrill vociferations of the women; but the soft bubble of the fountain in the centre of the room was quite lost sound of in the clatter of their scoldings.

Zirma was angry because Leila had been presented by Alfred with a new bracelet of English workmanship; it had formerly belonged to Mrs. Herbert, and Alfred had unclasped it from her arm one fine midnight, when, the two together in the balcony at Brighton, he had sworn to cherish it for ever as a memorial of the kiss he had been permitted to press on the round arm it encircled; but the passion that animated his caress at that moment had long since died away in his heart, and prudence (always the better part of all his other qualities) had survived it; so he packed the jewel up with his other possessions when he started for the Continent, fully intending that it should supply the place of any costly bauble his favourite inamorata might desire. Unfortunately, Mrs. Herbert had not twice given him the opportunity of securing such a costly memento of herself, and so Alfred was unable to satisfy the claims of both the fair denizens of his Turkish retreat.

"Thou whose yellow hair is as coarse as strings of matting, canst thou pretend to match it with a ruby?" said Leila, angrily, with a vicious twist of her own black braid, to rescue it from the clutches of Zirma's fingers.

"Thou most immodest! Thou who feedest chickens of both sexes without veiling thy face! Thou whose hair is dirt-coloured and unworthy to make a cushion for my feet!" screamed the angry Circassian, choking so with passion that she was unable to continue her string of invectives. "Come here;" and she dragged her rival to Alfred's feet, where they both assailed him with such a volley of words, screams, and tears, that he put his hand to his ears to deaden the din.

He rose to escape, but Leila hung about his neck, while Zirma clung round his knees, determined not to let him depart before she gained either a right to the coveted treasure, or to one similar to it.

"I tell you what," said Mr. Cadogan, as he extricated himself from the embraces that impeded his flight, and made towards the door: "you children of infidels are more clamorous than Christians—more avaricious than daughters of Israel. I will not visit you again for two moons. Go to Jehannen, both of you!" and he retreated hastily behind the crimson hangings that concealed the exit to the apartment, his temper ruffled and his arms aching from the effects of the energetic pinches Leila had bestowed on him in her efforts to detain him. The two beauties ceased wrangling when he was out of sight, partly because the absence of spectators always diminishes the zest of a quarrel, whether between women or dogs, and partly because Zirma became too incensed for words. A "woman scorned" is a dangerous enemy, to whatever clime she may belong; and Zirma's heart filled with sullen wrath, which boded no good to the slighter of her charms, should he come within reach of her vengeance.

Alfred made his way down to the landing-place, and hailed the *caïque* that was to take him to Constantinople. It was early morning, and those who are acquainted with the shores of the Bosphorus can imagine what a lovely scene greeted Mr. Cadogan's eyes as he stood awaiting the approach of the swarthy boatman to the landing-place. Festoons of fishermen's nets hung wet on the maple boughs that overhung the water; fruit, glowing between layers of vine leaves, lay piled up in the baskets that waited transportation to the market. Crowds of felucca craft darted swiftly through the heaving current, leaving foamy sparkles dancing in their trail.

As far as eye could follow the stream into misty distance, it beheld, rising above the blue depths of the river, terrace after terrace bright with flowers, the delicate spires of mosques gleaming in the clear air, hills, rich with verdure, and gardens that dropped rose leaves along the margin of the waters; cypress trees that rose dark against the gay glow of the shore—the whole suffused in that soft rosiness which is the characteristic of Eastern landscape.

Mr. Cadogan paid little attention to the beauty of the scene; he anathematised his two boatmen for being late in responding to his signal, and taking his seat in the *caïque*, was soon far on his way down the stream. He intended to come back to Mirghuen in two days' time.

23—2

"They will be cooled down by then," he thought, "and Zirma will be glad to welcome me on any terms." He little thought what kind of welcome the enraged Circassian was preparing for him against his return home.

When on the evening of the second day Alfred re-embarked at Tophana, a Frenchman, who accompanied him down to the quay, asked him when they should meet again, as they were both engaged in an important speculation, and Mr. Cadogan's presence at Constantinople would be required in a few days' time, in order that the latter might sign some papers relative to the business in hand.

"This is Tuesday," Cadogan said, reflectively. "When shall you want me here again?"

"On Saturday."

"On Saturday, then, without fail, I will be with you by twelve. Adieu!"

And Mr. Cadogan, waving his hand to his companion, got into his *caïque* and recommenced his journey homeward.

"What wicked-looking faces those boatmen have!" the Frenchman said, as he walked away from the quay. "I wonder where my friend Alfred goes to spend his evenings." But he thought no more on the subject until Saturday arrived, and then he had occasion to tax his memory to recall every word that passed on the occasion of his last interview with Mr. Cadogan, for the latter never kept his appointment; and, as day followed day without any tidings of him reaching Constantinople, those who knew him began to have anxious apprehensions on his account, feeling sure that some unprecedented accident must have detained him from keeping an appointment where his money interests were concerned. Their forebodings were increased when one day a packet from Mirghuen reached the hands of his French friend, announcing that Alfred Cadogan had never returned to Mirghuen, and begging that inquiries might be made, both of the members of Alfred's household and the boatmen who had been accustomed to transport their master to and from Constantinople. This packet emanated from Leila, who was frantic at her lord's prolonged absence, and who had reason to suspect that Zirma was in some way the cause of it.

The emissaries of Turkish law are prompt to act when actuated by hope of lucrative reward, and as it was important to Mr. Cadogan's French friend that the former should be proved dead or alive, no expense was spared to further the investigation. One of the *caïges* was secured (the other having made good his escape over the mountains), and as the captured man had no bribe to offer the police officers equivalent to that which awaited them at the hands of Cadogan's friends, he was first forced by threats of corporal punishment to own all he knew of the Englishman's fate, and then handed over to justice, to meet the reward of his crime.

The substance of the boatman's confession was contained in the newspaper called the *Levant Herald*, the only portion of it that was suppressed being the references made to the bribe with which Zirma had tempted "her master's servants into the commission of the crime that would rid her for ever of the pain of witnessing his attentions to her rival."

Those Europeans who interested themselves in Cadogan's fate thought it useless to introduce an element of scandal in the affair, to increase the anguish his friends in England would feel when they should hear of his unhappy fate; so they put aside all mention of his private residence at Mirghuen, and the paragraph in the *Levant Herald* merely expressed its regret that one of those foul murders, accompanied by robbery, that were of only too common occurrence, had again disgraced the beautiful waters of the Bosphorus. "The unhappy Englishman was first struck in the back, his pockets were then rifled, and his body flung overboard. The English consul was exerting himself to the utmost to secure justice to the assassins, while the regret Mr. Cadogan's loss would occasion in the mercantile world (of which he was so esteemed a member), and in that private circle of friends who bewailed his loss in England, would doubtless be as loudy expressed by the one as deeply felt by the other." The paragraph concluded with sympathising with every one who might be concerned in the matter, and cited a case of a young English midshipman having been attacked in a similar manner by his *caïges* during the period of our occupation of Turkey, only the middy was fortunate enough to be able to keep his assailants at bay with a revolver until he could obtain assistance. The paragraph in the *Herald* finally found its way in a curt form to England, but long before then it met Captain Adair's eye in the column of a French newspaper, which he took up carelessly from the table of a restaurant, where he was dining one evening in Paris.

The gas-lights glared hideously in his dizzy sight as he caught the full meaning of the words before him. The polite attentions of the *garçon* who waited on him were totally unresponded to during the next quarter of an hour, and that worthy man came to the conclusion that this English-man was more mad or *bête* than even Englishmen generally were.

"God forgive me for being so glad," Geoffry thought, as he stood on the deck of a Channel steamer the next morning, watching the shores of France growing dim to the sight. "I never thought another man's murder could make me feel so light-hearted; but I had no hand in it, and I cannot curse the ill wind that has brought the love of my life near me again!"

Lady Renshawe had left the bulk of her property to her nephew, James Lisle. "It was right," she said, "that the inheritor of her title should have sufficient means to dignify it; and now that the wild days of his youth were over, she doubted not that her nephew would be as worthy an heir as she could select." To Esty she left her jewels and a legacy of twenty thousand pounds; the principal to be lodged in government securities, and the interest thereof to be paid to Esther Cadogan's own order, through the trustees appointed for the purpose. The countess acknowledged she had previously arranged that Esty should be the inheritress of a larger portion of her wealth, but, taking into consideration the anxieties that might accrue to so young a woman from the possession of colossal property, she, the countess, had altered her intentions in favour of Colonel Lisle—a "pro-ceeding which, she was sure, would find favour in her dear grand-niece's eyes."

Esther was even more gratified at her father's accession of fortune than she was able to express in the cordial words and loving looks with which she hailed it.

"It would have brought *him* back directly," she thought, with a shudder; for with instinctive appreciation of her husband's character, she guessed what an effect the intelli gence of her being heiress of Lynncourt would have had on his movements. As it was, she feared her legacy might prove an attraction too potent for him to resist. It was not until three months after her grand-aunt's death that she learnt that Alfred Cadogan could never give further trouble in this world to friend or foe.

One day she was sitting alone in the upper drawing-room at Bruton Street, a different apartment from that in which she had made that miserable confession to Geoffry Adair. *That* room she never passed without a sick feeling of self-reproach in her heart; now she was waiting in the twilight for the return of her maid from a shopping expedition. Esty had come up to town unattended, save by this maid and a man-servant, for the purpose of making various purchases for her mother; they were to sleep in town two or three nights, and Mrs. Cadogan pressed her face wistfully against the dingy panes as she counted the lonely hours that must elapse before she could feel tired enough to wish to retire to bed.

She was thinking of the sweet scents that were blowing along the fringes of the honeysuckle lanes round Lynn-court, and thinking how pleasant it would be if a breath of them could penetrate into that smoke-dried, dirt-tainted court, into which the back window of the room looked, when she was surprised by hearing a ring of the bell, followed by the sound of feet outside the door. The foot-man's voice was heard in energetic protest.

"I do not know if Mrs. Cadogan would wish to see you, Sir; pray let me first announce your name;" but his re-monstrance was unheeded. The door opened, and Captain Adair entered the room. Their eyes met, and on this occasion the look of welcome was mutual.

CHAPTER XLI.

THE ACCIDENT.

"I hear my blood sing, and my lifted heart
Is like a springing water, blown of wind
For pleasure of this deed."

SWINBURNE.

ESTY and Geoffry sat in silence for some time, reading their happiness in the fire-light. A strange constraint came over them. He, on his part, felt almost afraid to speak of the feelings that were making his eyes dance. "Will she think that I speak too soon if I tell her all my heart now?" he thought. "Will she think it necessary to show any semblance of affection or respect to that dead man who came between us?" He could not decide the point at once, and yet every moment words trembled on his tongue, which when spoken must decide his future for ever.

Esty sat motionless and silent; the fire cast warm light on the silken sheen of her dress and on the little hands that lay clasped in her lap, but her face was in shadow, and Geoffry could not see the expression of it.

It was now nearly two years since they had parted affianced lovers under the shadow of the oak tree at Lynn-court. During a great portion of the time Esty had exerted all the strength of mind she possessed in the endeavour to forget him; perhaps the effort had never seemed so futile to her as it did now that she recalled it, while her rebel heart was bounding so exultantly at the release from the dreary penance she had imposed on it.

She tried to repress the throbs of what seemed to her conscience to be a somewhat guilty joy; she wished she could have been released in any other way than by so tragic a termination to that other man's life: she honestly deplored the cause, but do all she could it was impossible for her to subdue the happiness of her heart, while she felt the result in the joy now coming near her. She had striven to do well by Alfred Cadogan in the short time they had been thrown together, but he repulsed and slighted her; she had scrupulously endeavoured to put away from her the image of the man who loved her and whom she loved so well, and now the very self-control she had exercised in the past seemed to intensify the sweetness of her present tumultuous happiness.

There was still silence between them, for they neither of them cared to trust their consciousness to words; they heard only the lap of the flames against the bars and the faint sound of far-off wheels without.

"Esty!" he cried at last, in a low voice, that had somehow a sound of pain in it. "My Esty!"

She moved her face out of the shadow and looked at him.

"Come here," he said, imperiously.

Unceremonious as the injunction was, she obeyed it, and stood up before him with those "hearts' meteors," as Shakespeare so beautifully calls blushes, glowing in her face at every word he spoke.

"Tell me, Esty, if it were all coming over again, would you forsake me now and give yourself to another?"

"No," she said, her eyes flashing through her tears. "And you know I should never have broken faith with you only that ——" Her voice quivered, and she hid the shame in her face by sliding down through his arms to the floor, and hiding it between her hands.

"Esty, do you love me still?" he whispered. He touched her ear with his lips as he spoke, and for an instant everything seemed to swim before him in his heart's ecstacy at that caress.

She turned up her wet face towards him, and steadied her voice to answer him.

"I have never done otherwise; I have never ceased to love you. I have tried hard to banish you from my thoughts; I have prayed to forget you, but I have lived to know that only death or madness could have blotted out your image from my memory. If with a hard struggle I managed to pass a day without recalling you, you were avenged at night, when my thoughts were no longer under Reason's control. And the end of all the efforts that have wearied so many months of my life—of the days that were so cold and hopeless when not enriched with the thought of you, is this—that ——"

"That what, dear?"

He lifted her arms from her sides and wound their soft coil round his neck as he looked down into her eyes, waiting her answer.

"That I love you more than ever."

"Take care, Esty," he said, drawing her nearer to him; "take care how you deal with the man whose heart you have once nearly broken! Do not tell me you love me if there is a shadow of a doubt plucking at your heart to stop the words on your lips. Do not let the hunger of my love be disappointed with the lightness of the food it consumes. There must be no lie between us now. If there be a doubt left—if there be any wavering in your mind as to the path you wish to take—tell me, so that I may let you go, now and for ever. But if you love me as I love you—to the absorption of every other feeling—if you wish to compensate me for the last two years—say 'Yes, I love you,' and no human power shall ever divide us again. Which is it to be —Yes, or No?"

He released her from his arms for a moment, and the lapse of their warmth struck a chill through her frame; she shivered and held out her hands to him.

He caught her to his breast in an embrace so tight that she could feel the beating of his heart throbbing against her bosom, and took with a kiss of her lips her answer of "Yes."

The evening crept on—the moments melted into hours— the fire burnt lower and lower in the grate, and the room grew dark; while outside the roar of the London world came subdued from behind the ranges of courts and alleys.

To them the hours fled as minutes; the gathering darkness was unnoticed, for they read the light of love in each other's eyes—a light that blotted out all shadow. The rumbling of the wheels seemed hundreds of miles away; sorrow, anger, and misery, all were dissolved in the joy of the present. Thus together, what memory could poison those kisses?—what foreboding could still those wildly-beating hearts?

"To-morrow, love, to-morrow," murmured Geoffry, a few hours later, when he rose to go in spite of the detaining hand she laid on his wrist. "I *must* go, love; there is the license to be got, and a thousand other things to ——. I shall lose no·time now in securing you as my own. Good-bye, my darling, my wife! To-morrow I shall come again."

It has always been thus, has it not, oh shade of Cressid?

It is thy woman's eyes whose office it is to cast lingering glances after the lover who disappears in the morning mist through the city gates, till his form becomes but as a blurred speck to thy dimmed gaze. It is for him to promise to return to thee; it is for thee to wait with patience—to rejoice at his advent or to bewail his absence, according as fate and he shall ordain.

"To-morrow, love, to-morrow," Geoffry repeated, as he kissed her lips once more. Then he went, and she listened, with her face buried in the sofa-cushions, to the sound of his departing footsteps. When she went up to bed, she dared not let her thoughts rest either on past or future only, and in the happy trouble of her dreams that night she was haunted by the recurrence of his parting words, "To-morrow, love, to-morrow."

Two days afterwards they were married, and the old clergyman who made those twain one thought that he had rarely seen a lovelier pair of faces stand before his altar-rails. "A love-match," he said to himself, with a smile and a sigh, as he rose from his knees at the end of the service. "It makes me feel young again when I see faces like theirs paired together." And for an instant he saw his wife standing bonny and blushing before him, with all the wrinkles of thirty years' privation smoothed out of her face.

They were married by special license; and it was arranged that Esty should return home two days afterwards, to break the news to her family.

"I am afraid they won't like it," she said, fearfully. "They will think I ought to have waited longer."

"I think I have waited long enough!" her husband said, stopping the objection with a kiss. "And when may I come down to claim you again? I am not going to submit to a lengthened separation, I can tell you. You will go down on Monday, you will tell them on Tuesday, and I may come down—when?"

"The next day, I suppose," Esty said, with a rosy blush.

And her lover-husband thanked her with a look in which love seemed to brim over in his earnest, shining eyes.

"Oh, my Esty," he said, bending over her, as they stood once more by the fire-place at Bruton Street, "there isn't room in my heart to hold all my joy! I could kiss the clock for having told the happiest hour of my life. I should like to catch at the birds in the air; to sing aloud amid the roll of organs; to run along the ridge of a breezy mountain; to throw myself over it, burying my love and life in one crash. I am too happy, too happy!" And he let his joy run over in passionate caresses of her hair, lips, and hands. "What are you thinking of?" he asked, jealously, for she was silent, her face wearing a far-off look of dreamy happiness.

"Nothing," she said, turning the love in her eyes on him; "only some lines of Robert Browning's were running through my mind."

"What are they?"

> "What's the earth,
> With all its art-verse music, worth,
> Compared with love found, gain'd, and kept?

she quoted, with an exultant ring in her voice. "We are each other's now, Geoffry, in health and sickness, till death shall put his silence between us. It is a thought to go mad with joy on!"

When it was time for Esty to return home, Captain Adair saw his wife off by the train that was to take her to Lynncourt. He had not intended to escort her to the station; the young couple agreed, with commendable prudence, that Geoffry's appearance with her at the railway might be commented on unpleasantly if they happened to be recognised by any stray acquaintance. Esty recanted her prudence before she had got half way down to the terminus.

"I should just like to see him once more," she said, as she took her seat in the railway carriage. "I wish I hadn't,"—and then she checked herself with a blush and a thrill; for lo ! he stood close to her window.

"I couldn't help it," he whispered; "don't be angry, darling."

"Geoffry !" she stammered, confused with pleasure, "is it you ? " Then they linked their hands together and were silent for a moment. "You will be there on the *fête* day ? " Esty said, presently.

"What *fête* day, dear ? You never told me of one."

"Oh ! I forgot—and no wonder. There is to be a grand floral *fête* at Lynncourt on Thursday. You shall have a card for it, Geoffry, and then you can come anyhow, you know."

"I shall be sure to come; but I won't promise to go with the other guests. Good-bye, my darling; we meet on Thursday, then ? Good-bye, my wife."

A furtive look round, a kiss behind the shadow of the curtain, and the train rolled away, the young man watching it until it was out of sight.

"My wife," he repeated to himself, as he ran down the stairs of the station. Then he trilled out a joyful whistle as he remounted the horse that had brought him down to the station. He rode home along by-streets towards the West End, his reins rather slacker in his hand, and his seat less assured than common. He was so absorbed in thought, that he received one or two rather rough reminders from the passers-by as to "keeping his own side of the road." "Really I must think of where I'm going," he thought, with a blush and a smile. In another instant he would have gathered up the loose reins and urged his mare into a trot, when the latter shied at something on the pavement of a narrow street, and, swerving violently across the road, slipped upon the greasy stones, and rolled down, with her rider under her. The mare struggled to her feet, but the rider lay motionless where he had fallen, his white face marked by slow red drops, that dripped fast from a cut by the side of his head. There was a crowd round him directly, and, as is usual in such cases, the most extraordinary and inappropriate remedies were suggested in his behalf.

"Hot water," cried one.

"Cold," said another.

"Lift him up."

"Leave him alone."

"He's dead."

"No, he aint."

"I think there's nothing so good as a drop of brandy," said a devotee of that liquor, who thought that a drop or two might come his way if it were only set going.

A surgeon came up and examined the prostrate man.

"He's only insensible," he said, after a few moments' investigation. "He certainly is not dead, and we must take him home. Some swell, no doubt," he added, scanning the fine linen and high-bred face of his new patient.

They searched Captain Adair's pocket, and found his card with the address of his lodging on it. They took him home, and the surgeon, checking shortly the ejaculations and self-condolence of Captain Adair's landlady, saw that Geoffry was laid in a quiet back room, from which all sound and light were excluded.

"I wonder if there is anyone I ought to write to," the doctor thought, as he watched by his patient that night. "There is concussion, I fancy, and I can't yet determine the extent of the injury."

He was agreeably surprised the next day to find a decided improvement in the case. Towards the end of the second evening Captain Adair recovered his consciousness, and although there was still some fever on him, his doctor began to think the injury was much slighter than he had apprehended. The next morning he asked if there were any letters for him; but the servant had been enjoined to keep all papers from his master until the doctor had paid his morning visit, and ascertained the state of his health.

Lying rarely comes hard to a town-bred domestic. So

William swore, with the blandest expression of face, that there was "nothink at all for you to-day, Sir." Geoffry felt irritated and disappointed, and his fever increased so much with his worry of mind that he was a good deal thrown back by the time the doctor called again.

"You did quite right," the latter said, approvingly, when he heard of William's well-meaning mendacity. "He should have nothing to worry his mind for the next day or two; he is decidedly worse."

When on the Thursday morning William was permitted to put two letters into his master's hand, he was aghast at the effect it produced. Captain Adair raved like a madman, and when he heard of the ruse that had detained his letters from him (William was proud of the reticence he had observed in behalf of his master's health, and took no pains to conceal it) he struck the man to the ground.

"You may have murdered her!" the young man shrieked. "Oh, you damned scoundrel! Oh, Esty, Esty, I am coming! Oh, God! if it should be too late!"

He dashed down-stairs, and was out at the door before the astonished servant could recover an upright position.

"I cannot catch any but the 7.30 express, and that won't get down till 9," Captain Adair groaned, as he drove down to the same station where a few days since he had pressed his last kiss on Esty's lips.

"Shall I arrive at Lynncourt too late?"

CHAPTER XLII.

A TERRIBLE RESURRECTION.

"Oh, bringer of dire tidings, hide thine eyes,
Lest they be blinded by the pain in mine!"

A. C. S.

"I MUST tell them to-day," was Esty's uneasy thought when she awoke the morning after her return home.

She was very nervous, and looked at Christine wistfully once or twice, as though entreating her to discern what she had to communicate. It was irritating to see Christine moving so placidly about the rooms, singing little odd scraps of tunes and braiding her trails of hair languidly before the mirror.

"Oh, Chrissy!" Esty began once, and then she hesitated; for Chrissy, with an abstracted look, grasped her hair-brush in one hand and turned her blue eyes slowly on her sister.

"There will be two or three hundred at the *fête*," she said, musingly. "I shall wear blue and white. You will wear half-mourning, of course, as a widow?"

"Pshaw!"

Miss Lisle was rather astonished at her sister's petulance, but her mind did not dwell long on it. Her thoughts strayed to some one who was to come to the *fête*, and who would probably show more appreciation of the "blue and white."

"Only he says I am beautiful in anything." These sweet reflections diverted her mind from Esty; and while the latter wandered about like the unhappy spirits that are supposed to inhabit the never-resting birds of the Bosphorus, Christine brushed her hair the slower, and half closed her eyes in the charm of her meditations. Miss Lisle was, however, down soonest that morning, for, although Esty had been dressed some hours, she could not make up her mind to leave the friendly solitude of her chamber.

She was moving about the room, now turning over the pages of the books on the table, now fingering the lace-edging of a sleeve which had been left on a chair, when Christine suddenly re-entered the room, all traces of content vanished from her face.

" Oh, Esty ! " she began, and then she stopped.

" What is it ? " Esty cried, dropping the sleeve from her fingers.

" Oh, Esty ! " Christine spoke again with anxiety and terror in her eyes. " There is a letter, and I am afraid—oh, how can I tell you, my poor darling ! "

" Who is dead ? " Esty confronted her sister, and grasped her wrist. "Tell me quick," she cried, "or I shall be mad directly. Is it Geoffry? is it my ——"

Words failed her before she betrayed her secret, and her stuttering tongue and wild eyes supplied the rest of the question.

" It is not Geoffry," Christine said, hastily; "he is quite well for all I know. It is worse than that."

Esty's face relaxed and her fingers dropped their grasp on her sister's arm.

" Nothing could be worse than that," she murmured, in a low voice.

"Excepting eternal separation from him in this world," Christine said, in a voice almost as low, and choked with tears. " Esty, there is a letter from *him !*"

" From whom ? "

Christine shuddered at her sister's tone. "Don't look so, Esty ! " she cried. " It's too dreadful ! Oh, Esty, the sea has given up its dead, and Alfred Cadogan is coming back to you, my poor, poor dear ! "

She advanced towards her sister with outstretched arms,

24

but the latter receded from her, as though a horror were pursuing her.

"What!" she screamed, her face livid, her lips working convulsively. "Is this the news you have brought? *His* —wife? Not Cadogan's! No—no. I swear it—not Cadogan's! He shall never touch me again! Say it's false, Christine; I *know* Alfred is dead; he has been under water these six months. Hell could never have sent him up, only to torment me, a poor, heart-broken, miserable woman! What have I done? I—ha! ha! ha!—excuse me, Chrissy. Really I can't help laughing. Such a joke —such a very, very bad joke! Don't tell it to Geoffry, though. He doesn't like jokes: he told me so years ago. He might kill you, or dig up Cadogan, to be sure he's dead, you know; for if Cadogan is alive, Chrissy—what am I?— not your sister—not fit to—oh! —— "

In her paroxysm she flung herself down and beat her head against the floor. From incoherent raving she went into convulsions, and her unhappy sister, miserable and terrified, yet keeping her nerves well under control, hastened to obtain some hot water in which to immerse Esty's feet, and after applying two or three restoratives, had the doubtful satisfaction of watching her return to consciousness.

"Is it true?" the poor white lips lisped out, as the mind struggled back into misery.

Christine nodded her head. "But do not agitate yourself further," she added; "you will kill our mother if she finds you like this."

Her gentle yet firm manner produced its effect; and Esty's nerves continued tranquillised, although she stared at Christine with a most piteous expression of countenance.

"When will he come?"

"On Friday next."

"Ah, that's the day after the *fête*?"

"Yes."

Esty repeated to herself mechanically, "The day after the *fête*," then turned on her side on the bed where Christine had laid her.

"Leave me," she said. Like Dido, it "irked her" to

behold "the face of day." Neither could she bear to meet her sister's eyes, and she buried her face in the pillows. Her heart smote her, however, that she had spoken unkindly to this her faithfullest friend. "Kiss me, Christine —and yet, no, never mind. I did not intend sin, but ——"

"Go to sleep, darling, and rest a little," Miss Lisle interrupted. She feared that in the excitement of talking, the convulsions might recommence.

Esty obeyed, and lay silent for some time, staring at the wall opposite, while Christine moved softly about the room, closing the shutters and arranging a sleeping draught for Esty, which she left by the latter's side, with strict injunctions to take it in the course of the next hour. Then she left the room, and Esty, presently rising from her bed, emptied the proffered soporific out of the window.

"I could not go to sleep with this on my mind. What would it be to wake up and remember it? Oh, Geoffry, my poor darling, this is worse than death to us! Would that we could have perished in each other's arms two days ago! My punishment is greater than I can bear," she added, turning her pale face towards heaven. "My mistakes have all been crimes; but oh, let not the burden of them fall on him! Vouchsafe to lighten his load, and I will bear all and thank Thee. Mine was the sin; let mine be the expiation."

When Christine returned to the bed-room she was astonished to find her sister awake and composed. The latter offered to go down and join the family circle.

"How did you account for my absence?" she asked, somewhat anxiously.

"Oh, well, they were very eager to know how you bore it, and I said it was a shock to you, of course, and as you were unnerved and agitated, I had given you a sleeping draught."

"And how was it that ——" she could not go on, but Christine understood the implied question.

"He was picked up by a benevolent old Turk who was walking in his garden on the shores of the river. He saw the body float for an instant, and, fancying it might yet live, he instantly ordered his *caïque*, which, fortunately for

Alfred, was still in attendance, having only just landed its master at home, to pick up the drowning man. He was brought in, and was carefully nursed for three months, during a part of which time he was raving with brain fever. He is even now suffering greatly from the effects of his wounds, which have been obstinate in healing. He would have communicated his safety before, in order, he says, to spare you 'useless lamentation,' but he has been so ill and helpless, and—but here is the letter."

Esty could not repress a shudder as she recognised the well-known formal hand-writing. The concluding paragraph ran thus :—

"I fear the report of my death has been a dreadful shock to you. I feel sure that in your wifely devotion you have sacrificed beauty, and worn the deepest black and most cumbrous of widows' caps. You have doubtless also prayed for my soul, and have ere now extenuated my errors in the kindly manner in which one judges the faults of a departed servant. It perhaps gave you satisfaction to think that I was settling my accounts elsewhere than in the house of Cadogan & Co. A merciful Providence has preserved me in the greatest peril. I have heard of your aunt's death, and shudder to think what a narrow escape I had of meeting her in Hades. I wonder what she has left to my own precious wife. This I shall ascertain when I come home this week.

"Meanwhile, believe me your devoted

"ALFRED."

"Be sure and have my sheets well aired, and fires in my room until I come. Love to all."

Esty glanced at the first part of the letter.

"Friday—it is on Friday he expects to be at Lynncourt; then there is no time to be lost."

"What did you say?" Christine asked, not hearing distinctly Esty's muttered words.

"Oh, I did not say anything," Esty answered, evasively. "I am going down now to see papa and the mother."

She went with a steady, composed pace to give her morning greeting to her parents, and listened unmoved to all the comments they passed on the unexpected return of her husband."

" D—— the fellow!" Lord Renshawe said, testily.
"Wish he'd stay where he was. He'll be wanting me to
keep him here, and really there isn't room. Was much more
room for him in the Bosphorus."

But this speech was not uttered in Esty's hearing; it was
directed, as all Lord Renshawe's little discomforts of mind
ever had been directed, against his wife.

" I hope it may turn out happily," that poor lady said, nervously, as she cast furtive glances at Esty's rigid face and
meaningless smile ; " but if that be pleasure on her face it's
pleasure's ghost, it is so faint and wan."

The bag for the early post left Lynncourt at twelve mid-
day, and as the letter-boy passed through the park on his
way to the town, Mrs. Cadogan stopped him and slipped a
letter into the bag.

" There goes my last hope," she said, as she walked back
to the house. " My poor Geoffry, it will be very dreadful
for him !"

Her letter ran thus :—

" Cadogan is not dead—he is alive, and I am as vile as I
am wretched. Come directly you receive this. Every other
tie is now lost to me but the love that binds us to one
another. I was mad at first, but now I am stunned and
quiet; besides, I am waiting for you. You must take me
away, and we will live as strangers. The world will censure
us, but we will keep our souls white with God, and we shall
be—no, not happy, but less miserable than if I stayed here.
Could you not find me some situation with some good
woman? It would be better so. At all events, come
directly you receive this. I must have your counsel and
help. I would like to comfort you a little. Come and
take me away, for I will die sooner than meet that man
again."

CHAPTER XLIII.

WAITING.

"How dreary is the gulf! how dark, how void
The trackless shores that never were re-past!
Dread separation! on the depth untried
Hope falters, and the soul recoils aghast."

PARNELL.

"Poor unfortunate,
Whose crime it was on life's unfinished road
To feel the step-dame buffetings of fate,
And render back thy being's heavy load.

*   *   *   *   *   *

He who thy being gave shall judge of thee alone."

CAMPBELL.

T was with a throbbing heart and a wild hope in her breast that Esty ran down to meet the letter-boy on the morning she had calculated that Geoffry's answer would arrive.

Her anxious eyes discerned the little brown figure looming through the soft morning mist before anyone else's, and she walked down the path to meet him with a slow and deliberate gait. Had she followed the wild impulse of her heart she would have flown towards him, but she feared lest Lord or Lady Renshawe might look from their window and comment on her haste.

So she walked slowly, with a sickly affectation of indifference, as she turned round to call the dogs, or to pluck a blade of the tall grass that waved by the side of the palings.

When she got up to the post-bag, she could no longer resist the clutch of eagerness with which she grasped its contents, and her hand trembled so that she spilled the letters on the ground. A dreadful blank seemed to fall upon her as she picked them up, and in the first cursory glance failed to recognise the handwriting she sought.

She looked again, not daring to believe it true : once more—surely her eyes must be blinded by the pain throbbing through her head. "There *must* be one from him !"

But, no ; that first glance had not deceived her, and there was no answer to her appeal for help.

She walked up to the door, with an altered face, and had to encounter the fierce blue eyes of Lord Renshawe, who was exceeding discomposed at the particles of mud and gravel that had clung to the envelopes of his own letters.

He liked to examine the seal, the superscription, the corners of the envelope, and to guess the writer, before he chose to solve the problem by breaking open the letter. It is not, then, to be wondered at that he should feel indignant with Esty, whose carelessness, he considered, had deprived him of his legitimate and time-honoured amusement.

"On my word, it's too bad !" he exclaimed. "Look here, Elinor ; is this right that Esther should throw my letters into all the mud of the place? Not fit for a Christian to touch," continued he. "In future I will have the bag delivered to myself."

This threat alarmed Esty into making a humble apology, and a promise to be more careful in future. And thus she partly pacified my lord, who grumbled (he could not make up his mind to resign that luxury altogether) less loudly the rest of the breakfast-time.

Suddenly a scream of joy burst from Lady Renshawe. She held a thin, foreign-looking letter in her hand, which she waved frantically, amid the steam of the urn.

"James!—girls !" she cried, "what do you think ? Egbert ——"

"Well, what of him ?" said my lord, impatiently. "Do get on."

"Egbert is coming home !" she continued, excitedly.

"Only fancy! he is already at Paris, and will be here the day after to-morrow. Oh! I'm so delighted I don't know what to do. Read it—read it out, James, that the girls may hear what he says."

And with her fine grey eyes glistening with joy, she passed the letter on to Lord Lisle, who took it with his usual methodical manner, although a flush of surprise and joy lighted up his face.

It ran as follows :—

"Paris. Hôtel Windsor, August 4, 18—.

"My dearest Mother,

"How surprised you will be at reading the above date, and finding that I'm so near you! I am indeed all but home, and feel ten years younger at the thought of it.

"The fact is, my arm got so troublesome lately, that I was obliged to apply for a year's sick leave, that you and Esty might nurse me well again. Rather to my surprise, and much to my joy, they granted it, and I started immediately, overland.

"Dear old things! I long to kiss you all.

"Ever yours,

"Egbert.

"P.S.—Isn't it jolly? Don't worry about my arm; it isn't very bad.

"I hope to be with you some time on Friday. Don't send to S—— to meet me, as I can't say what train I shall catch. I will take a fly."

"Friday," said Lady Renshawe, meditatively; "and this is Wednesday. Two days more to wait!"

And now that he was so near, the mother began to grudge the few hours that must elapse before she should see the son whose four years' absence she had borne with the patience of a Spartan.

Everyone was so excited with joy that they had no leisure to bestow a thought on Esty's forlorn face and glassy eyes.

As soon as she could get away she crept up to her little room and locked the door. She then sat down on the edge

of her bed, too stupified with terror and pain to find relief
in her customary restless pacings up and down the room.
The bright morning sun streaming in at the window seemed
to mock the unhappy soul it could not comfort. This news,
which a few happy years before would have sent her about
the house as exultant as a lark, now served to bow her more
heavily to the ground. "How," she asked herself, "how
was she to meet Egbert?" Egbert, the affectionate brother,
the upright man? Egbert, whose career had been so un-
sullied, whose actions had been so blameless?

She heard, with the vague observance of intense misery,
the chirp of the birds outside the window, and the sound of
the cheerful bustle and excitement down-stairs.

Christine's clear young voice pealed up in a triumphant
rapture of song as she roved about the house. Like the
rest, she was in a fever of joy, and gave vent to her feelings
by making various changes and improvements in the house
which she supposed would be productive of additional
pleasure and comfort to Egbert. All the servants of the
household sympathised with and shared in the family re-
joicings.

The housemaids made a prodigious bustle in preparing
Captain Lisle's room; and the very scullery-maids commenced an arduous scrubbing down of all the back stairs,
as though anticipating a speedy examination of their clean-
liness (or the reverse) on the part of that gallant officer.

"Esty," cried Christine, from outside the window—
"Esty, come down and help me directly, you lazy thing
you!"

"I'll come directly," answered Esty, in a voice which she
felt to be dry and hard, in spite of her efforts to make it
otherwise; "wait a moment, dear;" and Esther darted to
her writing-case with a swiftly-formed determination in her
brain to write one more letter to Geoffry. "If that failed?"
—well! she did not dare to think of any alternative—she
would trust in this final appeal. She wrote hurriedly:

"Geoffry, what am I to think of your not answering me?

"I am sure that there must be some mistake; but it will
be a fearful one for me unless it be cleared up soon.

"Thursday is the day of the *fête*. You can have no

scruple in coming to it, as you have received an invitation. If I do not see or hear from you before the close of that day, I shall think I am indeed deserted by God and man. But, whatever happens, believe me that I am yours, and yours only, E.

"Come—for God's sake, come!"

She folded up her letter and sealed it, and then put it into her bosom, to await the chance of sending it. Having done this, she felt relieved. She had thrown the die, and at present nothing more could be done; so she bathed her white face with cold water, by way of trying to restore some colour to it, and joined Christine in the drawing-room.

"I am going to W——," said the latter young lady. "We want all kinds of things for the party. Will you drive over with me?"

Esty assented willingly; for this was the very opportunity she wanted for posting her letter.

Christine looked the picture of health and beauty as they rattled along the dusty road, the sunlight intensifying the bloom on her cheek and the glisten of her hair. She chatted merrily about a thousand different things, the exuberance of her spirits quite doing away with her habitual gravity.

W—— seemed full of life and liveliness as they drove in. The old red-brick houses looked quite bright in the morning sun, and the shop-windows shone resplendent in the dazzling colours the tradesmen had put out to attract the eyes of the passers-by.

Many of the shopkeepers paused, as they passed Christine's pony-chaise, to congratulate her humbly, but most sincerely, on the coming advent of her brother. They had heard the intelligence from the letter-boy, who had gained it from the servants at Lynncourt; and they always felt in some degree complimented by any intelligence of Captain Lisle. They were very proud of his success in life, and quite considered him as the representative of all the valour, proved and unproved, that W—— could boast.

As the sisters neared the post-office, a jingling of spurs and waving of plumes, and other warlike commotions, gave evidence that Captain Fleming was passing by with his troop of hussars. Esty felt sure that, in the glamour that would hold Christine's eyes till the gorgeous apparition had passed, she should be able to post her letter unperceived. She accordingly did so, and turned round in time to catch the look of devotion with which Fleming was bowing to her sister, who, on her part, was looking down stedfastly at her gloves, trying to seem as if she wasn't feeling conscious—an attempt in which she failed signally, as Fleming knew as well as possible that *she* knew that he was looking at her. He soon disappeared down the street, lost in the dust of the horse's hoofs, his gay accoutrements sparkling like a firefly in the hazy distance; and Christine having completed her purchases, they, too, returned home.   The rest of the day seemed weighted with lead to Esther.

She did not dare to lie awake that night, for fear her thoughts should drive her mad.   Only one more day to come, and that would decide all !

CHAPTER XLIV.

GONE TO HER DEATH.

"I told the clocks, and watch'd the waiting light,
And listened to each softly-treading step,
In hopes 'twas he; but still it was not he."

SPANISH FRIAR.

THURSDAY came, and still no answer from Geoffry.

This silence was worst of all to bear. Esty's young face was getting drawn and shrivelled. It had that painful expression peculiar to troubled youth: the marks of care and age seem so much more natural when accompanied by the wrinkled lines of threescore years, than when they draw down the dimples of nineteen or twenty.

Nothing but the unusual circumstances surrounding Captain Lisle's expected arrival and the approaching *fête* could have diverted suspicion from her so effectually. She knew this, and the feeling that detection was so dependent on accident made her more than ever determined that this state of things must be ended speedily—how, she had not made up her mind.

The day dawned on a world of excitement and preparation at Lynncourt. Lady Renshawe seemed to be all keys, as she hurried from room to room brandishing those formidable domestic implements in the eyes of the incautious passers-by.

My lord withdrew to his dressing-room to peruse the

day's paper, feeling inwardly in as great a tumult as the rest, but disdaining to show any outward sign of excitement, or to take any extra trouble on that account.

Indeed, trouble was a thing my lord hated always, whether in times of sorrow or pleasure.

"Esty," said her sister, "we must go and get the drawing-room ready. Come along."

Esty followed, and, duster and brush in hand, was soon engaged in her old occupation of dusting the ornaments on the chiffonier.

It was wonderful with what care and patience she followed the little dusty intricacies of the china shepherd and shepherdess. She had to clench their slippery waists very tightly in her hand, concentrating what mental energy she had left within her to forcing her nerveless fingers to do their work. The necessity of preventing any trace of agitation or pre-occupation in her manner made her go through her work with unusual care and precision.

She felt a kind of tenderness for these little ever-smiling china faces, whose rosy cheeks and bright eyes had formed her childish idea of perfection ; and it was with a shuddering dread that the thought floated through her mind that it might be the last time she should ever aid Christine in these innocent household occupations.

Christine, meanwhile, had filled the vases with flowers, taken off the covers of the chairs, put out the best albums, and dusted the piano and music-books. She then paused, duster in hand, to judge of the effect.

"That will do very nicely, I think," she murmured, in her soft voice. "What do you say, Esty?"

"Beautifully," said Esty, vaguely, giving the bowl in her hand twice as much friction as its slight coating of dust demanded.

"And now," said Christine, "we will go up and dress."

Esty assisted Christine to don the blue dress, so becoming to the latter's complexion, and then retired to her own room, and proceeded to dress herself with unusual care.

"She would like to look her best," she thought, "if Geoffry were to see her that day;" and she felt conscious that misery had made deep inroads on her beauty lately ; so she attired herself in white—a soft, gauzy muslin—and over it she put the fawn-coloured mantle which Egbert had sent her from India. Over the soft Cashmerean texture, dusky Asiatic fingers had woven innumerable silken flowers and hieroglyphics of the same colour as the groundwork. It fell gracefully round her girlish figure, and she looked very lovely when her toilette was finished, in spite of the paleness of her cheeks and the huge hollows round her eyes.

"Esty! Esty! I see some carriages coming!" screamed Christine from her room. "Come down, and we'll all go together to receive them."

Esther descended, and joined her sister and Lord and Lady Renshawe on the steps of the portico.

Carriage after carriage came rolling up, freighted with lovely women.

They came, smiling and bowing, accompanied by troops of adorers, whose services they had especially secured for the day; for we all know that a *fête champêtre* is a stupid affair, unless every Phyllis has her Strephon secured to her. If you trust to the chance of picking up a stray knight, you trust to a broken reed, and are likely to pass an exceedingly dull day.

Most of Lady Renshawe's visitors, being experienced ladies of fashion, had been far too wise to leave themselves wholly unprovided with an attendant, and so a large number of handsome faces and luxuriant mustaches came in their train to make their bow to the hostess. Among these, Esther's anxious eyes looked in vain for Geoffry Adair. By this time she had worked herself up into a belief that "he *must* come. Geoffry was as true as steel. He never could mean to desert her in her need. She felt sure he would be there soon."

But two o'clock—three o'clock struck, and still no signs of him.

The spirited strains of the military band, the hum of the voices, were getting strangely confused in her ears.

"It will be necessary to *act* soon," she muttered to herself, "instead of *thinking;*" and she turned to go into the house. She stole up the stairs unperceived, and walked into the painting-room, where she had passed so many hours of quiet happiness. Her own picture (a copy of Greuze's "Broken Pitcher") was still wet on the easel: there was the difficult piece of the white drapery, in which her hand had strayed into so many feeble lines, and to which her mother, by a few bold touches, had brought back somewhat of the resemblance of folds. There was the stool by her aunt's chair, on which she had sat perched as a child, reading Franklin's beautiful translation of the Greek plays, and watching the dark boughs of the cedar that peered above the window, wondering if it was of the same species as those used on Iphigenia's funeral pile. All the silent evidences of old occupations cut her to the quick.

"Will it ever look the same to them again when I am gone?" she thought.

She went into her mother's bed-room, and, kneeling down, kissed the pillow on which her mother's head had rested during the past night—rested in blissful anticipation of her son's arrival—in blissful ignorance of her daughter's misery and disgrace.

Esty took up a pencil, meaning to write a few words of farewell to the two women who had loved and cherished her for so many years; but she laid it down again.

"Far better they should think it a fit of temporary insanity," she said to herself; and, casting one last look round her, she quitted the room, and joined the party on the lawn.

It was a pretty sight to an unoccupied mind, those crowds of brilliant women, scattered like butterflies among the flower-beds, their little delicate feet cased in kid sinking up to their ankles in the velvety green sward, and the silvery laughter proceeding from their rosy lips making a pleasant echo through the warm summer air.

Christine went by, her fair face shaded by the most *espiègle* of little hats, and mantled by the most expressive blushes and smiles. She was leaning on Captain Fleming's arm, and the two might have served as a perfect personification of youth, beauty, and happiness.

Everything in this summer afternoon seemed in accordance with the perfection of their bliss. There was no cloud to darken the sun to them; no discordance in the music the wind carried to their ears; no poison in the fragrant atmosphere of the flowers round them.

"What a comfort that they are so happy!" thought Esther. "He will help to console her, whatever happens!"

They paused on seeing Esty, for they were so happy that they wished to convey the sunshine of their feelings to all around them, more especially to one so dear to Christine as Esther was.

"You look pale, Mrs. Cadogan," Fleming said, kindly. "Don't you feel well?"

"Not quite," she answered, slowly. "I could not sleep last night, I had a headache; but I shall be all right by the evening. Good-bye for the present," she added, "my head is getting worse, so I'll go and lie down."

"Poor Esty!" said Christine, and then added, with the unselfishness peculiar to her, "let me come and bathe your head. I will with the greatest pleasure!"

"Oh no," Esty answered; "I'd much rather not; but I'll go and be quiet a little. Don't let me be disturbed, and if I don't come down to dinner, make my excuses to mamma and the rest. Good-bye, my darling," she added, with an involuntary tenderness, which she could not repress.

And she disappeared through the trees from their sight, as they fancied to retire to her room, but in reality she turned her steps towards an arbour that commanded a view of the road.

She gazed wistfully out of the rustic little window, and saw that the shadows were sweeping in longer and broader masses over the park. The sun touched the bark of the trees with red golden light, and lit up the brown cattle with radiant patches as they passed lazily to and fro in the line of its beams. Soon these beams faded away altogether, causing a faint reflex of their glow in the clouds above, and the air grew colder as the grey shadows increased in intensity.

Hope was getting faint and sick in Esty's breast. When eight o'clock sounded from the church-bell, she knew that there could be no more looking into the future, and she rose to go, but first felt herself fain to go and have one more look at her home, and at those dear ones who had made the light of it to her.

The sound of voices had long since disappeared from the gardens; the bandsmen had gathered up their instruments and departed; the last carriage had rolled away in the distance, and Esty crept unperceived up to the dining-room window. Life within was shining in its full radiance and enjoyment :

> " Fires were crackling ; wine was bubbling
> Up to the top of its beaded brim ! "

Lord Renshawe was entertaining a large party of guests at dinner, and was pledging in a glass of sparkling Moselle the health of his son, Egbert Lisle: " whom he expected home hourly," he said. The table was dazzling with silver and glass. Through the spaces intervening between the ferns that drooped gracefully from the glittering épergne, Esty could detect Christine's fair hair and downcast head, and the sound of her merry laughter floating through the gentle hum of conversation, and the clatter of the knives and forks penetrated through the heart and ears of her unhappy sister outside.

With the unjustness of sorrow, she accused Christine of indifference and neglect.

" They don't care whether I am there or not," she said, bitterly. " They won't miss me ! "

She did not know that Christine had been repeatedly to her door, but finding it locked, had retreated on tip-toe, fearing to disturb her, and informing Lady Renshawe that " Esty was asleep," she thought; but " that she, no doubt, would come down after dinner."

Esty had taken the precaution of locking her door, wishing to divert suspicion as long as possible. She had no wish to be rescued ; her design once put in motion, half-measures could avail her nothing now. She looks at her mother, whose face is beaming with expectation, and who turns her head every time the door opens with a half hope of seeing her son. Nothing but the conventional propriety due to her guests prevents her from hastening to the window to watch. Had she done so she might have seen the white garments of her cowering and wretched daughter, instead of Egbert's upright, manly figure.

Esty pressed her face against the pane, and gave one last long, loving look at the inmates of the room.

" Good-bye all," she said. " Oh, my darlings, good-bye

25

—good-bye!" And with an unsteady step she walked away from the window.

As she passed by the corner of the house where the kennels stood, she heard some deep, low, excited barks, and a desperate scraping of gravel proceeding from them. These came from Oscar, a favourite dog of hers, a cross between a mastiff and bloodhound, who was nearly frantic at the idea that his mistress was going to take a walk without the accompaniment of his society, and vented his disapprobation accordingly. Esther went up to him and calmed his excitement, by kneeling down and putting her arms round his neck. His honest, soft, speckled jowl reposed complacently on her arm, while his tail still continued to represent the delight he was feeling by its agitated brushing of the ground.

"No! you can't come with me; down, Oscar, down!" she said, as his efforts to break away redoubled at her movement to go.

He sat down directly, in meek obedience to her voice, but she was hardly out of sight before his exertions to free himself became more violent, but the chain was stronger than he, and resisted all his efforts, and so it happened that a dog's wistful eyes were the last to watch her leaving her home.

Although Esther had never openly acknowledged to herself the course she would pursue this night, yet her instinct had never deviated from one point—and that was· Gardenhurst.

"It must not be here," she murmured; "it would make the place hideous to them." So she lifted the latch of the park gate and went out in the gathering darkness, on the road to Gardenhurst.

Through the mist, past the wayside cottages, whose glimmering lights gave evidences of life and home which she was never more to taste.

She walked with such eager desperation that she arrived at her destination ere half-an-hour had past.

The old gate was overgrown with weeds and lichen, and was so sunk into the ground, that it required some slight exertion from her delicate arms to raise it.

The whole place had the hush of desertion upon it—not

a single dog to bark—no bell to ring that would bring a human voice to answer it. There was no sound save the flutter of the birds who fled from the covert, scared by the unusual presence of a footstep near them.

It would not have been wonderful if she had felt scared at the loneliness and silence reigning round her ; but no, she had a pain in her head and breast, the intensity of which bade defiance to any outward circumstances, and she felt glad that there was no one there who could see her last disgrace.

She forced her way with some difficulty through the tangled masses of boughs and blossoms that overhung the boundary path.

The sweet scent of the azaleas lay on the place like a balm, and their glutinous petals fell on, and clung to her shoulders and hair as she brushed by them in her haste.

She had but one thought, one haven for her journey's end, and that was the round pond : in its dark waters she would bury all the remorse, the misery, and the feeling of degradation that had made life a hell to her for the last two days. She forced her way through thicket and briar, till at last she emerged on the narrow green pathway that still ran round the dark pool's margin. It had always been the most secluded spot in the grounds, and now that man had ceased to curtail and clip the luxuriant foliage round it, it had become doubly so.

There was only one narrow path open to it, and through that a neighbouring herdsman sometimes came to give an occasional meal to the swans, who lived there to suit the convenience of a neighbouring gentleman, who had too great a number on his own lake. As a rule, however, they subsisted on the dense green herbage of the pond, and it might be many days before they would be visited again.

Esther sat down amid the cool green reeds for a few moments' reflection.

Images of past happiness, commingling with present misery, came crowding with such rapidity through the wretched creature's mind, that she began to fear her brain would not be clear enough to offer up a prayer for pardon to that God whom she was about so grievously to offend. She pressed her head between her hands and tried to think clearly. To add to the agony sustained by this unhappy girl, let it be added that she was afraid to die ; afraid of the unknown gloom that lies over the unpenetrated depths of the other existence; afraid of the earthly degradation that meets our fallen dust in this world; afraid, miserably afraid, of the oblivion and silence which, after the first passionate wail of mourning is spent, close over the absent dead.

" Will Geoffry remember me ? " she thought, " or will he, if he grieves, take some other woman's hand to occupy the blank mine will have left ? "

She was sitting under a chestnut tree, with whose fruit she and Egbert used to pelt each other, as children.

What would she not give if she could obliterate all the intervening years, and see herself and her brother again as sunny-headed infants, playing in the chequered light under the green leaves ! She thought of Egbert, of his lengthened toil, and of the crown of honour that had rewarded his exertions; and then while grieving to think of all he would suffer at her death, she felt glad that she was not going to give him the still more bitter reproach of living. She thought of Christine, and her faithful and untiring affection.

Of her mother she dared not think ; of Geoffry she did: his image was too much woven into the present circumstances for her to be able, had she been willing, to obliterate it.

She remembered the happy youth she had passed here, of the pure and poetical fancies she had nursed among those fragrant blossoms until Geoffry came to turn her dreams to a reality. She thought of the glorious happiness of their first love, of the dreary hours of sorrow succeeding their separation, of their meeting again, when their love, as abiding as ever, had become a crime instead of a grace to their lives.

She went over in her mind the words of her wild entreaty to him to save her from this, and of the dread silence that had answered her petition.

This last remembrance gave the deciding impulse to her intention. She fell down on her knees. " Oh, Father ! " she said, " have mercy on an unhappy creature not fit to die, but more afraid to live ; forgive me and pardon me, if you can, and help my dear ones to bear the affliction this will bring on them. Oh, Lord, forgive me! Oh, God, have mercy on me!"

She got up and flung her arms over her head. "Oh, Geoffry! Geoffry" she cried. It was the last cry of a soul in its mortal agony, for as that scream passed her lips she fell headlong into the dark water beneath her.

A splash—a swirl of the troubled water—a convulsive gurgle—a trembling agitation on the part of the stream that floated over the body, that sank and rose and sank again, and all was still.

A silvery cloud passed by for a few seconds, and then the moon rose up, and shone with serene splendour over the scene of death.

There was nothing in this deserted place to feel either astonishment or sorrow at this terrible calamity.

The summer night was as calm, and the rabbit bounded as lightly over the path as before.

The water lapped as peacefully to the side of the pool, gliding over the smooth green leaves of the water-lilies, whose wax-like blossoms were closed from the night-air, and the swans, that had uncoiled their long necks from under their pure-hued wings at the disturbance in the waters, hid their heads again when they found that those other patches of white, heaving to the surface at irregular intervals, offered no injury to the legitimate denizens of that lonely pool.

Meanwhile a hackney carriage had rolled up to the doors of Lynncourt, and Egbert was being enveloped in such a storm of kisses and welcomes as almost bewildered his sight and senses.

With him came another man, whose face looked pale and worn in the glare that fell on it from the bright red blaze of the hall fire.

This man was Geoffry Adair, who after casting several furtive but anxious glances round him, laid his cold hand on Christine's arm, and drawing her aside, whispered in a scarcely audible voice, "For God's sake tell me, where is your sister?"

CHAPTER XLV.

WITH THE WHITE SWANS.

"Oh, Marianne, where art thou?
Thou canst not hear my bitter pleading!
Ah! couldst thou, thou wouldst pardon now,
Tho' heaven were to my prayer unheeding."

BYRON.

"FOR God's sake tell me, where is your sister?" Christine was recalled by this question to the recollection of Esty's headache, and felt a little penitent that she had not been up to apprise the latter of Egbert's arrival.

"Poor, dear Esty!" she said. "She is in her room; she hasn't been quite well to-day, so she is lying down. I'll go and see if she is awake."

"Aye do," muttered Adair, and he bounded up the stairs after her, feeling his anxiety quickening with every rapid step he took. But Christine, who knew of no reason for any particular hurry, and who was not aware that Adair was following her, could not resist turning into Egbert's room, to see if his fire was blazing, and if everything looked comfortable for his reception. Adair stood in the shadow of the staircase, grinding his teeth at the delay, and apostrophising Christine less affectionately than usual, as he heard the deliberate way in which she broke up the coals with the poker, and drew the curtains of the window; presently, however, her fair form gleamed through the doorway, and she walked down the dark landing towards Esty's room.

Geoffry followed her stealthily, and heard her try the door gently. Failing in her endeavour to open it, she cried out, "Esty! dear!—Esty! it is I—Christine! Egbert has come, and you must run down directly."

No answer! Christine paused a moment, and then called again, louder.

"Esty, wake up. I tell you Egbert is here, and Geoffry has come with him."

Still silent.

Christine was becoming a little discomposed, and, turning round in her perplexity, found herself opposite Geoffry's pale face.

"Oh! how you startled me!" she said, and continued :— "I have been calling ever so loud, and I can't make Esty hear! how soundly she must be sleeping!"

Soundly, indeed! oh, troubled sister with the fair face! So soundly that your appeal will nevermore elicit any response from her.

Christine began shaking the door violently, but still gaining no answer, began to feel a scared sensation come over her at the unexpected silence that followed her anxious queries.

"I hope she isn't worse!" she said, doubtfully to Geoffry.

He answered by putting her aside from the door, and by flinging the weight of his shoulder against it.

It fell open, but the room was too dark for them to distinguish anything.

"I can easily find my way to the bed," said Christine, and she groped along with her hands before her; Geoffry following the sound of her movement with terrible anxiety.

Presently her knee struck against the foot of the bed, and she stretched out her arms over its surface.

"*There is nothing here!*" she said in a voice in which terror began to mingle. "Where on earth can she be?"

"She must be found immediately," said Geoffry. And he ran down-stairs, followed by Christine, who somewhat recovered the tone of her spirits as they emerged into the light below stairs.

"What a goose I was to feel frightened!" she thought.
"I daresay she has gone down the other way!"

In the hall they met Egbert, followed by his mother, and
the men-servants, who were carrying up his luggage.
Egbert's handsome brown face was beaming with happiness. .

"Halloo! Adair," he cried; "has Christine been showing you your room? We are coming up to see Esty; they
tell me that ——"

Here he broke off in his sentence, for looking up, he saw
an expression on his friend's face that somewhat puzzled
him.

"What's the matter?" he asked in an altered voice.

"We can't find your sister," said Adair, "and I've reason
to think—I fear ——"

"Fear *what?* isn't she well? Where is she, Christine?"
(turning to his sister).

"That's just what I don't know," said she. "She isn't
in her room, and the door was locked!"

"Poor child," said Lady Renshawe. "If her head was
aching, I daresay she is walking outside, to cool it; and you
know, Christine, she often locks her door. So, no doubt,
she has got the key with her."

"Well! let's look all round the house first," replied the
latter. "Here, Sally! have you seen Mrs. Cadogan
lately?"

"Not since the afternoon, Miss," was the answer.

Christine again raced up-stairs, accompanied by Sarah,
and they commenced an active search, beginning with the
bed-rooms, and ultimately coming round the back way
through the dining-room to the hall, where the members of
the family were awaiting their return.

"Well?" said Egbert.

Christine shook her head, while Sarah said, with that
promptitude with which the vulgar delight to convey bad
news, "We can't find Miss Esther nowhere, Sir!"

Meanwhile Lady Renshawe had gone to the door, and
was calling out in a loud shrill voice, "Esther! Esther!"

"You will catch your death of cold, mamma," said
Captain Lisle. "Do come in. We will go and look for
Esty. I daresay she is walking in some of the paths, or

fallen asleep in one of the summer-houses. Besides, you must look after my father ; he don't seem well."

And, in fact, Lord Renshawe, who had been much excited by all the events of the day, had sunk into one of the hall chairs. His face looked blue, and he seemed unable to support himself. Lady Renshawe and Christine, much alarmed, assisted in conveying him up-stairs, while Egbert continued to give some energetic directions to those round him.

" I want some lanterns," he cried, " and six servants. Two will go with me, two with Captain Adair, and two with you, Williams, and it will be hard if we don't find her soon."

The lanterns were soon procured from the stable, and the party started on their search, each taking different routes, and Lady Renshawe and Christine, who had recovered Lord Renshawe from his fainting fit, looked out into the dark night from their window, and saw the group disperse under the shadow of the trees. The sound of their voices grew fainter in the distance as they reiterated the call of " Esther ! Esther ! " And then the two women, unable to bear the suspense and inaction of their situation any longer, gave a glance at Lord Renshawe, who was now sleeping quietly, consigned him to the care of Sarah, and, gathering up their skirts, they ran' into the darkness, also crying, " Esther ! Esther ! "

*   *   *   *   *

Half an hour had elapsed, and no trace had been discovered of Esther until Captain Adair paused before the door of that summer-house in which she had passed those last dreary hours of vigil.

Unconsciously to himself, he . was standing (just three hours too late) on the very spot in which her last hope of seeing him had expired.

His quick glance penetrated in a moment through the darkness round him, and he fancied he detected something white lying under the rustic seat.

" Bring the light," he cried, and he darted forward, and picked up the object.

It was a pocket-handkerchief, one of his own, and one part of it was torn and jagged, and stained by some small spots of blood.

"This could only have belonged to *her!*" Geoffry whispered to himself as he read by the light of the lanterns his own initials in the corner; but he did not know that Esty had bitten it through, and her lips also, while waiting there between the hours of six and eight.

Fresh steps and voices came hurrying through the dusky shadows, and Egbert and his party came up, their faces now pale with apprehension.

"*I* can't find her, Adair," he said. "In God's name, what is to be done?"

There was a pause for a moment, until Williams broke out with:—

"I have it, I know the way to find her! What fools we were not to think of it before."

"What! what!" said Egbert, impatiently.

"Why, the dog, Sir; Mrs. Cadogan's dog, Oscar. If she has not taken him with her, he'll track her anywhere."

"That will do," said Egbert, laconically, and the whole party turned towards the kennels.

"Better not all go," said Williams; "he knows me, and I'll let him loose, if you gentlemen will watch and see what path he takes."

So they waited under the trees by the path, while Williams went on his mission.

They watched silently for a few minutes, and then they heard Oscar's short barks as he bounded down the walk towards them. The dog seemed to be too busy to pay any attention to the party. He looked at them for a moment, and then went on diligently snuffing the earth in fifty different places.

They watched the vacillations of his search most anxiously, not daring to call his attention away, but feeling desperately impatient at the delay occasioned by his uncertainty. Presently Egbert cried out with a voice that had something of a thrill in it:—

"*Look!* he has got it!"

And, in fact, Oscar seemed to have quite made up his mind, and with his nose well between his paws, had darted through the gate they were holding open, and was plunging wildly down the park. Adair, Egbert, and two of the men gave rapid chase. The others came on more leisurely.

"No need to hurry so," they said; "he'll be sure to pull up presently."

They were right in their conjecture, for by the time they reached the last gate they found Oscar in a state of irresolution, his pursuers hanging anxiously on every movement.

The fact was, Oscar was debating between the two roads. One (as we know) led to W——, to which town he was accustomed daily to follow the pony-carriage; the other led to Gardenhurst and Brenwyn. To the astonishment of them all (excepting Geoffry, who dared not be astonished by anything) Oscar decided on the latter road, and soon disappeared from their sight.

"What, in Heaven's name, could take her this way?" Egbert exclaimed. "Can the dog have made any mistake, do you think, Williams?"

The latter shook his head.

"Not likely, Sir; he was so fond of Mrs. Cadogan. (That "was" sounded ominous!) Anyhow, it's our best chance for tracing her."

This was true enough, and they went on more quickly than ever. And thus it was that the high intellects and affections of man were compelled to follow with intense anxiety and entire dependence the animal instinct of a dog, who was pointing out the road by which they were to discover the lost sister and lover.

On arriving at Gardenhurst they found Oscar barking furiously at the shut gate, which was too high for him to jump over it, and too close in its formation to allow him to get through.

"Does any one live at the lodge here?" asked Egbert. "Any one whom Miss Esther would care to see?"

He did not consider the improbability of Esther's leaving her home to go such a distance to see any one, whoever it might have been, on the night of his arrival; but he could not even yet realise to himself the idea of any positive peril to his missing sister, and chose to imagine the only construction that could have been placed on her visit here.

For a moment the door (caught on a rusty nail) resisted his hand, and he pulled the bell at the side. He pulled it sharply, and it rang out loud and clear through the quiet night air, till its last tinkle died in silence among the shrubs without producing any kind of response.

Oscar was getting frantic, and was whining and scratching up the earth under the gate. Egbert applied his shoulder to it, but it opened with such unexpected ease, that he half fell forward.

In the surprise of the moment Oscar darted through, and had disappeared in the dense foliage round them before they could follow him up.

"Where to?" asked Egbert.

"We will try the house first," said Geoffry, "and if she (here his voice faltered)—if she is not there, we shall soon hear Oscar bark!"

Geoffry's heart had divined that which the others could not understand, namely, the reason that might have induced Esther to seek Gardenhurst.

He did not dare to think that she had come there to *die*, but the thought crossed his mind that some species of mental aberration might have caused her to wander from home, and that being the case, he could easily understand that instinct would lead her to haunt the scene of her happy youth.

To the house they went, but there everything looked unmistakably deserted; the shutters were all closed, and every door locked. The scene of past household happiness was void and cold, and as silent as the grave. Esther could have found no refuge there.

They all looked at each other in blank dismay, but presently they heard a distant bark, which indicated that Oscar was excited afresh by something : they hurried round the house and heard the barks more distinctly.

"This way!" cried Egbert, running down the old green walk he had not trodden since the days of his boyhood.

They all followed until they came to the end of the path. Then they listened again. The barks came from the left, and, with a species of scream, Geoffry darted down the narrow way, crying, "My God ! the *pond !* the *pond !*"

They soon reached the calm pool, round the sides of

which Oscar was running frantically. The trail had ceased with the water, and his part was played.

As they came near, Geoffry clutched Egbert's arm :—

"What's *that?*" he whispered, huskily; "that white *thing?*"

"Oh, Sir!" cried Williams, "that's only the swans: there are, two or three of them here,—look! I'll go and frighten it away." And he went, and kneeling down on the bank, plunged his arm into the water. "My God!" he cried, "it's a *hand!*" and he fell back with terror.

Geoffry was in the water in an instant, and Egbert saw him raise in his arms the inanimate body of his dead sister. The moon shone so brightly on the glossy face and dripping hair, as to leave no doubt of the identity, ghastly as it was.

They lifted her out of the water and laid her on the bank. Egbert seemed petrified, and could neither speak nor move; Adair had fainted, and him, too, the servants laid on the ground, a little higher up, among the dank reeds and dew-wet leaves.

"She must have died hard," muttered one of the men.

Egbert shuddered, and hid his face in his hand. She *had* died hard, for life was strong in her; but she was so determined to die that (as though fearing her courage might fail her) she had held her head down between her hands— for the water was nowhere deep enough to drown her, had she lifted herself up. Her gold chain had fallen from her fair neck across the back of her head, and the bracelets were hanging far forward on her wrists.

No description can convey any idea of the horror inspired by the sight of this dead girl, with all the appurtenances of life clinging to her! The soft white dress hung in wet, flaccid folds round her; the rings glittered brightly on her white, cold fingers; her whole attire gave evidence of the life and warmth in which she had moved but a few hours before.

Geoffry staggered up from the place where they had laid him, and knelt down by her side. "Esty! Esty!" he whispered, in a strange broken voice. "Esty! speak to me!"

"She will never speak again, Sir," said Williams, sadly,

as he rose from her side, where he had been attempting to
hear the beatings of that heart which had throbbed so
wildly a few hours since, but which was now so fatally still.
"She is quite dead," he continued, "and has been so for
some time, I should say."

"You lie!" howled Geoffry, so fiercely that Williams
recoiled involuntarily; "you lie, I tell you! She *can't* be
dead—Esty can't be dead!" and he bent over her and
kissed the cold forehead. "Esty!" he cried, "speak to
me! say that you live! tell me that I have not lost you!
Oh, Esty! Esty! I never got your letter till to-day. I
came as fast as I could. I came directly to take you
away with me, so that we may be happy together—we will
be so happy, dear—it shall atone for all. Oh, Esther, say
that I'm not too late!" No answer; no look of recognition
in those staring eyes, looking up through the mystery of
death into his own.

Egbert took him by the arm. "Come away, Adair," he
cried, almost fiercely, and pulling Geoffry away, he flung
himself down by the body, and listened first at her heart
and then put his fingers on her wrist.

Geoffry looked at him gloomily, but was not wholly convinced of his loss until Egbert lifted up his face, haggard
and pale with despair.

"She is dead!" he said; and then he hid his face on his
knees, and burst into uncontrollable sobs. "Oh, Esty, my
little sister," he moaned, "is this the way you greet me? is
this what I've been waiting for and hoping for all these
years? Why did she do it?" he cried; "what sorrow, what
sin, has driven her to this?"

Presehtly a recollection seemed to come across his mind.
"Adair," he said, fiercely, "what do you know of this?
You were uneasy from the first."

"Nothing!" muttered Adair, hoarsely. If Esther were
dead, no word from him should indicate the secret she had
lost life in order to keep.

Williams put his arm round Egbert, and lifted him up.
"My dear young master," he said, "there is something
more to be done. We must go home, Sir—somebody must
prepare her ladyship for this terrible event. Would it not
be better for us to be going?"

"Yes, yes! you're right," answered Egbert, who felt a sickening sensation come over him as he remembered the anxious faces at home.

Geofiry was still staring at her who lay at his feet, and took no notice of them until they came to lift her up. Then he ran to Egbert and grasped him by the arm. "Lisle," he said, "leave her with me for a few moments, I entreat you; let me talk to her alone for a little while."

Egbert turned round and looked at him sternly. "What was she to you, I should like to know?" he asked.

"What was she to me?" cried Geoffry, in a sharp tone of agony. "Do you ask *that?* Well, she was everything in the world to me. I loved her better than anything else, and she loved me, Lisle; and as you would have shown her mercy, I beseech you grant it to me."

Williams interposed. "Wouldn't it be better that you should go home first and prepare them?" he said; "and meanwhile the men can make up a kind of litter from the boughs."

Egbert hesitated. "Perhaps you're right," he said at last. He then took Geoffry aside. "You must not stay longer than a quarter of an hour."

"I will not; I promise it," was the answer; and after giving a few words of direction to the men, Egbert departed. His bowed head and grey coat soon disappeared through the dewy foliage, and Geoffry was left alone—alone with his dead love and her faithful dog, who could not be induced to leave his mistress, but who lay stretched out close to her feet, his head between his paws, and his eyes furtively looking round at every movement Geoffry made.

It was getting daylight, and amid

"The early pipe of half-awakened birds."

and with the cold, yellow light broadening over the horizon, he held his last tryst with the woman he had loved so dearly.

He put his arm round her head, and laid it on his knee. How strangely cold and stiff that young head seemed whose cheeks a few days since glowed at his touch, and whose hair used to curl round his caressing fingers in such soft, warm, clinging tendrils!

"Too late!" he said; "too late, my darling! Oh, if you could but have waited a little longer! oh, that cursed delay! that letter, that letter!" And he tore out a handful of hair in his agony. "If you were but alive," he murmured, "how happy we should be!" And he laid his lips on her cold, impassive cheek, and kissed it tenderly.

Ah, that kiss! If it could have come a day earlier, what a glow of comfort would it not have brought to that wan pinched face!

"If she could but have been spared this last sorrow!" he thought. "That she should have thought me unkind or careless of her misery! Oh, my God! my God! how could you permit this poor, helpless creature to be so crushed!"

He heard the voices of the men coming near. They were whispering in awe-stricken voices of "Mrs. Cadogan."

"Mrs. Cadogan?" muttered Geoffry. "Even in death is that name to haunt you?"

The servants began to approach with the litter, and Geoffry knew that his interview (strange interview, with one so silent, the other so passionate) was nearly over.

He pressed a kiss on her blue lips. "Good-bye, my own!" he whispered; "I shall never see you again, but I shall never forget you, never!"

He disengaged the chain from her wet, matted hair; at the end of this chain hung the locket he had given her containing his hair; he put it round his neck, and then laid down her head gently on the ground. He knelt then on both knees and said, "Good-bye, Esther; you have died in consequence of your love for me. Now listen to me, darling: I swear by the sky above me, and by you, my poor dead love, that I will never touch woman's lip again: and the memory of you shall last me as long as I live!" He rose up and called "Evans!" One of the footmen came up.

Captain Adair was very calm in his manner now; only he had a strange light in his eyes, and the sound of his voice was totally different from that in which he used to speak. It sounded harsh and broken. "Tell Captain Lisle," he said "that I shall stay at W—— for a few days, until he is able to see me; he will find me at the White Hart. I am going there now."

"Yes, Sir," Evans said; "and I suppose we're to take Mrs. Cadogan home?"

Geoffry shuddered. "Stay!" he answered. "I will help to carry her home—at least to the gates—there can be no harm in that."

And so they lifted her on to the rude litter they had fashioned, and, Geoffry taking his station by her head, they commenced their homeward journey.

The cool morning breeze played over the unconscious face, as that dismal procession paced the quiet country lane; they passed slowly through the peaceful fields, surrounded by the sweet scent of the hedges, whose fringes were sparkling with the early rime. The fresh, awakening beauty of nature seemed in strange contrast with the ghastly horror of the burthen they bore.

And so Esther Cadogan went home again, accompanied by the lover who had come too late to be of any other use to her; and the first sight that greeted those two poor women at Lynncourt as they watched from their open window (they watched still in silent horror for that which Egbert had warned them was to come) was the light flutter of the dress, which hung down over the side of the litter that was bringing them back the dead daughter and sister.

CHAPTER XLVI.

CONCLUSION.

"Sleep, widow'd eyes, and cease so fierce lamenting;
  Sleep, grieved heart, and now a little rest thee;
  Sleep, sighing words; stop all your discontenting;
  Sleep, beaten breast; no blows shall now molest thee."
                                        P. FLETCHER.

  "Death will lead her to a shade
  Where love is cold, and beauty blind."
                                        DAVENANT,

      "Here are no storms,
  No noise, but silence and eternal sleep."
                                        SHAKESPEARE.

T was a bright June day—a day joyous with sunshine, sweet with the breath of flowers—a day
which seemed to overrun with a sense of its own
gladness. The fountain at Lynncourt rose in a
spiral stream in the sun to break in a thousand glistening
drops over the wild grasses that threw such cool shadows
round the faun's dimpled marble toes. The air was filled
with soft whistles of birds; half-torpid insects crept slowly
across the golden gravel paths, until they were lifted by the
sun's influence to a brief but brilliant existence among the
flowers. It was a day haunted by the cooing of wood-doves,
by murmurs of bees, the cluck of farm-house hens, and the
lowing of cattle. Even the far-off call of the bird-boys, that
died away faintly behind the purple gloom of the Lynncourt

woods, did not chime in otherwise than harmoniously with the music of those summer hours.

The great breadths of sun and shadow that streamed over the massive frontage of the house seemed to steep it in calm —a calm unbroken by human intrusion : for there were no faces to be seen at the heavy-mullioned windows, no voices to be heard at the doors. Inside the house the same silence and desolation prevailed : there were none of the customary movements of servants along the corridors and passages. The one or two that did pass did so with stealthy steps, as though they were afraid of waking somebody—somebody who in this world might never again wake to step of friend or foe—somebody who was lying in a distant chamber of the vast house, with the sun playing as warmly on her marble face as though, like all else in nature, the poor motionless thing could rejoice in its genial warmth. In her bed-room, where the window turned towards the south, and where the scent of flowers came richest through the framework of magnolia leaves, lay Esty Lisle, her little hands stiff by her side, and the brown hair put away under the folds of the handkerchief that supported the serene dead face.

Yes, it was serene and untroubled enough now. The moonlit waters at Gardenhurst had reflected a face wild with agony and terror; but that was before they had sucked the poor, troubled countenance down amidst the roots of their own pure-hued lilies. When they "gave up their dead" to the surface again, the convulsion of pain was replaced by a quiet smile, and the agony and the remorse were transferred to the living who wept around her.

As she lay there, oblivious of how time was going—careless whether sun or shade rested on her brow—the wind that blew through the window lifted up a tress of hair that had escaped from its cerements, and fluttered it gently to and fro against the rigid line of her cheek.

At that moment the door of the chamber opened, and Christine, with heavy rims round her eyes and clenched hands, walked swiftly up to the bed. She had felt a great gulp in her heart when she saw that moving curl of hair. For a moment one of those wild imaginings—one of those faint hopes that may come across the most evenly-regulated minds—brought a thrill to hers.

26—2

"Esty!" she cried—and then, before the cry had died into echo, she knew how vain a one it was, and fell prostrate at her sister's feet. The birds twittered—the sun moved slowly from one window to another—the faint bubble of the fountain still made a pleasant murmur in the distant garden; but the dead face turned as impassive a regard on the beauties of the day as it did on the appealing anguish of Christine's eyes: henceforth it could recognise neither. The glories with which God graces the earth, the love that had attended her from childhood, and that had made life sweet to her, were all equally a matter of indifference to the dead heart that had forgotten everything and everyone. "Oh, Esty!—my Esty!" murmured Christine, as she pressed her hot face against the cold one of her sister. "If you could speak to me—look at me—but for one instant!" she sobbed; and then she fell on her knees, and took up and kissed tenderly the rigid fingers that lay with such a numb weight between her own feverish palms. "You will never touch me with your dear hand again—never look at me—never call me with your voice. My love cannot reach you now. Oh, my darling! you have gone away from me—far, far away—and were I to weep out my eyes over your dead face, I could not make it comprehend my sorrow, or wake to consciousness of my tears!" and Christine placed her arm as tenderly round her sister's throat as though it were still palpitating with life, and showered kisses and tears in passionate profusion over the benign, unanswering face. The sunbeams, that streamed through the coloured glass of the antique window-panes, flung curious hues over the floats of Christine's yellow hair, as it swept across the breast of the dead, and the summer air, that blew gently against her tear-stained face, seemed to mock her with its sweet content, bearing with it, as it did, the scent of mown meadows and the faint clash of the haymakers' scythes.

Christine loathed the sunshine, and felt sickened by the perfume of the flower and the song of the bird.

"What is it to *her* now?" she murmured, passionately. "What is light to her now—or sound—or love?"

The yearning in Christine's eyes, as she sat and looked love into her sister's purple-filmed orbs—the expression of intense desolation in her whole attitude—was in strange contrast with the silent peace that pervaded the aspect of the dead. Truly the poet has said, "'Tis the survivor dies;" and no one who could have gazed at the two sisters, in this their last interview, could have doubted but that the younger was the less to be envied.

"What is it?—oh, my God, tell me what it is!" and Christine, with a fresh access of agony, flung herself down by the bed, and stretched up her arms to Heaven. "What is this life Thou hast made so dear to Thy creatures—this love which makes Thy creatures so dear to one another—if *this* is to be the end of it all? What is this death that comes to destroy all that life has engendered, that love has fostered? It is cruel—cruel to make life, and the love so dear to beings whose doom is that they should fall away from both—making torn remnants of the hearts that survive them."

Then she looked at the sweet smile that still lingered round Esty's lips, and her incoherent ravings ceased.

"I was wrong," she said—"wrong to repine at *His* decree, since it will enable us to meet again where sorrow shall not cloud your poor eyes nor trouble your heart. I shall come to you, my darling; and when I am cold like you, there will be no more separation between us."

Then, with a shudder, she recalled the terrible thought that had glanced across her mind when she first caught sight of the burthen the men bore on their shoulders as they passed up through the dewy avenue to the front door on that dreadful yesterday morning. But she put the thought from her vehemently, and let her mind rest on the explanation Egbert had given her.

"It was fever, it was delirium, and she did not know what she did. My poor, poor dear, I should have kept better watch over her. She did not know where she walked, and there was no one with her, and the bank was so slippery. Oh!" she added, with a groan, "how can I ever forgive myself for my negligence! Had I kept with her a little longer it might never have happened. Hark! what is that?"

Full and clear through the summer-steeped air came the sound of the Lynncourt church bell as it began to toll the

number of Esty Lisle's departed years, and Christine, burying her head in the clothes, prayed with an agony of self-
abasement that God would be merciful to the poor erring
soul He had taken so abruptly from the harsh world to be
judged by an infinite compassion.

"Pity and pardon her, O Lord! Let all the pain she
suffered be sufficient penance for her sins. She was
human, and thus made by Thee to err. Thou who art
divine, judge not too hardly of the failings of Thy creation.
Pardon her, O Lord! Admit her to the glory of Thy
blessing; and so fit me that I too may one day partake
of it, and meet her dear face in the peace of Thy heavens."

And as the day waned, and the shadows deepened in
the corners of the room, and the dew fell thick on the
grass, Christine seemed to feel a foretaste of the peace
she implored, for the tears dried on her cheeks; and as
she sat there, with the dead hand still resting in her
own, her beautiful features wore a calm like that of the
face lying on the pillow before her.

"I shall see her again—I feel quite sure I shall see
her again."

Although Esty's shape lay there, it was observable that
her sister spoke of her as one far away. And was she
not far away? Aye, far away from all human sympathy.

"But I shall come to you," said. Christine, unconsciously paraphrasing the words of the Psalmist: "My
darling, you will never come back to me, but I shall
come to you."

And then she stood up and took a last kiss of her
sister's still smiling lips, and left the room, closing the
door gently behind her.

* * * * * * *

Years after, when the grasses round Esty Lisle's grave
had grown rank and tall under the dews and rains of
many seasons, and the clematis planted by Christine's
hand had crept up and o'ershadowed the tallest letter of
the name recorded on the tombstone, and when the
villagers had long ceased to look with any interest on
the inscription that described in brief terms the fatal
accident by which Esther Lisle lost her life, at the age

of twenty-four years, there still came an annual visitor to this otherwise forgotten grave—a friend whose footsteps crushed the wild luxuriance of flower and weed on every anniversary of Esty's death, whose hands reverently culled some blossom from the scented tangles of honeysuckle, to bear away on each visit as a remembrance of that green-stained tomb and its occupant. But the hand and the step were not those of a man. The heart that never forgot, the voice that prayed by Esty's grave until the voice itself was dumb in death, was that of Christine, her sister.

THE END.

PRINTED BY W. SMITH ND SON, 186 STRAND, LONDON, W.C.

4—7—77.